THE
SPACE FORCE
CHRONICLES

Fred Saberhagen

JSS
A JSS Literary Productions Book

A JSS Literary Productions Book
JSS Literary Productions, Albuquerque NM
www.fredsaberhagen.com

ISBN: 978-937422402
ISBN-13: 978-1-937422-40-0

First printing in this format, February 2018

Introductory Note

The stories in this volume were written early in Fred's forty-seven year career in science fiction and fantasy. I suppose they can be classified as military science fiction as they involve the Space Force. Certainly, they are also representative of anthropological SF. Fred's early optimism and his trust and respect for the ultimate good in humanity remained throughout his writing career. Fred continued anthropological themes in his early berserker stories, particularly in *Berserker Brother Assassin*.

The novellas The *Golden People* ('64) and The *Water Of Thought* ('65), were first published as Ace Doubles. *Golden* was expanded and republished by Baen Books in 1984. Tor Books published an expanded version of *Water* in 1981. The Tor edition contains a number of illustrations by award winning science fiction and fantasy artist Janet Aulisio.

The character connecting the three stories in *The Space Force Chronicles* is Boris Brazil, Spacer/Planeteer.

The note Fred added to *Planeteer* when the story was republished in the collection *The Book Of Saberhagen* nicely summarizes the way he approached his creative work.

> Each science fiction writer tends, I suppose, to work mostly in a rather small number of "worlds" of his own devising, each world being (usually) a future that can be more or less reasonably extrapolated from our own unlikely reality. Here's a look into one of my earliest worlds, that of the Space Force.
>
> --- Fred Saberhagen

Hope you enjoy.   Joan Spicci Saberhagen, editor

PLANETEER

FRED SABERHAGEN

PLANETEER

During the weeks that the starship *Yuan Chwang* had hovered in close observation of the new planet Aqua, ship's time had been jockeyed around to agree with the sun-time at the place chosen for first landing.

Boris Brazil saw no evidence of sane thinking behind this procedure; it meant the planeteers' briefing for the big event was set for 0200, and he had to get up in what was effectively the middle of the night—a thing to which he had grown accustomed, but never expected to learn to enjoy. Leaving his tiny cabin in a state of disorder that might have infuriated an inspecting officer—had there been an inspecting officer aboard interested in the neatness of cabins—he set forth in search of chow.

Brazil was tall and bony, resembling a blond young Abe Lincoln. He rubbed sleep from his eyes as his long legs carried him toward the mess hall. A distracting young squab from Computing sailed past him in the opposite direction, smiling.

"Good luck," she said.

"Is the coffee that bad?" It was the best facsimile of a joke he could think of this early.

But the girl hadn't been talking about coffee. Chief Planeteer Sam Gates had picked Brazil to go along on the first landing attempt, he learned when he met Gates in the chow line. He saw by the small computer clipped to Sam's belt that the other man had been up early on his own, double-checking the crew chief and maintenance robots who were readying their scoutship. Brazil felt vaguely guilty—but not very. He might well have been just another body in the way.

Sam Gates stood in the chow line swinging his arms and snapping his fingers, chewing his dark mustache as he usually did when nervous.

"How's it look?" Brazil asked.

"Oh, free and clear. Guess we'll have ground under our feet in a few hours."

Most of the *Yuan Chwan's* twenty-four planeteers were in the chow line, with a fair number of people from other departments. The day's operation was going to be a big one for everybody.

Trays loaded with synthetic ham, and a scrambled substance not preceded by chickens. Gates and Brazil found a table. Ten scoutships were going down today, though only one would attempt to land; most of the night shift from all departments seemed to think it was time for lunch. The mess was filling up quickly.

"Here comes the alien," said Gates, gesturing with his fork.

Brazil raised his eyes toward the tall turbaned man bearing a tray in their direction. "Hi, Chan. Pull up a a chair."

Chandragupta was no more an alien here than any other Earthman; his job had earned him the nickname.

"Good morning," said the Tribune with a smile, sitting down with Gates and Brazil. "I hope my people treat you well today." He had not yet seen one of "his people" and possibly never would; but from the moment high-altitude reconnaissance had established that intelligent life at an apparently primitive technological level existed on Aqua, his job had taken on substance. He was to represent the natives below

4

in councils aboard the *Yuan Chwang*, to argue at every turn for what he conceived to be their welfare, letting others worry about the scientific objectives that had brought the exploration ship so far from Earth, until he was satisfied that the natives needed no help or the mission was over.

"No reason to expect any trouble," said Brazil. Then, wondering what reaction he might provoke from his messmates, he added: "This one looks fairly simple."

"Except we know there are some kind of people down there," Gates said mildly. "And people are never as simple as you'd like them to be."

"I wonder if they will need my help," said Chan, "and I wonder if I will be able to help them." The job of Tribune was a new one, really still experimental. "in a few hours perhaps I will know."

"We're not trying to conquer them, you know," said Brazil, half amused and a little offended by Chan's eagerness to defend against his shipmates some people he had never seen.

"Oh, I know. But we must be careful not to conquer them by accident, eh?"

When Brazil got up to leave the mess, he could feel the eyes on his back, or thought he could. Here go the heroes, he thought. First landing. Hail, Hail.

And deep inside he felt a pride and joy so fierce he was embarrassed to admit it to himself—to be one of the first Earthmen stepping onto this unknown world.

***

Briefing was normal for a mission this size. The twenty planeteers who were going down into atmosphere, plus two reserve crews, slouched in their seats and scribbled notes and now and then whispered back and forth about business, concentrating so intently on the job at hand that an outsider might have thought them bored and distracted.

Captain Dietrich, boss of the *Yuan Chwang*, mounted the low dais in the front of the briefing room. He was a rather small man, of mild and bookish appearance. After working with him for awhile, one tended to treat cautiously all small men of mild and bookish appearance.

Tribune Chandragupta entered the briefing room through the rear door. The Captain eyed him thoughtfully. This was the first voyage on which he had been required to carry a Tribune; the idea had been born as a political move in the committee meetings of Earth Parliament, and had earned certain legislators reputations as defenders of liberty.

Captain Dietrich had no detectable wish to conquer anyone, having of course passed the Space Force psych tests, and he was willing to give the Tribune system a trial. After all, he could always overrule the man, on condition he thought it necessary for the safety of members of the expedition—though he was the only one aboard who could do so. But it seemed to the Captain that this placing of a civilian official aboard his ship might be only the start of an effort by the groundbound government to encroach upon what he considered to be the domain of the Space Force. Every time he went home he heard complaints that the SF was growing too powerful and cost too much.

"Militarism," they would say, over a drink or anywhere he met civilians. "We've just managed to really get away from all that on Earth, and now you want to start all over, on Mars and Ganymede and this new military base on Aldebaran 2."

"The Martian colony is hardly a military base," he would remind them patiently. "It now has its own independent civilian government and sends representatives to Earth Parliament. The Space Force has practically pulled out of Mars altogether. Ganymede is a training base. Aldebaran 2 you're right about, mostly; and we do have other military bases."

"Aha!" Now how do we know that none of these outlying bases or colonies will ever threaten Earth?"

"Because all spaceships and strategic weapons are controlled by the SF, and the SF is controlled by the psych tests that screen people trying to enter it. Admittedly, no system is perfect, but what are our alternatives?"

"We could cut down on this space exploration, maybe stop it altogether. It's devilish expensive, and there seems no hope it will ever relieve our crowding on Earth. What do we get out of it anyway that makes it really profitable?"

"Well," Captain Dietrich might say, "since you talk of militarism, I will ignore the valuable knowledge we have gained by exploration and answer you in military terms. We have the ability to travel hundreds of light-years in a matter of months, and to melt any known planet in minutes, with one ship delivering one weapon. How many races do you think live in our galaxy with similar capabilities?"

No Earthmen had met any but primitive aliens—yet. But people had begun to comprehend the magnitude of the galaxy, where man's few hundred-light-year radius of domination gave him no more than a Jamestown Colony.

"Assume a race with such capabilities," the Captain might continue, "and with motivations we might not be able to understand, spreading out across the galaxy as we are. Would you rather have them discover our military base on Aldebaran this year, or find all humanity crowded on one unprotected Earth, perhaps the year after next?"

Dietrich got a wide range of answers to this question. He himself would much prefer to meet the hypothetical advanced aliens a thousand light-years or more from Earth, with a number of large and effective military bases in between.

But right now it was time for him to start briefing his planeteers, who probably knew as much about Aqua as he, who had never driven a scoutship into its upper atmosphere

"Gentlemen, we've found out a little about this planet, the only child of a Sol-type sun. after watching it for six weeks. One point one AU from its sun, gravity point-nine-five, diameter point-nine, eighty-five per cent of surface is water. Oxy-nitrogen atmosphere, about five thousand meters equivalent. We won't try breathing it for some time yet. Full suits until further notice.

"What land there is, is probably quite well populated with what we think are humanoids with a technical level probably nowhere higher than that of medieval Europe. Several rather large sailing ships have been spotted in coastal waters. There are only a couple of long paved roads, and none of the cities are electrically lit on nightside. We don't think anyone down there can have spotted us yet."

Most of his audience looked back at him rather impatiently, as if to say: We know all this. We're the ones who found it out.

But the Captain wanted to make sure they had all the basic facts in proper focus. "Our mission is to make contact with the natives. To establish a temporary scientific base on the surface for seismic studies, biological studies, and so forth—and of course to learn what we can from and about the intelligent inhabitants."

The Captain raised his eyes and spoke as much to the Tribune as to his planeteers, "There seems very little chance of any permanent colony being established here, due to the native population on a very limited land area. This same factor would seem to preclude our establishing the temporary base in some remote area, without knowledge of the natives. So we will have to deal with them somehow from the start.

"I've never believed in the god-from-the-sky approach, and as you know, SF policy is to avoids it if possible. It falsifies from the start a relationship that may become permanent, even if we now intend it to be temporary. And he who takes godhood upon himself is likely to have to spend more time at it than at the business for which he came, and to assume responsibility for far-reaching changes in the native history."

The Captain paused, then looked at another man who stood waiting to speak, paper in hand. "Meteorology?"

"Yes sir."

On a wall appeared a photomap of the island that had been picked for the first landing attempt, an irregular shape of land about a hundred and fifty kilometers long by twenty wide. Air temperature at dawn in the landing area should be about fifty degrees F, the water a little cooler. There might be enough fog to aid the landing scoutship in an unseen descent.

Meteorology also discussed atmospheric effects on communication between scouts and the mother ship, and predicted the weather in the landing area for the next day. He paused to answer a couple of questions, and introduced Passive Detection.

The PD man discussed Aqua's Van Allen belts, magnetic field, the variety and amount of solar radiation in nearby space, and that to be expected on the surface. He spoke of what the natives probably burned for heat and light in the nightside cities, and confirmed the apparent absence of any advanced technology.

Biology was next, with a prediction that the island would show diverse and active life. It was near the tropics in the spring hemisphere, and green with vegetation. Scout photos showed no evidence of very large animals or plants. Some areas appeared to be under cultivation.

Anthropology took the dais to speculate. The people of Aqua were thought to be humanoid, but in the photos anything as small as a man was at the very limit of visibility, and the estimate of the beings' appearance was based on lucky shots of dawn or dusk shadows striding gigantic across more or less level ground. There was some massive construction, probably of masonry, in the one sizable city on the island. A seawall and a couple of large structures had been built on a finger of land that protected the city's small harbor, where sailing ships were visible.

Captain Dietrich came back to outline the patterns he wanted the non-landing scouts to fly. "The target island is pretty well isolated from the planet's main land areas, so if we put a base here it should have a minimal effects on native culture. Also, if we botch things up here, we may be able to move on and try again without the natives in the new spot having heard of us." He looked around at his men; the idea was strongly conveyed to them that the Captain preferred they not botch thing up. "Chan—anything you want to say? No? All right, board your scouts."

Brazil strode beside Gates out the door in the rear of the briefing room, passing under the sign that read:
MAYBE . . . . ANYTHING

Maybe they're real telepaths down there. Maybe they're a mighty race now retired from active competition and preferring the simple life. Maybe ...

Never mind. it was time to follow the planeteers' motto: *Go Down and Find Out.*

Gates and Brazil now faced a final quick Medical & Psych exam in a ship's corridor. Brazil had long since given up trying to startle the psych doc by giving to the inevitable weird question an even weirder answer.

"I'd swear you were sane if I didn't know you better," the doctor told him this time. "Pass on."

They fitted themselves into the suits of Armor, Light, Space and Ground, that had been selected for this job. The suits included among their accessories flotation bubbles that when inflated enabled the wearers to maneuver with supposed ease through water. The suits now received a quick semifinal test.

Captain Dietrich was waiting in the berth that was almost filled by the fifteen-meter-long stubby bulk of scoutship *Alpha*. Gates and Brazil juggled checklists and fishbowl helmets to offer him each an armored paw to shake. The Captain said something about good luck.

The two planeteers climbed through the scout's hatch, twisting sideways with practiced movements to meet the ninety degree shift in artificial gravity between mother ship and scout. Gates climbed on toward the control room while Brazil stayed to seal the hatch. On planet they would of course use an airlock.

Engines started. Ship's power off and disconnected. All personnel out of berth. Ready for sterilizing.

Lethal gas, swirling around the scout's hull, was mostly pumped away to be saved and reused. Then a blast of ultraviolet, more intense than the raw Sol-type sunshine outside, bathed the inside of the berth. No microorganisms must be carried down into atmosphere.

Strapped and clamped into control room chairs, ports sealed, watching the tiny world of the berth by video screen, Gates and Brazil were nearly ready. The berth door slid open on schedule, and what was left of gas inside went out in a faint puff of sudden mist.

The watery world that someone with little imagination had named Aqua, sixteen thousand kilometers away, filled the opening. A quarter of it was dayside, blue mottled white with patterned clouds; nightside was eerie with subtle atmospheric glows.

"Stand by one, *Alpha*," came over the radio. "A little trouble clearing *Delta*."

"Understand," said Sam Gates. "Hey Boris, I like those tridi stories at home. The chap just drives his ship up to a new planet and lands. The faithful crew stands around scratching their heads. 'Well, what'll we do now?' says one. Then they wait for the hero to speak up."

" 'Let's get out and look around,' " said Brazil, grinning. " 'O.K., but let's all be careful. Maybe we better close the door of the ship behind us.' "

Sam gave a rare smile. "And then one character takes his helmet off to eat a coconut. Only it turns out to be a chieftain's daughter."

"And they're all in the soup. They never seem to learn."

"Stand by, *Alpha*," said Operations over the radio, unnecessarily.

Gates pointed to the slim volume wedged under an arm of Brazil's chair, secured, like everything else aboard, against some possible failure of the artificial gravity. "What's the book this time?"

"Thoreau. I thought I might need a dose of philosophy if you get us stuck in the mud down there."

"Always meant to read the old nature-lover through some day." Gates nodded at the screens showing the waiting planet. "Wonder what he would have thought of all this."

Brazil looked at the image of the planet with the dawnline creeping imperceptibly across upper atmosphere as a rainbow of varying ionization and light pressure. He smiled at a sudden recollection, and quoted: "*Walden Pond*—let's see— 'A field of water betrays the spirit that is in the air. It is continually receiving new life and motion from above ... I see where the breeze dashes across it by the streaks or flakes of light. It is remarkable that we can look down on its surface. We shall, perhaps, look down thus on the surface of air at length, and mark where a still subtler spirit sweeps over it.' "

"He wrote that in the middle of the nineteenth century?" asked Gates, astonished. "Let me see that book when you're done with it."

"You're clear for takeoff, *Alpha*. Good luck," said the radio.

Scoutship *Alpha* outraced the dawnline by an hour to the island and eased down on schedule, without hurry, into thicker and thicker air, until it entered predawn darkness and fog. Gates used his radar for the first time, to work his way down toward the water a few hundred meters off the rocky coastline.

Aqua was Brazil's ninth new planet. But I won't forget this one, he thought in some corner of his brain not used for watching instruments.

And he was right.

***

The plan called for an offshore landing unseen by the natives, the concealment of the scoutship under water but near land, and the going ashore of Gates and Brazil in protective suits to make contact with the local intelligent life. Tight-beam communication was to be maintained at all times with the *Yuan Chwang*. A small video eye rode above each planeteer's left ear; whatever the eye saw was transmitted to the mother ship.

The versatile and roughly humanoid robot that accompanied every scoutship (and followed men onto new planets, but rarely preceded them) would be left in the submerged scout, and would bring it to the human crew if they summoned it by radio.

The *Yuan Chwang* was not orbiting Aqua, but hovering and trying to keep its great bulk invisible, fifteen or sixteen thousand kilometers above the island. The other scouts were cruising in upper atmosphere in the general area of the target island, observing what they could.

Aboard *Alpha*, detection screens picked out what looked to Brazil like the infrared pattern of smoldering fires and fainter body heats of a small village where the recon photos had shown a village to be. Gates worked the scout by radar to an offshore point about a kilometer from the village, which lay on the shore of a small cove. He dipped the scout low enough to put a sonar probe under water and get a picture of the bottom.

"Nothing strange down there," said Gates. "We'll go ahead."

Cutting in automatic stabilizers, he lowered the scout into and through choppy water and made slowly toward shore, while Brazil studied the ocean and bottom, trying to read half a dozen presentations at once.

Near the rocky upthrust of land, Gates let the little ship settle gently onto sandy bottom. He summoned the robot and told it to use enough drive to prevent the ship's sinking into the bottom. The robot got into the pilot's seat as the humans checklisted themselves into helmets, out of the control room, and into the lock. They stood with legs spread and arms raised while gas and UV sterilized their suits and the chamber. Gates nodded and Brazil opened a valve to let alien sea into the lock; in a few seconds they stepped out of the world of checklists and into dark water. Brazil lingered to feel that the lock door was secured behind them, let gas into his flotation bubbles, and followed Gates up through the darkness. Once something like a luminous smoke ring curled greenly past them through the water.

"Can you bliphate the distance phlooh that?" asked a voice from the *Yuan Chwang*, half strangled by transmission through space, air, and water.

"Hard to say; I'd guess only a few meters," Gates answered, waiting until his head had broken surface and he had taken a look around. Brazil was right behind him; he could barely see Gates' helmet above the water three meters away. The rough rock face of the coastline was only a deeper darkness at one side. They paddled toward it; waves sloshed them against it; they gripped it and began to climb.

Earthmen emerged onto the land of a new world, looking more like primeval lungfish than lords of creation. They climbed rock uncertainly and slowly and halted at the top of a small cliff. The suits were engineered for easy movement and reasonable comfort for twenty-four continuous sealed-in hours in almost any environment. Old Planeteers sometimes said soberly that they needed a suit on to feel comfortable; but they usually preferred to take the suit off before sitting down to discuss how comfortably they wore it.

15

"Let's wait for a little more light," said Gates' radio voice.

Brazil sat down beside a large rock and tried to see what was on the inland slope away from the cliff.

The sun was not far below the hilly horizon now and a gray predawn light made the scene gradually intelligible. A faint excuse for a road wandered along a few yards away, roughly paralleling the shoreline; it might be a cattle path that led toward the village. Beyond the road were fields with a a semi-cultivated look, holding orderly rows of squat bushes above a mat of low-growing vines that seemed to cover most of the ground in sight. Green hills rose beyond the fields.

The dawn brightened slowly. To Brazil, sunrises always brought awe, whether he saw them on an outworld, or on crowded Earth, or across the rusty deserts of the world to which his parents had emigrated and where he had been born. Sitting on this alien rock with sea water dripping from his armor, he thought: First Landing: it's like a First Morning. Let there be light.

"Light enough," said Gates. "Let's get started."

They walked on crunching vines to the road, heads swiveling constantly and air microphones tuned to high sensitivity. Brazil caught himself listening for the ape-howling that had accompanied each new morning on his last new planet. It wasn't good to carry such mental baggage on the job; he would have to unload it.

They paced along the faint road toward the village. The hard-packed brownish soil of the road held no informative prints of hooves or feet or wheels.

"Smoke ahead," said Gates suddenly. It was a barely visible vertical tracery in the sky, rising not far away.

The road curved around a. craggy little hill; when they had rounded this, the village was before them. Large rowboats were beached on the sand of a small sheltered cove. Forty or fifty meters back from the water stood about twenty huts, built mainly from what looked like mats of the groundvine. A small stream trickled through the village, flowing from the direction of a structure like a low fortress, that stood beyond the huts and was much larger than any of them. Its dark walls of dried mud or clay were surrounded by a considerable space cleared of all vegetation.

Brazil turned his head to one side and saw his first native. His stomach went cold and he said to Gates: "On the rock up there. Look."

The native was undoubtedly humanoid and had apparently been dead a long time. He was bound somehow with vines to the crag that almost overhung the road, four or five meters above the Earthmen, and around his neck hung a placard that looked like cardboard, bearing a short inscription in bold characters resembling Arabic. He had been a tall man in life, by Earthly standards, and long strands of pale hair were still in evidence.

"Get this?" asked Gates of the observers in the sky.

"Affirmative. You're going on?"

"Don't see why not."

"We never mind these 'No Trespassing' signs," said Brazil. with an attempt at flippancy he didn't feel. Dead men were nothing new to him, but this one had a considerable resemblance to himself and had, so to speak, sneaked up on him.

There were no living people yet in sight, but there were shrill cries from the village, and a small flock of hawk like birds with oversized wings sprang up from among the huts. The birds were green and vivid orange against the misty sky and flew circling over the village.

"Let's go," said Gates.

They went down the sloping road toward the huts, trying to look confident but not frightening.

At an open gateway in the wall of the fortified structure a figure appeared, a red-haired man dressed in dark jerkin and leggings and boots, with breastplate of silvery metal that matched the round helmet he carried in one hand. In the other was a spear. He stretched himself and yawned, and appeared to be trying to scratch his ribs with the helmet. He was still a good distance away and gave no sign that he had spotted two aliens in strange suits walking into his town.

The birds were more alert. The cries of the circling flock changed suddenly in tone, and in a moment it had become a living arrow launched at Gates and Brazil. The flock broke off just before contact, to circle the intruders in a blurred uproar of wings and claws, but several birds scraped the helmets, which were almost invisible in mild light, and came back to tear head-on at Brazil's apparently unprotected face.

The thud of impact was impressive; when Brazil's eyes opened from the reflex blink, the bird was flopping on the ground with something badly broken. He picked it up, intending to impress the natives with his friendliness by treating kindly their pet that had attacked him, and also to suggest to them that it was futile to attack; but it struggled and fought his armored hands so that he thought he was doing it more harm than good.

He set it gently down again as the first natives came blinking and shivering out of their huts to see what all the noise was about, some of them still pulling on scanty rags of clothing.

They were all of a type with the body on the rock, blond, tall humanoids with deep chests and slender limbs; in the living people were visible a dozen small distinctions of facial and bodily proportion that added up to an obvious but not at first definable difference from any Earthman.

The red-haired man of the fortress had ducked inside the gateway, which was still open. A domestic-looking animal with plumes on its head looked out at the strangers with interest.

The blond natives stood together in front of their huts, as if waiting for a group picture to be taken, gaping at their visitors in silence. The watchbird flock still screamed and flew, now in widening circles, having given up assault at least temporarily.

Gates kept moving forward until he stood near the center of the cleared space between beach and huts. Brazil stopped beside him there and they stood almost motionless, smiling, arms spread with hands open, in the approved position for approaching. Apparent Primitives who seem timid. The sun stood over the horizon, dissipating the morning fog.

Brazil became aware that the whole crowd was watching *him.* Only now and then did one shoot a quick glance at Gates, as if puzzled about something.

Gates spoke via throat mike and radio, scarcely moving his smiling lips. "You look like'em, boy. I think you better play leader. They may never have seen anyone dark as me before."

Brazil made the practiced throat-muscle movement that switched on his airspeaker and opened his mouth to begin the greeting of his public with soothing sounds. He was interrupted by Sam's voice in his ear again. "Coming from the fort."

Six Apparent Primitives who looked anything but timid were marching in sloppy formation down the slope from the walled structure, straight toward the Earthmen, bearing spears and facial expressions that Brazil could not interpret as meaning anything good. They were all red-haired and armored, muscular, well-fed, and bulbous-nosed, evidently of a different tribe or race than the blond hut-dwellers.

Brazil's barefoot audience watched the warriors' approach nervously and began to fade back into their huts. But one of the older men, who had been staring Brazil in the eye with an expression of intense and mounting emotion—the planeteer grew edgy at not being able to decide what emotion—now sprang forward to grab Brazil by the arm and harangue him with the first native speech he had heard, meanwhile looking at him with the gaze of a pleading worshipper.

The six red-haired warriors were very near and didn't look happy at all. They also seemed to be concentrating on Brazil.

With a cry as of great despair the old man tore himself away from Brazil and fled at top speed toward the huts. One of the approaching warriors threw his spear with a whipping, expert motion; it caught the old man in the back and sent him dying on his face in the sand.

"Well, I'll be—" Boris Brazil roared out the first Earth words into the air of Aqua.

The red-haired warriors stood before him, eyeing him with what he interpreted as incredulous contempt. One of them barked something that he thought he could almost translate: "What are you doing, you blond peasant clod, dressed up in that outlandish armor?" He probably looked more like a blond native in the suit, with his physical proportions somewhat concealed, than he would without it.

The one who had speared the old man started walking toward his victim, maybe to retrieve his weapon. Brazil started that way too, with no clear idea of what he was going to do, but with the feeling that the old man had appealed to him in vain for help.

As Brazil started to move, the five other spears were suddenly leveled at him. A hysterical blond boy ran out of a hut to kneel beside the old man and scream something that sounded nasty at the approaching warrior. Gates was standing motionless a few meters away. A spear thrust fast and hard against Brazil's chest with plain intent to kill, setting him back on his heels; a lordly voice from the *Yuan Chwang* said in his ear, "This is not our affair." Brazil grabbed the thrusting spear in his left hand, jerked its owner forward off balance, and delivered with his armored right fist what seemed the appropriate greeting to an Apparent Primitive Attempting Murder of Earthman.

The blow knocked the man out from under his helmet and dropped him to the sand. Spears rocked Boris from all sides, clashed and slid around his helmet. He caught a glimpse of the sixth warrior kicking the boy, knocking him over, and pulling a short axe from his belt for a finishing blow.

The arm swinging back the axe suddenly released it; the weapon spun through the air to land some meters away and the warrior sat down suddenly and nervelessly. Sam Gates had decided it was time for stun pistols.

Before Brazil had reached the same conclusion, the four remaining spearmen had given up trying to stick him through his suit and were grabbing at his arms to hold him. Gates potted two more of them, in the legs, with silent and invisible force. The remaining two abandoned the fight and backed away toward their stronghold with spears leveled, shouting what was no doubt a call for reinforcements. The man that Brazil had felled got up and tottered dazedly after them.

"Let's get out of here," said Gates.

Brazil's eye swept around. The old man was dead, the spear still in him. The young boy who had been kicked was lying unconscious right in front of a warrior who was going to be considerably annoyed as soon as he felt a little better. Brazil scooped the child up and got him over his shoulders in a fireman's carry and looked at Gates, who gave a sort of facial shrug.

They strode at a good pace out of the village, with the watchbirds screaming a cheerful farewell. A few Reds were milling around the gateway of the fort as the Earthmen went over the rise and out of sight, but no organized pursuit was yet visible. Once out of sight of the village they began a steady loping run, the small body bouncing on Brazil's shoulders. Gates called for the robot to bring the scout up to the surface at the shoreline.

"This is the Tribune," said a voice. "What do you intend doing with that child?"

"Saving his neck," said Gates. "Maybe we can learn something from him too."

Brazil was gasping when he finished the climb down the rocks to the shoreline and set his unconscious burden—no, half conscious now, with a swelling lump on the forehead—down inside the airlock. The outer door shut behind Gates and the robot had the scout underwater and moving out to sea a moment later.

Entertaining an alien aboard a scoutship was something the Space Force had learned to plan for ahead of time. A door in the back of a suit locker led from the airlock into the tiny Alien Room, into which Gates was feeding atmosphere from outside, via snorkel and remote control. When the room was ready,

Brazil carried the boy into it, sealing the door behind him. Gates could decontaminate in the airlock, and go to the control room. Brazil would have to wear suit and helmet for a while yet.

Medical was already on the communicator in the Alien Room when Brazil turned to look at the screen, after putting the kid down on the bed-acceleration couch that took up most of the room, checking the air pressure and setting the temperature up a few degrees.

"Kid doesn't look too bad," Brazil told the doctor. He smiled reassuringly at the boy, who was now fully conscious and lay watching with wide eyes and a growing yellowish lump on his forehead. He might be ten or eleven years old, judged by Earth standards.

"Keep him quiet. Gates is going to get us some remote X-rays. You try for a blood sample as soon as possible. Do you think we'll have to feed him?"

"Yes. If we can keep him for a week or two we should get the language and a good line on the local culture. We've got synthetic proteins and simple sugars on the scout, of course, so I guess he won't starve—but I'll try for your blood sample first. And listen, this may be important—I'm turning off the video screen now. When we use it again, keep anyone with red hair off it. Use blond, noble, handsome people like me if possible."

Brazil started to call Sam on the intercom, but through a valve into the Alien Room came sterile blankets and a painless blood sample syringe, before he could ask for them.

Chandragupta's voice came into his helmet: "This is the Tribune. I have little complaint of your actions so far, except that striking that man with your fist at least bordered on the use of excessive force. But I must forbid you to keep that child any longer than is necessary for his own welfare."

"How long will that be, Chan?" asked Captain Dietrich's voice, getting no immediate answer. "Would the boy be welcomed home, or speared like that old man, or what? I think we'd better learn the language and customs before trying to decided. And as for Brazil's hitting that man—"

A debate went on. Brazil listened with half an ear while he covered his guest with blankets and sat beside him, trying to inspire confidence.

"It's all right, sonny, it's all right." I hope. He patted the boy gently with his armored hand. That was the only treatment he dared attempt until he knew considerably more about the biology of his guest.

And the guest could be very valuable. Children made good subjects for First Contact as a rule, if they were not too young. Their minds adapted quickly to the alien. They caught on quickly to the game of language teaching. And they were likely to give an honest and direct view of their own culture.

Brazil handed the blood-sample syringe to the boy after locking the plunger. The kid took it after a brief hesitation, looked it over cautiously, then gave a sudden shy smile and said something that might have been a question. If his head was bothering him he gave no sign of it.

Brazil answered with some kindly nonsense and took the syringe back. He made a show of rubbing it on his own suites arm, turning his head to the other side as he did so. Then he turned the boy's head gently away and got his blood sample without fuss on the first try. He valved the loaded syringe out into the airlock, where the robot came to load it into a courier tube that would carry it up to the *Yuan Chwang*.

***

24

Earth and Aqua life turned out to be too alien to one another for infectious disease to pose a problem either way. Brazil shed his suit with relief.

The courier tube returned before sunset with containers of vile-looking gunk that Supply swore would feed the boy, whose name was approximately Tim. Tim tasted the stuff but looked unhappy, so Gates went out spear fishing. Tim was pleased with some of the assortment and ate it raw, while turning down the rest in disgust. He seemed to be suffering no aftereffects from the kick in the head, but Brazil did his best to keep him quiet anyway.

For the next few days the scout stayed well out at sea, mostly submerged. Brazil spent most of his time in the Alien Room, pretending to learn Tim's language almost as fast as he could hear the words, while the linguistically expert brains, human and electronic, aboard the *Yuan Chwang*, looked and listened over his shoulder. They forgot nothing, and spoke into his ear, prompting him on what to say next.

Tim became restlessly active after getting over his first awed fascination with video screen, doors, acceleration couch, and plumbing. When told he was aboard a ship, he wanted to see it all. Brazil kept the robot, at least, out of Tim's sight, and had to struggle to learn more than he taught. He played games with Tim to give him exercise, and to gather data on his physical strength and dexterity.

The hungry brains aboard the *Yuan Chwang* devoured Tim's language. Within two weeks they had fed it by memory tape to every planeteer. A few days of practice would give them command of it.

It was time for a major conference. The two planeteers on surface sat in with Captain Dietrich and the department heads above, via communicator, while Tim was confined discontentedly to the Alien Room.

"Gentlemen and ladies, we have a choice between two courses of action," the Captain began. "We can try again to establish relations with the natives of this island, or pull out and start over somewhere else. I think we can agree that our only major problem on this island is likely to be intercultural?"

No one disputed him. "I'd like to say that I hope we can find a way to set up a base on this island," said Biology. "That luminous water-ring was fascinating, though I'm not sure it's in my field. And that groundvine..."

"We can't complete our gravitic tables for this system without seismic measurements of the planet," put in Geology. "That island still looks like a good place to me."

"We've got the language here now," said Brazil. "Our First Contact tapes show the red tribe's speech is nearly the same as Tim's. And they're already trying to kill us on sight, so what can we lose by another try?"

Chandragupta said sharply: "The people of the island may lose, if we are not careful, Mr. Brazil. Indeed we may have caused substantial damage already, by inserting ourselves into a situation of considerable tension between two tribes— though any harm we may have done was accidental, and I do not blame anyone for it."

"Just what sort of damage can be attributed to our arrival?" asked the Captain.

"I think I can explain what Chan means," said Sociology, clearing his throat. "The data we have from Tim fit in with what we saw on First Contact. Everything indicates that the island is ripe for civil war.

"The picture is this: a local settled tribe, fishermen and part-time farmers—the Blonds, as we have come to call them—invaded and conquered by a warrior tribe of the Viking type, probably fewer in numbers. The invaders seem to have come from the smaller islands farther north. Perhaps they were driven out themselves by someone else. Now they have settled down here as a ruling class. Tim says this invasion was a very long time ago, before he was born, but that his grandfather—the old man who unfortunately was killed during our First Contact—could remember a time when there were no Reds on the island. I'd guess the invasion was about fifty standard years ago. We've seen no evidence of intermarriage, although in fact we've seen none of the Red women or children yet."

"Tim talks of a day when his people will rise up and destroy the Reds," said Brazil. "The dream of his young life seems to be to find a way to slaughter them wholesale. He wants me to lead the revolution. Someone has talked a lot of war and rebellion to him, that's for sure.

"Tim's grandfather thought I was a tribal folk-hero, come back from the great beyond in strange armor to lead them out of slavery. That's what the old man was talking to me about: I suppose that's why they speared him. It's on the tape, of course. Now I can understand it." Brazil fell moodily silent.

"I suppose the First Contact incident might have touched off a full-scale Blond rebellion?" someone asked.

"If conditions had been just right, yes," said Sociology. "Apparently they were not."

Captain Dietrich spoke up: "During the last few days we've made numerous recon photo runs at high speed and comparatively low altitude. If there was any open warfare in progress, we'd almost certainly have seen it."

27

"How about that body lashed to the rock?" someone asked after a brief pause. "Have we learned anything on that?"

"Tim can't read or write," said Sociology, "so neither can we, yet. So we don't know what the placard hung around the fellow's neck says. Tim says the Reds put him up there because they were angry at him. Seems reasonable, if not illuminating."

"Captain, I wish we had made such photo runs as you now mention before First Contact," said the Tribune.

"We weren't sure of their technological level then," said the Captain, a little wearily. "We didn't want them to spot us flying over. It's one of those choices you have to make. We didn't want to shock them by appearing as gods, remember?"

The discussion flowed on for a while. Finally Dietrich brought it back to his original question: "Shall we continue to try for a base on this island, or shall we move on?"

Chandragupta: "The question I must insist we try to answer, Captain, is this: How can we be helpful to the people of this island, where we have already interfered?"

The Captain: "Chan, we didn't come all this way to open a social service bureau."

"I realize that, Captain." Grimly. "Nevertheless, I consider our effect upon the natives more important than seismic measurements. I would like to ask if you plan to conclude an agreement with the authorities controlling those Red soldiers, for a scientific base on the island?"

"I'm considering it."

"I believe our doing so would in effect recognize their authority to live as they do, holding another tribe in slavery."

Sociology raised his eyebrows. "It would be unusual if slavery could not be found in some form at this level."

28

"Perhaps I should have been more precise. I consider it evil that a member of the ruling class should have it in his power to take at any time the life of one of the lower class, as we have seen here. I think we are bound to try to correct such a condition. Of course we shall not be able, nor should we attempt, to establish our idea of a perfect society. But we must try to set these people on the road to greater freedom and justice." Chandragupta raised his voice above several protesting ones. "We are already committed to interference here, in my view. We must now see to it that the changes we produce are for the better."

The Captain smiled faintly. "Are you arguing for the revolution, Chan?"

"I think you know better." The Tribune was somewhat irritated. "We could hardly expect the total effect of a general armed uprising to be beneficial."

"Just what do you think we *should* do, then, to start these people on the road to greater freedom and justice, as you put it?"

Chandragupta sighed. "I think we must first investigate them further, to learn how best to help."

There was a little silence.

"Anyone have a further comment?" asked the Captain. "All right, this is it. We continue work on this island. We try to stabilize native affairs on as just a basis as possible, and then deal for our base. Boris, you say Tim has relatives in an inland village who can hide him out from the Reds if need be?"

"All right. Take him to this inland village, tonight or tomorrow night. Talk with some of the adults there. Especially try to find out more about the political situation. Is there a Blond resistance group, how strong, and so on. Since we seem to be committed to some sort of interference here, we'd better get all the data we can, and quickly. Any questions?"

***

The following night was dark and foggy. Gates drove the scoutship silently and, as he hoped, invisibly over the island's hills toward the village of Tim's relatives. The boy acted as navigator, guiding an electronically presented green spot over a contour map of the island, with an air of sophistication. He had, he said, seen maps before, if not flying machines. But he was excited at the prospect of showing off Brazil in armor to people he knew, and telling them of the wonders he had seen. Brazil had given him orders to keep the scoutship's flying powers secret if possible.

Brazil changed the scale of the map to show only the area within a couple of kilometers of the village. Tim guided Gates to a clear landing spot, out of sight of the village but within easy walking distance. Gates brought the scout down quickly, probing below with radar and infrared, until the little ship settled with a crackle of crushed vines into a tiny hollow between hills.

The cries and movement of small life alarmed by their landing gradually quieted. There were no signs of human alarm.

Brazil suited up, for protection against dangers other than infection. He led Tim into the airlock, and paused for a final briefing.

"Now, who did we agree you should look for in the village?"

"First I will look for Sunto, who is one of my cousins. He hates the Reds and is not afraid of them. If he is not home I will seek Lorto or Tammammo, who are the junior headmen of the village. Only if I can find none of those will I talk to my female cousins, who do not understand these things. I will try to avoid Tamotim, who I think is still the boss headman here. He likes the Reds and tells them things. If I see no one who is safe to talk to I will come back here and we will talk over what to do next."

"And if someone stops you and asks you questions?"

"I will just say there is a strange man out here who wants to speak with someone from the village. I know what to do, you don't have to worry. I won't say you are our Warrior Spirit, or anything like that. Unless there are Reds in the village, who capture me; then I will cry out for Warrior Spirit and you will come and kill them, hey?"

"My name's not Warrior Spirit. And if you see any Reds, just come back." Brazil opened the lock's outer door and they stepped out and down into matted vines. "Remember, just say I brought you over the hills if anyone asks how you come to be here. No one else need know yet that my ship can fly."

"All right. Over that way is a path," said Tim, becoming oriented. "And that way is the village."

"Get going, then." Brazil sent him off with a gentle shove, and then stood quietly, testing the alien night with artificially aided senses.

The sound of Tim's bare feet faded quickly on the path.

"I'll take her up a ways," said Gates on radio.

"Good idea."

Brazil saw the dark bulk of the scoutship lift in silence that was almost eerie even to him, and drift up out of sight into fog and darkness. No stars to see tonight. Well, he had seen enough of them. For a while.

He moved off and found the path with his infrared lamp and waited just at one side of it. He hoped the kid wouldn't run into any trouble. About five minutes passed before the glass of

31

his helmet, set for infrared translation, showed him some large life moving toward him along the trail from the village. "One— two of them, Sam, coming this way."

"Affirmative, I have them now."

"Boro?" His native name, called in a soft voice from the darkness.

Brazil switched his air mike on again. "Right here."

Tim approached him. "This is Tammammo with me, Boro. He is a junior headman."

Brazil gave the second vague shape a slight bow, which Tim had told him was the ordinary greeting between equals. "Sam, keep a sharp eye out. We need to use a little light down here." Planeteers worked their air-mike switches for such asides as quickly and naturally as they used their tongues for speech.

"Understand."

Brazil turned on what he hoped was a dim and non-startling electric glow from a suit lamp, revealing a Tammammo bug-eyed at being called out of his hut at night to meet what he might think was the Warrior Spirit.

Boris greeted him in a matter-of-fact, businesslike way. Maybe the fact that he spoke the common language of the peasants put the junior headman more at ease.

Tammammo had heard a version of the First Contact incident which began with the Red garrison of the coastal village executing an old man for daring to worship the Sea God in a way reserved for rulers. Dying, the elder had called down a curse upon their heads, whereupon the Warrior Spirit of the Blonds appeared, and slew sixty Reds with a sweep of his arm— or perhaps it had taken several arm sweeps, the point was uncertain. A Red magician, called upon by the enemy, had evoked from somewhere a dark and evil spirit, also clad in armor. The Blond Warrior had departed to do battle with this other elsewhere, not wishing to devastate the entire island in the struggle, but he was expected to win and would return shortly to—and this point was whispered very cautiously—slay all the Red warriors and turn over their women and children to the Blonds as slaves.

Tammammo almost managed to look Brazil hopefully in the eye as he finished the tale.

Tim started to speak with the exasperated eagerness of a youngster to point out errors—or maybe in disappointment at being left out of the story altogether. But Brazil shushed him by putting a hand in front of his face. He spoke carefully to Tammammo.

"Junior headman—look at me carefully. I am only a man, nothing more. I am not a Warrior Spirit, or any kind of a god. I am only a man from a far land, who looks like one of your people and wears armor that is strange to you. Now I wish to speak in private with the leaders of your people—not with the headman who tells everything to the Reds, but to the leaders of your own people, who may not be known to everyone. Do you understand me?"

"If you say you are a man, so be it." Tammammo seemed to be shivering with more than the night chill. "The leaders you speak of—I do not know anything about such matters, except for stories heard by all. There is a man in the village who might know. His name is Sunto. I can tell him what you want when I meet him. Will that please you?"

"It will. And I think there is no need for you to speak of me to anyone else."

"I will not! I will not!"

"Then send Sunto here to meet me at this time tomorrow night. One thing more, junior headman—this boy goes to live now with his relatives in your village, I want you, Tammammo, to see to it that no harm comes to him from the Reds. As I said, I am only a man, yet I can do many things, I would be quite angry if the Reds were to harm this boy. Do you understand?"

Tammammo indicated vehemently that he understood. Obviously he wished himself a thousand kilometers at sea, or anywhere out of this situation.

"Tim, keep out of trouble. Go, both of you, and send me Sunto here tomorrow night."

Evidently it was not a Blond habit to waste any time in farewells. Brazil watched them out of sight, realizing suddenly he was going to miss having the kid around. "OKay, Sam, you can bring her down."

Trudging to where the scout was crackling down into vines again, Brazil paused and looked up with a sudden grin. "Hey, dark and evil spirit. How come you listen to what that Red magician says?"

"Shut up and get in."

***

Sunto appeared at the appointed place on the following night, escorted by Tim. This time the scout had not landed; Brazil was lowered the last few score meters by cable.

Sunto was less timid than Tammammo. He too had heard of the first contact fight, but was shrewd enough to realize how events could change in the seeing and retelling. He professed no doubt that Brazil was only a man, and a friend of the Blonds. Would he arrange a meeting with the Blond leaders? Certainly. Those leaders were meeting in the remote hills, three nights from now. Boro could come if he wished. There would be many large fires at the meeting place so it would be easy to find. Was Boro living in the hills now?

Did everyone know about this meeting, Brazil asked him. What if the Reds saw all those fires? Why had Tammammo been so timid in discussing Blond leaders?

Sunto did not seem to understand. He used several new words in trying to answer the questions. Eventually the idea came across that this was going to be a religious meeting, not political at all. He, Sunto, knew no more than that timid Tammammo about political matters. Of course the Reds would not interfere with this irreligious meeting; the Sea God would be angry with them if they did. True, the Reds controlled the Tower, but that didn't mean others couldn't hold meetings of this type, did it?

"Of course not," Brazil agreed soberly. He got a repeat on the time and place of the meeting, and went home to the scout.

They located the meeting without trouble, as Sunto had predicted. Brazil was lowered by cable again, a little distance away from the circle of fires in the hills near the center of the island. Gates held the scout overhead, ready for anything, while Brazil walked to the lighted area.

About fifty Blonds of both sexes were quietly busy with varied rituals within the illuminated circle. There were no detectable lookouts posted around the place, or any attempt at concealment.

Brazil watched for a little while, far enough away to be invisible to those near the fires. Then he walked slowly in on them, arms spread out in a gesture of peace. Gradually they became aware of him, the nearer people first. Within a few seconds all of them were standing still and watching. Then a. few of them moved slightly, opening a lane from where Brazil stood to a place near the center of the circle. He could see now a low structure of stone that stood there, a couple of meters square. It might be an altar.

"Any advice?" he subvocalized to the watchers above.

"Best thing I can think of is to bow in greeting and tell them to proceed with what they're doing," said some anonymous expert. No one argued with him. The final decision rested, as usual, with the man on the spot, the planeteer.

He accepted the advice offered, and it seemed to go over well enough. The attention of the Blond group turned from him to the central altar, where a few men and women began to perform some simple rites. The others stood watching with folded arms. Brazil folded his. No one was sitting down, and he resigned himself to what might be a long stand. He wished himself wearing Armor, Ground, Heavy, with powered legs that would let you nap standing if you wished.

Not that he wanted to nap now, although the ceremony teas had so far shown him nothing especially interesting. It had elements that Brazil had seen in life or on training tapes of a hundred primitive religions on a dozen planets.

But its climax was unique. A pair of muscular—deacons? Brazil could distinguish no one set apart as clergy—came from the darkness outside the waning firelight. They bore a, large and heavy pottery vessel that wobbled in their grip as if it held a quantity of sloshing liquid. Someone held a torch to illuminate the altar top. A slender tower about fifty or sixty centimeters high had been built of small flat pebbles, surrounded by a low wall of similar construction.

The men with the jar approached the rear of the altar and raised the vessel toward it, as a woman thrust a trough into position. They tipped the big jar evenly. What looked like clear water sluiced out of it, guided by the trough toward the pebble-tower. For a moment Brazil thought the little structure might withstand the flood, but some vital part of the base gave way suddenly. The men continued to tilt the vessel smoothly until it was empty. The tower toppled, taking with it part of the surrounding wall. It was washed piecemeal from the sloping altar by the last of the flood.

It hit them hard, Brazil could see, looking from one Blond face to another in the firelight. None of them stirred for a long minute. Plainly the collapse of the tower had some evil significance. Tower? Sunto had mentioned a tower, connected with the Sea God, and controlled by the Reds.

The Blonds gradually shook off some of their gloom. Again they were turning toward Brazil.

"Ceremony didn't turn out too well, I think," said the voice from the *Yuan Chwang*. "Just hope they don't blame it on you."

Once more everyone was watching Brazil, except for a couple of men who had begun to dismantle the altar. Might as well get started, he thought. He could pick out no one as leader, and so spoke out loudly to the group: "I am a man who has come from a far land, and I would learn what I can about the people here."

The faint stir and whispering among them ceased, and all watched him with guarded faces. There was only the fire glow and crackle, and the twittering background of animals or insects.

"This—" Brazil realized he had no certain word for ritual. "What you have done at this meeting is strange to me. If I can do so without giving offense, I would learn about it. Will someone here tell me?"

A light clear voice came from somewhere in the background: "Are you he of whom it is said, that he slew sixty Reds with a sweep of his arm?"

"It is said, but it is not true. I fought with six of them, but I slew none."

"You fought with six of them, yet none of them slew you." The still anonymous voice used a more subtle grammar than Tim had taught and had a slightly different accent. With his limited experience in listening to the natives, Brazil could not identify it as male or female. But it smelted of authority to him.

"My armor is strong," he said, answering the implied question. "And I had help from one who is wrongly called a dark demon, who is only a man like me, my countryman and friend."

"So have I heard it." The speaker moved forward slowly into brighter firelight—a woman. Not a girl, and not an old woman nor middle-aged. Not the kind that a man will follow with his eyes from the first glance, but the kind he will turn to see again a quarter-minute later, and remember. So Brazil thought of her at first sight, and only remembered with a start the subtle unearthliness of her face and body.

"So have I heard it, from those who were there and saw with open eyes." She came close to Brazil, dressed as simply as the others. She studied him. "You speak with the tongue of a simple Blond peasant."

"It was one such who taught me."

"You learned well. What is your name?"

"In your tongue it is best said as Boro. And what is yours, if I may ask without giving offense?"

She smiled. "Certainly, there has never been a god so fearful of giving offense. My name is Ariton. Tell these people whether you are god or man. I fear some of them will still not believe what you told Sunto."

Brazil loudly pledged again his membership in humanity.

Ariton waved her hand, and her people turned away. Most of them went to sit in a circle around where the altar had been. They began a low-voiced chant.

She walked with Brazil a little away from the group, and tried to answer his questions about the ceremony he had just witnessed. Her explanation was unintelligible with new words at first; finally he got her to simplify it enough for him to understand that the tiny tower on the altar had been an analog of a full-sized structure in the island's chief city. The big Tower was sacred to the Sea God. Now it was monopolized by the Red priests, and beside it the king of the Reds, Galamand, had built a castle. At mentioning the king's name, Ariton moved her foot as if grinding something into the dirt beneath her heel. Tim had sometimes done that when speaking of the Reds.

"And what did the water-pouring mean?"

"Maybe something bad." She looked at Brazil thoughtfully and raised a hand to touch his transparent helmet. "I have seen—before," she said, using a new word that he thought meant glass, from the context. "Now I will ask a question. Why could not the Reds slay you?"

"My armor is stronger than it looks."

"And why did you slay none of them?"

"There was no need."

"Those of my people who watched with open eyes say that you were angry at the killing of an old man you did not know. Why?"

Brazil pondered. "There was no need for his slaying, either, that I could see."

"Strong Red warriors could not hurt you with their spears," Ariton said thoughtfully. "And when they tried to seize you they were struck down by cramps and sickness, like swimmers who have entered cold water with full bellies. So the Sea God might ..."

"But it was not the Sea God. Shall we sit down here?" He gallantly let her have the low boulder that presented itself, and crunched his armored seat down into groundvine. The suit was a load to stand around in, even at point nine five gravity.

"Where is your dark companion now? And your ship?"

"He is not far. And our ship is near the island." Some water from the altar flood had run into the nearest fire, and the light grew dimmer yet. There was no word in Brazil's ear from above.

"It might be thought that you and your friend are only castaways."

He took the suggestion calmly. "It is not so. Our ship is near, with others of my people aboard. My countrymen and I travel to learn about new lands that none of us has seen before. We would like to live on this island for a little while, perhaps a few years, on some land your people do not use. We do not want to boss your people, or take anything we do not pay for."

"I have no land to give anyone, while there are Reds on the island." Ariton's voice was sharp.

"Some of my people will talk to the Reds, too, about using land. But we will not trade with a tribe that holds another tribe in slavery."

She was puzzled. "But who does not own slaves, if he can? If we could enslave the Reds, we would. Do you own no slaves at home?"

"It has been very many years since my tribe held slaves. A tribe becomes stronger when it does not depend on them. My people have traveled far and looked at many tribes, and it is always so."

"But if all were free to choose, who would do the mean and dirty work of slaves by choice?" Ariton looked at him searchingly.

Brazil gave a faint sigh. "True, someone must do such work—sometimes someone must be forced to do it. But even such lowly persons should be treated as members of the tribe, and not killed or beaten as animals would be."

"And if there are two tribes, as on this island?"

"Two tribes can live together as one, if their leaders are wise and strong."

"That is a strange thought to me. But then I have never traveled in the far parts of the world." Ariton meditated for a few moments before she spoke again. "Will you, Boro, go to speak with the Red King about this matter of land? You still look like a Blond, so maybe the Reds will try again to kill or imprison you."

Brazil thought it over. "I may be the one who goes. It is only chance that I look like a Blond. My shipmates are of varied appearance; some of them resemble Reds." He thought to himself: What planeteer looks most like a Red? Foley, but his hair isn't nearly the right shade. A little dye will fix that, if need be.

"I will go with you, when you go to speak to Galamand," Ariton announced.

Brazil was surprised. "Can you walk into his castle at will?"

"I think Galamand will see me if I call on him." Ariton smiled. "I am a high priestess of the Sea God."

***

Another conference began as soon as Brazil was hoisted home to his scoutship.

"Religion may give us a way to promote unity here." said Sociology. "Since Reds and Blonds both worship the same Sea God."

"We have that Tower located, by the way," put in Captain Dietrich. "And what's probably the Red king's castle, or at least his summer home. It seems too far from fresh water to withstand a siege. Where's that chart? Here, on this peninsula that protects the harbor at Capital City, a large stone structure. Right next to it, on the side toward the ocean, is the tallest building on the island, a tower about thirty meters high. Then there's a sea wall running the length of the peninsula, for protection against waves and maybe against invaders.

"Foley. you and Brazil will be visiting Galamand as soon as we can locate him. Get your hair died to match the Reds'. Maybe we can at least put over the idea that it's possible for Red and Blond to cooperate."

"I trust everything possible will be done to avoid another fight." Chandragupta wore a frown.

"We'll try," the Captain said. "Is anyone against sending a delegation to Galamand as soon as possible?" It seemed that no one was.

"Should we take Ariton along, as she suggested?" Gates asked the conference.

"It might make us seem to be committed as her allies against the Reds."

"No doubt that's what she wants."

"But it would bring the two leaders face to face, with us present."

***

Planeteer Foley, hair reddened, was flown down and transferred to scoutship *Alpha*, which lay out at sea again. Gates intended to hold himself in reserve, on the scout.

Hoping to find out where the king was, and to arrange to take Ariton to the planned meeting, Brazil almost literally dropped in, shortly after sunset one evening, on the hill village where she had told him she could usually be found.

No Reds were in evidence. Again a flock of watchbirds assaulted Brazil with futile energy. The Blond natives stared at him with some awe, but little surprise. They directed him to a building set against a hill.

It was a low structure of groundvine mats and rare wooden poles. Carved or molded masks hung in profusion at the doorway, the first artwork of any kind Brazil had seen on the island, except for the decorated armor of the Reds. He stood at a gateway in a low surrounding fence and called a greeting to the dark and open doorway of the house. In a few moments, a Blond man, unusually tall and carrying an oil lamp, emerged from the rambling building. He stood studying Brazil emotionlessly.

"I am looking for Ariton," Brazil repeated. The towering Blond somehow made him feel for a ridiculous moment like an adolescent suitor come to call on his girl and greeted by her older brother.

"Ariton has gone to Capital City," the man said finally. "To meet you or your countrymen there when you go to visit the king of the Redmen." Again the grinding foot-motion at mention of Galamand. This man conveyed a suggestion of insolent freedom and power to Brazil. It was impossible for him to think of this man or Ariton as slaves.

"Is Galamand now in his castle beside the Tower of the Sea God?" Brazil asked.

"Yes." The Blond man paused, then seemed to reach a sudden decision involving Brazil. "Come with me." He beckoned with his lamp and led the way into the house.

They followed a passage leading back toward the hillside. The open rooms they passed contained things unknown to Brazil, things carven and feathered and stained. More temple than home, certainly.

"Here." The Blond turned aside suddenly, and stooped to roll up a floor mat. Buried among mats of groundvine that filled a hole evidently of considerable depth, were row upon row of spears, simply made but strong and sharp.

"When your king comes to this island." said the Blond, showing powerful white teeth above his beard, "he will find ready help to topple the Reds from power. Not all my people are willing to live the lives of animals. Long have we planned and waited. The Reds are fewer than we. Each year they stay more within their forts and their walled city and each year hurt us more, with killings and beatings. We will be ready to help you."

Brazil took a deep breath. "If you want to help me help your people, you will not rise armed against the Reds. You will agree to live with them as one tribe, when they also agree."

The man stared at Brazil for a long moment, then gave a short and nasty laugh. "When they say that will be the day when they are helpless."

"Remember what I say, if you wish your own people well." said Brazil, turning to leave. "Let there be no armed rising against the Reds."

"Not yet," said the Blond in a cold voice. "Not yet for a little while."

***

Brazil and Foley stood among tall bushes and grass on a hillside with a fair view of the town whose name translated into Capital City, just after sunrise on the next morning. They wore heavy ground armor, in camouflage colors. They studied the city before them, adjusting their heavy glass faceplates for telescopic vision.

Capital City was plainly divided into two sections. The Reds dwelt on a hill at the far side of the harbor from the watching planeteers, in an area surrounded by a defensive wall. Their buildings were of stone or mud brick, and a number of Blond servants could be seen going about menial tasks.

In the Blond section, on lower ground and closer to Brazil and Foley, no Reds were visible except for an occasional squad of patrolling soldiers. These stuck close together, looking grimly over their shoulders. The houses were built mostly of dried groundvine mats, though some mud bricks were used.

Beyond the Blond section were the docks. The water of the harbor was studded with the low shapes of fishing boats, and, larger, a few of Galamand's war galleys.

"Well—shall we march?" asked Foley.

"Might as well. I expect Ariton will know we're here before we've gone very far."

Brazil moved his legs. The suit servos drew power from the tiny hydrogen fusion lamp in the backpack; the suit legs churned the massive shape ahead. The wearer had the sensation of moving in light summer clothing, but he could plow through heavy bush and small trees if he chose. Brazil and Foley had no wish to leave a trail of destruction, so they picked their way with care to the nearest road and set out toward town.

Ariton met them in a narrow street before they were well inside the town. She stared hard at Foley when Brazil

45

introduced him, but gave him a common greeting-word in a pleasant voice. "Sunto is waiting with a boat in the harbor," she told them. "It is the shortest and easiest way to Galamand's building."

The planeteers followed her through narrow, winding streets toward the harbor, ever a center of apathetic, curious, hopeful, or pokerfaced stares from the Blond slum-dwellers. None of the Red patrols came within sight, which suited Brazil fine.

Sunto was waiting at a low dock, in a crude and lopsided rowboat fashioned of reeds. "Hope the blasted thing can hold us," said Foley on radio. "It'd be a long swim from the middle of the harbor."

The sun was still bright in the morning sky, promising a warm day. Galamand's castle rose forbidding across the harbor, beyond the fishing boats and the moored biremes of his navy. Above and beyond the castle rose the slender stone Tower of the Sea God.

The rowboat held up as Sunto propelled it across the calm water of the harbor, straight toward the landing steps at the base of the castle. Reds appeared on the steps, watching. Their number grew as the boat approached.

"Galamand will have heard of you, of course," said Ariton. "I think he will be eager to see you for himself. Of course he may decided to kill you." She observed them.

"I don't think he will harm us," said Foley. From inside heavy ground armor they could remonstrate gently but confidently with Galamand while he boiled them in oil or his cohorts attempted to bash in their faceplates with axes. It would require a local Archimedes and considerable time and effort for any technologically primitive power to do them serious damage.

But Ariton wore not much of any clothes at all. Foley asked her: "Do you think you will be safe?"

"The priestess of the Sea God is safe even from Galamand," she answered absently. Brazil thought she was worried, but not about herself.

He scanned the ranks of grimly watching Reds as they neared the landing steps. "Is Galamand among those?"

"I do not see him. No doubt he awaits you in the great hall inside."

The boat wallowed up to the landing. Ariton nimbly hopped out and made it fast with a rope of vine. A couple of Red soldiers halfheartedly leveled spears in her direction, but no one moved to stop her. Brazil and Foley disembarked and stood quietly, giving the Reds the chance to look them over and make the first move if they felt like it. There were no Red women or children in sight.

Ariton moved her hand in an intricate gesture, in the air above Sunto's head, then touched his head briefly. "Now they will not bother him—for a while," she said to Brazil. "Well, let us go on and try to see the king."

A sword-bearing Red who might be an army officer stepped forward. "King Galamand has been told that you are here. Stand and wait." He eyed Foley with unconcealed and unfriendly curiosity.

Some of the Red troops looked Brazil over and commented among themselves with openly truculent contempt. His blondness was plainly visible through the faceplate. He looked back at them, deadpan, and unobtrusively moved to inflate his suit's flotation bubbles. Giant red swellings ballooned around his shoulders and torso. The soldiers stared and fell silent.

A few minutes passed. Brazil was deflating his bubbles as a more elaborately costumed Red appeared, and imperiously beckoned the delegation to follow him into the castle.

The few Blonds visible inside the walls had the look of the lowest of slaves. Now a few Red women and children were in evidence, but these retreated rapidly of out sight of the visitors. The complex of walls and buildings making up the stronghold had been built of heavy stone, with little if any mortar used.

The great hall was a high chamber about thirty meters by ten, dimly lit by smoking torches and small, high windows. It was crowded by Red men of varied appearance. Across the far end of the room stood a solid wall of tall soldiers bearing shields and leveled s

"Stand and wait here," said the distinguished Red who was acting guide, indicating a spot not far from the leveled spears. He disappeared into the crowd at one side.

Brazil and Foley turned casually around as they waited, studying the chamber and the Reds in it. No attempt had been made to surround the visitors closely. The door by which they had entered still stood open. Ariton stood waiting between the planeteers, with utter calm.

Another important-looking Red appeared before them; but it was somehow obvious that he was not the king. He held his hands clasped before him and owned a nose remarkable in size even for one of his tribe. "Do you bear weapons?" he demanded, looking from Foley to Brazil.

"We do," said Foley, "and we are not the only men here who bear them." He tried to give his speech the accent of a Red.

"You must give me your weapons," said the chamberlain. "Then you may advance and prostrate yourselves before the king."

"We will greet the king in all friendliness," said Foley. "But the law of our own nation forbids us to do him homage, or to give up our weapons."

The chamberlain hesitated a moment, then began to screech at the Earthmen threateningly. He raved and glared and waved his arms, jabbering so fast he became almost unintelligible. Yet Brazil got the impression the man was trying to avoid direct personal insult. It was a masterful performance of denouncing their disrespectful behavior but not themselves.

"Let's wait him out," Brazil subvocalized to Foley via radio. "Maybe they just want to see if we bluff. It wouldn't do for the king himself to try and fail."

The planeteers stood silent a full thirty seconds longer, glaring stony-eyed back at the speaker. The harangue gave no sign of slackening. "Better squelch him," Brazil said at last. Evidently the torrent of words was going to continue until they reacted to it in some way. Brazil did not now want to give the impression that Earthmen had infinite patience. The squelch might be better accepted coming from the "Red" planeteer.

"Silence!" Foley bellowed, after turning up his airspeaker volume. He got what he called for with magical suddenness. Ariton wore a pleased smile.

"We have come here to talk with a king, not to listen to you," Foley went on. "If King Galamand is not pleased to receive us today, we will return tomorrow. Our business is important."

"Get out of the way," said a firm voice from behind the wall of soldiers. "Let them come here."

The ranks of soldiers opened, but stayed within spear-thrusting distance on either side. Brazil, Ariton, and Foley advanced toward the man who sat alone upon an elaborately carven chair.

The man upon the throne was not ordinary. A vast scar sliced across his face, nearly obliterating one of his eyes. He was approaching middle age, not big for a Red, but thick-limbed and strong. Upon his breastplate was worked in relief an image of the Sea God's Tower.

Foley opened his mouth, doubtless meaning to register a complaint about the way the chamberlain had spoken to them. "Greetings, great king," was all that came out. Galamand's bright blue eye seemed to nail you with more effect than if there had been two.

"Greetings, great king," said Brazil. Ariton stood between the Earthmen, saying nothing but watching Galamand haughtily.

The king ignored her and spoke to the armored planeteers, looking from one to the other. "I bid you welcome," he said perfunctorily. "Does your king send greetings to me?"

"He does indeed," said Foley. "And would send you gifts, as is our custom. But in some lands it is considered an insult to present such gifts immediately."

The king raised an eyebrow, and his mouth twisted slightly. Brazil spoke up: "Oh, there are such lands. King Galamand. Not many, but a few."

The blue eye fixed on his. "I thank your king for his greetings. Is he Red or Blond?"

"Neither," said Brazil, truthfully enough. "In our country men of different colors live together peacefully."

The king nodded toward Ariton. "You bring this woman with you. Why?"

"I have come with these my friends, to speak for my people," she said, flaring up at him. "And I speak also to the Sea God, as you well know."

Galamand seemed faintly amused. "Do you speak against me to the Sea God, woman? Your words are not strong enough. The Tower still stands against the waves. The sea-sound is faint in my ear, and soothing as I go to sleep at night. Will you arouse the Sea God to destroy me?"

Brazil heard the faintest stir and mutter among the soldiers on either side; evidently the king's words might be thought a provocation to the god. Galamand swept his blue eye around, but said nothing to his men.

He spoke again to the planeteers: "And you are this woman's friends?"

"We would be friends with Red and Blond alike."

Galamand digested the statement swiftly and without comment, and changed the subject. "Your ship is swift and hard to see; my ships have circled the island every day since you first appeared, and have not found it. Now I admit this puzzles me."

Brazil answered: "As you say, great king, our ship is elusive and very swift. It is not the wish of our king that our first visits here be seen by many ships upon the sea."

"And why do you come here at all?"

"We seek always the knowledge of new lands, oh king," said Foley. "Some twenty or thirty of us would like to live on this island for a year or two, on some small area of land that you who live here now do not need. We are willing to pay for this privilege. But we do not want to deal with a government engaged in civil war, under which two tribes contend against each other; or with a king who holds another tribe in slavery."

"No one contends against me here and lives." Galamand spoke quietly and distinctly. He gave Ariton his twisted grin and asked: "Is it not so?"

It stung her deeply, and her voice rose loud: "Your day is not forever, Redman. One day your children will be our slaves, if you beget any before you die. We will—"

Brazil's voice rose over hers. "That is not what *we* want! That would yet be war and slavery."

Both native rulers looked at him, for the moment united against the outsider. Then Galamand asked quietly: "How would you have us live?"

"As one tribe."

Galamand narrowed his operational eye and scratched his beard. "You spoke of payment, for the use of land. What do you mean to offer?"

Foley answered: "To the ruler of a peaceful land we would offer, to begin with, a great quantity of cord, much stronger and more lasting than your vines, to make excellent fishnets, oh king."

"And weapons?" The king's voice was casual and gentle.

"A quantity of swords and spears might be included—"

"You do not carry swords or spears."

"We carry them for trade." They could be made up.

Galamand's blue eye did not waver from Foley's face, but his right arm shot out toward the nearest guard, and his fingers snapped. The haft of the guard's spear was instantly in his grip. The king stood up and thrust the spear, butt first, toward Foley, at the same time holding out his left hand open.

"If you are men who deal in spears, then I will trade with you. I offer in trade this good Red spear, for that weapon you wear at your side."

Foley assumed a deeply troubled expression. "Oh great king, we have no wish to anger you. But we must refuse to trade our weapons. If we did so, the anger of *our* king would fall heavily upon our heads. And against *his* anger we have no defense."

"And against mine?" Galamand's voice was still gentle. So is a lion, when not hungry or offended.

"We have our weapons, which we cannot trade, great king," said Brazil, with punctilious courtesy. The blue eye lanced at him and he looked right back down the shaft of it, while from the corners of his eyes he watched the spearmen carefully. Galamand too must have received accurate intelligence about the First Contact, if he could identify the butt of a stun pistol as a weapon.

Galamand grounded the butt of the spear and stood drumming his fingers on the shaft. "Fishnets," he said meditatively. "Your great king has then no weapons to spare? I would reward you well if you were to convince him that he has; or if you were to act, shall we say, on your own ..." He reached into a pouch at his belt and brought out a lustrous pearl-like jewel, bigger than a grape.

Foley shook his head slowly. "Oh king, it cannot be. If you offer us the riches of the whole island, still we will give or trade to you no weapons, save such as you can make yourselves."

Galamand tossed the spear back to the soldier and seated himself again. "And your armor? I admit I have not seen such glass."

This time Brazil joined in the head shaking.

"Strange men," Galamand mused. "You say you will not trade with a ruler who holds another tribe in slavery. I will not ask you why. I have not asked for any trade with you that would pay me in fishnets, and I want none. While the waves spare the Tower, the Sea God supports me. I am king upon this island. My slaves are my slaves. When you are willing to trade something worth while for the use of my land, you may come back again and speak with me."

"Suggestions?" Brazil radioed.

"Leave without argument," said a voice from above. "We can analyze what we've got and try again."

Ariton stood proudly erect while Brazil and Foley bowed deeply to the king, who told them with a straight face that he was providing them with an escort back to their ship, that no harm should come to them on the way.

"They'll see the scout unless we can shake them," Brazil radioed, starting out of the throne room.

"Guess we'll have to give them a minimum marvel to look at," said Gates' voice. "There's a suitable deep cove just outside the city, about four kilometers from where you are. Just walk south along the shore? I'll bring the scout up partly out of the water for you to get in, and let them get a good enough look to be sure it's a ship and not a sea monster. Okay?"

"Good idea," said Captain Dietrich. "A submarine will startle them some, but it should further convince them we're not spirits who just materialize."

Ariton walked with the planeteers out of the castle; they stopped at the landing steps to pick up Sunto, who was much relieved to see them. When told they were leaving by land, Sunto climbed out of his half-waterlogged rowboat, and said to a Red soldier standing guard nearby: "I leave to you as a gift the noble craft which you have praised so highly." And he ground his foot against the stone stair. The Red glowered but said nothing.

The walk out of the city was uneventful. Within an hour the four of them stood on the steep sloping shore within the chosen cove, with Galamand's heavily armed honor guard watching very carefully from a little distance and a Red galley casually standing by off shore.

Foley was telling Ariton that a ship would soon come to take Brazil and him on board, but she and Sunto would have to stay on shore. She agreed calmly, and watched the horizon for the ship, with some puzzlement.

Brazil turned to Sunto. "The Tower of the Sea God is very important to your people and the Reds, is it not?"

"Yes." Sunto did not seem especially interested in the subject. "It is our old belief that as long as the Tower is not destroyed by the waves of the sea, the Sea God smiles upon the rulers of the island, whoever they be."

"What if the waves should knock the Tower down?"

Sunto smiled wryly. "Then I think you would see upon this island the one tribe for which Ariton says you asked the king. For the Tower to be so destroyed would mean the Sea God thinks the rulers of the island evil. The destruction of his own Tower is to be his last warning before he overwhelms with waves the entire island, slaying everyone on it and carrying the evildoers down to be frozen forever in the ice at the bottom of the sea."

"Get more on this!" said an excited radio voice. "Foley, ask Ariton about the Tower, she should be a real authority. Gates, hold that scout underwater for a minute.

Brazil asked Sunto: "Do you think the Sea God will ever destroy the Tower?"

Sunto looked out at the ocean soberly; it was dull and placid in the sun. "May I never see the day—but I am a practical man. Whoever is king will surely see to it that the sea wall of large rocks is kept strong at the base of the Tower, to break the force of the waves. Someday, perhaps, a very great storm ... but there are great storms every year. The Tower has stood for many years."

"Is the season for great storms coming soon?" Brazil felt the vague beginnings of what might be a valid idea.

"No, it is just past. Now is the time of the steady-but-not-too-strong winds."

"That checks," said Meteorology from above.

Sunto continued: "Also, the Tower stands on a straight shoreline, and the Sea God hurls his waves most strongly against the points of land that jut out into his domain."

"That is true in all lands," said Brazil absently. He had just the start of a plan to scare these people into co-operating, by making the Tower seemed threatened by a storm. It might be just possible to induce a violent storm. But what would it do to the rest of the island? The scheme seemed worthless ... "That is true in all lands. As it is true that the waves come in nearly parallel to the shore, no matter from which point at sea the wind is blowing. And the reason is the same ..." Brazil fell silent, as if in a sudden dream.

"Why, that is so, but I have never thought about it," said Sunto in surprise. "Truly, the waves are like women, for men watch them long and understand them but little."

"... that they travel more slowly as the water beneath them grows more shallow," said Brazil with a far-away look. He gave a sudden laugh at the sight of Sunto's startled face. "Waves, I mean, not women. Sunto, tell me this. If the Tower were destroyed by some means other than the waves, what then?"

Sunto gave the Blond equivalent of a shrug. "Why, the Tower would simply have to be rebuilt, and the king would gain merit in the Sea God's eyes by rebuilding." He thought for a moment. "Maybe the Red king would rebuild it on some inland hill; where no wave could ever reach it, and so make his rule safe."

Brazil nodded as if satisfied.

***

Twenty minutes later he sat with Foley in scoutship *Alpha*, gratefully peeling off chunks of armor. They faced on a segmented screen the debriefing assembly of their peers and bosses, electronically gathered to analyze the visit to Galamand. The astounded natives who had watched the two planeteers enter the submarine craft were by now no doubt attending their own conferences on the subject.

"First, tell me this," Brazil invited, eyes alight with an idea. "Does it seem likely that a massive assault of ocean waves on this Tower might make these people willing to try getting along together, at least for a while?"

"I would say yes, based on what Ariton told me," said Foley.

"It might well give us a start in the right direction," said Sociology cautiously.

"An assault of ocean waves, you say," Captain Dietrich frowned. "Not of forcefields, explosives, chemicals or sonic vibrations."

"Captain. I think there's a chance it can be done with this scoutship. and not by directing any of those modern weapons against the Tower."

"I am afraid I would have to forbid the use of such weapons against the natives, on principle." said Chandragupta grimly.

"The idea is not to wreck the Tower," said Brazil, "but to make the natives think that the Sea God has decided to wreck it."

"That Galamand's no fool," said Gates. "He's probably thinking up antisubmarine devices already. And how are you going to stir up suitable waves with a scoutship?"

"I'm not going to stir them up, exactly. And I don't think Galamand will notice a submarine acting a good many kilometers out at sea."

"Brazil, are you drunk?"

"No, on duty. Another reason for getting this situation settled. Now we'll need some information from Oceanography. And a weather forecast of such massive solidity that we can all lean on it—one that includes a steady ocean breeze here."

***

Trofand, Red priest of the Sea God, and chief caretaker of the Tower, was awakened by the sound of the waves, to which he always listened with half an ear even when asleep. The sound was now too loud for his liking.

He arose from his pallet and was dressing in the stone-damp darkness of his chamber in the Tower's base when he received a shock. A streaming puddle of cold sea, water flowed against his bare foot on the floor. He hastened to light a candle from the smoldering brazier that fought uselessly against the permanent dampness of his bedchamber.

By candlelight he saw with distress that water was entering in multiple thin streams through chinks in the massive masonry of the inner Tower wall. It was something that happened only in the heaviest storms. The booming roar of the waves pounding the heavy sea wall outside seemed to be increasing, and now brought him to the beginning of real fright. In ten years in the Tower he had never heard it so loud. A mighty storm must be raging, though the season for them was past, and the weather signs had given no indication of any approaching tempest.

Trofand was nearly dressed when an underling came with a torch, pounding on his door and opening it with a minimum of courtesy. "My lord, the waves, the waves! They are very bad."

"I have ears, fool. Someone should have called me sooner. What are the signs of the storm's length?"

"My lord, there is no storm."

Trofand started an angry retort to the foolish statement, but something in the pale frightened face before him made him pause. Fastening his belt, he led the way out of the chamber to the stair that climbed to the Tower's top.

It was true, he realized, emerging into the predawn darkness atop the Tower. The sky was clear. The wind was steady in direction from the sea, but it was not strong. The surf at the Tower's foot should be fairly gentle.

He thought he felt the stones of the Tower quiver underfoot with each leisurely watery smash.

An assistant was at his elbow, speaking with a worried voice. "My lord, what shall we do? The signs are that the wind will rise throughout the day, and remain steady in direction. If the waves become yet higher—"

"If they do, we will deal with them. The Sea God is not our enemy. Go rouse out the Tower slaves. Conscript more if need be. Have them stand by the fresh slabs of rock, ready at dawn to strengthen the seawall. Then go you to offer the day's sacrifice to the Sea God. But do not take too long about it."

"I obey." The man was gone in an instant, down the stair. Other junior priests of the Tower huddled about Trofand in the chill night, in the light of a dim torch, looking to him for guidance.

Well, a I was right about that. Trofand said to himself. He was thinking of the extra stones, weighing many tons apiece, that he had long ago ordered to be kept on rollers in the courtyard. They were constantly ready to be moved to reinforce the seawall in case a storm of unprecedented violence should threaten the Tower.

Now, another question: should he order the king awakened? After all, the Tower seemed in no immediate danger, and Galamand might grumble if he were waked up for something unimportant. But he might have the man boiled alive who failed to wake him for a real emergency. It was not a hard decision to make. "You—go rouse the king. Tell him I say that waves threaten the Tower. Tell no one else."

"I obey."

King Galamand was beside Trofand within a few minutes, looking over the parapet and frowning at the strange intensity of waves that were driven by such a modest wind. He observed the preparations that had been made to reinforce the seawall at dawn, and then turned and struck his fist against the parapet. "You did well to call me. But these stones have stood throughout my lifetime, and I say that they will stand yet a good while longer." Trofand saw him outlined against the first gray light in the east.

The Blond slaves, whipped on by overseers, now began to roll the mighty rock slabs into position to reinforce the seawall. It would be dangerous work. But slaves could be replaced, while the Tower—.

There was an outcry somewhere inside the Tower. In a minute an exhausted runner appeared, helped up the stairs by others. In near panic he leaned against the stones beside the king. "My lord, the seawall—the wall away from the Tower, up and down the peninsula—"

"Is it breached by waves? Where?"

"No, my lord." A gasp of breath. "I came along the wall, after carrying your message conscripting slaves—"

"Well?"

"Elsewhere, my lord, the waves are small. Only here at the Tower do they rise abnormally, as if in raging anger. As if the Sea God has grown angry and—uh!"

Galamand's vicious backhand blow knocked the man sprawling. "Enough! Do not preach the anger of the gods at me, or I will show you what anger is! I am the king!"

The king turned away to peer, with Trofand and the others, at the waves beating against the seawall at a distance from the Tower. The fast-brightening dawn revealed that the messenger had spoken the truth.

***

The news was out, Brazil saw, as he strode along the seawall road toward the Tower and the fortified complex of Galamand's castle. A puzzled Ariton walked between him and Foley. Reds and Blonds stood in little groups along the wall, commenting on the waves that were assaulting the base of the Tower. Faces turned toward them as they passed, but ever turned back again to the greater wonder of the waves.

Each long swell marched in from the clear horizon of the ocean, foaming up and curling over as the depth of the water below approached the height of the wave, to smash itself finally against the rocks piled in shallow water at the base of the seawall. But in the sea before the Tower, each incoming rise of water seemed to squeeze itself together along its long axis, rising to at least three times the height of the waves elsewhere, before it piled up in a foaming fury of discriminating violence against that part of the seawall.

Ariton paused at her first sight of this, whispering something that might have been a prayer. "You knew of this?" she asked Brazil. "This is why you brought me here?"

"I'm taking you to talk to Galamand," Brazil evaded. "I think if you and he can't come to some agreement soon, there won't be any Tower left for either of you to use. You have lived near the sea all your life. You know the strength that is in large waves."

"What do you mean?" She stared at him, half afraid. "Do you speak for the Sea God?"

"We are only men," he answered innocently. "But do I not understand your gods correctly? Is it not so that the Sea God may destroy his own Tower when there is great strife in the land and evil rulers, as a final warning before he destroys the entire island?"

After a long moment she took her eyes from Brazil's face and turned toward the Tower. "Come, whoever you are. It is my place to be there now."

"Is this really going to work?" Foley radioed while they walked. "I mean that Tower isn't built out of pebbles, exactly. And it's stood through a lot of storms."

"On Earth," answered Brazil in professorial accents, "wave forces have been measured at over thirty tons per square meter. Engineers will not build a shoreline structure on Earth without carefully considering local conditions regarding the effect we are now employing. Besides, the idea is to scare Galamand and the lady here into cooperating, not to actually wreck the Tower. That would probably kill someone, and I hate to think what might happen in the panic."

At the castle gate, the guards were almost looking over their shoulders at the Tower as they halted the three visitors and sent word to Galamand of their arrival. Within a few minutes a guide appeared to escort the visitors to the bare top of the Tower.

Brazil could see by the flags above the castle that the wind had increased slightly and was holding a steady direction, as Meteorology had promised. If only we were gods enough to control the weather in an area of a few square kilometers, thought Brazil. We can come a hundred light-years to stick our noses into our neighbors' business, but if the weather doesn't quite suit our schemes we can only wait until it does.

Galamand scoured them with his single eye when they had climbed the stairs to the Tower's top. The king paused in his pacing amid a group of high-ranking Reds. "Come you to preach the Sea God to me also?" he inquired in an ominously quiet voice.

Ariton looked about her. "Where is Trofand?"

"He has gone to offer sacrifice in the chapel below," said the king, a tinge of amusement in his voice. He leaned against the parapet with thick arms folded and his back to the sea as if in contempt." He has rather suddenly remembered to take his religious obligations seriously."

"Human sacrifice?" asked Brazil. He hadn't thought of this possibility.

"He considers that course," said Galamand. "But I think the Sea God has lives enough for one day." He moved his head to indicate that they should look over the parapet.

In the cold boiling hell of surf at the Tower's foot a hundred Blond slaves or more struggled on the slippery rocks, straining on levers and vine ropes to move an enormous block of stone into the surf at a place where the waves had weakened the wall. With each torrential ebb and surge of water, Brazil saw, a pale object in the surf was drawn out and hurled in near the rocks, buried in foam and tossed up again—a fish-pale thing that had blond hair and no longer any face. And there was another—and another …

No Blond slave or Red overseer took any apparent notice of the drowned men, much less attempted to pull them from the sea. Every living man down there was concerned too intently with his own footing on the treacherous rock.

"Take it easy, old man." said a voice inside Brazil's helmet. Oh, this Brazil is a wonder, a red-hot planeteer, said a louder voice inside his mind. Just trust him to come up with a great scheme to set everyone on the road to happiness without bloodshed. That's important, no bloodshed. Well, you can't see any blood down there, can you?

Now that's enough. Shut up and get to work, there's a job to finish. "Why does the surf attack only the place of the Tower, oh king?" he asked, turning, stony-faced.

The blue eye studied him. "Had I a ship so cunningly built as to travel under water, I might discover why." Galamand turned to his aides. "Send boats and divers out beyond the white water. See if anything strange lies under the surface."

"The old boy's uncomfortably shrewd," said Foley on radio. "Doesn't seem likely they'll search the bottom eight kilometers out and eighty meters deep, though."

Boats and divers soon appeared in the sea a few hundred meters out from the Tower, and made a show of investigating underwater conditions. It was not a really dangerous job for such skillful sailors and swimmers, out there where there were no rocks to be dashed against. But the Red seamen seemed to approach the job with a vast reluctance. Their faces turned often toward the Tower, as if in hope that the king would recall them.

Time passed. By noon the wind was obviously gaining strength again.

"I go to join Trofand in the chapel," said Ariton to the king, as if daring him to stop her. He pulled at his beard and appeared not to hear.

When she had gone he ordered food brought to him. His aides grew continually more gloomy. They looked often at the king, but sought to avoid his eye.

Galamand was amused to see the planeteers drink their lunch from tubes inside their helmets. He asked if their suits had sanitary facilities too, and roared with laughter when he was told they had. But the laughter had a forced sound in the wind.

The wind grew yet stronger, though it was still far from a gale. Down below, a wave got under a forty-ton slab of rock just right and skipped it like a flat chip against the base of the Tower itself. Stones split and flew; one fragment spun almost to the Tower's top.

The next wave poured through the gap in the seawall, like the paw of a giant beast forced into a hole to grope for prey. The next tore free another huge stone from the edge of the hole. The bones of the Tower quivered.

Slaves and masters at the Tower's foot scrambled desperately to move another massive rock into a defensive position. Brazil saw it was a futile thing for creatures weak as men to attempt. One roaring curl of water caught a Red, who dropped his whip and grabbed at the slippery rock to save himself. Brazil saw the upturned face, the eyes seemingly looking straight into his own, the mouth open as if to yell. The next wave tore the man away and dragged him out of sight.

Galamand was roaring orders for more slaves to be brought. "You have strange powers and weapons," he demanded suddenly of Foley. "Can you help me now?"

Brazil pulled himself out of a hideous fascination with what was happening down below.

"And if we can?" asked Foley.

"It might be that the agreement you sought with me could be quickly reached." The wind tore at Galamand's words, and shot spray past his head, here thirty meters above the normal sea. A small wave-tossed rock clattered against the parapet, as if shot from a giant's sling.

"Then order those men from the sea down there," Brazil demanded. "And give your word to make of Red and Blond one tribe."

"Then you can cure this," barked the king. "And it may be you have caused it!" The other Reds glared at the Earthmen; some weapons were drawn. Then cries came from the stairway, distracting attention.

Ariton and Trofand were suddenly at the top of the stair, in ceremonial robes half sodden with sea water.

"My king, the Sea God pours his wrath into the very chapel. I—" Trofand jumped back, as if he thought the king's sudden lunge was directed at him. But Galamand seized Ariton, had her arm twisted behind her back and his dagger at her throat in a moment.

"Sacrilege! Sacrilege!" howled Trofand. The other Reds looked on, wavering, wide-eyed, undecided.

The king swung Ariton to face the planeteers. "Now, aliens," he roared. "Cause the waves to cease, and quickly, or I will butcher this so-called queen with whom you ally yourselves. You seek to put her on a throne, but I alone am king. And so I will remain!"

"My lord." Ariton's low voice stopped the king in surprise. Doubtless it was the first time she had used any title of respect to him. "My death will not save our island. But I will marry you and bear your sons, if that be the only way to save it. And we will live here as one tribe."

For the first time in his experience, Brazil saw Galamand taken aback. But it was only for a moment.

"No, I'll not have it! I am the king here, I alone. Not you, or the aliens, or the Sea God himself, can order me, do this, do that!"

Trofand moaned and covered his face; every other Red was visibly shaken by the king's defiance of the god. Brazil felt a sudden turn of sympathy for Galamand, losing to forces he could not comprehend, cutting himself off now from his own followers. Be ready for the moment ...

The sea-flung stone, the size of a grapefruit, actually missed Galamand's helmeted head by only a few centimeters, and flew on to bounce off the opposite wall and down the stairway. The jolt from Brazil's quick-drawn stun pistol took the king in the head about one second later, when all eyes were on Galamand. No native doubted that the rock had grazed the king's helmet and caused his sudden collapse. Brazil's pistol was reholstered as quickly as it had been drawn.

The Red priests and soldiers stared at the fallen ruler in awe. Plainly he had been struck down for blasphemy. None of them moved to aid him. Foley went to him, pulling out his first aid kit and beginning a quick radio conference with the medics of the *Yuan Chwang*. The stun-jolt should wear off in a matter of minutes; a carefully chosen tranquilizer administered now should ease the situation then considerably.

A Red officer of apparent high rank spoke almost imploringly to Trofand. "We will obey you, my lord. Is there any way to save the island?"

The priest looked uncertainly at Ariton. Brazil asked her: "Will you now marry the king, as you offered, and so unite your people with his?"

She rubbed the arm that Galamand had twisted, and frowned. "There is no need for that now. The Sea God has rejected him. With your help, I will be ruler—"

"Do you want the Tower to stand?" Brazil cut her off brutally. "Remember, too, that the Red soldiers are still strong, and perhaps not eager to serve you."

She nodded, meekly wide-eyed for once.

Brazil turned to Trofand. "Can the marriage be performed as soon as the king awakens?"

"If he can be made to agree to it: I see that the Sea God has spared his life, for now his eyelids move."

"I think he can be made to agree," said the high-ranking officer, grimly. "I think it is time we had a certain heir to the throne, and also an end to this unprofitable fighting in our own land."

Brazil switched off his airspeaker, with throat muscles beginning to quiver with the relaxation of tension. "Sam, start cutting down that hump. But stand by to rebuild, until I give you the word that the honeymoon has started."

Eight kilometers out at sea and eighty meters below the surface, scoutships *Alpha* and *Omicron* braced themselves on water-filled space, and thrust noses equipped with jury-rigged bulldozer blades against the mound of mud and sand rising from the bottom, the mound they had carefully constructed in the same manner the day before. It was not much of a mound for size, really, and unimpressive-looking to any but an oceanographer. But it shallowed the water above it, and so it slowed the waves, refracting those from one certain direction, focusing them as a lens treats light, causing them to converge on one small area eight kilometers away.

***

Boris Brazil opened his eyes. He had not been asleep. He was slouched in an easy chair in an alcove of the recreation lounge aboard the *Yuan Chwang*, and Chandragupta was standing looking down at him.

"Do you mind if I ask what you see behind your eyelids, my friend?" the Tribune asked.

Brazil was not quick to answer.

"Perhaps you see drowned men." The Tribune sat down facing Brazil and spoke with quiet sympathy. "My friend, you have what must be one of the most difficult jobs in the known universe; you must be a researcher, a diplomat, a fighter, a linguist and a survival expert, by turns or all at once. And I know I have left out many things. I think you do very well in your job, considering that you are no more than human. We all agreed that your plan of threatening the Tower with waves should be tried. I still think it was good. It has set the islanders on the road to unity, and so no doubt averted more suffering than it caused."

"Thanks, Chan." Brazil stretched, and uncoiled slowly from the chair. A little humor came back into his face. "I'm going to play it as lazy as I can for a couple of days." He straightened his off-duty semi-uniform and said, half to himself: "Maybe I'll just mosey over toward Computing and check out—something. Hmm—"

"Boris?" Foley's voice was heard before he came into sight. "There you are. Scout just sent back word from over nightside: they spotted one of those luminous water-rings over there; this one's fifteen kilometers across. Our regular standby crew is out, so Gates wants you in the briefing room on the double. Oh yeah—" Foley gave an uncertain smile. "He says: 'What would Thoreau have to say about that?' "

Brazil's answer was probably inaccurate.

THE GOLDEN PEOPLE

THE GOLDEN PEOPLE

PART ONE

Chapter One

Fourteen-year-old Ray Kedro was backed up against one of the mural-painted walls in the Middle Boys' recreation yard doing what he could to defend himself, when twelve-year-old Adam Mann first saw him. Adam glanced up from the electronic pages of Space Force Adventures, and watched for a few moments with a playground veteran's indifference. Then he realized that the six kids facing Ray had more in mind than the routine taunting and roughing that they were likely to hand out to any newcomer. This time some of the guys were really hot about something.

Most of the angry bunch were a year or two older than Adam, and all but one of them were taller. But he was widely respected on this territory. He folded the comic book, the electronic pictures on the thin plastic pages darkening into lifelessness as he did so, and stuffed it into his pocket. Moving in the slightly swaggering gait that he had recently developed to what he considered near-perfection, he walked toward the group.

"What goes on?" Adam demanded. He had dark eyes that were often, as now, belligerent, medium brown hair with a slight curl in it, and a nose that had not been broken—not yet at least—but looked as if it might have been.

73

"He's a snooper." Big tough Pete swung out a long arm and slapped the new kid again. "He can read your mind. He's gonna be singin' for the bosses here—"

"I'm not!" The new kid was tall for the age-group of this yard, but thin, with incongruously good clothes that were dusty and rumpled now from his being pushed around. Mussed blond hair fell over blue eyes that looked scared but still didn't blink at being slapped. He had a handsome face, almost delicate, and bleeding now a little along one cheekbone and from the nose. But he didn't look to Adam like a sissy, only like a guy who couldn't understand what it was all about.

"He made them dice move!" another guy standing beside Big Pete put in. The tone made it a deadly accusation.

"You wanted me to play with dice!" the new kid shouted back at them. To Adam he still looked more angry than afraid. "I had to show you first what I can do. If I play dice with you, you'll have to trust me—"

"Play dice, play dice!" Pete mimicked, in a changing, cracking voice. Whenever Pete's voice betrayed him in that way, making him sound funny, he got mad, and now it made him madder than ever.

The guys were all yelling and waving fists. Adam was suddenly scared, in a cold, clear way. Not so much afraid of getting hurt, but that these guys he knew could get so wild over something like this. Some stupid nonsense that didn't matter. It didn't sound like the new guy had really done them any harm.

Adam was beginning to understand, vaguely, or he thought he was. There were, there had always been, a few people in the world who could move dice in more subtle ways than with their fingers, move dice or other small objects using their minds alone. The same people, or others with unusual mental powers, could perform other tricks, equally unsettling. Parapsych talents, the books in the Home library called such abilities. Up until only a few years ago hardly any scientists had believed that such things existed. And Adam had never to his knowledge met any of the rare folk who were so gifted.

The little mob was surging forward, bent on destruction. On impulse, Adam shoved his own strong and stocky body in front of the new kid, and knocked down big Pete's upraised arm. "Let 'im alone!"

Big Pete halted, gaping. "Why?"

"Because I say so!"

Pete gave an angry grunt, and swung. Adam's reflexes and timing were already superb; his head moved safely out of harm's way, and his own right fist was already in a good position to hit back. He got enough weight behind his counterpunch to flatten Big Pete's nose.

Furious and clumsy, the little mob closed in on Adam and the new kid. Something hit Adam, hard, on the side of his head. In a daze, he found himself flat on his back on the playground's genegineered grass, looking up at a ring of faces filled with hate and excitement. In a way, though he knew better, it seemed to Adam that they were all playacting, they couldn't be serious about this great stupidity they were engaged in. A part of his mind kept wanting to laugh at the foolishness of it all, even while he kicked and struck up at the lowering faces, and feet kicked back at him.

Then the recreation yard monitors came, running and shouting threats, from wherever they had been goofing off. They were older teenagers, full of strength and energy once they got started, and they arrived just in time to break up the fight before anyone was killed or crippled.

***

Half an hour later, sitting on a cot in the infirmary, waiting to get his lumps patched up, Adam listened with some satisfaction to the moans and curses coming from the next cubicle. That was where they were working on Big Pete, and from the snatches of the medics' talk that Adam could hear, it sounded like maybe Pete's nose was really broken.

Beside Adam sat the new kid, holding a coldpack to his head. His battered and dirty face was still handsome, but an empty, stunned look occupied it now. He was quivering faintly.

Adam asked him: "What's your name, guy?"

"Ray Kedro." The kid pulled in a deep breath, that helped him regain a measure of steadiness. He looked at Adam. "You may have saved my life today—I won't forget it." He tested a loose tooth gingerly with his fingers. "You're name's Adam? I hope this doesn't mean a lot more trouble for you."

Adam tried to laugh with a split lip. "Hey, they won't do much to us for fighting. Long as nobody got killed. Some extra duty probably is all. I was about due to hang one on Pete anyhow. Hey, was all that true, about you being a parapsych?" It was the first time Adam had ever tried to pronounce that fancy word, but he felt pretty sure that he had it right.

Ray hesitated, looking at him closely, then nodded. "I have—some of those—talents."

"Dice?"

"I could if I tried, I suppose."

"What about reading minds?"

The other shook his head. "You just don't reach into someone else's thoughts, for no good reason. It'd be like… well, like doing the dirtiest thing you can imagine. I mean, I wouldn't like it any more than the person I was reading would."

76

"Huh." When Adam heard it put that way, it sounded more intriguing and at the same time more repulsive than before.

As if encouraged by Adam's reaction, or lack of one, Ray went on: "Maybe you *can* do it, but you don't. Of course if the other person wants you to get into their mind, and tells you so, that's different."

"Huh." Adam considered. "Hey, you know, I read somewhere once that any parapsych who could move dice with his mind could kill people too, just as easy. You know, just grab a little valve or something in their heart—"

"No." Ray's voice was flat and certain. "The talents don't work like that, they won't kill."

"They won't, huh?"

"They never have. There've been people who have tried it, but they just make themselves sick. Oh, someone might find a way to do it someday. Someone who was evil enough and worked at it. There are a few very rare cases—but those are spontaneous combustion—" The blond boy broke off, smiling suddenly, wincing as he did. "If I had any kind of a knockout punch, I'd have used it out there today."

"Hey, yeah, I guess."

***

Adam's prediction about the degree and type of punishment for fighting in the recreation yard was proven accurate. All those who had been involved in the playground brawl were given extra work, beginning the next day after school.

Assigned to work together, using a sonic machine to clean the walls and floor of a long corridor tiled in white and green, Adam and Ray talked again.

Adam asked his new acquaintance: "You know anyone else who's a parapsych?"

"Yes. Ninety-nine of them, to be exact."

"Ninety-nine!"

Ray paused thoughtfully. "Ever hear of a doctor, a medical researcher, named Emiliano Nowell?"

Adam tried to remember the name. He looked through daily news printouts sometimes, on days when he didn't use up all his reading time on library books and adventure comics. And he read news magazines when he could find them. "Emiliano Nowell. Isn't he the guy who bought out an old Space Force installation way out on Ganymede, and set up a place there to do research? Why'd he go way out there?"

"He wanted privacy. Not to be bothered."

Adam could understand that. "And he was raising kids there out of bottles, until the government found out about it, and... Hey. Are you—"

Ray was mechanically guiding the cleaning machine along, not really looking where it was going, but not looking at Adam either. "Yes, I'm one of his kids. The law took us all away from him and Regina—that's his wife—and split us up, put us all in different Homes while they try to figure out what to do with us next. We can still touch minds with each other, now and then."

"You were raised way out on Ganymede? Wow."

"Not for very long. We were all brought to Earth about ten years ago. Doc owns quite a bit of real estate here too."

Adam was fascinated. He stared at Ray. "You look— human, like everyone else."

In the blue eyes deep pain was visible for just a moment. "We came from human seed, from human cells."

"Then what's the difference? I mean…" Adam was confused. Somehow he would have expected anyone he met with parapsych talents to be around three meters tall, and look like either the hero or the villain of a hologram thriller. Of course if he thought about it, that was crazy.

Adam was still curious, but he didn't know what to say now. He realized that he had just given offense by implying that Ray might not be human, and he was trying not to do so again.

Ray asked him: "Do you know what genes are?"

"No. Oh, wait, maybe…"

"They're little parts in the center of a living cell. Of all the human cells that make up your body. They decide everything you inherit from your parents: the way you look, your potential intelligence, and your parapsych potential too. What Doctor Nowell did was find a way to make forcefield manipulators small enough and controllable enough to use them to work on genes directly. Get right in and move the molecules and even the parts of molecules around. He experimented first on animal cells, and then on human. When he thought he had the technique perfected, he rebuilt a hundred fertilized human egg cells. And then he stopped."

"Why?"

"He says he wants to wait a quarter of a century, to see how his first batch turns out—that's us—before he does any more. Meanwhile he's keeping his techniques a secret, and some people are unhappy about that."

"Then you're what they call Jovians, in the news sometimes."

"That's right."

"He rebuilt you to be perfect, huh? You don't sound too happy about it."

"I wouldn't say perfect... I don't think Doc tried for that. What does perfect mean? Anyway, if we were, I don't think the world would like it. Whatever he tried for, Adam, we're very lucky. A lot of people are still born crippled."

Adam was silent for a while, working away with the cleaning nozzle, attacking stubborn stains on battered tile. This new kid Ray gave him a lot to think about. Ray talked with fancy words and a kind of accent that Adam supposed meant he had been brought up a long way from public Homes. But that way of talking sounded natural, for him.

Ray too was silent, as if he were thinking something out. Then he suddenly spoke up again. "Look, Adam, if things go right, the way I think they will, and I get out of here pretty soon... how'd you like to come to Doc's place for a visit?"

Adam almost dropped the cleaning nozzle. "You mean to Ganymede?" For Adam at twelve the Space Force and its activities were a holy cause; but space travel of any kind seemed to exist only in an alternate universe from the one he really lived in, something to be glimpsed only in stories and dreams.

Ray smiled. "No, no, none of us have been out there for years. I meant come to Doc's place here on Earth. That's where we've been living most of our lives. It's mostly one huge building, a little like an expensive boarding school. There are legal reasons why Doc doesn't want anyone but his own kids to live there permanently, but you'd be a welcome visitor."

"Gee, I'd like to see it. You sound like you're sure he's going to win all this court stuff and get you kids back with him again."

Ray's smile broadened. "I know him pretty well."

80

Chapter Two

The windows of the big laboratory room were wide, and open, and unbarred, and they framed Virginia mountains blue with distance. The giant chair in the middle of the room looked quite a bit like one that Adam had seen, and occasionally occupied, in the Home's infirmary. In that chair at the Home all the kids were tested once a year, and those with suspected brain damage sometimes received treatment. It, like everything else at the Home, looked worn and scrubbed, while this chair, like all the other equipment here in Doc Emiliano Nowell's laboratory, looked modern and expensive.

There were other and still more drastic differences between the two establishments. Here, the unbarred windows looked out from every room, onto what seemed to Adam like kilometers of green trees and grass and gardens. It was hard to believe that one man owned it all, even though Ray and the other kids had assured Adam that the boundary of the estate fell short of including those blue distant mountains.

At the moment Adam was sitting in the giant chair himself, trying to get comfortable under a huge metal helmet that had been let gently down until the probes it carried inside it sank through his brown hair, just to the point where they began to tickle his scalp.

"Doc, can I ask you something?" he wondered aloud, a little timidly.

"Sure. As long as I don't have to guarantee an answer." Doc—everyone around the place, children, servants, lab technicians, seemed to call his that—was a tall, lean, graying man, presently wearing a laboratory coat. He was seated halfway across the large room, in front of the psych-chair's

81

control panel. He had, with Adam's ready permission, begun to put the young visitor through a series of physical and mental tests. Doc wanted to do this, as he had said, just out of curiosity. The two were alone, for the moment, in the lab.

Adam hesitated once more, then put his question: "About how much money have you got?"

Doc Nowell had a contagious laugh. "I thought you might be getting worried about the machine. Or wondering what position emission tomography meant." A little earlier, Adam had been reading those words aloud, from the equipment used in the last test. "How much money, huh? Well, Adam, let's just say that I'm too rich to be pushed around in court. My wealth is sufficient for my purposes. Which makes me a rarity among scientists... or among human beings in general, I suppose."

"That's neat, Doc."

"Yes, it is." Watching the panel in front of him, Doc paused to make a note on paper. "Oh, I haven't earned my money from society by probing for the secrets of life. No. It's mine by inheritance. Candy and chewing gum, mostly, a couple of generations back."

Halfway down one of the room's long walls, a door slid open, and a girl entered the laboratory. Merit Creston was a year younger than Adam, which made her by about three years the baby of Doc's hundred genengineered children. The ages of most of the others were clustered closely together, and ranged up to seventeen. Adam was, at least by strict chronology, a visiting child among adolescents. But he, who had come as an infant to the public Home, could scarcely remember ever thinking of himself as a child. His teenage hosts had obviously enjoyed a vastly different upbringing than his, and they impressed him as being mentally more grown-up than any group of adults he had ever encountered. Still, they were all so good at saying and doing the right thing that the visiting twelve-year-old rarely felt out of place.

Merit stood there in the doorway of the psych lab, wearing white shorts and a white blouse and a kind of footgear that Adam had learned were called tennis sandals. Merit's slender figure was developing already. Her face, in Adam's opinion, was—well, beautiful. And her hair had a kind of glint in it that made it really unlike the color of any other girl's hair that Adam had ever seen.

He knew that in a year or so he would start wanting girls in a physical way, like the older guys at the Home. What he felt about Merit now wasn't really that. It was something more—or maybe something less, Adam didn't know which. All he knew for sure was that he felt something powerful, and felt confused and strange whenever he tried to think about it.

Eleven-year-old Merit greeted him now with a giggle. "Hi, Ad. You look like you're getting your hair set."

Adam grunted. The problem was that he wanted desperately to say something witty, to show he didn't mind if she teased him a little, but he could think of no words at all. Suddenly he remembered there were a hundred telepaths, or at least potential telepaths, within a few hundred meters of him. Now he could feel his face getting warm. Why in hell did she have to stand there giggling at him—

"I think you'd better leave, young lady," said Doc, raising his head from his control panel. "You're a disturbing influence just now."

"All right, Grouchy Doc," said Merit. She spoke as if humoring some elderly and harmless relative—but she didn't argue. "Call me if he's mean to you, Adam." She winked at the boy in the chair, and gracefully closed the door behind her.

"So long," Adam called out, lamely, at the last moment, as the door was already closing. Suddenly he felt angry with Merit, irritated with Doc, with Doc's wife Regina, with the whole crew of these people here, who had so damn much more going for them than any group that Adam had ever met before.

The lean man in the lab coat sighed, bending over his control panel again. Then he straightened up. "Let's try something, Adam." With an air of decision, almost a theatrical gesture, Doc raised and let fall a hand, extended finger touching one of the panel switches. Adam could feel no change. Doc said: "I want you to close your eyes now, and imagine a black screen, waiting for a picture."

Adam closed his eyes. "What color is the screen?"

"Make it white. Okay? Got it?"

"Good. Now, just let the screen stay there, and listen to the story."

He was about to ask Doc what story, but there was no need. Right on cue, a recorded voice began to reach Adam's ears, coming to him through the helmet. In soothing tones the voice started telling him about a man named Caesar, who at some time, evidently long ago, had loaded an army onto a fleet of eighty ships, and sailed off with them for Britain.

"Keep your eyes closed, Adam," said Doc's voice, coming through the helmet too, as the storyteller paused. "Now, as you listen, try to imagine an ending for the story, and guide the story to that ending. Understand?"

"No sir, I don't think so. How can *I* change the story? Isn't it recorded?"

84

"You don't have to change it, really. Just give it a try. The effort should make some things happen that I can observe. All right?"

Adam shrugged, the helmet rustling on his scalp. He felt a faint tug. Somehow the probes in the helmet had taken hold of him, and he hadn't even noticed it until now. "Yessir, all right."

The whispering voice resumed its narrative. Caesar and his army poked around Britain, exploring and getting into trouble. They lost some of their ships in a storm, and fought against blue-painted warriors who liked to ride in chariots and hurl javelins. Adam didn't think much of Caesar, whoever he was, or had been. He seemed to have had no good reason for going to Britain and bothering the people who lived there.

Eyes still shut, Adam concentrated on trying to change the story. But, of course, the narrator's recorded voice just droned on. Adam didn't have anything to do with deciding what it said.

By now, the imaginary white screen in Adam's mind had been forgotten. If he were telling the story, he would have made up a different course of events, disliking Caesar as he did.

If only...

Just suppose... that some of the offended Britons could have sneaked into the invaders' camp, bent on revenge. Right into Caesar's tent, why not? Adam could see them clearly now, half a dozen men, not blue-painted but wearing robe-like garments, pulling out their knives suddenly and attacking. And Caesar reeled back and let out a hoarse scream, and his clothing was all blood. And Caesar's eyes closed, then opened, fastening on one of his killers. And...

"Kai su teknon!" The shouting voice broke with its emotion.

At the sound of the shout, Adam lurched upright in the giant chair. He was vaguely aware again of Doc Nowell's laboratory around him. But still at the same time, like watching a reflection in a window, he was still able to see the inside of Caesar's tent. Caesar had disappeared, along with his killers, but something—Adam knew it demanded his full attention—stirred the fabric of the tent flap.

Now the head of a handsome man was thrust inside the tent. The man's forehead was high, under a fringe of dark hair, and his features were noble and impressive. But something about him was very wrong, frighteningly so. Adam knew that before he had the least idea of what the wrong thing was. The head intruded a little farther into the tent, and now with horror the boy saw that it was borne on a long, scaly, reptilian neck. The body supporting that neck was still blessedly hidden by the flap of fabric making the tent door...

... and now, all around Adam in the vision, people were gathering. There might have been a hundred of them surrounding him. All of them, women and men alike, were giants, godlike in their beauty and power.

And a single human figure came pushing its way through that awe-inspiring assembly. It was that of a stocky and powerful man, much more ordinary than the rest, except that he was wearing what might have been some kind of elaborate spacesuit. The face of the man in the spacesuit was clearly visible through the faceplate. It was solemn in its expression, but Adam thought that there was a habit of humor in the eyes.

"My name is Alexander Golden," the stocky man in the spacesuit said to Adam. Then he turned toward the long-necked creature with the human head, and swung his arm as if to strike at it—

And then, abruptly, Doc Nowell's psych lab, its enclosing walls and equipment-loaded benches, was again the only visible reality. The psych helmet had already been raised from Adam's head, and Doc was standing close beside the great chair, looking at him intently.

"What happened?" they asked each other, speaking simultaneously.

It was Doc who answered first, putting on a faint smile that might not have been quite genuine. "Well, you went to sleep, that's what happened. Sometimes my stories, recorded or otherwise, have been known to have that effect on people. But what did you experience?"

Adam related as well as he could what he had seen and heard. As if it had been a true dream, some of the details were already starting to go.

He concluded: "And then the last man said that his name was—Alec Golding. I think. Something like that."

"It's fading?" Doc's tone was sharp.

"Yeah. Like a dream."

"The face of the man in the suit—you say you saw it plainly. Do you know him? Ever see him before?"

"No. I don't think so." It was hard to be sure. Now that last face was going too.

Doc hesitated, on the brink of saying something else. Then he turned away to shut things down at the control panel.

He turned back. "*Kai su teknon* is Greek—means something like 'you too, my child.' It's what Caesar is supposed to have cried out when he was stabbed, though that didn't happen in Britain—you know who Caesar was?"

"Nossir. When I read it's mostly about the Space Force."

"Damn. Oh, it's not your fault. The Space Force is a worthy subject too, I suppose, but—don't they teach you anything at that Home?"

"They say next year they're gonna reorganize the school."

"I should hope so... anyway, Caesar was quite a famous man. He's in the minds of a lot of other people down through the centuries, and his death-scene is one of the classical results we get from this test. Though I must say not one of the more common ones. You picked it up either from me, or directly from the past. Shows you have at least a fair amount of parapsych potential, certainly more than I do myself. If you had begun training very early, you might have become quite adept."

Doc walked back to the great chair in which his subject was still sitting, and rested his hands on one of the padded arms. "Adam, you interest me. Your biological inheritance is— superb. Almost equal to that of my children here. Whoever your parents were—you said you don't know."

"Nossir. They never could find out at the Home. Someone just left me there, when I was a baby."

"An unlucky start, in many ways. I was about to say, whoever your parents were, they at least blessed you with a superb genetic inheritance. One quite good enough to enable you to overcome environmental difficulties. You could, for example, become an outstanding athlete. But I think you have too good a mind to be satisfied with only that. We're going to have to make sure that your schooling is improved. And there is definitely some parapsych potential—but you may be happier with that undeveloped."

Adam didn't know what to say. *Almost equal to that of my children here.* He thought of Ray, backed up against the playground wall.

***

Out of the hundred Jovian kids, as the news media had christened them, only Merit and Ray ever became anything like close friends to Adam. The others, all of them at least slightly older than Ray, were always pleasant enough to Adam on his visits to Doc Nowell's estate. But when they were out of Adam's sight he sometimes had difficulty in even remembering their names and faces.

* * *

... and now the physical wanting was over, for the moment. In a way, for Adam, it hadn't been much different from what happened when one of the girls in the Home became available and willing. And in another way it had been very different indeed from that.

Adam lay watching Merit, who at the moment was lying on her back with her eyes closed. It was a summer afternoon, and the two of them were on one of the small, isolated roof-terraces of Doc Nowell's huge house. Their clothing was on the tiles at the foot of the lawn-furniture lounge on which they lay, Adam's garments scattered in savage haste, Merit's folded almost neatly.

"For a minute there," said Adam, and had to pause at that point to find the right words. "It felt like I was in your mind."

"Mm," said Merit, and turned her face a little more toward him. Her lips smiled faintly but her eyes did not open.

"Is that what it's like," Adam asked abstractedly, "when Ray or one of the others—?"

Merit's eyes came open now, but they were looking over Adam's shoulder, not into his face. He turned.

Ray was there. Adam hadn't heard the only door to the terrace open or close, but Ray was there. He didn't laugh, or even stare at the couple on the lounge, the way any of the guys at the Home would have done. He didn't show embarrassment either. Adam couldn't read the expression on his face at all.

89

Merit was at first alarmed to see Ray. Not because her clothes were off, because her first move wasn't to hide herself. Instead she jumped up halfway from the lounge, getting one foot on the deck, as if to be ready for anything. Adam watched her for a moment, then scrambled to do the same.

All Ray said was: "It's all right, you two. Really. It's all right with me." And there was still that strange look on his face, that was to stay in Adam's memory almost as indelibly as the image of Merit's body did. And Ray turned away and left them alone again, departing in an ordinarily noisy fashion by the ordinary rooftop door.

***

On his first encounter with the Jovians in a group, Adam had noticed that most of them seemed to look up to Ray in some subtle way, even though Ray was among the very youngest. Once Adam thought: Ray's a late model, with all the tested improvements built in. Then he felt vaguely ashamed of having such a thought about his friend.

Adam returned to Doc Nowell's estate for at least a dozen visits, at irregular but gradually increasing intervals, over the next five years. Repeated tests showed Adam's parasych potential to be fading steadily, and eventually Doc gave a shrug and announced that he would test him no more. Such withering away of parapsych abilities was more common than not, he assured Adam, in normal human subjects. It hadn't set in yet in the hundred subjects of his genengineering work; whether it would or not remained to be seen. Parapsych talents had never been established as dependable effects in any segment of the general population; Doc still hoped that with his hundred kids the story would be different.

Somehow the estate, the school, and the people who worked there seemed a little less familiar every time Adam returned; and except for Ray and Merit, the Jovians, though still friendly, were slightly and subtly more remote.

Adam paid his last visit to Nowell's estate at the age of seventeen, proudly wearing the uniform of a Space Force recruit. On that occasion he opened an unlocked door, one that he had opened often enough before, and walked into a room where he thought he might find Merit. She was there, all right. With Ray. Adam stopped silently in his tracks and stood watching them, without comprehension.

Hand in hand, eyes closed, Ray and Merit were floating together in the air, more than a meter above the floor. Their eyes were closed, and they gave no sign of being aware of Adam's presence. After staring at them for a few more seconds he retreated, from the room, shaken.

He would come back later and talk to Merit. Now he decided to find Doc. The halls of the great building, and the grounds around it, were nearly empty of people. Most of the hundred unique children were out in the world, making their way as adults. As far as Adam knew, they were having invariable success. And no small part of their success, he thought, was the way in which they were managing to fade gradually out of public attention.

A worker told Adam that Doc was in the laboratory. When Adam slid open the psych-lab door, he saw Doc sitting alone at his desk near the center of the room, just sitting there with his hands folded. There on the desk was a picture of Regina, Doc's wife, killed last year in a pedestrian stampede while she had been visiting New New York.

When Doc realized the door had opened, he looked up and jumped up and came over quickly to shake hands. "Well, Adam!" His eyes lighted when he took note of Adam's uniform. "So, it's up and out for you! I knew you'd make it."

"Thanks, I guess I always thought I would."

"I don't suppose you're sorry now that your PS talents eroded. From what I've seen of the Space Force psychological tests they seem to weed out almost everyone who has such talents, even in rudimentary form; I know that a couple of my own kids tried to enter and were turned down."

After greeting Doc, Adam mentioned the levitation he had just seen.

Doc nodded, without surprise. "I've seen that one. I once saw about twenty of my kids bobbing around in the air at once… it apparently requires a trance-like state that keeps them from doing anything else at the same time. And what good it will ever do them I don't know."

"There must be some other… " Adam gestured vaguely.

"Applications? Maybe there are. I no longer try to teach them anything, Adam. I just try to keep up with everything they're doing. And I can't." Doc paused.

"I'm sure they'll do great things."

"Yes, well, I hope so. That was the idea. I love them all, Adam, I tend to worry about them like a parent. And now, already, a lot of them are out in the world… what kind of lives they're going to have in this world I don't know. And what are their lives going to mean to humanity, after all?"

The aging man and the young one looked at each other, two mere humans, wondering.

"But come in, Adam. Have some coffee? Tell about the Space Force, how it strikes you now."

But he hadn't got far in his relation when Doc, who seemed scarcely to be listening, interrupted: "Often, I wonder, Adam. Was there some—some force, some universal, natural law, acting through me, when I pushed my microscopic tools into those living cells, and tore down and rebuilt molecules?"

"I don't know." The young man felt sorry for the old one, and puzzled by his evident quiet distress.

"Are these kids of mine really the next step up from humanity?"

"Oh. Is that what's worrying you? I don't know, Doc. You can be damn proud if they are."

Unexpectedly Doc scowled. "Proud of what? Of being used?" He fell silent, making an irritated gesture. "Forces and laws," he said obscurely, with something like disgust. Frowning made his face look more lined, considerably more lined, than Adam remembered it. Adam wondered if possibly the mind developed lines and wrinkles too.

"She was incurably sterile, you know," Doc said. Now he was looking back at the picture on his desk. "We could never have any children biologically our own." Then he looked at Adam again, and brightened, with a visible effort. "Well, enough of that. You're going to the Academy, hey? How soon will you have a chance to try to get into planeteering? I remember how you always talked of that."

Chapter Three

The chance to get into planeteering had not come easily, but it had arrived at last, only after Adam had spent four years at the Academy, and three more at other assignments.

Then planeteering school. After that, his second exploration mission took him to the world that was shortly afterward named Killcrazy, by the survivors among the Earth-descended men and women who had been in the first group to land upon it. But Killcrazy was behind Adam now, along with the homeward-bound starships, and the Terraluna transport run, and the shuttle down to New New York. Ahead of him were thirty glorious days of leave, with Alice. Then the two of them were going together out to the enormous Space Force base located in the Antares system. Alice had a job in the science analysis section, and the baby would be born out there, a spacer right from the start.

Adam had met Alice only a year ago, and had married her only a month before he had to start out on the Killcrazy mission. But Alice understood. She was Space Force herself, as were her parents before her.

This time, coming home, it was fun for once to encounter the roaring confusion of the great city. At the shuttle port in New New York Adam came dodging his way nimbly through the crowd, a thick-limbed, brown-haired, strong young man of average height, swinging a heavy travel bag. He wore a dress uniform that hadn't seen much use to date and a new ribbon on his chest. Alice had written something about his coming home with the decoration on, and so he was wearing the uniform instead of civvies.

As Adam emerged from a pedestrian entrance of the shuttle port into canyon-like city streets, he saw a headline flashing on a media kiosk:

JOVIAN SUPERKIDS—
WHERE ARE THEY NOW?

The headline was quickly, replaced by a giant three-dimensional picture. The face of Ray Kedro, blond and ruggedly handsome, looked down in a multiplied image from each of the kiosk's panels. Adam hadn't seen Doc, or Ray, or Merit, or any of the other kids, for a long time now. For years. He recalled having read and seen news stories from time to time, to the effect that most of the Jovians were intermarrying with each other, that most of them seemed to be blending quite smoothly into society, tending to avoid publicity, not making waves. The suggestion of the stories was that the hundred born, or decanted, out on Ganymede, were after all not that much different from the rest of the world. Very bright and capable people, yes. But...

Pushing his way through the crowds, Adam wondered about Merit, what she might be doing at this moment. There had been a time...

With a small start, a sensation almost of guilt, he recalled that Alice was almost within reach now, waiting for him. She was certainly no Jovian. And for that Adam was thankful—though he had never made the effort to analyze just why.

The heavy travel bag felt feather-light in Adam's grip as he changed slidewalks for the last time, stepping onto the one that would take him to their little sublevel apartment. Going right home this way was certainly better than trying to meet her in the spaceport swarm. People had been queued up there at all the communication booths, so he hadn't delayed to call her from the shuttle port. Anyway, Alice knew when his ship was due in.

Adam surveyed the endless hive of tiny dwelling units through which the slidewalk carried him, private cells stacked high and wide, their ranks staggered and their walls insulated in an effort to grant the occupants some diversity and privacy. On Antares Six they would have better quarters than this. There wouldn't be any outdoors there for the baby, not for some time at least, except for, as Adam had heard, a little domed-over garden. But that was really about all the outdoors you got in New New York.

Adam dialed his private combination to let himself into the tiny apartment. He put the travel bag down and moved stealthily, hoping against hope to achieve surprise. Ready to jump at Alice the moment he spotted her, he tiptoed into the bedroom, and then the kitchen. No one.

It was in the kitchen that he found the note.

Darling—suddenly I can't wait to see you, so I'm going to the spaceport. If you find this, I've missed you, and the joke's on me for being impatient. Sit tight and I'll be home soon. Love XXXX Me

He sat tight for an hour, savoring his impatient joy. He looked at Alice's clothes, hanging in the small closet, and touched them tenderly.

The phone chimed.

The screen at first showed only an official shield. Then a man's voice spoke: "Spaceport Authority. I'd like to speak to Spaceman Adam Mann, please."

"Speaking."

Then a man's face, the expression that it wore bringing the first cold blow of fear: "Is Alice Dexter-Mann your wife?"

"My wife. Yes."

"I'm sorry to tell you that there's been an accident."

Adam afterward could never remember exactly what else the man on the videophone might have said. He raced in a nightmare through the bright anthill of the city, back to the shuttle port. Traveler's Aid. They told him where to go. In the Port-master's office, there were sudden grave, guarded looks when Adam gave his name, looks of sympathy and hidden triumph: *It happened to you, not to us.*

After hearing the words several times, from two different people, he began to realize that Alice was dead. The surgeon on duty at the port said that the baby was dead too, though she had ripped it out of Alice's body, trying to save it.

"We did all we could for her, spaceman. Sometimes it still just isn't enough..."

A policewoman sat with Adam and talked to him calmly and gently, trying to bring him through the first shock. She tried to answer his questions. It had been a violent and deliberate attack, right in the crowded port. One suspect had been seized, but then the people who might have been witnesses had all melted away without identifying themselves.

"These teenpacks—I don't know what the answer is, spacer. We do all we can. This year the big thing for some of them is to hunt pregnant women. Last year it was something else."

"Who's your suspect?" Adam's stomach had turned sick and his knees weak. But still the truth hadn't really, totally, sunk in.

"I'll show you. He's a real prize."

The policewoman let him look through oneway glass at a young man who sat slouching on a bench. The suspect's body had grown out of adolescence. But the appearance of him, the look in his face and eyes, suggested that his mind and soul had long since ceased to grow, that now they only wriggled, caught like baby worms on some unknown fishhook. Greasy pigtails framed the masklike face. The oddly-styled leather jacket was lipstick-marked with obscene clan symbols.

Adam opened the door of the detention room and stepped through, moving too fast for the cop beside him, who was left reaching after him with one outstretched arm. There were other police, men and women, in the detention room with the suspect, and they looked up at Adam's entrance, wondering.

"This one did it?" Adam's knees were no longer weak.

The sneering young mask-face held out insult like the groping hand of a blind man, trying to touch someone with it. "Sure, fatherman. I must have did whatever it was:"

Now a large and gentle cop was standing close beside Adam, soothing him and standing in his way. "Easy now. Maybe it wasn't him at all." The other cops were standing around a communicator, going on with whatever they had been doing. But they each kept an eye out for the bereaved young spaceman, watching him with pity and calculation, ready to lead him away if he should become violent.

Little they knew. Adam's brain and body had absorbed the Academy training in personal combat as if he had been designed for that purpose and no other. He might have gone on to world class competition in the martial arts, except that his feelings for them had always been mixed. Arm-twisting stuff, he sometimes called that sort of activity, with a certain contempt that proceeded from a blend of distaste and fascination. What he really wanted was to be a planeteer. But before leaving the Academy Adam had acquired the ability to be more effectively violent than almost any of the instructors.

Now the impersonal trained-in combat computer offered one of several feasible plans: three quick strides to the target, then the certain kick with the left foot, a blow with the right fist. Impacts that would break bone and crush nerves. As like as not the shock waves that the target's brain received would be enough to kill. The police were not wearing their stunguns in here; even so, their numbers and positions in the room could make it an interesting technical problem. But Adam doubted that the police would be able to stop him. The target might react to some purpose by the time he reached it. He doubted that a great deal too.

"Come along." The large cop's gentle hand was resting on Adam's arm. "We'll find out, if it was him. We'll find out."

The pig-tailed youth, looking at Adam, said: "C'mere, fatherman. I got a present for ya." He giggled, and made a gesture that meant nothing whatever to Adam.

Adam waited for whatever spark it would take to set him off. Once before, as a teenager defending himself on a street near the Home, he had killed with his hands. But why had he bothered to defend himself, that time? He didn't understand it now. It had done him no good, for now his life was gone.

He felt no reluctance to kill, but no spark came. His life was gone. His loss was beyond all paying-back, and made all action pointless. He let himself be turned around and led away. He was very tired now. It would be good to get home at last and...

It sank in a little more. Alice was dead.

When he did get home, there was her silent note, still waiting for him on the table.

***

The Space Force looked after its own. Adam had scream-it-out grief therapy, and then for a while tranquilizers, and after that grief therapy again, this time that of a different school.

He went on with the motions of living, and then, one day, he began to go on again with living itself.

After a tour of duty as instructor in personal combat at the Academy, his revised orders finally came through for Antares.

PART TWO

Chapter Four

The footsteps, those of one person hurrying, came to a halt just outside the messroom door. The door slid open, and the face of the courier ship's captain appeared, wearing its usual expression of faint disapproval.

"Antares Base is on alert, gentlemen," the captain informed his two passengers; and then without waiting for an answer or comment he was gone, perpetually hurried footsteps fading.

Adam Mann looked up and across the chessboard at his new boss, Chief Planeteer Colonel Boris Brazil, and asked: "Suppose it's just practice?"

"I suppose." Brazil slouched in his chair, a tall, lean, blond, bony-faced man, unmoved by the news. "Or maybe something scared 'em. Maybe they heard old spit-and-polish was coming." He nodded after the courier's captain, whose way of running his ship had not earned the Colonel's respect during the days of voyaging. "Anyway, we'll soon know. I concede a draw," Brazil added, nodding cheerfully at his hopeless chess position.

***

One good thing about putting the whole base on alert, thought General Grodsky, was that it at least got him up into a ship again, even if it didn't get him out from behind a desk. Nothing could do that, it seemed.

His logistics only grew more complex when an alert was on. He then had to hold most of his available fleet off-planet, while keeping the emergency repair facilities on the surface of Antares Six still ready to function at full capacity, as well as maintaining skeleton crews of people at the other Space Force installations around the system, all under his command. But none of this, somehow, ever cut down on what was still called paperwork. It seemed to the General that at least as much of the data processing as before came shuffling its way inexorably after him, a many-tentacled monster of information; and Grodsky wound up still spending most of his time at a desk.

The door of his inner office aboard his flagship opened now, and his secretary came in, carrying more things that he was going to have to deal with.

The first item in his stack was something Grodsky had been looking for, and he pushed the rest aside. "Molly," he told his secretary, "get Colonel Brazil in here to me as soon as he's on board." The courier with Brazil aboard had begun to transmit its routine, official messages from Earth as soon as it appeared in normal space within reasonable radio range of Antares Base. But Grodsky wanted to hear from the Colonel the unofficial news of attitudes and rumors at home; and he wanted even more urgently to get Chief Planeteer Brazil briefed quickly on this new Fakhuri thing.

***

Spaceman Adam Mann was kept waiting for several minutes in Grodsky's outer office, but the young man remained standing during that time; the fact was that he felt too keyed up to sit down. Then the inner office door, through which Colonel Brazil had already passed, opened again and a young woman in uniform stepped out. "The Colonel asked me to lure you in," she said with a tolerant smile. The impression she conveyed was that she had known the Colonel for some time, and was willing to make allowances.

Adam marched into the inner office, where General Grodsky was sitting appropriately behind a massive desk, while Colonel Brazil meanwhile perched quite inappropriately on a corner of the same piece of furniture. Brazil hardly appeared to notice Adam's entrance; he was staring into space, as if at some new and fascinating vision that he had just been shown.

Adam marched straight to the desk. "Spaceman Mann reporting, sir." He threw the General a sharp salute.

Grodsky returned the gesture carelessly, but gave Adam an intent look. "At ease, Mann. Colonel Brazil thinks you can fill a vacancy in the planeteering crew of this flagship."

"Yes sir." Adam was well aware of that, and it was exactly why he was keyed up. He hadn't thought, still didn't think, that his being given the job was really in doubt. But if the General himself was taking an interest in the matter... "I hope the Colonel's right, sir."

In the middle of the largest relatively clear area on the General's desktop there was a personnel file; Adam recognized a permapaper copy of his own service record, which Colonel Brazil had been carrying around with him and had somehow managed to dogear slightly. Grodsky picked up the file now and began to study it. Almost immediately the General looked up with a frown. "You've had only two missions, Mann?" He turned to Brazil. "Boris, I don't know..."

Brazil, paying attention now, was wearing one of the more subtle forms of what Adam had come to recognize as his I'm-one-up expression. "Read on a little farther, sir. One of those was the rescue job on Killcrazy."

"Oho." The General checked the record again, and looked back at Adam with new respect. "Were you with the party that went into the crater?"

"Yessir."

Grodsky paged his way deeper into the record and read on. "Boris found you teaching hand-to-hand combat at the Academy. Well, that would fit the team's needs. Krishnan—the man you'd be replacing—had a high combat rating. Hm, I see you've married a Space Force lady. Congrat—oh." The general raised his eyes again. "I'm very sorry."

"Sir, I was intending to stay in planeteering before that happened. I'm really eager to get back to it now."

The General nodded, his eyes probing Adam's as before. Then Grodsky gestured to a chair. "Sit down, Mann. I've already told Colonel Brazil the reason for this alert we're on. Now I'm going to show both of you."

Grodsky picked up a small control unit from his desk, and swiveled his chair. The lights dimmed in the office, and a holographic stage slid up in front of the large viewscreen that occupied most of one of the office walls. "This recording," the General announced, "was made about two standard months ago, aboard the *Marco Polo 7*." Adam recognized the name of a deep-space exploration ship.

There were no titles or preliminary information at the start of the three-dimensional video recording, except the routine security classification label. Not so routine in this case—top secret. Adam hadn't yet seen many of those.

The recording itself began with some solid-looking symbols on the stage, which he was able to recognize as representing the astrogational co-ordinates of some star system or other deep-space celestial object, no doubt those of some system that the Marco had been sent out to investigate.

More data about the system and its chief components followed, presented in a routine symbolic form. It contained one star, a sun remarkably like Sol, whose light had been blocked from Earth since before the beginning of recorded Earthly history, by a narrow, twisted cloud of opaque interstellar dust. This Sol-like sun and its planets, all of them as yet unnamed, lay on the advancing frontier of Earth-descended humanity, right on the edge of the thirty million cubic light year volume of space which that ambitious race had somehow managed to more or less explore, marking out a small enclave within the end of one arm of the Galaxy's spiraled bulk.

"We're skipping a lot of early details of the survey," said Grodsky in a quiet voice. "Planet Four looked very good, from a distance. Fakhuri went in for a closer investigation, according to standard operating procedure, and—well, you'll see."

The stage now effectively placed the three men watching aboard the control bridge of the *Marco 7*. The three-dimensional picture, made in the course of routine recording of periods of key activity, was centered on a dark, intense-looking man who sat in the ship commander's acceleration chair.

"That's Fakhuri. A good man," Grodsky commented firmly. The General paused, and then went on: "At this point, Planet Four still looked almost like a moonless twin of Earth. Which it continues to do in many ways, but... now they're launching the scoutship. Remember, Fakhuri is following survey SOP and he hasn't used any radar yet."

Explorers going out from Earth and Earth's advanced bases had yet to encounter any aliens technologically sophisticated enough to be able to detect a radar probe. But if any such existed—and it seemed inevitable that there must, somewhere in the Galaxy—there was thought to be no point in warning them prematurely that they were under surveillance.

As if looking over Fakhuri's shoulder aboard the *Marco*, now cruising some four hundred thousand kilometers from Planet Four, Adam Mann and Colonel Boris Brazil watched and listened as the scoutship, piloted by Fakhuri's Chief Planeteer, made one swing around the planet at about a hundred thousand kilometers, and another slower one at about twenty thousand. Both passes were uneventful.

During his swing at two thousand kilometers, the Chief Planeteer who was flying the scout solo reported observing something strange on the land surface below him.

"Like a lunar ringwall, or a half-buried foundation for a building eight or ten kilometers across," said the radio voice. "Lots of clouds there—I couldn't get a very good look."

Fakhuri's image rubbed its dark chin. "Make a lower pass over it."

Six seconds passed, while the finite speed of radio carried the ship commander's order on a tight beam down to the speeding scoutship, and brought the answer back.

"Roger. Descending to six hundred klicks."

The magnification of Fakhuri's screen showed a tiny dark scoutship creeping across the blue and green and brown of a sunlit alien continent. Then the scout almost disappeared against the background of a dark blue ocean.

"I'm jumping forward again in time," said Grodsky. "We'll pick up the recording again—here."

They were still observing the image as if looking over Fakhuri's shoulder. "Coming up toward that ringwall again," said the planeteer's voice from the little scout below. "I'll go right over it, this time. Leveling off at six hundred klicks. Should get a little atmos—"

And that was all. The radio beam from the scout had for some reason been broken off. Fakhuri turned his head, this way and that, looking for a reason. He pressed things on his panel, trying to extract information from one instrument or another.

Seconds later, another watcher on Fakhuri's ship cried out: "He's falling, out of control!" A closeup of another screen showed how the motion of the scout's flight had changed, from a nearly horizontal creeping to the steep curve of a dropped stone.

"Golden! Do you read me?" Fakhuri was shouting.

And yet another voice: "Radio beam's unlocked, sir, we can't reach him."

"Get us right over him," ordered Fakhuri, reaching with one hand for a red stud prominent at one side of the panel before him. At the bottom of the image on Grodsky's holographic stage appeared the words: RED ALERT CALLED ABOARD MARCO POLO 7. There was justification. Scoutship drives did not fail, communications between scout and mothership simply did not break, not by accident, not just like that.

Now, through a low cloud cover, the huge ring-wall formation on the planet's surface became partially visible in the *Marco's* powerful scopes. The ringwall looked like stone, perhaps once splashed molten, perhaps deliberately piled. Details were still obscure, though the starship was accelerating powerfully in normal space, very quickly getting closer to the planet.

The screens on the *Marco's* bridge showed the scoutship as an almost invisible dot, tumbling toward the ringwall formation as if toward the center of a target.

"No sign of his escape capsule."

"Radio still out, sir."

"Radar," Fakhuri snapped. "Track him. Planeteering, have that standby scout ready. But don't launch yet."

Grodsky said to the onlookers in his office: "Watch now, here it comes."

Fakhuri's image switched its viewscreen to pick up the radar image when the bouncing pulses brought it back. The seconds of unavoidable distance delay crept by.

"Can't pick up any flash of impact optically, sir. Maybe he hasn't cra—"

The echo came. Fakhuri's screen showed only electronic hash for a moment. Then the radar computer gave up its search for a small moving target, and dispassionately showed the waiting humans exactly what it saw, the problem it was having to contend with.

Some watcher on Fakhuri's ship cried out: "Captain!"

The radar picture electronically frozen on Fakhuri's screen held him—and now Adam—frozen in disbelief. Not the expected rough semblance of the Earthlike planet shown by the optical scopes. Nothing like that—here instead was a bright spheroid, looking smooth and opaque as a steel ball, more than a thousand kilometers greater in diameter than the planet it shrouded.

Fakhuri quickly switched his screen back to present the image brought in by the optical telescopes. Planet Four still reflected the radiation of her own sun as naturally as Earth reflected that of hers—again Four appeared innocent and friendly in her bright aura of oxygen atmosphere, plain and ordinary behind a tattered white film of clouds where her spherical shape curved closest to the *Marco.*

"Evasive action!" Fakhuri ordered. "Around the planet!" If this world was shielded from radar, it might well be armed in other unimaginable ways as well. Anything might be about to come up from it.

The brutal acceleration of evasive action was evidently too much for the *Marco's* artificial gravity, for Fakhuri's chair now folded itself protectively around its occupant. The chair also put forth to the control panel a pair of artificial arms, slaved to the captain's motor-nerve impulses.

"Passive detection still blank screen, sir." That meant that the *Marco's* instruments could detect no artificially produced radiation from the planet.

"We lost him in the surface clouds, before we moved," said an astronomer's shaken voice. "Never got any indication of an impact where he went down."

"Radar gear checks okay, captain, I don't know what—"

"Pulse again, then! give me the whole planet again."

The *Marco* was over nightside now. The planet showed in the optical scopes as a vague dark bulk, embraced by a thin bright crescent. Then that image was gone, as Fakhuri switched his screen to receive the radar image again. The pulses would be hurtling down again toward the planet... down... down... back... back...

The marvelous thing flashed from the screen again, electrically beautiful. The only difference on this side of the planet was at the point antipodal to that where the scoutship had disappeared. Here, the radar-outlined, metallic-looking, optically invisible surface curved steeply down to meet the planet's land surface, in an amplexicaul depression, like the dimple around the stem of an apple. Fakhuri sat staring at it, as if the wonder of it was stronger than alarm, for him.

But there were standing orders for exploration captains. Any technologically advanced strangers encountered were to be treated with the utmost caution. One starship could carry a weapon capable of destroying a planet in minutes. There was of course a chance that the scoutship pilot might still be alive; but one of Fakhuri's mechanical slave-hands was already moving, slamming down on a stud marked EMERGENCY FLIGHT.

The flight had been toward Antares, not Earth; no possible trail must be left toward home.

***

The holostage in Grodsky's inner office went blank momentarily. Then the General said: "This is the planeteer who was lost, Mann. Colonel Brazil knew him."

On the stage there appeared the figure of a heavily-built, cheerful-looking man. It was a picture made outdoors somewhere that showed its subject, walking quickly, wearing a planeteer's groundsuit, carrying his helmet under one arm.

"Alexander Golden, Chief Planeteer," said General Grodsky. His tone was oddly formal, as if he might be wondering what the name and title ultimately meant.

The secretary, who had re-entered the office a few moments earlier carrying some papers, had paused to watch, and now had a question. "Did he leave a family?" she asked, gazing into the stage.

"No." Grodsky rubbed his eyes. "As I recall from his records, he grew up in some institution—like you, Mann. Never married. Very able spaceman."

"And an able planeteer," put in Colonel Brazil. After a moment he added: "Another happy bachelor bit the dust. Not many of us left. I guess I met him two or three times."

Adam was staring at the last frozen frame of Alexander Golden on the little stage. Something about it was bothering him. "I... think I might have met him, somewhere." But the vague sense of recognition eluded Adam and vanished when he tried to pin it down. He shrugged.

As the holostage dimmed down completely and the lights in the room came up to normal, Boris shifted around on his desk-top perch to face the General. "Well, boss, what do we do?"

"We go back there," said Grodsky, swiveling his chair back to face his desk, and the two visitors in his office. The General's face was lined and tight-looking. Obviously Fakhuri's discovery was in his lap. The situation could not be managed from the distance of Earth, not when it took forty days by courier ship for a message to be sent and answered. No Earth government would be foolish enough to send more than broad instructions to Antares base, and in this case there was little doubt of what those instructions were going to say.

"Now," said Grodsky, getting down to business. "That forcefield, or whatever it is, around that planet—let's start calling it planet Golden—the field around planet Golden seems to me a flat impossibility. Consider:

"First, it almost entirely envelops an Earth-sized world. Second, the passive detection crew on the *Marco* were able to pick up no trace of it. Third, it allowed a scoutship to enter, but

110

only as a falling object. It cut off the scout's engines, its radio, and possibly everything else aboard.

"Gentlemen, we've nothing like that, anywhere!"

After a little silence, Brazil spoke up, casually. "Are we taking a fleet when we go back?"

"I think not. I think just three ships. A whole fleet might look like an attack, to—them. Whoever they are." The General shrugged. "If they even exist. We have no proof that this—field—is not a natural phenomenon. Golden couldn't see it without his radar on, and he just drove right into it."

"And just accidentally happened to drop right into that ringwall," said Boris. "That was just coincidence, right?" No one answered him, and he went on: "If I ever drive a scout near that thing, I won't be so damn sneaky about it. Next time we go in radiating the whole damn frequency spectrum in every direction. If someone spots me, it won't be by accident."

Adam couldn't tell if the Colonel was serious about his announced plan or not.

"I intend to take a very good look around there before anyone drives near it again," said the General grimly. "Boris, I want you ready for the best job you ever did, if and when we do go down on Golden. You can pick any planeteers you want, from any crews in the fleet."

"If you mean to launch from just one ship, my own people are as good as any."

The General looked at Adam, then back to the Colonel.

"My crew will be up to full strength now," Brazil added casually. Adam felt a sudden surge of pride and loyalty, about which he would never speak.

Grodsky considered a moment, then nodded decisively. "All right. Mann, consider yourself aboard. You can go look up your quarters, or whatever you have to do."

"Yessir!" This time Adam's salute was even sharper than before.

When the doors of the inner and outer offices were both closed after him, he took a quick look up and down the long main corridor of the flagship to make sure that he was unobserved. Then he snapped his body into a flip, a somersault in the air without touching his hands to the deck. He walked away grinning widely.

He was still quite a young man. For a time, in time, even the murdered love could be forgotten.

***

When the young Spaceman Mann had gone out, leaving the two of them alone, the General said thoughtfully: "Boris, I wonder if we can really function as a military outfit." They both knew, everyone knew, that the Space Force was organized and equipped and trained for exploration, not for conquest. It had never faced a real war, or anything remotely like one. Who knew what would happen if one came?

"I do believe that courier captain thought me unmilitary," Brazil answered. "And all I had done was—well, never mind. You really expect we'll get into a fight this time, boss?"

On an impulse, Grodsky flicked on his big view-screen. The hellish red bulk of nearby Antares seemed to fill the room. Then the slow rotation of the flagship brought into view the tiny green companion star, and then the other multicolored sparks, cloud behind cloud of them, reaching ever farther and dimmer out to infinity.

"This time, or the next," the General said. "Sooner or later."

Chapter Five

General Grodsky's flagship was a big craft, fast and tough, designed for battle as much as any ship could be when battles between ships were virtually unknown. The outer hull of the flagship formed a sphere almost a kilometer in diameter, and like most Space Force ships it bore no permanent name. Its code designation for this mission was Alpha One.

After a couple of days' passage in flightspace from Antares Base, the flagship appeared in normal space near the Golden system, at a couple of astronomical units' distance above the north pole of Golden's sun. After an hour of general observation from that vantage point the flagship began to move again, staying in normal space this time, traversing a curve that in three unhurried days would bring the explorers aboard into the close vicinity of Planet Four.

Alpha Two, also custom designed, was a much smaller ship, built for high interstellar speed and long range observation. It winked into existence near the point in space where Alpha One had previously appeared, just as One began to move sunward. Two would alternate with Three, its twin, in observing the activities of One and in carrying news back to Antares Base.

At a distance of thirty million kilometers General Grodsky ordered his first radar probe of Planet Golden's surface. He found the enveloping forcefield to be exactly as Fakhuri's recordings showed it, covering the world entirely except for an area of a few hundred square kilometers at most, where the field came down in its amplexicaul curve to meet the land surface of one continent. With that verification in hand, Grodsky turned his flagship away from Golden, and spent a standard month in methodical preliminary survey of the system's seven other major planets. On none of them, nor on any of their major satellites, did his teams find any indication of the presence of intelligent life. Or anything at all to suggest an explanation of Planet Golden's unique and mysterious field.

The preliminary system survey completed, Alpha One returned to the near vicinity of Golden. And now the crew of explorers focused their instruments with great interest upon the surface formation that resembled a lunar ringwall.

The Ringwall, as the human observers began to call it, occupied most of a roughly triangular river island eight kilometers across, at the confluence of two great streams in a country of low, rocky hills and subtropical jungle. The big island seemed always to be at least partially obscured by clouds and low mist. And infrared observations of the area were perpetually fogged as if by volcanic heat.

For all the observers above the atmosphere were able to tell, the irregular polygon of mountainous walls might be titanic architecture, now partially obscured by jungle growth as well as by mists and clouds. Or it might still have been accepted as an accidental formation. But, if the ambiguous feature were truly accidental, was it only by another accident that it lay exactly at the antipodal point from the place where the Field curved down to planet surface?

And careful study of Fakhuri's optical recordings showed that, of all the planet's area, Golden's scout had apparently fallen directly into the Ringwall, scoring a kind of crazy, inexplicable bullseye. Another accident?

Wherever the scoutship or its wreckage might be, optical observation from the flagship could detect no trace of it. And the Field continued to prevent all other kinds of observation.

114

Colonel Boris Brazil, in the first scoutship launched from Grodsky's flagship toward Golden, drove twice around the planet, keeping about fifteen hundred kilometers above the upper surface of the Field as it was outlined for him by his radar. True to his promise, Colonel Brazil had his ship continuously radiating a wide assortment of signals.

There was no response from below.

That evening, ship's time, the Colonel knocked at the door of Adam Mann's tiny cabin, and on hearing a response from inside slid it open. "Alpha Three should be in the system tomorrow, Junior," Brazil announced. "Two will be heading back to Antares; we're sending a robocourier over to her in a couple of hours with mail, if you want to send some."

Adam was seated at the small desk that folded out of the bulkhead. "Thanks, I was just writing one." He paused. "How did it look today from down there?"

"Everything looked a lot closer. Here, I'll drop that in the mail bag for you." Leaning in the doorway, the Colonel shamelessly inspected the address on the envelope he had just been handed. Then he held it down at his side, snapping it between long nervous fingers. "Tell you what, Junior, you get ready for a little ride tomorrow. I want someone along to make sure that my scout keeps transmitting on all fifty frequencies. Briefing at oh-five-hundred."

"Roger!"

"Don't look so damned happy. It's disgusting. My good planeteers will be driving their own scouts tomorrow." Boris started to close the door, then paused, waving the little envelope. "Say, this Doctor Emiliano Nowell you're writing to— isn't he the one who had that secret biological lab on Ganymede years ago? The geneticist who started all that Jovian superkid business?"

"Yeah. I used to be invited to visit his estate on Earth a couple of times a year. Got to know some of them. Tell you about it sometime."

Boris's brows rose over his innocent blue eyes. "You move in exalted circles," he whispered, and made his exit.

***

In the morning, Colonel Brazil was all business from the start. "This reminds me a little bit of a mousetrap," he was muttering, as he sat strapped and cushioned in the left seat of the scoutship's little control room, staring at the radar screen in front of him. Alpha One was now something more than a million airless kilometers above the scout; the fair true surface of Planet Golden was only a few hundred klicks below.

The radar showed the smooth hump of the Field rising high above the scout on all sides, rising higher and higher as Brazil drove the small ship down in a slow descending spiral. It was as if they were dropping into the vortex of a whirpool, a solid maelstrom carved into some fluid invisible to human eyes. The walls of the funnel around them constricted gradually as they descended into it. Below them, a circle of planet surface some fifty kilometers in diameter was shown by radar as free of the Field, and to all appearances this comparatively small area was open to normal landings and exploration. The free area was mixed-looking countryside, to the eye indistinguishable from the land immediately surrounding it.

"I don't see any bait," said Adam. He was buttoned into the right seat, alertly watching a multitude of screens and indicators. "But we're here, aren't we? Maybe an obvious trap is bait enough for the curious."

116

"Now's a fine time to propound that theory," Brazil growled. "How d'ya read me, Alpha One?"

The distance delay. Then: "We read you loud and clear. Good picture."

Adam had an excellent imagination, which in his line of work was not always an asset. Right now he could readily imagine the Field-funnel around them closing in on the little scoutship with a sudden snap, dropping the ship rocklike with them inside it to share Alexander Golden's fate. But the Field did not snap shut. The Field did not move at all. No change of any kind had been observed in it since Fakhuri's first recorded sighting.

A few hours ago, long probes with loops of current-carrying wires attached to them had been lowered into the Field from a hovering scoutship. On the wires' first contact with the Field the electrical currents in them had instantly ceased. But mice and other small forms of life, lowered into the Field in sealed boxes, had survived the mysterious condition for several minutes without any apparent ill effect. If Golden had survived the crash of his ship—that seemed a vanishingly faint hope —he might still be alive.

The field-free area of the surface, that the explorers from Earth were now beginning to refer to as the Stem, lay in the low north temperature zone, on Planet Golden's second largest continent. Below the scoutship, Adam's viewscreens showed rolling, open plains, covered with a probably grass-like plant. The main themes of biology were repeated, sometimes with startling fidelity, from one world to the next, all across the explored Galaxy, wherever closely similar environments obtained in terms of gravity and chemistry, pressure and radiation. Here, patches of deciduous-looking forest were

117

scattered over a line of hills that grew into a range of mountains some kilometers north of the Stem. One of the wide, winding rivers of this continent ran in several places briefly congruent with the intersection of Field and planet surface. But this, again, seemed accidental.

"Enough for today," said Brazil abruptly, when they had cruised for ten minutes at about two hundred kilometers' altitude. "Let's ease up out of this hole."

***

On a sunny afternoon a few days later, Adam and Boris were scouting again, cruising within a kilometer of the surface, now with the feeling of being part of the world below. The starship overhead was of course invisible to them beyond the sky.

Early summer was warming and brightening Golden's northern hemisphere. The screens showed a view of green plains and forests that made the scoutship cabin feel stuffy.

"Makes me feel like I want to get out and go camping," Adam commented.

Brazil only grunted. He was easing the scout still lower, losing altitude at a rate of a few meters per second. The small ship slid forward through the clear summer sky at a couple of hundred kilometers per hour.

"Looks like a herd of large herbivores over there." Brazil was pointing to a scattering of animate dots on the plain ahead. Under moderate magnification these became deerlike creatures—another major interplanetary evolutionary theme identified on Golden. As the scout drew closer the lenses showed that the deer-like creatures had developed their own variation on the theme, in the form of stretch-able necks. In a few minutes the scout passed directly over the herd, gliding on

118

the invisible force of its silent engines, still too high for its presence to alarm the animals.

Adam continued to sweep the landscape below the scout, and the air around it, with his instruments. He even scanned nearby birds suspiciously several times. "I don't see any Field-generating superbeings."

"Maybe they've all dried up and blown away. Are you keeping one eye on the Field, Junior? I have most of my attention on it."

"Ah, roger. I have one screen on radar."

But the Field only waited indifferently, whether they watched it or not. The smooth cliff of it rising up around them on all sides, as motionless as stone.

Boris drove the scout steadily lower. Inside another hour they were circling the Stem area just off the deck, dipping below hilltops and nearly brushing trees with the bottom of the scout's nearly-spherical metal hull. Some of the flora below them stood fifteen meters tall and closely resembled the hardwood trees of Earth.

As their altitude decreased, Boris slowed their speed as well. Now the scoutship was moving not much faster than a man might run. Birds, singly and in squawking flights, fluttered out of its path, their cries coming plainly into the cabin through the outside microphones. On the ground an occasional animal fled, or crouched snarling in the scoutship's moving shadow.

Brazil said: "Looks like a big trail over there, going down that ravine toward the river."

"Animals only?"

"Maybe." Boris turned the scout, and drove it down the ravine, going lower and slower than ever; and there was the little village, no more than a cluster of teepees whose colors blended with the muddy earth. The themes of Galactic life extended to humanity, on many worlds, and that the native humans on a planet as Earthlike as this one should morphologically resemble their cousins from Earth came as no real surprise.

But the native dwellers on Golden, or this sampling of them at least, were less sophisticated. For a long second, naked humanoid figures stood about their village in frozen poses, gaping up at the approaching scoutship, a gigantic mass of bright metal drifting silently through thin air; then the people below dropped fishnets and cooking pots and exploded into frenzied motion.

"Wow—get all those cameras going!" Boris ordered as he turned the scout again, taking it out over the river and there backing it slowly away from the village. "We'll disappear for a while—starting a major panic isn't going to do us any good."

And now the delayed voices from Alpha One began to gabble in the ears of the two planeteers in the scout, urging them to turn viewscreens on this or that detail in the fast-emptying village.

***

Joined by other scoutships carrying other planeteering teams, Colonel Brazil and Spaceman Mann made one approach after another to the Stem area during the next few days. There were interesting discoveries, but no truly surprising ones, and none that appeared to have any direct connection with the Field. Nor were there any observable changes in that mysterious phenomenon. Whatever unknown powers there might be on Golden appeared to be still indifferent to the presence of the explorers from Earth.

There arrived a morning when Colonel Boris Brazil, with Spaceman Adam Mann aboard, launched early from Alpha One, and drove his scoutship down into the Field—free funnel leading to the planet's surface. On this flight the Colonel circled the Stem area only once, to let the red sunrise at surface level catch up with his measured descent. Then he drove toward a grassy hill near the river, a spot that had been carefully selected on an earlier trip.

The scout sank gently; landing struts extended themselves to touch down in the grass. The little ship settled quietly to rest on the hilltop.

The two men inside it examined the outside environment carefully, with eyes and radar and infrared. Here and there life moved, in the grass, in the tall reeds and bushes along the shore, and under the surface of the river.

Life moved, apparently going about its own business. Still nothing challenged their arrival.

"No reaction. Alpha One," said Brazil finally.

"Roger, proceed as briefed," said the delayed voice.

Brazil turned in his seat, and fixed Adam with what a stranger might have interpreted as an angry stare. "Well, Junior, I need a body outside, to lure these Field-formulating superbeings into my snare. Get your ass moving."

Adam unfastened himself from his chair and stood up, already wearing his groundsuit. He gave his boss a half-smile through his faceplate and moved from the control cabin to the final decontamination chamber, in which he stood with his suited arms raised and legs spread, while poison gas and ultraviolet sterilized the outside of his suit, a last step in the effort to protect native life against possibly dangerous Earthly microorganisms.

121

Adam was going to be First Out. First Out, on *this* planet, where Total Investigation was a certainty. He had to remind himself that such an assignment didn't necessarily mean that he was the best planeteer around. Without argument, it meant he was expected to be one of the best.

***

A hatch opened in the seamless-looking hull near the base of the landed scoutship, and a short ramp extended itself to the ground. A human figure, anonymous in an armored groundsuit, appeared in the opening. The morning sun glinted on its faceplate as the figure walked slowly down the ramp and into the kneehigh grass. A representative of Earth-descended humanity had set foot upon the soil of yet another planet.

Adam's boots left a dark trail in the dew-silvered grass as he walked a slow circle, going completely around the scout. The sun was well clear of the horizon now, and he could see for kilometers in every direction. There was not another human being in sight, or, at the moment, even an animal, with the exception of a few birds high and far away to the south. The looming amplexicaul curve of the Field was of course still invisible to his eyes. The Field appeared to make no difference at all to anything that he could see. There was hardly a cloud in all the kindly blue vastness of Golden's sky.

He had a sense that the whole planet was—not exactly watching him, maybe, but still aware of him, even if only in the back of its collective mind. Aware and waiting for what he might do.

"How's it going, Mann?" asked General Grodsky's voice. A majority of the hundreds of people aboard Alpha One, all of them who had the chance, were probably watching the video relay, sent to them through the scoutship from the tiny camera in Adam's helmet.

"Fine, sir," he answered. "It just looks good." The words were of course inadequate, but at the moment, with no new facts to report, such words were the best he could come up with.

According to plan, Adam now turned his back on the parked scoutship, and walked about fifty meters to a place from which he could look down-hill to a bend of the river. A heavy growth of short trees and tall reed-like plants lined both banks closely. On worlds where native human beings existed, rivers were considered good places to spot them, traveling, fishing, or just getting a drink. In his mind Adam quickly ran through the basic procedures for first contact with Apparent Primitives. But at the moment there were no Apparent Primitives in sight.

As Adam turned and started to walk away, a small creature sprang away out of the long grass near his feet, giving him a start. More startled than its human discoverer, the thing went bounding away from him like a jackrabbit, down the slope toward the river. By all appearances it was an inoffensive herbivore. After the first few meters of its darting flight it began to tumble clownishly, leaping and playing with the exuberance of an otter. Near the heavy bush by the river the small animal stopped, looking back uphill at Adam with apparent good cheer.

Adam returned the look, grinning downhill. Then he gazed around him again at the peaceful river and hills and sky. He surprised himself, with a wish to—well, to pray. He was not ordinarily a consciously religious man. But now he felt a wish to pray, maybe to Whom it May Concern, that this world, new to its discoverers, could be treated right by them, that good would come from their discovery. It was a strange moment for Adam, one in which he felt himself in communion with—with the powers of the universe, perhaps. He had rarely had a similar feeling in his life, and never since Alice—

Something huge was moving, very quietly, down in the thick bush by the river. Then it burst into the open, a massive, bloated-looking quadruped that pounced with startling speed. The rabbit-thing was taken by surprise. One heavy clawed foot caught it in the middle of its first frightened leap, and crushed it down into the grass and dirt, where it wriggled helplessly and let out shrill faint screams.

Its prey secured, the big animal paused, speed leaving its movements as if a switch had been opened. The predator was a little smaller, Adam thought, than an adult hippopotamus, but just as graceless.

Adam thought that he had seen this large species before, or one very closely related to it. But those sightings had been distant ones, to which he had paid little attention amid the superabundance of new things to be observed. He had really seen nothing of the species but its gross overall shape, until now.

Now, when this specimen turned its head and looked up the hill at Adam from only fifty meters away, he felt a chill, even armed and armored as he was. Because the face of the gross beast was human. Not just a close resemblance. Almost exactly Earth-descended human in all its features, enlarged though they were to fit the massive head.

Adam could hear Brazil muttering something; his own shock was shared. Adam dialed magnification into his faceplate. Now, inspecting the beast's face at an effectively closer range, he could see that it was covered with very short pale fur, from a distance resembling light-colored human skin. The red-rimmed yellow eyes of the animal were human in configuration, down to the smallest visible details of the lids and lashes. Something about the lids gave the eyes a look of arrogance, and above those haughty human eyes there rose a smooth shield of some horny substance, in a shape that in a man might very well have been described as a noble forehead. But behind this frontal shield the skull sloped off sharply into a dark and matted mane—there was no room for a proportional brain behind that mask-like face.

There was nothing like an animal's snout on that flat face, but a human nose instead. Not even the great width of the mouth, the heavy jaw, or even the size of the omnivorous teeth—bared now in a sudden yawn—could destroy the impression, the illusion, of man-larger-than-life. Nor could the ears, half-hidden by the mane, and curving along the head in a shape that looked neither human nor animal. Only when the eye reached the longish scaly neck did the illusion fail.

Over most of its body the big animal wore the hide of an elephant, gray and wrinkled, scantily clothed with a thin coat of greenish-black hair. The feet were obviously weapons, half-adapted for gripping and clawing as well as for locomotion. Mud was beginning to cake dry on the thick legs of this specimen, and a trickle of green slime drooled from a corner of the frowning mouth. Omnivore, thought Adam. It must have been feeding on some river plants, and then it decided to go for a morsel of meat.

With his right hand on the butt of his holstered sidearm, he stared back at the creature. The mask-like face, taken by itself, would have to be called handsome—there was no other word for it. But when Adam saw it on the beast, the total effect was so hideous that he half wished, perhaps more than half, that the thing would charge him, that he might have a good reason to kill it.

"Ugly thing there," said a fascinated voice in Adam's helmet. "What's that it's caught?"

"Rabbit-theme," he answered, without taking his eyes from the bigger creature's face. "I think probably mammalian."

The big animal now turned its full attention back to its victim, bent its long neck slowly and chewed with delicacy. The faint screams went to a higher frequency. Adam thought: *Like an Earth housecat, playing with a victim.* But on a deeper, stronger level, he was thinking also: *Come on, you obscenity, come up where and try that on me. Come on.*

But he was a damned fool, to be upset by the sight of one animal eating another one. He watched a little longer, answering a few more questions from above, then turned his back and went on with his job.

An hour later, when Adam had finished the rest of the scheduled First Out procedures, and was back in the control room of the scoutship, he found Brazil looking at him with an oddly fascinated expression. The first thing the Colonel said was: "I wonder why your big playmate out there didn't have wings."

Adam let himself sink into the right-hand seat with a tired sigh. "Wings? Why?"

"The original did; Geryon was his name. Remember? Or don't you like to read?"

"Jur—who?" But something in Adam's memory stirred faintly. Was it something he had read? Or something else?

But what?

"G-e-r-y-o-n." The Colonel spelled it out. "A thing Dante met when he was visiting the Inferno. It had the face of a just and kindly man. And wings. Among other attributes."

Adam gave a half-laugh. "He encountered it in a likely place, I think. Kind of took me by surprise, out there."

Chapter Six

By the third standard day after First Landing, scoutships were shuttling in an almost continuous pattern between Alpha One and the tiny accessible area of Golden's surface that the explorers had come to call the Stem. As everyone had expected, General Grodsky had decreed Total Investigation here; that meant that eventually everything within reach on Planet Golden was to be sampled and studied. Planeteer teams had already begun analyzing the air, the water, the soil, and many of the smaller forms of life. As yet no attempts had been made to obtain specimens of the larger animals. For one thing, the human natives might be inconvenienced or outraged by such activity, and for another, until more had been learned by observation there was at least a theoretical chance of getting an intelligent, non-primate-theme human being in the game bag by mistake. A very few such races were known to exist in the Galaxy, of intelligent beings therefore classified as human, but with no more physical resemblance to Earth-descended humans than to marigolds or mollusks.

The indications so far on Golden were that life here held at least fairly closely to the commonest Galactic theme patterns for Earth-type planets. Beside the natives who were obviously intelligent beings in the primate theme, there were deer-types and giraffe-types to be seen grazing on the green plains. Species

127

of large animals strongly centered in the cat-theme of Galactic evolution had been observed, preying as might be expected upon the larger herbivores. And here on Golden, as on every habitable world that explorers from Earth had yet examined, there were also apparent exceptions to the standard Galactic themes—here, most notably so far, the species of large omnivores that were already being called geryons.

Day and night the radar equipment of the Earth-descended explorers never ceased for a millisecond to scan the Field. But still the Field was never observed to move or change. Every attempt to measure or analyze it had so far proven fruitless, as every technologically advanced instrument brought into contact with it died on contact. The Field simply existed, as it had since Fakhuri's first sighting, shrouding the planet completely except for the tiny Stem area of the surface.

On the third day after First Landing—Golden's rotation was only very slightly slower than that of Earth—a small group of women and men in protective groundsuits approached on foot the invisible but very sharply defined line where the Field came down in a nearly vertical wall to meet the soil of Golden.

These planeteers carried with them long wired probes, similar to the ones that had earlier been lowered into the Field from a scoutship. It was soon discovered that at ground level the result was the same. Electrical currents died as soon as any part of the wire carrying them was introduced into the Field. The surface of the Field was soon found to be very smooth in every region tested, and very sharply defined. The anomalous condition—now a favorite term of description—was soon shown to extend, in the same plane as aboveground, for at least a few meters below ground level. Plans were begun for deeper exploratory excavations.

Electrical devices of any kind invariably went dead when they were shoved across the invisible boundary. Yet the boundary appeared to mean nothing to birds and animals, or to the native people who like the birds and animals were observed passing in and out of the Field at will, with the bioelectric activities of their bodies presumably unaffected by it.

"Do you know what the word is on Golden?" asked Adam through his groundsuit's airspeaker. He was sighting carefully into a radar instrument as he spoke, and a moment later he began to drive another marking pole into the soft ground, just inside the newly charted boundary of the Stem.

Kwame Chun Lui, the only planeteer on this mission who was less of a veteran than Adam, moved his electrical probe a little further on, positioning it in accordance with Adam's gestures. "'Presumably'?" Chun Lui offered. "I hear the physicists are having it programmed into their writers on a single key."

" 'Apparently' is the one I had in mind," said Adam.

Small Earth animals, pushed into the Field inside a wheeled cage, showed no immediate effects from the exposure, and gave no sign that they were even aware of a change in their environment. But the second time the experiment was tried, and on a number of tries thereafter, the small padlock securing the door of the animals' cage fell open. On examination the locks showed no sign of damage, nor could they ever be made to repeat their bizarre behavior outside the Field. A whole new set of experiments, having to do with the behavior of mechanism inside the Field, was launched.

Levers, screws, and other simple machines, when not part of any complex system, were always observed to perform normally inside the Field. But anymore complex mechanical combinations or systems tended to display wildly erratic behavior. A fine antique chronometer, put at risk by the devoted scientist who owned it, was almost—but not quite—certain to run at the wrong speed, or even backwards, when it was pushed across the border.

No pattern was apparent. Within the Field, the law of complex machines was Chaos. Hope for the life of Chief Planeteer Golden, never bright, faded again; it seemed that the complicated mechanism of his ejection capsule could never have carried him free of his falling scoutship.

Any forcefields that the explorers from Earth were capable of generating simply ceased to exist at the boundary of the Field. And beyond that border, many non-biological chemical reactions, especially the more complex ones, could not be induced to conduct themselves properly.

Over there, atomic clocks and power supplies failed quite dependably, as if their impelling isotopes had been turned to lead. Over there, a fusion power lamp flared out like a cheap candle—someone wrote that as a note and then deleted it. On the contrary, a cheap candle over there burned perfectly well. Yet the high-tech devices could always be made to resume proper operation again as soon as they were pulled out of the Field; and counters in the Stem picked up faint normal background radiation, probably from natural sources, coming from across the border.

Over there, fire burned as always, when kindled in wood or grass by lightning or by human hands, employing primitive means. Over there, animals and plants and people lived, and lightning darted when a rainstorm came. Nature and primitive invention alike appeared to be quite unperturbed by the Field's

130

presence. Only the advanced technology of the explorers from Earth was affected.

Some of those explorers concentrated their observations on the native branch of humanity. Men, women, and children were seen at a distance, repeatedly moving from Stem to Field and back again, without the least visible awareness of any change, or even of the fact that any boundary at all existed. Of course the native humans wore no groundsuits, complex with valves and circuits, and depended upon no machines more advanced than the knife or the bow.

The local people fled at every tentative approach of an explorer. The explorers did not try at all to press the issue. Brazil and his people had plenty to do as it was. Diplomacy, for the time being, could wait.

No objection was offered to the presence of the explorers; the hypothetical Field-builders failed to materialize. After several days Grodsky brought down his flagship to a mere fifty thousand kilometers or so above the Stem, and the distance lag in communication between the flagship and its people on the surface practically disappeared.

The odd Ringwall structure around on the other side of the planet, antipodal to the Stem, remained a mystery. New photos of the Ringwall taken from just above the Field at that point showed essentially no more than the first pictures of it had shown. The Ringwall was an irregular polygon of mountainous cliffs, several kilometers across, above which the lower atmosphere seemed always to be hazy enough to blur detail. If it was indeed to be classified as architecture, there was no other building on Golden anywhere near its size. Neither were there sizable cities anywhere on the planet, or large ocean-going ships, or cities big enough to make space-farers' beacons in the night.

***

There came at last a lull in the explorers' efforts to gather still more data, a pause while human brains and computers tried to digest the mass of detailed information they had so far accumulated. Brazil and almost his entire planeteering crew went up to attend a meeting on Alpha One, leaving just Adam Mann and Kwame Chun Lui, with a single scoutship, on the surface of the planet.

"You're the boss until I get back this afternoon," Colonel Brazil told Adam on departure. The Colonel glowered. "May the mighty spirits protect our cause on Golden."

Adam and Chun Lui were not to remain idle. They began hopping in the scout around the perimeter of the Stem, following a circular path more than a hundred and fifty kilometers in diameter, repeating earlier tests with probes and meters to see if anything about the Field had changed since the tests began. There was no sign that it had.

Shortly after midday, Adam looked up from his drudgery with marker poles and electric probes, and commented: "More of the damned things."

A hundred meters away, on the other side of the boundary, three geryons had just come over a hilltop. Now another of the beasts appeared on the hill, and presently two more came into view at one side of it.

"They're after something," said Adam. "That's how they hunt anything bigger than a rabbit—in a pack." He had been watching them whenever he could, beyond his normal duties of observation; he felt a kind of private fascination.

"After us, maybe?" Chun Lui wondered. The geryons' dead-looking yellow eyes were turned down the hill in the general direction of the two men.

"Maybe they are. All right, let's go back to the ship for a while. I wouldn't care to start messing around with weapons right here at the edge of the Field."

"Roger." Chun Lui pulled firmly on the rope that he was holding. The rope's other end was tied around the ankle of a humanoid robot, and the robot lay fallen on its face just beyond the line of marking poles that defined the Stem-Field border. One of the routine tests now used was to send the robot walking into the Field and haul it out after the inevitable collapse. Someone in one of the departments on the flagship had evidently thought it would be an informative procedure. Now, as soon as Chun Lui had dragged the heavy metal body back into the Stem, animation returned to it. The man-shaped thing climbed to its feet and took an unsteady step back toward the boundary.

"Halt, Otto," Chun Lui ordered in a crisp voice. The machine stopped in its tracks obediently. Its lenses, halfway eyelike projections on the front of its head, moved slightly, watching the animals on the hill.

"Carry this back to the scout, Otto." Adam told it. "And these things." The robot turned, picked up the indicated equipment, and strode purposefully toward the scoutship, which waited about forty meters inside the Stem.

Adam and Chun Lui followed, carrying the rest of the gear and looking back over their shoulders. The geryons were now moving slowly toward them in a spread-out line.

"Hey, it's not us they're after," said Chun Lui when the walking men had almost reached the scoutship. "Looks like they've caught—" His eyes went wide behind his faceplate, and he stopped so suddenly that Adam almost walked into him.

Adam spun around, just as the machine called Otto hurtled past him, running faster than any man could run, accelerating like a racing motorcycle back toward the boundary of the Field. Fifty meters beyond that boundary the geryons were now ringed around a native child who danced in panic, looking too terrified to scream. The robot's programmed compulsion to protect human life drove it toward the animals, into the Field. At the boundary it instantly collapsed again, tumbling forward in the grass with its momentum.

Adam was only vaguely aware of hearing the first excited comments from Alpha One. Already he had turned and barked to Chun Lui: "Get in the scout and man the turret!" Then he took off running back toward the animals on the hill, the servo-powered legs of the groundsuit churning him forward as fast as any unburdened human sprinter.

He stopped only a couple of paces before he reached the Field. The heavy machine pistol, as if by itself, had already come out of the holster and into his armored hand. Fifty meters up the slope the child—looked like a little girl—was trying to dodge out of the geryons' circle, but the gray bodies moved with graceless, efficient speed to block her in. Adam could see the irregular white teeth in the girl's open mouth, and hear her thin wailing cry.

He thumbed the pistol's safety off and locked the optical sight onto the largest geryon as it moved. He fired a burst that should have torn its backbone out. The tracers snuffed out when they hit the Field, and thin trails of smoke curved down into the grass not far beyond the boundary. There was a faint pattering disturbance on the far side of the line, as if he had tossed a handful of gravel over.

The geryons ignored the demonstration. The largest of them had caught the child's arm in its teeth now, and Adam could see the blood. The others hovered ponderously, as if impatiently waiting their turns to bite.

"Fire the turret!" Adam shouted. "For effect!" It occurred to him that main turret fire might kill the child, too, if indeed the beams managed to break through the Field at all. But to try it looked like the only chance.

"What's going on?" General Grodsky's voice asked loudly in Adam's helmet. Then that voice was drowned in a burst of noise, as the sharp, nearly invisible beams stabbed out from the scoutship's main turret. The air thundered around Adam, and his armor glowed in the mighty splash of heat that billowed up and down the Field's surface from the point where the beams struck it. On the Stem side, the grass at Adam's feet went up in smoke, while centimeters away, across the invisible barrier, the blades stood green and fresh.

Several of the animals on the hillside turned their heads and looked toward the scoutship, as if the sound of the blast had annoyed them.

"The siren!" Adam shouted. "Turn the siren on!"

Another geryon had caught the child in its teeth now, and was nibbling at her delicately. Her rising scream was drowned with all other sounds when the scoutship's siren climbed to a full-volume howl. Adam turned off his air mikes, and realized that Grodsky was shouting questions at him.

"Native attacked by animals, inside the Field," he called back. "We're trying to help."

Adam did not really hear what the General said next. The effort to help was not succeeding. The siren did not greatly distract the beasts. Now Chun Lui was trying an optical laser in their eyes, but the beam began to diffuse as soon as it hit the Field. The geryons snarled and squinted and turned their heads away from the glaring light. They kept on with what they were doing, like starving animals at food.

But it was not food they wanted, only bloody sport. Adam caught another glimpse, between massive gray bodies, of the child, and could see only too well that she still lived.

If he entered the Field in his groundsuit, valves would malfunction and he would collapse at once, unable to breathe. He brought an arm in from its groundsuit sleeve and had two fasteners loose inside his helmet when the General's voice blasted at him: "Mann, what are you doing?"

"Going up there."

"No! That's an order! Fasten your helmet!"

A third fastener fell loose. "There's nothing else left to try."

"Chun Lui, stop him! Stun him!"

Adam dashed toward the Field, which he expected would protect him from stunbeams. Once across the border, he would have to get his helmet off very quickly, to let himself breathe, then run up the hill and distract the animals. And get the girl to the scout. There might be some chance yet—

The paralyzing beam from the scoutship struck him before he could reach the line of marker poles, and the grassy ground swung heavily up to hit his faceplate. His groundsuit was poor protection against the scout's heavy projector at this close range. But somehow he rolled on one side, reached out an arm. If he could drag himself across… it was surprising that he could move at all…

The beam struck him again, and his body went dead as ice. The last thing Adam saw before darkness came was a geryon looking down the hill at him, frowning haughtily, displaying red-stained teeth.

Chapter Seven

Alice was holding out her arms toward him, crying for his help. But Adam could not reach her, because the terrible fight in the playground was still going on and he was still trapped in it, pinned up against the wall that was covered with painted murals, unable to break free. Then he was flat on his back. Strangers with hate-filled faces had surrounded him; they were looking down at Adam and shouting hate, for he was somehow odd or different. They kicked at Adam and he tried to hit back at them, but his arms had gone heavy and numb and useless. Then the faces were gone, all of them except one—

—the face of Kwame Chun Lui, who was bending over him. Adam was lying on his back in his bunk in the scoutship. His helmet and groundsuit had been removed. He could tell from the way the ship felt around him, and from the quality of background sounds, that the ship was still parked on the surface.

"Wha—" He sat up with a grunt, and then almost toppled over sideways before he discovered that he was still half-paralyzed. "Uh. How long—?"

"You've been out about an hour," said Chun Lui. Standing back a pace from the bunk now, components from the scoutship's medical kit in hand, he looked relieved and at the same time a bit wary. "I had to do it, Ad. Good thing Otto still had that line tied to his ankle; I reeled him in, and he carried you in through decontamination."

Adam said something vulgar, and let himself flop back on the bunk. He added an obscenity, and repeated it several times. "Why didn't you use that damned thing on them instead of on me?"

Chun Lui's voice was quiet. "Well, I tried it on them, Ad. It did no more good than the main burner."

Adam swore aimlessly once more, and then made another effort to sit up, this time with somewhat better success. He sat there on the edge of his bunk, stamping his feet, trying to rub and flex the woodenness out of his thick arms. There had been a chance, some kind of a chance, to help the kid, and they had stopped him. It was all he could think of.

The large communication screen on the bulkhead lit up, with General Grodsky's image glaring sourly out of it at him. "Well, Mann. Since you disobey orders, I presume you possess some information about the conditions there that you didn't have time to explain to me. Let's have it."

Adam stared back doggedly. "Sir. I just wanted to help that kid."

"You think I didn't want to help her?" The screen seemed to vibrate slightly with the volume of the General's voice. Then the volume dropped, but the hardness grew. "What was your next step going to be, exactly?"

"I was... going to go on up the hill, sir. To do what I could."

"What you could." Grodsky almost smiled, projecting mock satisfaction now. "Would you outline for me, please, just what that was going to be?"

All right, he was in trouble. Adam told himself that he didn't give a damn. Yet he did, but what else could he have done?

He replied to the General: "Distract the animals. Try and get the little girl away from them. Try to get her downhill to the scout again. Where we could give her medical attention."

"How many of those animals were there?"

"Half a dozen, maybe. Sir."

"And you were going up there unarmed, to take their prey away from them." The General made it sound totally insane. Well, maybe it had been insane. No doubt it had. All Adam knew was that he had been unable to keep from trying. If the situation came up again, he'd have to try again.

The volume of Grodsky's transmitted voice had decreased now by another level, but the tone had become if anything more vicious. "That Field you were so eager to enter, that air you were so anxious to breathe, are still completely unknown in terms of what their effects on an Earth-descended human being will be. Did you learn nothing at all on Killcrazy? Wasn't everything there innocent and peaceful in the first days of exploration? Are you utterly stupid, Mann? We've already lost one planeteer here, and I don't—"

"How about that little girl?" Adam heard himself shouting back. "Does she fit on your scorecard anywhere?"

Violence appeared behind Grodsky's angry eyes. The possibility loomed suddenly, real as a brandished club, that a commanding General's awesome authority in the field was about to be invoked with crushing impact. Adam was suddenly afraid. He knew that the General would have been legally justified in ordering him shot, for disobedience in the field. He wouldn't be shot now, of course; the emergency was over, the situation stabilized. But he might be tried and imprisoned. He might be kicked out of the Space Force. He might be sent back to Earth to some meaningless desk job. Damn it, he had done what was right, and would do it again. But the girl was dead by now, and he wasn't, and he was getting a little scared.

But the General's club of authority—though it had been figuratively lifted from his shoulder—did not strike. Grodsky, as though with the purpose of impressing everyone with the need for caution and control, made his own anger disappear. Adam had observed before, with a touch of envy, how the high brass all seemed to be able to do that.

General Grodsky, his own intentions now as well hidden as a poker hand, asked Adam in a controlled voice: "Have you got anything more to say?"

Adam drew a deep breath. "Sir, apart from humanitarian considerations, it could help us to get on with the natives, to have pulled one of them out of trouble."

"Sure it could," said Grodsky, not impressed for a moment. "Or, that girl might have been a ritual sacrifice, and saving her might have ruined our chances to get on, as you put it—apart from humanitarian considerations. But that's not the main point. The main point right now is that when I give an order it must be followed."

"Yessir," said Adam, meekly. He was beginning to dare to hope that he might survive. "If I was wrong, I... was wrong."

"You were wrong, dammit."

"Yessir..."

"But what?"

"But... I was left in command down here, General, and there occurred what I judged to be an emergency, and I took what steps I thought were best."

There was a silence, long enough for Chun Lui to put in a few words. "Sir, with the turret firing and all, it's possible we didn't hear all of the General's spoken orders very clearly at the time."

Adam nodded. At the same time, Colonel Brazil, for once no trace of humor in his long, bony face, appeared behind Grodsky on the screen.

The General was considering the situation silently. Then he said: "I'm reserving judgment, for the time being, on the incident that's just happened. We'll carry on from where we are."

There was a little silence. Then after a moment Chun Lui said: "Sir, I think sooner or later we're going to have to fight off those beasts in self-defense. More and more of them keep hanging around, watching us. And they seem to build up their courage in large groups."

Grodsky nodded, confirming that the chewing-out was going to be allowed to turn into a planning session. The tension in the atmosphere drained rapidly as the General turned around. "Boris, those animals do seem devilish hard to frighten, don't they? Of course we can defend ourselves against them within the Stem, but I want to hold the killing of any native fauna to a minimum, at least until we know—"

"Seven humans are approaching the scoutship on foot," interrupted Otto's robotic voice.

Chun Lui quickly switched the viewscreen to show the scene outside. Six naked warriors, armed with bows and bone knives, were approaching the landed ship with an air of timid determination. The one woman stumbling along in their midst wore a wrap of cloth about her hips, and was nearly hysterical with grief. The woman bore in her arms what the geryons had left of the little girl, and the woman's body and her legs were stained with the child's blood.

Brazil's voice from the screen said: "I would suggest one of you two down there go out and say hello to the people, since it appears they finally want contact." The Colonel turned away briefly and could be heard exchanging a few muttered words with Grodsky. Then Brazil went on: "Mann, you're still the ranking planeteer down there. Take charge."

And may the mighty spirits aid our cause on Golden, Adam thought. *All right; here we go again.* He stood up. His legs almost betrayed him.

"Damn. Chun, help me up to the left seat, will you? Then you go out and talk to them."

Chun Lui assisted him. "Sorry I had to use that stun beam on you, Ad."

"Dammit, quit saying you're sorry. It's all right. Just shut up and get outside quick."

The seven natives knelt before the groundsuited figure of Chun Lui when he descended to greet them formally.

* * * * * *

Dr. Osa Yamaguchi, head of Linguistics, was getting up in years. Whether as a result of her advancing age or not, she sometimes adopted a didactic manner, irrespective of her listeners' rank.

"They're undoubtedly appealing for our help against the geryons," she informed General Grodsky, meanwhile tapping the papers and other records arrayed on the conference table before her. The language of the local people—the Tenoka, they called themselves—was now well on the way to being understood, at least well enough for some practical conversation. The job had taken several weeks of recording and computing and study, since Tenoka was not a simple tongue and the native speakers of it had been dwelling mostly on one subject.

"That's definite?"

"Yes."

Grodsky turned to the head of Anthropology. "How does it look to you?"

"They're not really too surprised at our presence, though they've never seen anything like us before. They accept us as some kind of demigods." The Chief Anthropologist was a small man named Pamon, usually vague of manner and sometimes indeterminate in his appearance. He tended to absorb the behavior of whatever people he was working with; already he was sitting with his hands clasped in the fashion of a Tenoka warrior, though he had not yet seen one of the Golden natives except on a screen.

"So, they ask our help," Pamon went on. "I gather they've had more than the usual trouble with geryons lately. The beasts don't often attack healthy adults, and it seems probable that they can tell when a human is armed. For a child, or even two of them together, to leave the village unescorted is quite dangerous; and yet the children do. I suppose they must, to learn the adult skills."

"Girls too?"

"Perhaps. Or, she might have sneaked out just to watch our planeteering work, just out of curiosity." Pamon sighed.

Grodsky frowned. "Have they any taboo against killing these particular animals? I don't mean to slaughter 'em wholesale, of course; no telling what that might do to the ecology. But if the beasts are cunning enough to avoid armed adults, it occurs to me that we might find a way to teach 'em that from now on attacking children is dangerous also."

"No taboo against killing them, General. But they're doubtless hard to put away with primitive weapons."

"I think we can educate 'em," said Colonel Brazil, breaking a thoughtful silence.

"We have made this magic-doll, in the semblance of a child of your people," Brazil announced a few days later. He spoke in the Tenoka tongue, in which some days of intensive training had made him almost fluent, and he was standing outside his own scoutship on the surface of the planet. "The doll has no spirit of its own. When we wish it, the spirit of one of our warriors will enter into it. Thus we hope that the geryons will come to fear the children of your people."

The Tenoka delegation, twelve or fifteen strong and including both men and women, shifted their feet uncertainly. Strong Breather, who seemed to be the most influential available leader, grunted thoughtfully. Pierced Arms, the local shaman, gave no sign of what he might be thinking, at least no sign that Boris could interpret. Pierced Arms was daubed over most of his gaunt, aged body with colored goo, and the scarred loops of tissue on his arms and shoulders were strung with feathered cords.

The entire Tenoka delegation kept looking at the semblance of a child. A modified small robot, it stood with its back almost against one of the scoutship's extended landing struts. About a meter tall, the robot had been transformed into a tolerably good likeness of a naked native youngster, though if you looked at it closely it was obviously not alive. A breeze now stirred the realistic hair; otherwise the small figure was motionless. When turned on, it answered to the name of Shorty.

"I will tell you now," Brazil resumed, "how we of the far land of Earth plan to help our friends, the Tenoka. As is well known, the Tenoka are fearless warriors; if they see any one of their tribe in danger, they will rush fiercely to help."

Two of the fearless warriors listening to him giggled suddenly, holding sun-darkened-hands over their mouths. Strong Breather looked at them sternly, but his own mouth twitched. Wait a moment, thought Boris—did I use the word for 'fiercely' or 'drunkenly'? But in any case it seemed no great harm had been done.

"This magic-doll," he went on, "will not need the help of the great Tenoka warriors. Our magic within the circle of our power is stronger than any number of the geryons. Therefore if you should see this seeming child pursued or attacked by geryons tomorrow, you must make no move to interfere. Will you inform all of your people of this?"

Strong Breather and Pierced Arms exchanged a look. Then Boris got the chin-thrusts and grunts that meant agreement.

Brazil added: "And tomorrow all of the real children must be kept in the villages, so there will be no mistake."

Again the leaders of the delegation signified that they were willing.

Now came what might well be the most ticklish part of the negotiation. "You have brought the used blankets, and the clothing worn but not washed." Brazil made it a statement and not a question; he could see that they had brought the stuff along as requested, tied into a bundle. But such things were often considered potentially powerful tools of magic against their owners. Pamon had been worried that the Tenoka might refuse at the last moment to turn them over.

The technicians aboard Alpha One had given Shorty no odor of his own, but had provided the robot with a plastic skin that would absorb any smells it came in contact with after activation. The plan was to immerse Shorty in the bundle of Tenoka-redolent cloth for a day. To a geryon, smell might well be a more important sense than sight.

"Take up the cloth things now," Boris instructed the Tenoka, "and wrap the child-doll in them, so it may convey to the geryons the danger of attacking your children. Tomorrow you may take back the things."

After a brief pause, and another exchange of looks with Strong Breather, Pierced Arms stepped forward and delivered a sing-song harangue to Shorty, who received it stoically; then another to Boris, who understood not a word of either speech.

But apparently this did not matter. The old man untied the bundle of laundry and began draping it around Shorty, piece by piece.

***

"Well, you're the combat expert," Brazil said to Adam in the grounded scoutship that evening. "Ready to go tomorrow?"

"All set." Adam glanced at the puppet chamber that had come down with Shorty from Alpha One, and now filled most of the scoutship's living space.

Right now the puppet chamber resembled an empty shower room, its glass walls enclosing enough space for a man to stand or jump or turn a somersault, but very little more. When the power was turned on, the interior of the chamber was filled by a fine, three-dimensional grid of forcefield lines. The grid recorded every instantaneous position of a human operator inside the chamber, data that could then be passed on by radio to Shorty or any other yesman, allowing a robot to be controlled exactly by the human. There was a return transmission also. Whatever experience presented itself to Shorty's electronic senses would be radioed back to the puppet chamber, and translated there into forcefield effects, with their intensity modified as necessary for the human operator's safety and comfort. A forcefield floor in the chamber acted as a treadmill, and continually modified its shape to imitate whatever terrain was under the yesman.

Shorty was now standing in the scoutship's airlock, still wrapped in the Tenoka bedding and garments. Adam had spent some time in practice with the puppet chamber, marching the small yesman around in the vicinity of the scout. It had not taken long for him, with his reflexes, to regain the walking gait and habits of childhood, with his legs effectively reduced to about half their adult length. Shorty also possessed a kind of autopilot mode, useful for steady travel, in which the robotic brain took over control of legs and balance.

"I'd just like to get started on the job," Adam added. Then abruptly he got up and paced, moving restlessly in the little space that was left outside the puppet chamber.

Since there was scarcely room for two men to walk about, Brazil sat down at the table. The Colonel produced a deck of cards from somewhere, and began in an abstracted way to deal out two hands.

Adam stopped his pacing and watched the fall of cards. "Two-handed poker?"

"Not necessarily. Look, Junior, don't find some new way to go wild tomorrow. Grodsky and I are both sticking our necks out quite a bit by keeping you on the job after what happened."

Mann stared at him for a moment, then said "Thanks" as if he possibly meant it, and spun away with nervous speed to pace again. He came back and stopped. "It's just that I keep thinking about that kid."

"I know." Brazil's own life was not yet very long, as years were counted, but it was crowded with experience. "You'll see a lot of bad things in this job. You can't get too involved."

"But I was involved. I was right there."

"You did what you could."

"Yeah."

"Possibly we were wrong to stop you. Maybe Grodsky made a mistake there. He's only human. But maybe you made one, you're only human too."

"Yeah." Mann was looking at him in a new way, as if the Colonel had somehow managed to make a previously unnoticed point. "Yeah, we're stuck with being only human, aren't we?"

Brazil blinked at him. "Right." It was good that he had made some point, but... the Colonel decided to let it lie. "Now bring back some geryon ears tomorrow, and as a special reward I'll stop calling you Junior."

***

Adam dozed, on the borderland of sleep. When he got tomorrow's job out of the way, when he had smashed some of those damnable animals and taught the rest a lesson, maybe things in his life would somehow straighten out. Planeteering would once again mean everything to him that it had once meant—or that he had once thought that it was going to mean. Back in the days when there had been more meaning to a lot of things. Before Alice had been...

In sleep, Alice's face came again to drift before him. She cried out again for help, only to be replaced by the image of the mangled Tenoka girl.

"Turns out she was an orphan," Pamon had told him. "The woman who carried her to your ship was a widow, acting as a foster parent, supported by the tribe. Interesting institution."

Later there was another dream, this one involving yellow teeth.

Chapter Eight

"Overseer reports another group of five animals, coming this way, bearing about one-two-oh," said Colonel Brazil. He was speaking over the scoutship's intercom system, and referring to an aerial survey of geryons within the chosen area of the Stem. "Range about a klick and a half. That makes twenty-two of the beasties within reasonable walking range. Be nice if you could get 'em all chasing after you."

"I'll walk by and give them the chance," Adam answered, He was standing inside the puppet chamber, trying to persuade the skin-tight operator's suit to stretch into something like a comfortable fit. "Let's hope they feel like playing."

"Ready for chamber power?"

"Roger."

"Power coming on."

Adam reached up to the top of the chamber, unhooked the operator's helmet from its suspension there and fitted it carefully over his head. The helmet covered his eyes and ears completely, effectively shutting out surrounding sight and sound. Blindly he worked to get the mouth control, that managed certain of the robot's functions, comfortably positioned where his teeth could operate it.

Adam let his arms drop to his sides. Color swam and steadied before his eyes, forming shapes and illusory distances, becoming the inside of the closed outer door of the scoutship's airlock. The background noise changed subtly in his ears.

The illusion was well-nigh perfect. Both sight and hearing assured Adam that he was now standing inside the airlock, inside Shorty's metal body, only a meter tall and still wrapped in the Tenoka cloth. He shrugged the stuff away from him, thinking himself probably lucky that the yesman had been provided with no functioning nose.

Adam stepped forward one child-sized stride, and raised one of his/Shorty's little arms. The stiff latch of the airlock door eased open at a touch of Shorty's baby-sized finger, steel-boned, electrically muscled, powered by a tiny hydrogen fusion lamp in Shorty's chest.

Adam-Shorty toddled down the short landing ramp. He was barely able to see over the tallest grass.

"Robot," Adam said, and let his legs relax, as the chamber controls read the code word, and the chamber forcefields tightened to support his human weight. The robot brain had taken over the routine business of making step after step with the yesman's legs. This might be an all-day job, and there was no point in wearing himself out hiking. Adam steered with the sterile-tasting mouth control, and with a light biting pressure held Shorty's speed to that of a walking child.

Tall grass flowed easily by him, the long blades still bearing traces of morning dew.

"Bear about ten degrees left," said the voice of the aerial observer in his ears. "You're going to find the first group, four beasts, about two hundred meters ahead, moving down a little ravine, very slowly."

Adam bore left as directed. He looked up into kindly blue. After a bit he was able to spot Overseer. If geryons were aware at all of distant scoutships, they ought to be accustomed to the sight of them by now. This one presumably would mean nothing in particular to the animals.

Adam didn't want to run right into the four animals ahead. He preferred to go past them and let them stalk him, if they would. They were cunning creatures, and the lesson was to be spelled out for them precisely and plainly. Death-beams or bullets might not be connected in the geryons' minds with the seeming child they were, Adam hoped, about to attack. Therefore beams and bullets would not be used.

He came to the ravine where he had been directed to go, and toddled along the top of the high bank. Soon he saw the four geryons, all adults, moving slowly along, grazing in sparse cover at the bottom. Adam-Shorty gave no sign that he had seen them. He walked past and let them become aware of him, then turned away from the ravine.

"Where's the next bunch?" Adam whispered into his helmet mike. Then he chuckled at himself for whispering.

***

Ninety minutes later Adam-Shorty had fourteen of the animals interested enough to follow him. The geryons were moving in a widespread formation that still seemed to be trying to give the impression of aimless drifting. Adam, taking care to keep the little robot well clear of the Field, was headed now toward a certain eroded slope above a bend of the river. There was plenty of rocky ground there to offer the firm support that Shorty's tiny feet might need, and there was a small box canyon that also figured in the plan.

He cast a quick look back over Shorty's shoulder. The geryons, at a distance of a hundred meters or so, were following him a little more obviously now, a slow certainty of intention apparent in their movements. Less frequently now did the omnivorous animals stop to graze, or pretend to graze.

Adam took a quick count—there were fifteen of the animals, three or four of them only half grown, with scaly-looking bodies and heavily furred legs. The faces of the adult females among the group were those of lovely but unhappy women. The males had men's faces with a look of nobility about them, slight variations on the face of the first geryon that Adam had ever seen.

The illusion was intense of his actual presence out there on the plain, a child small and alone before gigantic predators. How many real children had turned to discover that the things were following them, how many real children had run and tripped and screamed...

The illusion was heightened further as Adam took Shorty's legs back under his direct control. The rocks of the chosen slope were not far ahead. Out of nervous habit he felt with the yesman's hand for a holster at its side. Then he grinned to himself. Shorty did not carry sidearms. Or need them.

As he neared the stony area, Adam began to run, imitating the movements of a frightened child. Glancing back at the animals, he saw them drop all pretense of innocence and give chase. They were probably clever enough to know that a child might be able to find a sheltering crevice among the rocks.

Adam-Shorty toddled into the chosen box canyon only a few seconds ahead of the geryons, then turned and stood as if frozen in despair, near the center of the steep-walled natural trap. His pursuers came crowding after him through the canyon's narrow entrance, snapping and shoving to get ahead of one another. None wanted to be left out. One child was not going to provide much sport for fifteen geryons.

Adam continued to stand as if paralyzed by fright, while the huge gray beasts first settled a pecking order among themselves, then waddled to form a ring around him. As soon as the ring was closed, they began to tighten it, moving almost as if in practiced ritual. Some moved toward Shorty with high dainty steps, looking down their human noses at him as if in righteous pride. Some crept forward on their bellies, scummy tongues lolling from their frowning mouths, an effect that ruined the nobility of their fine men's and women's faces.

Adam could feel his breathing quicken and his hands tremble. The sun beat down upon the barren arena. The pack around him gurgled and howled, but only softly.

He made Shorty run to and fro in quick uncertain rushes, as if he were seeking hopelessly to escape. He was no longer entirely pretending; he could feel himself living as a Tenoka child, out there alone in the canyon.

Now the animals' deadly circle was less than four meters wide. Adam had to fight down genuine panic. He made Shorty spin wildly, and cry out in his high child's voice.

Something struck the yesman from behind. Shorty's legs were slaved to human reflexes, so he was knocked on his face. Adam felt the impact, scaled down by the feedback system, as a pat between his shoulder blades. He made Shorty roll over on the ground, and stared up at a circle of nightmare-handsome faces. He could feel his living breath sawing in his throat, and could see the kindly sky, the sky remote and indifferent beyond the sinuous gray necks, the clustered evil power.

The thought came flickering through Adam's mind: How many in all the universe, have seen the universe this way—

A massive foot was coming slowly down on Shorty's midsection—not with any weight on it. A dead victim would be no sport at all. Adam had to choke off a scream as one huge head, human-masked, sank toward Shorty's face. The unspeakable mouth was gaping over him. Now, he thought, now, and he thrust up an arm, and the big yellow-brown teeth closed deliberately on Shorty's child-sized fingers.

He closed Shorty's fingers on one big tooth, yanked it out like a thumbtack, and flipped it away.

Adam heard his own near-hysterical laugh at the reaction he saw in the geryon's face as the long neck whipped up and back, away from him. Another similar head loomed over Shorty, lowering uncertainly. Adam drove an arm up, hard and fast this time. Shorty's fusion-powered arm was slaved to follow Adam's. The metal fingers stabbed through thick neck hide, and drove on spearlike through yielding tissue, until Adam could feel in his fist the greater hardness of the neck vertebrae. He clutched at bone, and squeezed, and had the sensation of crumpling paper in his hand.

He had Shorty out from underneath the thing quickly, before the mountainous convulsions of its death had ceased. Before the other animals could make up their minds that now it was time to run, Adam maneuvered Shorty between them and the narrow entrance to the canyon.

Startled and confused, unable to sense any familiar danger, the geryons ran in circles within the high-walled box, raising clouds of dust in the sunlight. Moving rapidly at last, they jumped and plunged and bellowed. And now the biggest animal turned toward Shorty, looking past the yesman to the one way out of the canyon. Adam-Shorty blocked the path, even as the animal charged him with a snarling howl; in a flash the geryon looked to Adam like the one that had been first to bite the little girl.

He leaned forward, bracing Shorty's feet on firm rock footing beneath him. The geryon did not try to avoid the small figure in its path. The impact that came through to Adam felt like a swat from a pillow, and in it he could distinguish a sudden snapping yielding, that must mean that heavy bone had broken. The geryon fell sideways with a hideous scream, and the pack that had started to follow it halted again, its members colliding with each other in confusion.

Adam-Shorty strode toward them. Most of them scattered before him, not yet in panic, but wary, not knowing what was harming their kind. As one of the bigger geryons dodged past him he caught it by the tail in Shorty's mangling grip, braced his feet on rock again and swung the two-ton squirming mass around hand over hand to face the yesman. The huge head came around biting; Adam swung Shorty's fist with all his strength. Much of the geryon's head vanished in a gory explosion, spattering the other beasts nearby. They howled and turned to frantic flight from Shorty, scrambling in every direction to escape.

Adam pushed his latest victim aside and stamped after the animals on Shorty's tiny feet. With horror he saw that a couple of geryons were already climbing the steep canyon walls, their efforts so fueled by desperation that it looked as if they might succeed.

He grabbed up a loose rock the size of a basketball, and let fly with it at one of the madly scrambling animals. The yesman's throwing arm was slaved to human speed, so the impact was not all that Adam had hoped for, but still the target beast came sliding and rolling down the slope.

Picking up some more rocks, Adam trotted Shorty forward. Something feral and howling took over completely

155

now inside his own skull. The world shrank to a rocky arena where time was hate...

"Don't forget to bring us a sample for Biology," someone's voice reminded him.

"What? Oh, sure." Adam turned Shorty back to the first beast that he had slain—it was about the least damaged of any—grabbed it by one leg, and began to pull it toward the canyon exit. He noticed that his arms were all red, glistening and slimy. "I need a bath," he muttered.

"Huh? You're still here in the scoutship, remember?"

"Sure—I mean I'm sweating." I'd better pull myself together, he thought, or Psych will be examining me half to death.

The carcass that he was towing caught and tore and abraded on rocks. Shorty could pull the leg right off if the operator wasn't careful, and naturally the biologists wanted a specimen that was in reasonably good condition.

Already the scavenger birds were gathering overhead. They came from kilometers around in no time.

Adam stopped, got Shorty right underneath the hulk, and lifted it. It did not feel heavy to him, but it was an awkward thing to handle. The awkwardness was worse after he got out of the canyon and away from the rocky slope. Now the ground was softer under Shorty's tiny feet, and the burdened yesman kept sinking into the soil. Even when Shorty sank waist deep, almost swimming in the alien earth, Adam could still plow ahead with little physical effort.

The dead beast wobbled repulsively in Adam's grip, the geryon head trailing on the long broken neck, the human face that was no longer handsome abrading away on the ground.

156

He, Adam Mann, or someone else, would probably have to repeat today's performance, over and over, until every geryon that survived in the Stem had learned to fear and flee from Tenoka children. A good cause, but an unpleasant job.

The "touch" of the dead bulk became suddenly so repellent that he dropped it.

"Pretty tough going here," he said. "Can't you send a scout or a copter?"

Presently a voice from Alpha One reached him. "All right, a couple of biologists are coming down anyway, and they can pick up the specimen right there. They'll be there in a minute or two. Good job, Mann."

As soon as he saw the scout descending, Adam abandoned the dead geryon and began walking Shorty in the direction of his own scoutship. Blood was drying thickly on the yesman and swarms of insects were beginning to follow it. The parallel themes of Galactic insect life were strongly supported here.

He trudged on, a little metal man under the enormous sky of Golden.

PART THREE

Chapter Nine

The man in the canoe, gliding on the tranquil river, lifted the hand-carved wooden paddle out of the water, and a moment later lowered the small outboard motor into operating position at the squared-off stern. The canoe was handmade too, of bark and wood, designed in the native Tenoka style, except for that square stern. Now, as the craft glided from Field to Stem between moss-grown marker poles, the outboard purred smoothly into life, propelling Adam Mann toward the small boat dock at Far Landing.

People from Earth, as it had turned out, could live perfectly well on the surface of Golden without benefit of groundsuits. They could live perfectly well inside the Field, as long as they were willing to leave all high technology behind them. One implication of that was that seven years ago a certain Earthman, if he had been allowed to take the risk and remove his groundsuit's helmet, might have had some small chance of saving a certain Tenoka child from death at the fangs of timid monsters.

Or, on the other hand he might not.

After seven years, Adam Mann no longer remembered that day's horror very often, or thought about it at all that much.

An Earthman like Adam Mann, who a few years ago had surprised the few friends who thought they knew him well, by resigning from the Space Force, giving up an enviable career to live a mostly primitive life on one particular strange planet— well, such a man with his planeteering experience might have made himself wealthy on a raw world just opened to colonization. In fact, everyone who learned of his decision to resign from the Space Force assumed that that had been his motive.

If it had been, he didn't have a lot of wealth to show for it as yet. Nor any great prospects of much in the foreseeable future. But he was doing all right.

A couple of hours earlier on this mild winter morning, Adam had looked out of the window of his isolated cabin on the Field side of the river, and had seen a shuttle descending to the

Stem City spaceport. The civilian starships were coming out to Golden more and more frequently now, bringing with them tourists and adventurers and business people from Earth and a hundred other worlds. Three hundred thousand colonists were now living in Stem City, amid a continual roar of construction. On Earth demand was high for certain exotic products of this world, among them natural furs. Furs like those in the silvery bundle that rode in the bottom of Adam Mann's canoe.

No road had yet been built between Stem City and the Far Landing dock, but copters had begun to fly the route on a regular schedule. Adam could see one such aircraft just landing on a meadow behind the dock. The aircraft sat there with its rotor quietly idling, while a few people dressed entirely in plain black clothing disembarked from the passenger compartment. They stretched, and looked round them, and then got to work unloading from the copter's cargo bay an assortment of small containers and primitive tools. There were spades, hoes, and axes. Adam knew some of the black-clad folk, though these particular individuals were too far away at the moment to identify. They were religious colonists, who had planted themselves back in the wilderness, a few kilometers beyond even Adam's cabin.

There was only one traditional-looking tourist getting off the copter this time, a blond woman who was wearing jeans and a bulky jacket against the chill of the mild low-latitude winter day. The woman separated herself a little from the black-clad folk, and appeared to be looking round her as if uncertain what to do next.

Now she raised to her face what Adam supposed were binoculars, and swept them around until they were aimed at him. They stayed fixed on him for half a minute.

159

All right, girl, he thought. *We'll see about you. Just as soon as I get these furs checked in.* Lately he had encountered several examples of an interesting phenomenon, the attractive female tourist from Earth or from some other heavily civilized planet, who was ready to be briefly fascinated by the half-savage fur hunter and his peculiar world.

The copter landing area passed out of Adam's sight, behind a rank of riverside brush. The canoe was nearing the dock, and Adam swung his outboard up out of the water and shut it off. There was only one real building at Far Landing, a lonely trading shack of log construction. Outside the shack's door, a couple of Tenoka men were standing, in their usual costume of almost nothing at all, arguing about something with the bored-looking Space Force guard. The Great Council of Tenoka subtribes had granted their friends from far-off Earth theoretically limited rights to occupy the Stem area, and had in exchange accepted a mountain of trade goods and the permanent right of free medical care for any Tenoka who could reach one of the new hospitals in the Stem. So far the Tenoka appeared to be generally still satisfied with the bargain they had made.

Adam tied his canoe up beside a new and very similar Tenoka craft—it had a squared stern and a motor too—and tossed his bundle of furs up onto the dock. From the corner of his eye he could see that the blond woman was approaching, from around the corner of the trading shack, but he finished his tying-up before he raised his head to look at her.

When he raised his head he stood still. Very still indeed, for a long long moment. "Merit Creston," he said then, softly. It had been years, too many years, but as far as he could see at the moment, Merit had scarcely changed.

160

Merit was standing above him, laughing down at him, laughing very much like a little girl who has just successfully carried off a joke. Adam hopped up onto the dock beside her. The smile on his own face felt strange, as if, somewhere along the line and without his realizing it, smiling had become abnormal.

"Adam, it's been so long." She took his hands in hers. Merit as an adult was just about his own height, her hair as uniquely blond as it had been in girlhood but cut somewhat shorter now. Her body in maturity remained as graceful as ever.

"Too long. Much too long. I wonder that you know me." He took stock of himself: long-haired, bearded, none too clean. He was dressed in hunter's clothes, some of native leather, with a long hunting knife of Earth steel sheathed in Tenoka leather at his belt. "You know I quit the Space Force."

"Yes, I'd heard that." Merit looked out across the wide placid river, where a sky free of human technology arched down to a horizon that was notched only by the trees of the winter-brown forest. "I wondered why—now I think I can see the reason. Or part of it, anyway. It's so beautiful here."

As he remembered, Merit was not one who used that word lightly or often. He asked, seriously: "How are you?"

Merit looked back at him, studying him carefully. Or maybe the impression of care being taken was only a result of her turning her head to free her eyes of a strand of wind-blown hair. "Fine."

"And how are Ray, and all the others?"

Merit smiled faintly. "All well, as far as I know. Ray is fine too, he's here on Golden. We both arrived this morning."

"Welcome to my planet!" In sudden jubilation Adam cried out, and lifted Merit into the air—hey, this was Merit! She

161

squealed, a vulnerable and almost childlike sound, carefulness forgotten. And he kissed her.

Then Merit was resting easily in the circle of Adam's arms, eyes examining eyes at close range. She said: "Someone else was on the ship, traveling with us—my husband."

"Well." It hit him hard. For just a moment, it really hit him hard. He hoped he didn't let it show. He said: "I'll congratulate the lucky man when I meet him. Felicitations for you. Does he beat you frequently?"

Merit gave the little girl's laugh that he remembered. "Hardly at all."

"Would I know him?"

"Oh, I don't suppose so." Merit disentangled herself gently from his embrace, and stood gracefully trying to keep her hair from blowing in her eyes. "I don't know why you should. His name is Vito Ling. He's a physicist, specializing in field theory, and he works for Earth Universities Research Foundation."

"Then he's not one of Doc's kids? I don't remember the name. And tell me, how is Doc?"

"No, Vito's not a Jovian." The remnant of Merit's laughter faded from her face and voice. "Doc's dead, Adam. Suddenly, about a year ago."

After a moment he asked her: "How?"

"A heart defect. Evidently it developed rather rapidly, between his regular checkups. He was alone in the lab when he collapsed. By the time someone found him—it was too late."

"And no one—none of you—sensed—" Adam made a gesture of futility.

"None of us. They're so undependable, our parapsych talents. Usually most undependable just when they would seem to be most valuable. Maybe it was…"

"What?"

"I was going to say that maybe the reason we sensed nothing was because Doc felt no fear at dying. No wish to tell us anything. His life with us was a hard one, in some ways, I'm afraid."

Adam squeezed her shoulders. "That was the life Doc chose, the one he wanted." He took Merit's arm and they walked along the dock. "So now tell me about your life, my lady."

Merit's cheerfulness returned. "I'm here partly just to be with Vito. I must admit he's taken up most of my life for the past two years. Now naturally you want to know what he's like. He's tall, and dark, and brilliant, and quick-tempered."

"And not a Jovian."

"No. I said not."

Adam asked it bluntly. "Since he's not a Jovian, does it ever bother him to be left out, when you and the others start with your parapsych tricks?"

"We don't try to make our friends feel that way. Did you ever feel that way?"

"Yeah. I did. I know you don't try. You're right. But even so..."

There was pride in Merit's eyes. "And Vito won't let it bother him. His ego is neither small nor fragile. He won't see anything more in Jovians than gifted humans."

"*Are* you anything more? I can remember Doc soul-searching over that."

The question did not seem to surprise her; but she replied to it only with one of her own. "Do you want us to be?"

"I don't know. I've thought about it, and I don't know. I suppose you and Ray and the ninety-eight others are all still just one big happy family, too."

Merit shrugged. "We have our differences. We always have. But in a sense, yes, I think we're definitely like a family, if you can imagine a family of a hundred people. Maybe all the more like a family because we do have differences, and surmount them. I suppose Ray is really the father now."

Their walk had reversed itself where the riverside path began to grow difficult, and now their course brought them back to where the bundle of furs still lay on the dock. Adam scooped the bundle up, and said: "Let me take care of these." Merit came into the trading shack with him, and observed with interest the transaction between Adam and another Earthman behind a counter. The clerk opened the fur bundle and examined each item closely, then wrangled briefly over quality and prices before noting down the amount to be credited to Adam's Stem City bank account.

Adam, folding his paper receipt into a pocket, waited until he was outside again with Merit before he asked her: "Where are Ray and your husband now?"

"They went straight from the spaceport to the physics lab, at some place called Fieldedge. Scientists to the core. I told them I'd rather try to look you up first, and see some of the scenery at the same time. Since Earth people are rather confined here—or most of them choose to be—I thought I could probably find you with a minimum of trouble."

"Glad you did. Very glad." Adam paused. "You said that you were here partly just to be with your husband. What else?"

"For one thing, I have an obvious interest in seeing what had become of you. But there's something else, too. Geryons."

"Geryons. That's right, the last time I saw you you were getting into exobiology, weren't you?"

"Yes, I'm into it, as you say, rather deeply now."

164

"In fact—wait a minute. There was somebody named Creston mentioned as a source in a couple of references, last time I was over at Stem City library trying to look something up."

"The accused stands before you. It wasn't geryons you were looking up, I trust, or I couldn't possibly have been quoted as a source. I find the idea of them fascinating—the face, of course—but I've never even seen one outside of a holograph. I'd like to begin a study, though."

"Their faces, yes."

"You see, it's occurred to me that their faces might be less a result of chance than an example of interspecies parallelism on different but closely similar worlds."

"I wondered about that too. I had to study some of that evolutionary theme theory, of course, for planeteering... so, Ray's here taking an interest in the Field. I wonder what he thinks of it. What do you think?"

"About the Field? I don't know what to think." Merit looked out over the river, past the distant line of marker poles, then closed her eyes briefly. "I don't sense it there at all. I haven't been able to sense anything about it, since we arrived. Though I suspect Ray may have... do you know if anyone with parapsych talents has tried to investigate it?"

"I know of a few civilians who claimed to be making some effort along that line, years ago. As far as I know, they had no success. But of course they weren't Jovians... what are your plans? I mean right now?"

"Right this moment? I don't really..."

"Then how about a canoe ride? You can enter the Field directly and experience it first hand. Not that there's really anything to experience."

165

"Oh, yes. I'd like to!"

They walked back to where Adam's square-sterned canoe was waiting. The Space Force guard on duty in front of the trading shack looked up from his weary debate with the two Tenoka long enough to nod familiarly to Adam.

As they got into the canoe, Merit remarked: "It looks like the Space Force is going to trust me not to start any trouble with the natives."

"You're with me." Adam untied the canoe and shoved off from the dock. "And the Space Force usually humors me, because I'm still something of a privileged character with the Tenoka. They identify me particularly with the help we gave them against geryons, back in the early days. Of course if I ever get far enough from the Stem, well beyond Tenoka territory, things are going to be different. There are quite a number of other tribes out there, who I gather don't much like the Tenoka or their friends." The outboard started purring.

Merit was trailing her fingers in the water. "I presume this is safe to do. Nothing's going to come along and snap some of my fingers off?"

"Don't hear me yelling, do you?"

The Far Landing dock was falling behind. Ahead of them, open wilderness expanded.

"Adam, are Earth-descended people ever going to be able to see much of this planet?"

"Frankly, I don't think so. I don't believe we know any more about the Field today, really, than we did on the first day we ran into it."

"You don't seem unhappy about that situation."

"Actually, I suppose I'm not."

Merit was laughing again. "I can see already that you and Vito are going to hit it off just great. Oh, wow. He's all charged up with theoretical ideas, schemes on how to solve the problems that the Field poses, in what he still likes to call general field theory. I think he spent most of his time on the ship worrying that someone else would have the Field completely figured out before he got here."

Adam found himself smiling, grinning broadly, and then enjoying a laugh too, for what seemed like the first time in years. "I'd say he may have a few days yet, before someone beats him out. Now hang on, here we go."

Already the canoe was closely approaching the line of marker poles, at a place where that line went marching almost straight across the river, at right angles to the banks. Adam turned off the motor and let the small craft drift on its momentum toward the boundary.

He grinned at Merit. "Look at your timepiece," he suggested. Her expression brought back to him memories of her as an—occasionally—wide-eyed little girl. The flat silvery plate that she was wearing on her wrist went totally blank a moment after the invisible border had been crossed. Then numbers and other symbols reappeared on the small surface, but seemingly at random, flickering on and off erratically.

Adam was on the point of asking Merit why she wore the watch at all; no Jovian in his memory had ever needed an artificial chronometer just to know what time it was, only perhaps for the exact timing of a race or some scientific experiment; and this particular instrument didn't look as if it was intended for such purposes. But the convincing idea at once suggested itself to Adam that the timepiece was a present to Merit from her husband, who when he gave it to her had not

167

known her as well as Adam did. At the thought, Adam felt a moment of superior pride, mixed with an uncertain amount of jealousy.

With a sigh, Merit at last raised her head from contemplation of the confused chronometer and looked around her. "I still can't sense anything different here," she murmured. "Are we bound for anywhere in particular?" She sounded as if she would be satisfied either way.

"If you've got about an hour to spare, I'll show you where I live."

***

When they were quite near the Field-side shore, Adam spotted something moving in the bushes there, and rested his paddle for a moment, watching alertly. Two Tenoka children, a boy and a girl, came out into the open as soon as they saw that he was aware of them. Then they stood on the shore giggling and dumb with shyness, impressed by the strange woman in the canoe.

"You have a couple of admirers," he told Merit. "Wave to them."

Merit and the two children had a waving good time until the canoe reached Adam's little dock. At that point the kids vanished back into the leafless winter brush, too shy to approach the stranger closely.

He led Merit up along the well-worn narrow path, that wound a hundred meters up the side of a low bluff, to the shelf of land near the top where his cabin stood. The cabin was built mostly of native logs, the chinks between logs filled with local clay and sealed with a little liquid plastic. The small house, hardly more than one room, had a shingled roof that had been

168

sealed with plastic in the same way, and a chimney of clay and stone.

Merit appeared to be enchanted by his home.

But a thought struck her. "How do you lock up when you leave?"

"I left the latchstring hanging out this time. There, see? Any of my local friends who happen to come along can walk in, but animals are kept out."

"Don't the Tenoka ever steal?"

"Rarely from a home. Quite rarely. And anyway I'm something of a privileged character, as I told you. If the tourists get much thicker out this way I may need to devise some more protection." He swung open the stout wooden door, that moved easily and silently on its Earth-fabricated hinges of neat modern metal, and gallantly bowed his visitor in.

Merit, following Earth custom, slipped off her shoes at the door. Once inside, she was instantly fascinated by his hearth and hewn furniture, and by the couple of trophies he had mounted on his walls. The heads were of different species of large carnivores, evidence of Adam's bow-hunting prowess.

A small fire was still burning, to which Adam now added fuel. The cabin was reasonably warm.

Merit was gazing at a mounted head. "Leopard-variant theme, I take it."

"Though it doesn't really look that much like a leopard at first glance. Right. You're the expert."

"But the rug—it isn't real fur." It covered much of the rough wooden floor.

"I bought the rug in Stem City," he said. "Keeps my feet warm, when there's no other way." He was still standing just inside the front door, and now he gently made sure that the door was tightly closed, and pulled the latchstring in, not wanting interruption. Then he went to Merit, and turned her around so they were face to face, and pulled her gently, firmly against him.

She didn't pull back. She didn't argue, or protest, or say anything at all, but after a moment he knew that it was never going to be any good like this, not with her.

He said: "You didn't always say no."

"I wasn't always married."

Adam raised his hands to her shoulders, and held her that way, still very gently. He said: "I guess this husband is pretty important."

Smiling, Merit hugged Adam as if she were his sister, with a kind of tired tenderness. "I'm glad to hear someone say that," she told him.

And so it seemed that someone had said otherwise.

Chapter Ten

The outboard purred faithfully into life as soon as they had re-passed the line of markers in midstream. Adam asked: "Back to Far Landing?" He could be calm; he knew it wasn't over yet between him and Merit.

Her voice was ordinary, and he supposed she knew it too. "Vito and Ray were heading for a place called Fieldedge, and since it's a physics laboratory I've no doubt they're still there. Is it far?"

"Fieldedge. No, not far, just a few kilometers. And we can take the boat right to the door." Adam headed the canoe downstream.

Ahead of them the river curved deeply into the Stem. Falling behind the canoe, the line of marker poles marched in their great steady circle toward the river's wild bank, up onto it, and on away from the water, vanishing from sight.

Now the land on both sides of the river bore new roads, a number of new buildings, and a great many enigmatic surveying markers, bright-colored poles and pylons. People and machines were at work at scattered sites on every hand, clearing nature from the land's surface and building what they wanted in its place. Adam sat silently in the stern of the canoe, steering with the motor. Merit occupied the seat ahead of him, her trousered knees aimed at him but her face as often as not turned away, while she took in the sights of the new land around her.

Watching the beauty of her face, the curved grace of her body as she turned from side to side, Adam tried to imagine that they had grown up together in some normal family, that Merit was his sister.

The effort failed totally.

***

After curving majestically almost two kilometers into the Stem, the river's course bent back to the Field again. The great circle of marker poles reappeared, marching toward the water and into it, here crossing a bend of the river at an acute angle. Just where the line of markers came closest to the Stem bank, a large new building of concrete and glass jutted out over the water, projecting deliberately across the invisible line. The relatively small portion of the laboratory building that extended beyond the markers into the Field had been constructed mainly of simple interlocking plastic slabs, resting on stone piers.

The canoe was still several hundred meters away from the building when Adam saw three men walk out of a door on an upper level of the structure, to stand on an esplanade steeply terraced above the Fieldedge dock.

* * *

Vito Ling's mind, energized now by anger, was working with the speed and skill of an acrobat's warmed-up musculature, juggling mathematical equations and shuttling values in and out of them. Every calculation he could make assured him that Kedro had been right: they should have insisted that the time-quanta device be redesigned, before they agreed to leave Earth with it. Of course, it was too late for design changes. And in its present form the device was not going to be of the least help to them in understanding the nature of the Field.

What really angered Vito most was the fact that Kedro had been a step ahead of him again. This time they had really been on the same side, arguing against the false economy of the Research Foundation administrators. But he, Vito, keen to come to grips with the Field directly, had been willing to give in to the administrators, for fear that otherwise they might call off his trip to Golden altogether; and Kedro on the other hand had remained firm in his opposition, only yielding at last, gracefully when he did so, to the opinion of Vito Ling who was supposedly the senior scientist.

It was as if Kedro had been using some precognitive talent to foresee their present trouble. Of course with the Jovian Kedro, something of the kind was possible. But looking back, Vito had to admit to himself that parapsych talent would not have been necessary to have predicted the trouble, the blind alley in which they already found themselves with their experiment. Looking back now, melding what he knew of physics with what he knew of the behavior of administrators, he was able to see it himself with perfect clarity. But only Kedro had been as certain of the result when looking forward, not letting himself be blinded by impatience or anything else.

The perfect intellect, thought Vito, angrily, watching Kedro's massive tapering back as the Jovian man moved ahead of Vito out the door at the side of the Fieldedge lab. The perfect man—or would Kedro perhaps object to being called a man? Would it be better to say the perfect being?

Vito was jealous and angry, and angrier because he knew himself to be thinking unreasonably.

"Well, we can't be sure today," said the calm voice of little Dr. Shishido, director of the Fieldedge lab, coming outside behind Vito. "Tomorrow, we are certain to learn more."

Vito suppressed an angry answer. They certainly knew enough now to be able to predict total failure for the time-quanta gadget in its present form. And if it failed, after much investment of time and money, what chance did they have of learning anything of importance without it? He might as well turn around and go back to Earth tomorrow.

He wouldn't do that, of course. Having come this far, he would stay on for a while, and try.

Ray Kedro, his fair hair stirring in the faint breeze, was leaning on a railing overlooking the small dock and the broad river, and had apparently given himself up to staring across the width of moving water. It was as if the Jovian were trying to pierce the mystery of the optically invisible Field with his unaided senses.

The hero posing, Vito thought. Challenging the mystery too great for mere humanity to solve. Well, we'll see. I don't admit a damned thing about your so-called Jovian superiority, and Merit is my wife, and she enjoys being my wife, and wouldn't trade her life with me for anything that you could give her. And I bet that fact gripes you yet, for all you act like her older brother.

And I hope you're reading my mind.

Then, for some reason, a recurring question nagged at Vito: Why, really, didn't Merit yet want to have a child? Early on in their relationship they had agreed they would. But now...

Little Dr. Shishido, who had been last out of the lab, came to stand between Vito and Ray Kedro, drawing deep breaths of the mild winter air. "Why don't both of you come and have dinner with my wife and me tonight?" the lab director asked. "And bring your, er, sister, of course, Dr. Kedro." No doubt about who Shishido considered the senior scientist to be. "We're looking forward to meeting her. And, ah—"

"Maybe I'll bring my wife, too," said Vito.

Ray turned round, sensing minor difficulty, "Ms. Creston I expect will be glad to attend, in both capacities. You're right, of course, Dr. Shishido, Merit and I do usually consider ourselves as siblings for social purposes."

"Er, yes. That's what I was..."

Shishido actually appeared to be made somewhat nervous by the Jovian superman's mere presence. *Damn fool*, thought Vito.

Out loud he said: "I usually consider Merit as my wife. We find it works out well. We'll be glad to come." It took him an effort right now, gritted teeth, to achieve even that modest degree of civility. Temper, if you could only watch your temper, friends sometimes said to him. To hell with them, he'd like to show them what real temper was.

But with another effort he managed to ease his mental wrestler's grip on the problem of the Field, and started to take notice of the new world surrounding him.

174

A stair led down from the open space where the three men stood, down to a small dock where a couple of the indigenous people were sitting, onlookers without any visible purpose. The country on this side of the river looked to Vito like it was only beginning to be settled, and that on the other side was to all appearances utterly wild.

Kedro, still gazing out over the water, said: "Doctor Shishido, I think you're going to meet Merit before this evening."

Only now did Vito really notice the small boat that had been slowly and steadily approaching from upriver, with two figures in it. The two people were still too distant for any certain identification, but one of them was a blond woman wearing a bulky jacket that certainly looked like Merit's. The other appeared to be a man, and not a Golden native.

Had Merit hired a boat? But she had said something about going to look up a childhood friend. Yes, some former planeteer who had lost his wife.

The three men at the railing watched in silence as the boat drew near, heading right for the dock. There was no doubt now that the woman was Merit. She waved up at them cheerfully, said something to the man who was with her, and then hopped out nimbly on the dock. Her companion was a rough-looking character, bearded and dirty, and wearing a knife at his belt. After one glance up at the three men watching, and a quick wave, he busied himself with securing the canoe. Then the two native men came over to him and began a conversation, while Merit started up the stairs.

Vito stood at the top of the stairs, looking down at her, while she climbed toward him, smiling happily.

"Who the devil is *that?*" It came out rougher than he had intended.

"An old friend." Merit suddenly looked worried. "His name is Adam Mann. I told you about him, darling."

The anger rose up in Vito, a flame finding new fuel. "Didn't lose any time getting cozy with him, did you? He looks like a tramp. Is he another of your parapsych friends?"

"No—no." Merit was shaken. She appeared to be too surprised by his outburst to know how to react to it; somehow that only made him worse.

"So, you got off the ship and went straight to see him." The wrong words, meant to hurt, came out with perverse ease, like lines well-studied for a play, even when Vito knew that they were wrong.

"Yes, Vito, I did that." Merit, as usual, had needed only a moment to regain complete control of herself. Still she was angry too. "And I even went to visit the cabin where he lives. So be angry if you must. If you can't grow up. You could decide to trust me."

"Oh, I could, could I? And what would happen then?" *How good it would be, how really fine, to find some reason to hit someone.* And meanwhile Dr. Shishido, looking more and more worried, was hovering almost beside them, watching the argument. He kept making little fussing starts of movement as if he yearned to interfere. And Kedro still stood at the railing, now looking down at his huge hands clamped onto the wood, determinedly minding his own business.

It was just at this point that the Earthman chatting with the natives on the dock below looked up at them all again and smiled pleasantly. To Vito, at the moment, there was no doubt of

176

what that smile meant: *She came straight to me, and I took her to my cabin, and what are you going to do about it?*

Vito growled in his throat, and started down the stairs. Mann, or whatever his name was down there, was shorter than Vito and a little lighter probably, but the bastard was carrying a knife, and if he wanted to try using his knife Vito right now didn't give a damn.

"Vito, no!" Merit clutched at his arm belatedly as he went by her, and it afforded him minor satisfaction to be able to tear his sleeve free of her grip without a pause. Skipping downstairs with the unthinking balance of the natural athlete, he knew in the back of his mind that he was wrong, dead wrong and going overboard. But this was one of those times when temper just got out of hand, and afterward there could always be apologies.

He heard and ignored Shishido behind him, the little scientist raising his voice in some ineffectual protest. Then Vito hit the bottom of the stairs, and bounced along straight toward the man who owned what must be a very attractive cabin. The two natives saw Vito coming, and the way he looked, and they hastily backed away to stand with folded arms and wooden faces.

At close range, he could see that Mann was well built, with a deep chest and strong arms; good. There wouldn't be much difference in weight after all. Mann's pleasant smile had changed to a look of startled caution.

Vito stopped just within his own long reach of the bearded man. "Have a good time with my wife today?" he asked. He felt his lips drawn back, the blood beating in his head, the muscles in his face hurting a little. He felt his fists big and hard, and his feet ready to shift, quickly and lightly.

"Yeah," said Mann, plainly. He was squinting at Vito with his head a little tilted, as if he were trying to understand something.

Vito said a filthy name and shifted his weight and stabbed his left arm out in a well-aimed jab that shot past Mann's instantly moving face. The second jab missed too, and the hard overhand right, thrown without having the range at all, missed so badly that Vito almost fell down.

He lost sight of Mann for just an instant, and spun around with his guard up. But Mann was only shuffling backward away from him. A clumsy-looking man of about average size, his arms down, still puzzled. "What goes on?" he asked, seeming no more than annoyed.

Vito moved after him, with cold precision, and no lessening of the urge to strike and destroy. He shifted and feinted, like the good amateur boxer that he was, but drew no response. He moved in with another left jab that also missed those unblinking elusive eyes, and a long hook that touched only air, and then a looping right that was stopped when his forearm caught on Mann's, which came up with unhurried speed and felt like a wooden club

Vito stood there for a long instant, with his right arm caught and his left out of position, his feet somehow misplaced and his balance failing as Mann's forearm pulled him slightly forward, and he knew he was ripe to be clobbered, by someone who knew how.

But Vito wasn't clobbered. Mann disengaged at once and stepped back again.

"Keep it up, bud, and I'll chuck you in the river," he said in a flat voice. "Pretty cold this time of year."

Vito too stepped back this time. He was breathing heavily. Merit was calling something to him. From the sound of her voice, she was almost in tears. Shishido like an angry schoolmaster was saying: "Here, now! Stop it, you two!"

And now Vito's rage was burning out quickly, not with fear or frustration, though he began to feel both of those, but as if the fuel were being cut off. He backed away carefully from Mann, turned and headed for the stairway.

The draining out of anger left him shaky, going up the stairs. Oh, by all the Laws, he thought, I really popped my circuit breakers that time, He stopped and half-turned once on the stairs, intending to try to say something to Mann; but what was there to say?

Keeping his back turned to the dock, Vito climbed on. At the top of the stair he muttered some futile apology to Shishido, who favored him with a look of sad pity as he went by. Vito plunged right on into the lab; he had to be alone for a minute.

What kind of a damn fool am I? he thought. What have I done to Merit now? I never blew up like *that* before in my whole adult life.

He leaned against a generator that was still humming itself down slowly into silence after the day's futile experiment. After a few seconds he heard the door behind him, and then Merit's blessed footsteps.

***

"Adam, the way you look seems to prove that going native here is healthy. I should have come to try it years ago." It was Ray Kedro who said that, Ray grinning as of old, looking down from his great height and engulfing Adam's right hand in his own, almost crushing it in greeting.

"Seeing you and Merit again was what I needed," said Adam. Ray was looking stronger and handsomer than ever. Somehow he even gave the impression of being still bigger than the last time Adam had seen him, as if he might have kept on growing after the age of twenty or so. But it wasn't really an increase in physical size, Adam decided. In controlled dominance, perhaps.

Adam was introduced to Dr. Shishido, who went through the motions rather blankly, his mind obviously elsewhere. As director of the lab he probably had a lot to think about, when his physicists started trying to pick fights with strangers. Merit had already followed her husband inside.

"Do you suppose we had better postpone our dinner engagement?" the little administrator asked Ray. Shishido was still looking almost fearfully after Vito and Merit.

Ray told him: "Sorry about the demonstration."

"It's not your fault, Dr. Kedro." Shishido dropped his voice. "Tell me, is he—?" He concluded with a nervous motion of his head toward the closed laboratory door.

Ray puffed out his breath faintly. "Vito really isn't himself just now. There have been problems, some of which you know about... I regret to say that I think you're right about the dinner. Should I call you about it tomorrow?—maybe we can arrange to get together then."

"That would be best, I suppose."

"Good." Ray shook his head, as if trying to dismiss a nagging thought. "Right now I'd better start trying to get back to town. I have an appointment in half an hour to see General Lorsch. Ride in with me, Ad?"

"Sure."

While walking beside Ray toward the meadow where the shuttle copter waited, Adam remarked: "Merit's husband is not himself just now, you said. I can believe that. Why would she have married a total madman? What's going on?"

"It's a long story, Ad. Bureaucracy and frustration are only part of it. Among other problems. I didn't want to go into it all in front of Shishido. I'll tell you the whole story, sometime."

They walked the next few paces in silence. Then Adam commented: "So you're going to see the General, not wasting any time. She hasn't too much to do these days. There isn't very much Space Force left on Golden."

"I'm not wasting any time," Ray agreed, looking gently serious. "Not here on Golden. I don't think that there's any time left to waste."

And though he tried fiercely, Adam could not persuade him to elaborate on that.

Chapter Eleven

"Why are you people so anxious to get the Space Force completely off this planet?" General Lorsch made her voice deliberately casual. "I know you're putting pressure on Earth Parliament."

A woman whose rather shapeless body never managed to look well-fitted in any uniform, she still sat with practiced ease behind the huge desk she had inherited some years ago, along with the mysteries of Golden, from General Grodsky. Grodsky was currently serving in a high-placed staff job back on Earth. There were times when General Lorsch would have been quite ready to change places with him.

The only other person in the General's private office at this moment was the Jovian, Ray Kedro, who was sitting in an equally relaxed attitude in the big visitor's chair on the other side of the desk.

"General Lorsch," said Kedro, "I just got off the ship from Earth this morning. I've come to Golden as the representative of several organizations, so I'm not sure what you mean by 'you people'."

Lorsch consulted a scrap of paper on her generally untidy desk. She said offhandedly: "Oh, those organizations, yes... I have the list here. You represent the Research Foundation, of course, plus a hotel chain, plus a mining corporation. Plus one or two others."

"Is there anything wrong with my representing them?"

"No. Not necessarily. Though *I* wouldn't want to represent them all. Most of the people on this roster, probably all of them, have schemes to get rich quick, and some of them would like a freer hand in trading and dealing with the natives here... when they've made their profit, of course, they will then pull but, leaving a mess for someone else to worry about."

"You may be right about them, General, in some cases at least. My representation of them on Golden is limited. And it has a purpose."

"I'm sure it does. And I know I'm right. They have put similar schemes into operation on other planets."

"I—we Jovians—have had nothing to do with those schemes. I would only suggest that here, on this planet where we are somewhat involved, you might wait and see if those companies don't manage their affairs somewhat differently. More to the benefit of all concerned."

"If I waited to be sure of the result, it might well be too late."

"Not necessarily, General. It would depend to a great extent on how the contracts were drawn, wouldn't it?"

"Perhaps... but let that go for the moment. Even that is not my first concern just now."

"Then what is, ma'am?" Kedro, she thought, could find just the right note of politeness.

"I'll tell you what. There's recently been extra heavy pressure on Earth Parliament to get us—the Space Force—to leave Golden. And I don't mean just pressure from the mining corporations and so on that I've just been talking about. That kind of thing we expect, that's routine. This, as I say, is extra. And it comes from you people, always from you, and you know who I mean. Jovians. Now why is that?"

Kedro had been gently nodding his understanding throughout her speech. Now his eyes seemed to be asking her to understand him too. He said: "To me, the concept of 'my people' extends a long way beyond my ninety-nine siblings. I consider that my people are the human race. The whole Earth-descended branch of it, at least."

"I might say the same thing about my own feelings," commented the General drily. She made her chair creak, rocking gently. Sometimes the creak unsettled visitors, and she had an urge to see if Kedro could be unsettled. "But what I have in mind now is a certain sub-class of that large group, the very one you first mentioned. Namely you and your gene-altered friends. Your siblings, if you want to call them that, though I understand there's no direct biological relationship among you. In the popular phrase, the Jovians."

"You should not view us as opponents," said Kedro. His manner was still thoroughly calm, his tone almost reproving. He seemed to be skirting the edge of the attitude of someone who lays down moral rules and then expects to have them followed. "General, I think that your organization and mine can help each other, to the benefit of the entire human race. And I don't mean just the Earthly branch of it."

"Fine!" Lorsch pushed forward a carved box on her desk, offering Kedro several versions of Antarean cigars, an invitation which was politely declined. The General chose one of the smaller variants for herself, and lit up. Then she leaned back, still rocking and creaking a little. Then she asked again, patiently: "Why do you people want to get the Space Force off this planet?"

Kedro said imperturbably: "I think you are no longer needed here. I think that the Field itself adequately protects most of the natives of this particular world from exploitation. Adequate local laws, and improved contracts in the case of some of the people you mentioned, can protect the rest, here in the Stem area, which is the only place the Space Force can protect them anyway. I also think that the best place for the Space Force is elsewhere, out on the real Galactic frontier, exploring new worlds and in general doing the job that it was created to do."

Lorsch drummed her fingers on the desk. "Golden still is a frontier. What we have here is a small beachhead on an unexplored planet, though Earth people who live here for any length of time tend to get used to having the Field surrounding them and think of it as something natural. I wasn't in favor of opening the place up for colonization so quickly, myself, but... that's been done now. You're going to work on the Field at the lab. Do you think there's any hope of our physicists being able to solve the Field, manage it, push it back in the near future?"

Kedro shook his head, a thoughtful but definite negative.

Lorsch went on: "So, we're still very much on the frontier here, even though as you must know we've explored for a dozen parsecs beyond this system in every direction, trying to find more evidence of the Field-builders. So far, no success."

"I don't know that there are any Field-builders," Kedro replied.

The General was surprised. "You say it's a natural phenomenon, then? Why?"

"I don't know that that's the right answer either... well, stay on Golden if you like, General. Not that you have to ask my permission. I have not much influence in the matter, whatever you may think. But if this is, as you say, still a frontier, then I wonder why you haven't done more frontier work here over the last few years. Has the Space Force ever made any serious attempt to explore this planet's surface away from the Stem?"

Lorsch's cigar was burning itself out, forgotten in an ashtray. Her chair was still. "There have been a few scouting expeditions, necessarily made on foot—neither horses nor native animals have worked out as well as we had hoped for transportation. We intend to send out more expeditions eventually, probing deeper."

"I'd like to go along on the next one that you do send, General. It might be possible to make some observations away from the Stem that would materially help the physicists' work at Fieldedge."

"Well." Somewhat surprised, Lorsch thought it over. "Maybe something can be arranged along that line." It didn't hurt to say that much, at least. "I'll let you know if a suitable chance should come up while you're still on planet."

"I intend to be on Golden quite a while. Why did you call me in here today, General? Just to ask about my lobbying efforts back on Earth?"

"You weren't forced to come when I called. You're a practicing telepath, aren't you? Do you need to ask me about my motives?"

"I need no special parapsych powers to read your hostility. General Lorsch, you must know something of how telepathy actually works, as opposed to the popular ideas. You must realize that the idea of probing your mind is as distasteful to me as it must be to you. And I can assure you it's not a very reliable way to obtain information."

"You have tried it, then."

Kedro ignored the question. "Now why do you think I want you and your people to leave Golden? So I can make myself governor? Dictator? Or enrich myself by smuggling?"

The General shook her head. "No." Her voice was weakening a little, and with a conscious effort she made it stronger. "I don't really think you people want such things, except maybe in an incidental way. You people don't work to become conspicuous rulers, and you're not ostentatious about your wealth. You'd much rather stay behind the scenes, and marry each other, and cooperate with each other to accumulate indirect control over all kinds of human activity."

"I might say the very same things, and just as accurately, about the Space Force, General Lorsch. Are those things evil when we do them, and good—"

"It's not the same thing at all, dammit!" Lorsch, to her own surprise, could feel her self control slipping. "It's simply not true that we try to control all kinds of human activity. And we don't consider ourselves to be more than human!"

Kedro looked down at the floor for a few seconds. His handsome face was sad. When he raised his eyes and spoke, his voice was soft and almost tentative. "Why should you be tempted to consider yourselves more than human, General?"

"Do *you* think *you're* more than human? Homo Superior? I've heard that you do!"

"Do you believe that I am human, General Lorsch? Or even something less than that, perhaps?" Kedro's voice this time was still low. But it was no longer soft, or tentative.

Seconds slid away in silence. Lorsch, trying with unexpected difficulty to frame her answer, felt an impression growing on her with the speed and force of nightmare. It was the impression that what sat and spoke with her in her office was not a man in any sense, but rather an elemental force, a materialized law of the universe that had taken on a slightly larger than human form, and might at any moment take on a different and more disquieting form than that.

While remaining physically calm, the General found herself somehow—unable? unwilling?—to move or to speak. And her inner being froze and screamed silently in fright at the prospect of confronting directly, seeing clearly, the alien being, the god, who sat facing her across her desk.

Part of the General's outer mind was able to say comfortingly: Nonsense, this is just a foolish notion that's taken me. Nothing is really happening. I can move and speak whenever I like. Of course I can.

She looked into Kedro's compassionate blue eyes, and her ego cowered and whimpered: *Is this how a pet feels, a dog, when it looks up at—*

187

"Well, do you?" Kedro prompted, in an ordinary voice, and the instant he spoke the spell, or whatever it had been, was gone.

"Do I what? Oh. No, I can't admit that you're more than human." Lorsch moved slightly in her chair, to prove to herself that she could do so. Her uniform adhered to the chair irritatingly. The words of her answer almost stuck in her throat. But still, everything was normal again. Except that she was perspiring. It was only a big man who sat there, across her desk. A big, handsome, and extremely dangerous man.

"Then isn't your fear of us a touch irrational?" Kedro's voice was as reasonable as any voice that she had ever heard. "Really, we have the talent to get what we want by ordinary, legal means. Power? We don't especially want the responsibility of governing, this planet or any other. And even heavy manipulation from behind the scenes, however it might be accomplished, implies responsibility.

"We *do* like to guide the world of Earth-descended humanity just a bit, keep it when we can from making certain catastrophic mistakes. Show it values that it might otherwise miss. We'd like to be able to do a better job of guiding."

Kedro shifted in his chair, leaning his perfectly proportioned bulk forward, resting one elbow on the desk. He was smiling now, his handsome eyes narrowing in friendly, almost irresistible intentness. "Think of the good that we could do if we had, working with us instead of against us, all the wealth and power and organization of the Space Force. Or even a part of it. Say the Wing that you command, here on Golden..."

The General could very easily visualize the benevolent giants, golden in their virtue, superior to natural humanity. From their height above the struggling confusion that had given them birth, the Jovians saw far into the future, far and accurately, discerning a thousand dangers and warning their parent race against them all. The godlike powers of the Jovians' superior minds won victory after victory, over ignorance and disease and human misery, victories gladly shared with mere humanity... and now the golden people turned toward General Lorsch, seeming to plead: *Help us, help us to do these things. For your own sake, help us.*

The dream of glory faded. Of course Kedro had been projecting it somehow into her mind. Lorsch started to say: "Oh how I wish—"

She meant to finish: "—we could do that."

"—I could believe you," was what she said.

Kedro leaned back from the desk. He lowered his face into his hands for a moment and rubbed his eyes. He looked tired when he straightened up in his chair again. Tired, but not diminished.

"I wish you could," he said, and got to his feet. "Was there anything else?"

The General shook her head. She felt that she might commit some spectacular failure if her confrontation with this—visitor—went on any longer.

Kedro towered over the desk. "Let me know about the expedition, please," he said. "Really. If and when it ever gets organized." And he walked out of the office.

It was over. The General sat quietly for a minute, pulling her nerves back together. Trying to pull them back. She was all right, she was functional, but she suspected she would never be quite the same again.

When she got up to check the cameras and recorders hidden in her office she found that all of the machines had unaccountably stopped functioning and that nothing of the interview was preserved.

Chapter Twelve

Adam Mann stood stretching and yawning in the open doorway of his cabin, looking out from inside with a comfortable small fire at his back. He was gazing upon yet another mild winter afternoon with something like contentment—though it was a different sort of contentment than he had enjoyed, or had thought he was enjoying, a few days ago. Satisfaction with cabin life was mixed now with a new restlessness.

Merit was here. Only a few kilometers away.

Ever since he had joined the Space Force, the idea of living on Earth or some other crowded planet had repelled him more and more. Then the Space Force had lost its attraction too.

What Adam really wanted, when he looked at it squarely, was to be a Jovian, to have Merit for his woman and Ray and the others as his peers, as his brothers and sisters in a sense. But he was not going to become a Jovian, no matter what he did. Therefore it was necessary to adopt some other life. Until a few days ago the cabin and the rough, chancy existence of a fur-hunter had been, for the time being at least, quite satisfactory.

Merit was here, only a few kilometers away. But there were other women in the world. Many others, in the plurality of available worlds. Tenoka women, themed close enough to Earth-human for fun, still separate enough for there to be no worries about fertility and responsibility.

Adam stretched again. Tonight he intended to go into Stem City, and enjoy one last little fling before he left to spend a week alone up in the northern mountains. One more good haul of fine furs should be possible before spring.

Someday the tribesmen who lived up there, distant cousins of the Tenoka, might try to kill him, just to steal his marvelous bow, compounded of magical Earth materials. That risk, he thought, was not yet too great. But what was the risk of going into town tonight, to seek out another man's wife and at least spend as much time as possible with her? Because that's what he was intending to do. There was no use trying to lie to himself about it. And in fact he doubted very much whether he was starting for the mountains tomorrow, either. Not while she was here.

Out of all of them, the entire hundred, Merit was the one, the only one so far as Adam knew, who had chosen a non-Jovian to marry. And when she did that, she picked out a man who lived on Earth like an Earth-descended human being, not one who had turned into a hermit on an alien world—

Someone was approaching the cabin. It was a single person, walking quietly but not sneaking. Thin ice in a small shaded puddle crackled underfoot. He or she was coming along the faint path that followed the top of the river bluff, from the direction of the nearby religious colony. Again Adam heard movement, and saw small birds fly up from the brush near the path.

He knew that he had an enemy or two in Stem City, among the hoodlums settling in there on the fringes of the fur business. Then there was Tooth Biter, the Tenoka he had once caught stealing. Without moving from his position in the doorway, Adam reached an arm along the inside cabin wall to take his twenty-five kilo composite bow down from its pegs. He set the

191

bow on end just inside the doorframe, and reached again to slide a broad-bladed hunting arrow out of the hanging quiver.

Then in a few seconds he saw the white robes, marked with the symbol of the cross. Adam put back the weapons, and stepped out in smiling welcome. "Father, glad to see you."

Father Francis Marti was young and small; at first glance, he might have been a theological student lost in the woods. His hobby was studying the native wildlife of Golden, while his work was in a parish in Stem City. There, as he had once told Adam, the geryons' faces were sometimes even more convincingly human than were the faces of the geryons out here in the wilderness.

Now he might have been greeting a favorite parishioner. "Adam. Are you keeping well?"

"Still alive. You trying to convert your religious competition over there?" Adam nodded in the direction from which the priest had come. The colony of black-clad folk were back that way, only a couple of kilometers distant.

Father Marti appeared to consider the question seriously. He said at last: "No. I have been trying to warn them—some of them travel frequently alone and unarmed in the woods. Maybe their patriarch would listen to you more readily than to me."

Both men glanced toward the end of the right sleeve of the priest's white robe, from which no hand emerged. Father Marti did own quite a good right hand, but it was complex enough that the metal and plastic joints of it tended to freeze up or exhibit other bizarre behavior whenever he wore it into the Field. He usually, as today, left his right hand in the city whenever he visited the wilderness. Father Marti too had once walked in these woods unarmed. But then had come his wrestling match with a small geryon. Since then he came with the sheath of a Bowie knife hanging on his belt, ready for a left-hand draw.

"I'll talk to them tomorrow," Adam said. *Before I leave for the mountains,* he thought. *I really had better go. Then why don't I tell the Father I'm making one more hunting trip this winter? Because I know I'm not going. I mean to stay here instead and hang around another man's wife. Being merely human, I always lie to myself.*

"Father..."

"What is it?"

But there was nothing, really, to be said.

***

In the late afternoon Adam heated some water and got cleaned up and dressed to go into the city. He had no very extensive wardrobe, and wore a modified version of his usual garb. According to what he could see of himself in his small metal mirror, he looked like a tourist trying to look like an old settler. Not, he supposed, that it made any difference anyway.

By the time he had paddled and motored himself across the river to Far Landing, darkness was at hand, the million distant lights of Stem City starting to come on against the night. The shuttle copter rose from the meadow behind Far Landing into the last fading fire-glory of the sunset. The only other passengers this trip were a tourist couple carrying cameras and wearing tired, vaguely disappointed expressions. Maybe I shouldn't have washed up and changed clothes, Adam thought. He pictured himself boarding the copter in a begrimed hunting shirt, saying to the tourists: "Me half Tenoka. You take picture?" He grinned.

When he was on his way to look for Merit, he could feel good about his life.

***

The first thing he did on reaching the city was to try to call the Lings at their hotel—she had told him which one they were staying at. But they were out. They might, Adam supposed, be dining tonight at the home of one of the Fieldedge scientists, but he had no way of looking for them there. Stem City's rapidly multiplying places of entertainment were a different matter. He would give some of those a try.

Already the center of the only city on Golden strongly resembled that of a resort town on Earth. If the buildings here were not yet quite as tall as those on more crowded worlds, the money flowed at least as freely. People who traveled this far from Earth or anywhere else to seek amusement had plenty of money to spend.

Adam started on a round of bars, working his way outward from the exact center of town. He actually drank only a small amount. Neither alcohol nor other drugs had ever assumed any great importance in his life.

While smoking an Antarean cigar in a place that featured the worst music he had heard in at least a year, he happened to glance out through a large bubble window a hundred meters above the street. Kilometers distant, out near the northern perimeter of the Stem, there stood the newest tower on the planet, four hundred vertical meters of steel and stone, bathed at night in searchlights of changing color. A huge sign flashed pictures, first frothy bubbles pouring from a glass, then a couple dancing side by side, then the name of some entertainer blazing out, and then the cycle started over.

Yes, Adam thought, quite likely. It was the newest hotel on planet, advertised as top-status. Built on a hill that was still outside the burgeoning city proper, the tower looked up to the northern mountains in the distance, whence the savage fur hunters could look down at it in wonder. A Fieldedge scientist might well consider such a hotel the ideal place to take off-world visitors. Anyway, Merit would certainly not be here where Adam was now, listening to this subhuman music.

From the center of Stem City an enclosed, multi-lane slideway stretched all the way out to the new resort. FASTEST WITHIN TEN LIGHT YEARS! advertised the slideway's entrance signs. The dully-gleaming, black-surfaced lanes bore a thin scattering of passengers. Adam stepped from lane to lane, out to the express walk that moved nearest the stationary central divider, and was whistled along at highway speed. People going the other way blurred past him, just on the other side of the air-buffered plastic barrier in the center.

There was clear plastic overhead, too, a shield against weather. Every two hundred meters or so, glass or composite observation platforms had been bubbled out from the slideway's structure, otherwise mostly enclosed tunnel. These platforms were accessible from the slow outer lanes, and gave day or night a good view of the Stem country. Much of the Stem was already lighted at night, sketched in with roads and markers for future development even where there were as yet no buildings. Soon, Adam expected, the city was likely to fill the Stem completely; at which point the developers would be sure to want a new treaty with the Tenoka, and then an expansion of development into Field territory. Which, Adam thought drily, should be fun to watch.

Now a pair of teener boys came hurtling past Adam on the other side of the center divider. With an expertly violent throw, one of them heaved something over the barrier as they came shooting toward him, some object that was caught and spun in the air buffers but still came past Adam's dodging head at sixty or seventy kilometers an hour, to land on the strip that he was riding and make a long streaked splash of something messy. For a second he thought of chasing the kids, but decided that would be a waste of time, whether or not he was able to catch up with them.

As he drew near the outer terminal, the flow of the black solid surface under Adam's feet began to slow and thicken, like water in a deepening river. Soon all the lanes were moving at the same low speed, and he walked forward to the splendid entrance of the Pioneer Hotel.

Ten copied pairs of Ghiberti's gigantic bronze doors opened into nothing that at all resembled the baptistery at Florence. The huge lobby inside was decorated in Imitation Primitive, with fake logs roaring electrically in fake fireplaces, and a few real furs and other trophies on the walls. Adam made a mental note that he might find a good market here after his next hunting trip. There were no geryon heads on display; he had yet to see one mounted anywhere. With the beast's body gone, the look was just too overwhelmingly human. It occurred to Adam that Merit would probably have something to say about that, too, when he had another chance to talk to her. It occurred to him also that Poe said it once: *Even among the utterly lost, there are matters of which no jest can be made.*

He realized a need: someone that he could talk to.

Tourists moved through the lobby, coming and going.

"Welcome to Golden, sir, we hope you enjoy our world," said a voice near Adam's ear. A pale young man, evidently an employee of the hotel, was standing beside him. "Were you desirous of a room, sir?"

"No." He would have to pick tonight to dress like a tourist, well, if he had come in his ordinary clothes they probably wouldn't have let him in.

"Entertainment and refreshment on the one hundred and first floor, sir, companionship available one hundred and two. High speed lifts to your right. Hope you enjoy your stay on our world."

"I hope so too."

He got off the lift at one hundred one, to find himself just under a crystal roof exhibiting the stars, and walking directly into the restaurant-bar-dance floor-whatever. Anyway it was a vast dim circular area containing people who had come here to be entertained, with fake trees and rocks making divisions everywhere, and pathways that were supposed to look like forest trails winding everywhere among the trees and tables. In places the ceiling was invisible, except for the way it contained rolling clouds of some light vapor, again shot through with multicolored light. There were probably several hundred people scattered about through the enormous room, but still it was not really crowded. It would take some searching to locate anyone here.

Sidestepping robotic waiters in the form of rolling trolleys, and a human hostess who appeared to be entirely naked except for her multicolored body paint, Adam made his way to an observation bubble—Stem City architects never seemed to tire of such constructions—that bulged out over the side of the building. There were several tourists standing and sitting in the bubble, some using the radarscopes that let them see how the funneling sides of the Field hemmed in the Stem on all sides and mounted up above. Three or four hundred meters below, the surface of the Stem was aflame with all the colors that humanity was able to get out of electricity. Rivulets of people and vehicles crawled everywhere, many of them going apparently in circles. *I stand here like Dante on the lip of the Pit, thought Adam. I need a Geryon to fly me down.*

Bah.

Instead of calling for a geryon, Adam went back to the bar, and bought himself a drink, and pinched one of the hostesses, who seemed to be expecting some such attention. Thoughtfully rubbing his fingers together, feeling the slippery body paint they had picked up, he looked around.

There they were, at a table a good distance off. There was Merit, talking and laughing and gay, wearing a kind of gown that Adam hadn't seen on anyone before, that was probably the latest fashion on Earth or somewhere else, or would be the latest fashion there next year. There was little Shishido of the Fieldedge lab, with a woman, her back now turned to Adam, who would, doubtless be Shishido's wife. And there of course was Vito Ling, a lean, strong man, a handsome and energetic and restless-looking man, laughing now at something that Merit had just said.

If I go over there, thought Adam, maybe he'll try again to hit me. Probably that would be easier to deal with than some other things that could happen.

"This time I think it's safe," said a magnificent, familiar voice at Adam's elbow.

He turned to see Ray Kedro.

"Well, that's what you were wondering, isn't it?" Ray asked, grinning down at him. "I don't have to probe your subconscious more than six or eight layers down to detect that."

"Hello," said Adam, and relaxed, or tried to relax, leaning on the bar. He experienced, as usual, a sudden wave of mixed feelings on encountering Ray. "Good old Vito Ling didn't give me a chance to say hello, the other day. Damn, he can't always be that touchy, can he?"

"He's not," said Ray, and paused thoughtfully. "Actually he's a pretty good guy." Ray paused again, and a faint smile appeared on his face, evoking old days at Doc's school, old shared pranks and adventures there when Adam visited. "Pretty good for one of you ordinary second-rate human types, that is."

"Yeah, sure." Adam turned back to the bar.

"He is. Merit picked him out, didn't she?"

There was a pause, in which Adam thought he could feel the slight intoxication of his evening's drinking fading prematurely. "Right," he said, not able to think of anything else to say. He wondered if Ray could tell how he, Adam, felt about Merit, and intended to try to do with her. He wondered how Ray felt about her himself. Wondered, and couldn't guess.

"We've already got serious trouble at the lab," said Ray. "And it's been getting Vito down." He ordered a drink from a robotic creature that appeared behind the bar, and Adam got himself another. The area behind the bar was all colored lights and shadows, and music, much better than some that Adam had heard recently, was coming from somewhere.

"What kind of trouble?" Adam asked, sipping.

"Mainly because of an expensive gizmo that the Foundation sent with us from Earth. It was supposed to be just what we needed to unravel the mystery of the Field. But it just flat won't work. Vito and I both told the administrators back on Earth that it should have been constructed differently, but they wouldn't believe us. They were wrong." Ray swallowed half his drink. Suddenly Adam couldn't remember if he had ever seen Ray take alcohol before.

199

Adam asked him: "So, you haven't much hope of success now with the Field?"

"We might have had a good start on it, if our gadget had been properly designed." Ray appeared to brood. "Now, we'll have to find another way."

"Another way?"

One of the naked hostesses, on the customers' side of the bar, was approaching Ray. When she got close enough to touch him on the arm, and he turned to face her, her professional smile suddenly altered. It was as if she had been awed despite herself by the Jovian man's size and masculine beauty, suddenly confronted at close range.

When the hostess finally opened her mouth to speak, Ray closed it for her with the lift of one massive finger under her chin. "You might come back and look for me again in a couple of hours," he told her. His voice was abstracted, as if his thoughts were elsewhere. The girl backed away, the professional smile almost totally gone, until she bumped into someone and the spell was broken.

There had been music in the background all along, ever since Adam had walked in from the lift. Now the instruments suddenly blared up louder, and more colored lights began to focus upon a wide central stage.

"So." Ray's eyes considered Adam. "Something drew you to settle on this planet—when, about four years ago? Something keeps you here. When I first heard you were living here, that you'd quit the Space Force, I thought it was the Field. But that's not it, is it? Not directly."

"You're right." Adam tasted his drink. "Something. And no, not the Field exactly. I don't know if I can define it. But the

Field's what brought you here. Or is it? What does this planet mean to a Jovian?"

"You're as perceptive as ever, Adam." Ray slouched easily, elbows on the bar, leaning there like a crouching lion. "No. The Field isn't really all."

"What else?" asked Adam. Then an answer occurred to him. "In your case, because someone built it. That's it, isn't it? It's the Field-builders who are on your mind."

"They are. Increasingly." Ray downed the rest of his drink. "Let's go over to the table. I don't think you'll have to dodge any more punches."

Ray was making fascinating statements, opening topics and then dropping them. That wasn't really his way, as Adam remembered. Adam still leaned on the bar. He wasn't ready to drop this one. "That's it, isn't it? It comes back to the Builders. Why did they create the Field, and where are they now?"

"Why? I think they created it—just to see what would happen when someone else, like—Earth-descended humanity, discovered it. And where are they now? I think that they're not too far away." Abruptly Ray pushed off from the bar. Not really looking to see whether Adam was following him or not, the huge man led the way toward the distant table where the Lings and the Shishidos appeared to be having a genuinely good time, celebrating something. Celebrating what, Adam wondered? Certainly not the laboratory failure he had just heard about. Certainly not the near-fight on the dock.

"Do you think the Field could be a parapsych effect?" Adam wondered aloud, suddenly, as they were skirting the low stage. The stage was occupied by frenetically dancing girls whose skins were covered with colored lights and almost nothing else, and Adam felt a little idiotic walking almost among them, discussing parapsych effects.

Ray turned to answer, the lights playing indirectly on his face. "If it is, it's a damned good one. They've integrated it with effects of the physical sciences. That's a little beyond what we can do. So far." It sounded like that, maybe, was the main point of what he had been thinking about. He turned again and moved on.

Vito Ling was the first person at the table to see them coming; the tall physicist's face took on an anxious look, and he scrambled to his feet and stuck out his hand to Adam. "Sorry about the other day. Really sorry. I had no reason to act that way, no excuse at all." He was obviously sincere.

"It's all right—no harm done."

"I'll say not. I'm just lucky that you're cooler than I am."

The handshake was firm. It might be easy to get to like this character, Adam thought. That was all he needed, that would make things really nice. Oh, yes.

Merit, delighted at the truce, got up to greet Adam with an old friend's kiss. He sat down in the chair Ray pulled up for him, between Merit and Ray. A drink was poured for him. He was introduced to Mrs. Shishido, at close range a nicer-looking woman than he had expected. Mrs. Shishido beamed at him.

"Well, now!" said her small husband, also well pleased to see peace. "Well! Mr. Mann, I understand that you are actually the first human being of Earth to ever set foot on this planet—except perhaps for the unfortunate Golden. And you've been living here for some time now? I wish that I might have been able to meet you sooner."

Shishido was genuinely interested in the planeteering history. The others were too, once the subject had been raised.

Adam began to talk of the earliest days of the Space Force exploration of Golden, telling as an eyewitness of the first experiments with the Field. He could speak well when he wanted to put forth the effort, and now he had a willing audience.

Vito Ling and Dr. Shishido listened with complete attention. Ray stared into space, but Adam felt that he was absorbing every word. The eyes of the two women stayed on Adam's face. The noise and visual confusion of the Pioneer Hotel faded into a vague background.

When Adam paused, Vito let out a sighing breath, and shook his head. "I wish I'd been here then!"

"It's still the same planet, outside the Stem," said Adam. "That's what I like about Golden. We haven't been able to ruin it. And it's still the same Field that we saw then."

The physicists began a three-way argument among themselves, each for slightly different reasons damning the theories and activities of the Research Foundation. Meanwhile, dancing was in again this year, and Adam danced with Mrs. Shishido, though he didn't feel much like it.

Then he led Merit out onto the crowded floor. The music was part of an uproar, that was about all you could say for it. Bodies jostled them this way and that.

"How's the geryon research going?" he asked.

"Slowly. I don't know if I can even call it research yet. I've been to your local zoo and library."

"They do a pretty good job, I think. I helped the zoo people collect some of their specimens, last year." Merit dancing beside him was silent, as if her thoughts were wandering. He asked: "What brought you to the Pioneer Hotel?"

"The Shishidos' idea. I really don't mind a place like this—about once a year." She didn't ask Adam what had brought him here tonight; probably she knew. Instead she asked him: "How do you like my husband?"

"I guess I like him."

"I love him, Adam. And he's a good man." Something was definitely worrying her. "And what more important things than those is it possible to say about anyone? About you, or Ray, or anyone else?"

Adam said nothing, important or otherwise. He held Merit gently and chastely in his arms, at the proper times during the dance, or tried to do so, while they were bounced around like fools on the stampeded dance floor. This was what he was going to get from her. This much and no more.

When there was a pause in the dancing, and the two of them got back to the table, Adam looked carefully at Vito for signs of another jealous fit. But Vito only smiled vacantly at both of them and went on with the scientific discussion of the Field.

Adam sat and listened to the scientific argument, meanwhile sipping on another drink. Now the alcohol in his bloodstream was easing him past the level of slight exhilaration, to the point where there seemed to be a certain amount of electronic noise in his brain, and concentration was needed to drive clear signals through.

Ray and Merit. Always his friends, right from the start. More than his friends. And yet at the same time always above him, above the rest of humanity too. Merit and Ray, their ninety-eight... siblings, Ray called them sometimes. Kin? Clan members? In Adam's opinion there still wasn't a good word. Maybe that was by design, to make the Jovians appear to outsiders as less of a cohesive group.

Not pretending to be superior. Not pretending anything. Not claiming a birthright above common humanity for the purpose of boosting their own egos, or to maintain themselves somehow in power. Adam might deride, or fear, or feel contempt for people who claimed superiority for such purposes, but he would never envy them.

And the truth was that he did envy the Jovians. They were superior, standing together above the world. Suddenly he wondered if there were any little second-generation Jovians as yet. It would be very strange, he thought, if there were not.

Some words caught his ear. The subject of table conversation had shifted, and he broke into the talk of Golden's possible future. "Hold on, this planet may be pretty well populated already."

"Primitive," said Vito. "Oh, I don't mean that we should talk all over 'em. But there must be enormous uninhabited areas out there, hey? Practically whole continents."

Adam said: "I really wouldn't think so. Of course it's hard to tell, from pictures taken from above six or seven hundred kilometers. The Field seems to cause random distortion of detail."

Ray chuckled softly. "I wonder how random it really is."

Chapter Thirteen

Adam got to his feet; he felt a little drunk, maybe more than just a little, and the sensation was unpleasant as well as unfamiliar. "Well, glad to have seen all you people. I feel the urge to move on." Merit looked up at him with an unreadable expression. The other people round the table made their several protests and offered their farewells, and he started away from

205

them. From near the elevators he looked back, across the room's activity. Ray was standing, resting one giant muscular hand gently on Merit's head, while she sat with her eyes closed and face relaxed, looking as if she might be sound asleep. The others round the table watched the two Jovians, not understanding any more than Adam did. And we never will, thought Adam.

Abruptly Ray left the table and walked toward the stage, which was empty now of dancers and musicians. Adam turned his back and found his way to the wall near the elevators, where in an alcove stood a discreet machine, dispenser of sobering pills. He gulped down a pill, and looked around again. Vito and Merit, who was lively again, seemed to be getting ready to leave, and Ray was seated at a piano beside the stage. Adam recalled suddenly that there had almost always been beautiful music, live or recorded, to be heard at any time somewhere in Doc Nowell's enormous house. And it would be like a Jovian, Adam thought, to play fine music now, in a place like this, amid such noise that no one else would be able to hear it.

It struck Adam that the drunken uproar was noticeably diminished. In the vicinity of the stage, a circle of heads were now turning toward the piano. The ring of quiet polarization widened. Even where he stood at the wall, Adam could hear some of the piano notes. And now he could hear more.

Ray's music flowed out to where the night sky of Golden was curved around the bubble windows. *I've never heard this*, Adam thought. *What can you call this kind of music? What is it?* He moved forward into the room again, until he stood gripping the back of someone's chair.

He can do this, too, Adam thought. They can do this.

206

The vast room, or most of it, was almost quiet, expect for the music that Ray Kedro played. Somewhere at the far side of the room, among the distant trees and rocks, one person sobbed, loudly and drunkenly. Then a door opened in the wall near Adam, and a fat man in evening dress came hurrying out, as if the silence had alarmed him. Then the fat man too stood quietly listening.

Experience this, said the music. *Feel this—you can almost touch it now. This is what life is about.*

No. Adam turned away, heading again toward the elevators. How would you know, Ray, what human life is like?

Adam's mind felt blurred. The alcohol and the sobering pill were fighting it out in his bloodstream.

The elevator door closed on him, shutting him in, cutting off the golden sounds. He was alone in the car going down. I usually am alone, he thought. You stupid drunk, he told himself, why don't you go off somewhere and cry?

There were only a few people in the hotel lobby when he reached it. Adam looked at his timepiece. It was two in the morning. He hadn't realized that it was so late.

He stepped out of the lobby onto the black and dully gleaming slideway. His head was full of vague thoughts, none of which really demanded his attention. The slideway shot him back toward Stem City, carrying him past observation platforms and alcoves. In one of these large recesses eight or ten young people were dancing to some music of their own. They had set up a screen on which the image of some retchsinger was contorting itself in three dimensions and unnatural color. No, at second glance it appeared that the screen was attached to a built-in, coin operated video that they were playing. Something new here every day.

The rest of the observation niches were empty as Adam glided past them. There were only a few people on the slideway, most of them riding in what looked like a grim hurry on the faster center strips.

Far ahead of Adam, going in the same direction as he was but on the slowest outer strip, a man and a woman moved along arm in arm. At a distance they looked like Merit and Vito; they were certainly dressed the same. But how could Merit and Vito possibly have got ahead of him?

Just as the couple were passing one of the observation alcoves, four figures erupted from concealment inside it. Like a pack of wild teeners, swinging fists and weapons, the four charged the couple from behind. The man and woman were both knocked down. Already they were being dragged off the slideway and back into the alcove.

The cold combat computer had flicked on automatically, and Adam was already hurtling forward, running in a curved path over slower and slower strips toward the alcove. He pounded off the slowest strip just in time to see the top of one pigtailed head vanish down through a utility trapdoor at the rear of the bubble-walled enclosure. The attackers were gone.

Vito Ling lay on the deck of the observation platform, twitching, wide-eyed, dead. His face and head were covered with his blood.

A few meters away... Merit...

Adam turned her over, to lie face up. She was unconscious, but she was alive, with no injury that his frantic examination could discover. A pulse throbbed in her wrist as Adam's shaky fingers held it.

He looked away for a moment, toward the closed trapdoor. Would he have a chance of catching anyone? But no, he had better stay with Merit. He looked back at her.

Adam screamed, as his legs thrust him erect, away from the figure on the deck. His hands came slapping up to hide the world from his eyes.

Instead of Merit, he had seen Alice on the deck, pregnant and butchered and dead.

Behind his closed eyes, his mind scrambled for truth, some kind of truth that he could cling to. Fearfully he uncovered his eyes, looking toward the place where Vito—

Had been. Vito's body was gone. There were no bloodstains there on the deck now. Nothing.

Numbly Adam looked around. No Merit on the floor. No Alice either, of course not Alice. And no Vito Ling. No pigtailed attackers. Adam Mann was alone in the alcove, breathing hard and trembling.

A couple of people shot by on the fast strip of the slideway, paying him no attention.

Hallucination. Forcing himself to think, to act, Adam walked to the rear of the alcove and examined the trapdoor closely. It was locked shut, and a thin film of unmarked dust lay around it and over it, along with a little windblown litter. It looked as if no one had used the door for days at least.

Hallucination. He stumbled out onto the slideway and resumed his journey. He was shaken, hardly aware of what was going on around him. To think that he sometimes envied others their parapsych powers...

But what could have brought on this experience? He had never had anything like it in his life before. Probably his feelings for Merit—relating her to Alice—but of course it might have

209

been genuine precognition, which would mean that some time in the future, Merit and Vito would travel this way, and would be attacked.

Shock hit Adam again. Merit had said something like: "I don't mind a place like this—about once a year." It wasn't likely that she and Vito would be on Golden that long. It wasn't likely, Adam thought, that they would return to the Pioneer Hotel before they left. Tonight it was going to be, of course, tonight.

In a slow unthinking way Adam had moved again out to the rapid strip; now he spun around and raced back for the immobile utility walk along the outer edge of the slideway. He had to get back to that alcove—or might the attack be going to take place at a different one?

Looking down the long slideway toward the Pioneer Hotel, he could now see Merit and Vito in the distance, approaching arm in arm, gliding toward him along the slow outer strip.

Adam reached the utility walk and sprinted back toward them. His view of them was blocked by vending machines on the walk ahead of him. How far was it to that alcove? God, it mustn't be far, the attack and killing took only a few seconds.

A lone man went by on the slideway, turning his head to watch Adam run, then turning away with determination, minding his own business.

Adam ran.

There was a scuffle and a faint outcry from close ahead. Adam rounded a vending machine and came dashing into the alcove. A figure at the rear was just putting coins into the video machine to turn it on, bringing the retchsinger figure gigantically alive upon the holostage above.

Vito Ling was not dead on the floor, he was still more or less on his feet, but he was being held in that position. One of his arms was being twisted behind his back by a tall powerful young man in teener garb, while another one stood before him with a brassknuckled fist drawn back, holding Vito's bleeding head up by the hair while turning his own head to look at Adam. The fourth attacker, who appeared to be more or less directing matters, was a short, lightly built man with a face lined well beyond the teenpack age. He looked around with surprise at the sound of Adam's entrance, then put a smile on his face and stepped toward Adam.

And there, behind the short man, Merit was lying on her face, just as in the vision.

The short man stepped forward. He was a cocky little character with dangerous eyes. But now he was going to do his imitation of polite reasonableness.

"Friend, we really don't need no help here," said the short man to Adam in a pleasant voice. The other three had paused, waiting and watching to see if there was going to be a real distraction.

Vito looked like he might be going to die.

Adam did not move or speak.

The short man said to Adam: "I mean the lady had a touch too much to drink, you know, and it's just a friendly little argument."

Adam leaned forward a little. At the end of his run he had automatically come to rest with his feet just the right distance apart for balance and quick movement. He could feel the strength ready in his arms, that were hanging loosely in front of him, and he could feel his chest heaving with the exertion of the run and with the build-up of adrenalin.

Alice. And now Merit. Twice in one lifetime. But now he had them in front of him. He watched the short man's eyes, and smiled at him.

"I mean," asked the short man, in a new tone, one meant to frighten, "why be a dead hero?"

When nothing happened, he stepped forward, making his voice friendly again. "Let me explain—"

Adam observed the short man's subtle shift of weight in stride, which meant that the right knee was going to come up for Adam's groin. The combat computer guided Adam's sidestep, and launched his right fist in what would have been a clumsy sucker punch if it had not come with almost invisible speed from a standing start. The blow took the short man on the neck under his left ear, and lifted him onto his toes. He fell, rolled over, and lay face down on the deck without moving.

The retchsinger image tore off its shirt, and jittered in its plastic cage. Its mouth opened and noise came out.

"Get him!" ordered the man who had been feeding the retchsinger coins, the lean figure standing close under the noise and light of the machine.

The two who were holding Vito let him drop and came at Adam, spreading out to get him between them. Their faces also were too old for teeners. Adam defended cautiously when they closed in on him, and in the first blurred second of savage motion and impact he knew they were a professional team. It was all he could do to keep himself alive and spin out from between them.

The lean figure in the rear came forward, cursing impartially at them all. "*Get* him, I said."

Adam had two seconds to look at Merit again. Still she had not moved.

The two big men regarded Adam with awe, and paused before coming at him again. One of them was flexing his wrist, where the edge of Adam's hand had caught it. The man was getting his fingers to work again, but his length of metal pipe had bounced away and was riding the slideway to Stem City.

"Come on!" urged the lean one. "Quick!"

Adam started a move at the biggest man, a subtle feint intended to fool a good fighter. The man jumped back a step as Adam spun round. He caught the lean man moving in, with a side snap kick that hit him in the knee like a swung hammer. One more down.

The giant with the brass knuckles was almost quick enough; Adam felt a scrape across his forehead as he dodged the swing. Then he was stepping in, hitting with backfist, knuckles, elbow. He thought that he had never hit anyone or anything so hard before.

And now the big character who had lost his pipe weapon was the only one besides Adam still on his feet. Still flexing his sore wrist, the big man backed away, no longer a workman going at a job, but a man with the fear in him. He was shaking his head a little. This one knew, this one appreciated •what was going to happen to him.

The man took a last look into Adam's face, and turned and ran for the slideway. Just at the edge of the alcove Adam caught him from behind. The two went down, with Adam on top; the man beneath him strained and squealed and then his neck was broken.

Adam turned round in a crouch. The lean opponent had overcome the pain of his knee enough to pull out a gun; and Vito, battered almost to death, had got up to throw himself at the enemy and save Adam from a bullet.

Vito had luckily managed to bang the lean man's sore knee, and the two wounded were struggling feebly against their injuries and against each other. Or, they had been struggling, for by now Adam had crossed the intervening space and kicked the lean man in the head. The head on its lean neck bounced through one vibration like a punching bag on its mount, and then was still.

Bloody and gasping, Vito just stayed sitting on the deck, staring ahead of him. Adam, gasping if not bloody, stood beside Vito looking warily around in all directions, ready to meet the next threat when it came. People were still going by on the slideway, passing the alcove scene and looking in at it, then turning away with a desperate blankness in their faces, eager to not-involve themselves. Adam eyed the passing people cautiously. But it seemed that none of them were going to turn aside into the alcove and try to hurt Merit any more.

In a few moments he had regained a certain relative sanity, and went to look after her. She was just stunned, he thought, just as in the vision. She was undoubtedly breathing, and now she was even turning her head a little from side to side, and her blood was still pulsing safe inside its warm tender vessels. Adam touched her face with one of his terrible hands. A living face. Yes, Merit had to be alive, because the universe still had to be a place in which a man could live.

The jukebox was still playing. Probably less than two minutes had passed since the start of the fight. But suddenly the voice of the retchsinger was silent. Adam looked up to see the image swallowing, drinking from its bottles of colored liquids, meanwhile twisting its body in time to the throbbing music, its sculptured belly muscles writhing.

Then the image raised its arms and the music crashed toward a climax. The imaged body snapped forward, and with a heaving groan projectile-vomited a streaming rainbow of bright color that splattered and filmed the inside of the plastic cage.

**

Vito Ling lay looking up from his hospital bed. A hundred thin insulated wires led to the helmet in which his head was cradled, but he was aware of his visitors and perhaps he was trying to smile at them. It was hard to be sure.

Adam kept watching Merit as she sat beside the bed holding Vito's hand. Her eyes seldom left her husband's face, and when she spoke to her husband her voice was sometimes not loud enough for Adam to hear it clearly. Vito was unable to speak to answer her, but his eyes kept coming back to her face and he appeared to be listening to what she said.

After a while, Adam got up and left the room.

Ray, his face looking tired, was waiting out in the corridor, where small bubble windows glowed with a wintry dawn.

"Looks like he's going to make it," Adam told him.

Ray nodded. "I've just been talking to the doctor in charge." Then he made a gesture of futility. "You saw it coming, fortunately, but I saw nothing. Nothing. Parapsych talent, the undependable. How can we build on it? And yet we must."

The two of them stood talking there in the corridor for a little while, not really saying much, until Merit, smiling tiredly, came out of Vito's room. She took an arm of each of them. "He seems to be doing as well as we could hope. He's going to make it, I'm sure now. Let's all get some rest."

Two plainclothes detectives met them just as they were passing the waiting room. "Mr. Mann, we'd like another few minutes with you, if you please."

215

Adam shrugged wearily. The small bandage pulled at the slight cut on his forehead.

"We'll wait downstairs," said Ray exchanging looks with him. He moved away, with Merit leaning on his arm.

The detectives watched them go, then faced Adam. One said: "We checked up on your Space Force background. I guess it is possible that you laid out those four hoods all by yourself."

"I'm glad to hear it. I was worried. Mind if I sit down?" He stepped into the waiting room and took a chair. Physically he felt weary. And he felt a little giddy, lightheaded, almost cheerful. Merit was all right. Merit was all right. Nothing else mattered very much.

The other detective asked Adam: "What do you think those four men wanted?"

"Looked to me like they wanted to kill Vito Ling. But you'd better ask them."

There was a brief pause while the two detectives exchanged glances. "Three of them are dead," one finally informed Adam. "It's not certain that the fourth one is ever going to think straight again. You hammered him pretty good. They say an artery in his brain gave way."

He knew their eyes were probing him to see what he thought of the carnage he had wrought, but he had been looking down at his hands when he heard the words and he just kept looking at them. The fight seemed unreal to Adam now. At last he looked up. "Can't say I'm especially sorry. I guess there are a lot of members of the human race I just don't give a damn about any more."

The two detectives had sat down facing him across the little waiting room, that was otherwise empty. One of them sighed. "Well, can't say I'm sorry either. They were all professional strong-arm boys. Two just arrived on Golden last month, two have been here for a year. They worked a lot for gamblers."

"We're growing into a big city," Adam said.

"Does Dr. Ling like to gamble a lot, do you know?"

"I couldn't say. I just met him a couple of days ago. But he's only been on Golden a couple of days. I doubt he's had time yet to run up any giant debts and refuse to pay them."

"Yeah." The detective sighed again; it made him sound as if he were surprised and saddened by the kind of things he kept running into in his job. "Know any other reason why anyone would want to kill him?"

Maybe me, thought Adam. *I want his wife.* Or maybe there was something else. His imagination showed him the president of the Research Foundation on Earth, tired beyond endurance of Vito's complaints, calling in the hired killers. He smiled (for Merit was safe, and he could smile) and said: "I have no idea, no."

And something was still worrying Merit, something besides the mere fact of her husband's being nearly killed. Well, he, Adam, intended to find out what it was.

"We understand Mrs. Ling is a Jovian, is that correct? One of those…"

"Yes. She's one of those."

"She's a telepath, then, isn't she? But she didn't foresee the attack?"

Adam felt annoyed. "They don't go around reading people's minds right and left. And once the action started she must have been stunned before she knew there was anyone approaching. Any danger."

"Stunned expertly," said a detective. "Very expertly. The doctors say there's no sign of any damage now."

"Yes?" Well, there were ways in which that could be done. "Meaning what?"

"What do you think that fact means?"

"Someone wanted her husband dead, but not her. Is that all? I'm tired."

Again the police looked at each other. "That's all for now, Mr. Mann," one said. "You're not being charged with anything, of course. In my personal opinion it'll smell a little sweeter here with those four gone."

"There'll be four more—or eight," said Adam, moving wearily away. "Lots of opportunity on Golden."

Chapter Fourteen

"It's this damned Jovian business," said General Lorsch. She was sitting behind her desk and looking at Boris Brazil through tired eyes. "Probably that fight episode on the slideway, with the Jovian woman involved, is somehow tied in with all the rest of it." With one hand she pushed a carven wooden box across her desktop to the Colonel. To Brazil it looked like Grodsky's old desk, but the Colonel wasn't going to try perching on a corner of it today.

He silently accepted the invitation to smoke, and took a little time to get his chosen cigar fired up. Time in which he could also do some thinking.

He was glad to be back on Golden again after a seven year absence, even glad in a way that the Field was still unconquered. But not everyone was so happy, evidently, or he wouldn't have been called back. He hadn't met General Lorsch before today, but he doubted that she normally appeared as worn and harried as she did right now.

"Excuse me, General," Brazil asked, "but is the problem really just these hundred Jovians?"

"Yes, it's basically just the Jovians, even if there still are only a hundred of them." The General, toying with a small cigar of her own but not lighting it, managed a smile. "From your viewpoint, Colonel, maybe I sound a trifle like a monomaniac— but you don't really know anything about these people, do you?"

"The Jovians? No ma'am."

"I didn't either, until very recently. Now I've been through one interview with Ray Kedro—he's evidently their leader, to the extent that they have a leader—but I can't communicate what happened during that interview as evidence. There are the intelligence reports."

She could, thought Boris, at least have talked to him about that interview, since it sounded so important. Maybe later he would push to hear about it.

As for the intelligence reports, Boris had already read through some of the printouts that were now scattered about on the General's desk. The Colonel glanced down again, skimming quickly over certain paragraphs:

"—Jovian organization has penetrated every branch of Earth society, probably including the Space Force. Their economic power like their political influence, is indirect but enormous—"

"—can they be considered subversive? If they would lead or coerce humanity, they have given no real evidence of what direction they would choose."

Subversive. Boris frowned at the word. He knew that there were people, in the Space Force as elsewhere, who could see subversive plotters behind every rock. There were also a few very real people, real terrorists, who for one reason or another plotted violence and destruction of the government. Usually, as far as Boris could see, it was not really because of anything in particular that the government had done, but just because the government was there, and terrorists in love with violence and destruction had to have some target, and big important targets were more fun.

And some of the terrorists might, for all that Boris knew, be Jovians.

The most urgent-looking message on the table read:

—EVIDENCE INDICATES JOVIAN CONSTRUCTION ILLEGAL STARSHIP ON GANYMEDE. GANYMEDE INSTALLATION NOW DESERTED JOVIANS UNFINDABLE IN SOL SYSTEM. PROBABLE SPECS OF SHIP CONSTRUCTED HERE FOLLOW:

The ship appeared to be a big one, and if the specifications given in the report were accurate, it mounted certain generators and other equipment generally reserved for exclusive use in weapon systems. It looked like the Jovians had built for combat.

"Neat trick, putting together a starship in secret," Boris commented. "One like this, especially."

"They're pretty clever people," said the General drily. "The authorities on Sol System didn't realize that the Jovians were up to anything on Ganymede until all the Jovians known to be in the system began to head that way. By the time we really took notice that something was up, they were in their starship and gone."

The situation was a complete dustcloud to Boris. He leaned back in his chair, puffed gently on his cigar, and said: "So, they're all out joyriding in their outlaw bird. I take it you expect them to come here, to Golden, ma'am, since you pulled me off another job and had me brought here and are telling me all this."

"I do expect them to show up at Golden, yes."

"I see, ma'am. What'll they do when they get here?"

"I wish I knew." Lorsch shook her head, and threw her own tormented cigar away, still unlighted. "I have three ships..." The General let her words trail off, then added: "I've asked Antares for some reinforcement, just in case. Three more ships. Don't know if I'll get them."

"You're expecting a fight, then?"

"I want to be ready for one."

"And just what am I here for, ma'am?"

"You're here because you know something of the planet and the situation, Colonel. And according to the records, you also know this fellow Adam Mann."

Aha. "Adam Mann. Yes ma'am, I remember him. He worked for me as a planeteer at one point. Right here on Golden."

"So the records state. What did you think of him?" Brazil pondered. "A good man, basically. Not— well, not an ordinary man, even for planeteering, where we tend to get—an assortment."

"Yes," the General responded drily. The reputation enjoyed, or endured, by the planeteering profession was nothing new to her. But she was thinking now of something else, of Adam Mann specifically. "I don't know if he's working for the Jovians, or just friendly with some of them, or what. In any case he probably knows them at least as well as any non-Jovian alive. I'd like to talk to him, find out if he's disposed to be helpful to us, and, if he is, consult with him. If he isn't—I'd like to know that too. And he's not always an easy man to talk to, or so I've been told."

"So you'd like me to try. All right. I'll talk to him." Boris got up out of his chair and took a quick nervous walk, the length of the office and back. Standing in front of the desk, he said: "It's the Field, of course, that's the special thing about Golden. If the Jovians, or anyone else, could control the Field, obviously they could control the whole planet. And any other planets where a Field could be established."

"Yes, I've thought about that, Colonel. That's an obvious answer. But I'm not sure the truth is that direct and simple. I tell you, every time I think I've figured out what they're up to, something—"

The intercom chimed, with muted elegance. The General answered it. "All right. Have him wait a minute." She raised her eyes. "Colonel, Mann's here now."

***

Coming into the inner office, not knowing why the General had asked to see him, Adam stopped short at sight of the unexpected face. "Well, I'll be—Boris!"

Pumping his hand, Brazil said: "Look, when I told you to go out and scout, I didn't mean you had to live five years in the woods. You can come in now, there's a settlement here."

The two of them shared a modest laugh, and there was an easing of tension. They had asked each other the usual questions people exchanged during the first stage of a reunion, while the General, smiling benevolently but guardedly, watched from behind her desk. Adam, noting her scrutiny, felt more and more certain that he knew what this meeting was all about.

Brazil had hardly changed, to the eye. He was still planeteering, of course, and Adam suspected he was now in chronic trouble with certain of his superiors, enough trouble at least to have prevented his promotion, while at the same time his reputation for getting results kept getting him what Brazil considered good jobs, interesting assignments: Maybe the Colonel really preferred not to be promoted into dullness.

"There're women chasing me on most of the old planets—the only time I get any rest is on the new ones," said Boris, who would have a lot of new planets behind him now, and a billion and one more ahead of him if he could keep going that long. And Adam was sure that the Colonel would try.

"Where was your last one?" Adam asked, beginning to feel the old lure again himself.

Boris glanced at the woman who sat patiently observing them from behind her desk. He said: "A good long way from here. I sort of got pulled off the job."

"Oh?"

"To come here. Certain of our leaders"—he wasn't indicating whether General Lorsch was one of them—"think that the human race here has a Jovian problem."

That announcement was, by this time, no real surprise to Adam. He said: "There're only two Jovians on Golden, that I know about. So what—?"

They told Adam about the Jovian starship, built secretly on Ganymede and now departed Sol System for parts unknown. Adam was puzzled. He had heard no hint from Ray or Merit of the existence of a Jovian interstellar craft, in Sol System or anywhere else.

"Well, if they built it, they must have had a good reason," Adam said at last. "They wouldn't just break the law..." He gestured, trying to find the word he wanted. "Casually. You know, cynically. Not just for their own personal profit."

223

"They might break it, though," said Boris.

Adam looked at him. "Anyone might, who thought there was enough at stake. I seem to remember that you've bent a rule or two from time to time."

"How long since you've been on Earth, Mann?" General Lorsch asked him.

"I take it you've been looking over my record, General, and you probably know how long. It's been years. Why?"

"People can change, even your Jovians. There's good evidence to indicate that during the past few years they've been behind a number of dirty deals, on Earth and the settled planets. There's more evidence that they're out to weaken the Space Force, reduce our influence. Have a chair, won't you? Want to look at some reports?"

Weaken the Space Force—ah, so that was the capital crime! Adam opened his mouth for an angry answer, but Lorsch looked so tiredly determined that an angry answer seemed certain to bring on an angry argument and that seemed futile, so he forebore. He could argue anytime; right now he wanted to learn more. Silently he accepted the chair the General had indicated.

Boris was waiting, watching him silently.

The General pushed a pile of paperwork on her desk, evidently the reports that she had mentioned, toward Adam slightly. She watched him too.

"I've known Ray Kedro since we were kids."

Adam finally told them both. "I'd trust him with my life."

Boris asked: "How well have you known him, Ad?"

"Well enough. As well, I suppose, as you can know someone who—you know what they are?"

Boris spread out his hands. "We don't know that, not in the same way you do. Maybe our suspicions are all wrong. Can you explain why?"

"I've never known one of them to do a mean thing." Only at this moment did Adam fully realize that fact himself; and with the realization he could feel his anger growing. "I've known people to beat *them* up, for the crime of being different. That's our way, isn't it, the way of the great human race?"

"Sometimes," said Boris. "But I have to put in a good word for my employers, in spite of all their blunders that I bitch and moan about. As far as I know, the Space Force has never deliberately exploited or injured an alien race."

"We've never before met another race we had to look up to." Adam paused, feeling a little embarrassed by what he was going to say. "Only the Jovians. They're like our children, growing up and getting ahead of us in the world. I think we should be proud of them."

"I see," said General Lorsch, tiredly, after a little while.

***

Later that day, when Adam entered the hospital room, Vito was sitting up in bed and working at feeding himself, apparently enjoying fair success at the job through the helmet with its hundred wires was still on his head. The tiny probes inside the helmet were keeping his injured brain going, stimulating and guiding a healing process. Some of Vito's cranial bone was still in the hospital's deep freeze, awaiting the right time for replacement.

Merit, sitting at bedside, looked up at Adam's entrance, and reached up a hand to him; he was able to hold her hand while he stood there getting the routine chatter of greeting out of the way. There was a newsprintout open across the patient's

225

knees, and Adam could see one item headed: SEEK MOTIVE IN SLIDEWAY ATTACK. And below: Police Probe Jovian Angle. But as far as Adam knew, no one had really found an angle yet, Jovian or otherwise. In a few days the item would be out of the news, and half-forgotten.

Which would suit Adam fine. He moved a few centimeters closer to Merit and put a hand on her shoulder.

"I'd like to take your lady out on a little sightseeing trip this afternoon," he said to Vito. "Give her a chance to relax."

"You do that," Vito responded instantly. His voice sounded all right, though he obviously still had to be careful about moving his head. "She needs that. Look at her, all worn out, looks worse than me. Bring me back a picture or two, hey Hon? Send me a nice thought, maybe, from out there?"

Merit looked at them both. "I will," she said.

When she had stepped out of the room for a moment, wanting to talk to one of the doctors, Vito said to Adam almost truculently: "She'll be safe with you. Safer than with me. Some good I was for her the other night."

"Hey, you probably saved my life by jumping that last guy, remember? And what could you do, with four of them?"

"You did all right."

"I'm a kind of well-trained freak."

* * * *

The most easily reached Tenoka Village was a couple of kilometers inside the Field. Riding the shuttle copter out with Merit on the first leg of the journey, Adam brought up the subject of his own unsuspected parapsych powers.

"There's a mystery for you. Why did I have that precognitive experience? I've never had, seen, done, anything like that in my whole life before."

226

She had listened to his account of the experience carefully. "I don't know what to tell you, Adam. People throughout human history have occasionally had such experiences. Usually—they don't have any vital effect, either on the person who goes through them, or anyone else."

He sighed. "Everyone says how undependable parapsych powers are. I guess the accepted wisdom is in this case right. You and Ray and the others—it's all fading away for you, right? That's what I've heard."

"We don't do those things as casually as we once did. I'm not sure that the power to do them is fading for all of us. Is that a village, over there, behind those trees?" Now the copter was descending.

From the shuttle landing place Adam and Merit hiked along a trail that he knew well, past the line of marker poles, here placarded with warnings to tourists. Essentially the signs cautioned them that from here on they would be in Field and on their own.

The appearance of the villages near the Stem had changed substantially over the last few years, as had the lives of those who dwelled in them. Now, nearly all of the Tenoka teepees were made from tough Earth fabrics, and nearly every Tenoka fire heated a cook-pot of Earth metal.

The warriors of this particular village greeted Adam warmly, and eyed Merit and her camera with greater toleration than most tourists received, since she was with him.

"There have been signs and omens, Geryon-Slayer," said one of the elders, speaking in his own language. "Even now Pierced Arms lies in trance. We have been expecting you, for he foretold two visitors for today."

"Did you get that?" Adam asked Merit.

227

She wrinkled her forehead. "Not too well." There was nothing unethical in a telepath's "reading" a message that was available to the ears anyway— and, as Adam understood it, nothing particularly unpleasant to the reader. But thoughts formed in an unknown language were apt to be difficult.

When Adam translated for her, Merit was interested. She asked: "Could we see this medicine man? Do you think it's genuine parapsych or fakery?"

"Probably fakery, if I know old Pierced Arms, and I think I do... but then, I thought I knew myself, before I started catching glimpses of the future. Well, we can try."

Adam turned to the elders and addressed them in their own tongue. "How about if we see old Pierced Arms? Would it be possible? Might scare my lady here a bit."

They smiled and took the bait; very little was so sacred to the Tenoka that it could not serve as the basis for a practical joke.

"He speaks messages now," whispered an attendant, as Merit and Adam were ushered into the darkened lodge. This one, consecrated to magic, was made of real skins. Surrounded by a large assortment of magical paraphernalia, with oil lamps burning at his head and feet, Pierced Arms lay tossing on his pallet. The body of the medicine man was daubed with colored clay in intricate patterns, and strings of feathers were laced through the loops in his wrinkled skin. Now his eyes were open, now they were shut. His arms and legs twitched, and he breathed irregularly and jabbered strange words.

"I don't quite get that dialect," Adam whispered.

Merit closed her eyes. "I can get something out of it. Yes. I think—a message from one man to another, here on Golden. They're distant relatives, and they live a long way apart.

Congratulations, I think, one is saying to the other... congratulations on I don't know what. Something will be sent. A present. But both men are surprised at being able to communicate in this way. It doesn't usually—"

Her eyes opened. "And, Adam, wait. There's something else going on, in the background." Merit was excited. Not quite worried; alert.

Then she was silent for a moment, and Adam said: "I think you're right about the messages being passed, somehow." He was fascinated. "I've never seen this before, though I've heard stories."

Merit pressed his hand, urging silence; she was concentrating intensely.

The shaman was beginning a new message now. His voice changed in tone as he did so, and shifted to a language that Adam had never heard before. Neither could Merit really follow it this time. Then quickly there was another shift. More talk followed, more minds were tapped. There were greetings between more people who were surprised to find themselves in mental communication—usually the subjects were not really astonished, though. It was something not unknown to the natives of Golden, this type of communication, but it was something rare. When they found themselves unexpectedly in mental contact, they exchanged greetings, or occasionally threats. Sometimes the exchange consisted of obscure words and ideas that neither Merit nor Adam could understand.

Once, when Pierced Arms paused longer than usual between messages, Adam paused to open the tent flap and look out. He was getting restless. "We'd better start back soon. It's going to be getting dark—"

Merit gripped his hand, suddenly and hard. But it was Pierced Arms whose voice boomed out a second later, louder than before, commanding, uttering perfectly accented words and sentences in the preferred language of Earth's Space Force and most of her colonies.

"Raymond Kedro, a message for him," Pierced Arms almost shouted. "My name was Alexander Golden, and I speak to warn the man from Earth called Kedro. He closes his mind against me, but he should hear. If he persists in what he plans for this world, he must fail. People will die, other people will suffer. Kedro himself may die—"

Merit raised fists to her forehead. Her scream was an elemental, primal sound, that had to have been driven out of her by some force greater than the mere shock of the words, of any words. The scream was so loud that it made Pierced Arms awaken, with a start.

Adam held Merit tightly while she recovered. The Tenoka at the door of the lodge were giggling quietly at the joke's excellent though long-delayed success.

"Merit. What was it? Merit—?"

"Adam," she whispered, "Ray was here—his mind—fighting something—"

"Hungry," muttered Pierced Arms, sitting up and scratching his lean old ribs. "Much talking always makes me hungry. Where's my worthless elder wife? Ha, Geryon-Slayer, you bring a woman to hear me speak? No matter, she can help prepare the food. Wife!"

"Merit, brace up," Adam murmured in her ear. "We'll talk later. Right now we'd better be good guests."

And she did brace up, immediately. If an ordinary woman had recovered with such speed from screaming fright, you would think she had been acting.

Chapter Fifteen

The string twanged sharply, and the arrow from Earth went humming away from Ray Kedro's thirty-five kilo bow. After a flight of thirty meters the shaft punched almost exactly into the center of the bright blue bullseye. The target, concentric rings of color on a soft plastic disk, hung from the stump of a branch on a tree at the edge of a clearing. The clearing was no more than about a hundred meters from Adam's cabin.

"I have no doubt about one point," said Ray, as he drew a second arrow from the new, fancifully decorated quiver on his back. "What you heard from the medicine man was genuinely intended as a message for me. I take the message seriously. And I'd prefer that you tell no one else about it."

The two men were completely alone in the woods at the moment, there being probably no other human beings within a kilometer in any direction. Merit was at the hospital, where she was spending most of her time these days. The medical reports were good, and Vito was due soon to be released.

"I won't tell anyone else about it if you say so," Adam said. "But why not?"

"Humor me."

"All right. But the Space Force is going to hear about your message anyway, through the Tenoka."

"I suppose they will. But let's not confirm it." Ray nocked his second arrow on the bowstring and took quick aim. A moment later another shaft sank into the bullseye, close beside the first. At archery, as at everything else, he was superb.

"And the communication was from Alexander Golden," Adam said, meditatively. "Pierced Arms said that name very plainly. And I don't understand it at all."

"I don't believe the message really came from Alexander Golden, but through him," Ray answered calmly. "Or through what's left of him, more likely."

Adam paused in the act of reaching for one of his own arrows. "What?"

Ray was looking at him soberly. "Even before I left Sol System I was vaguely, distantly aware of very strong parapsych activity, here on this planet and around it. Yes, I know, the enormous distance. But the mind, the Jovian mind at least, is not entirely constrained to obey the laws of physics... and since I arrived on Golden I've been able to confirm the parapsych activity. There's more of it here than there is on Earth, or anywhere else I've been. It may be that there's something natural about the planet, that induces or promotes it. You never had a precognitive experience before you came here, did you?"

"No... but what is all this activity that you detect here? What's the source?"

"Some of it emanates from these native people. The Tenoka here and around the Stem area, and others of their species around the planet. But the preponderate amount of parapsych action on Golden comes from the beings you have called the Field-builders." Ray studied Adam's reaction, and added: "Oh yes, they're still around. Very much so."

It was Adam's turn to shoot, but he still stood with his bow forgotten in his hand, staring at Ray. "If that's so... then you're the first person from Earth to ever make contact with them."

Ray smiled faintly. "Except for the unfortunate Alex Golden, of course... but they don't want such contact, Adam. They prefer to hide from us, from both Jovian and Earth-descended humanity, and study us at their leisure. And more and more..." Ray came to a halt, gazing at Adam in an abstracted and unhappy way.

Adam had a premonition of fear. "What?"

"Just that they hate us, Adam." Ray's voice had fallen almost to a whisper. "I can see the sickness in them. I become gradually more and more aware of what they are capable of doing. I admit it's a touch frightening... more than a touch, I must confess. They try to bury the sickness and hatred deep in their minds but there it is. I don't think Merit is able to make contact with them at all, which is perhaps just as well."

"Frightening, yes," Adam muttered. He remembered Merit's scream in the medicine man's lodge. "And the Field-builders are still right here, on this planet? You're really sure of that? I mean if you can contact them at the distance of Earth..."

Ray nodded. "They're here, all right."

"But where?"

"That question was not so easy to answer." Ray had another arrow drawn now, as if automatically getting ready to shoot again, but once drawn the shaft rested in his hand ignored. "By the end of my first day on Golden I had determined that they were somewhere in the other hemisphere. And I was also sure that Alexander Golden does not exist any longer. Not as a human being, anyway."

"What?"

"No, he's not human any longer. I can sense what they're like, Adam, the Field-builders, I can tell it by the things they do.

233

To people here and elsewhere. And by what they'd like to do to us. But they're a little cautious. We're quite strong."

"Ray. Gods of all space, Ray."

"I know, I know. Most likely all that's left of Golden by now is a sort of telepathic frequency converter, a bridge over which messages can be forced from their minds to those of ordinary Earth-descended humans, or to the Tenoka."

Adam was listening in horror.

It was as if Ray were reluctant to speak, to reveal the horrifying things, but was able to see no other choice. "I've seen... sensed... the Field-builders' dungeons, Adam. The torture chambers, where Alexander Golden still exists—I can't really say that he still lives—along with other prisoners. By now I've determined more precisely where they are, over on the other side of the world from here. Not stone walls with chains hanging from them, no. And not physical torture, or not that particularly. They—the ones you call the Field-builders—have solved somehow the old problem. How does a being, determinedly evil, use parapsych talents to inflict pain? And how can one maim and kill... with the mind alone..."

Ray's voice had grown grim, and now it almost quivered. His expression had darkened. Adam had never seen or heard him this way before. Now the huge man paused, staring into space. Suddenly Adam saw him as tired and strained, living under a burden that would have been too great for any ordinary human.

"Alex Golden was an Earthman," Ray said suddenly. "As I am." He looked at Adam suddenly. "Those who have done what has been done to him are on this planet. And I intend to call them to account."

"You—?"

Ray smiled at Adam. "General Lorsch thinks that we Jovians consider *her* our enemy."

"If you don't—and if you have some definite knowledge of the Field-builders—why not tell her the truth?"

"I've tried to do so, Adam. She and I once enjoyed a very private chat. More private than the lady realized, because I turned off the spy devices in her office. And then I even used what we call projection to present our case. That method gives me very considerable powers of persuasion." Ray grinned faintly, and Adam had no trouble believing him. "But she's a tough lady, Adam, and a stubborn one—and even if she could be persuaded to come to terms with us, she could not for very long deceive or disobey her superiors, and we would still have to deal with them."

"Look, Ray—even if she doesn't like you, I don't see why you can't tell her what you've found out about the Field-builders. About your contact with them. Did you try to tell her that? And why shouldn't we tell her about this message that purports to be from Golden?"

"No, Adam. I didn't try to tell her that." For the moment Ray sounded less like an old friend, and more like a patient schoolmaster. "Because there is nothing that she or the Space Force can do about Alexander Golden, or about the Field-builders either—at least not while the Field still covers the Ringwall, over on the other side of the planet."

"That's where they are, then." Adam almost whispered it.

"That's where they are... what we must do with General Lorsch is get her to prepare for a fight—let her think, if necessary, that we are the ones who must be fought. Then we shall convincingly uncover the real enemy."

"Uncover them how?" Adam paused. "You mean you can control the Field?" If it were anyone else talking to him… but it was not anyone else. He found himself ready to believe anything of Ray.

"Not yet," said Ray calmly. I don't expect to be able to control it from this side of the planet."

"From the other side, then… the Ringwall again?"

"That's right."

"But how are you going to get there?"

It was as if Ray had been waiting for that question, as if everything he had said up to now had been calculated to lead up to it.

"Watch," the huge man said.

A moment later, Ray's heavy bow dropped to the muddy ground; the hand that had held it was gone, had winked out of sight along with the rest of Ray. Ray Kedro had vanished completely, as if he had never been.

Teleportation. It had to be that. One parapsych effect that Adam had never seen before, that no one he had heard of had ever seen. He had heard or read somewhere that not even the Jovians were capable of it. Some authorities went so far as to say that there was not a single properly authenticated case of teleportation in all of human history.

But what else could it be? Now teleportation… Adam looked to his left and right, and behind him, and he was still utterly alone.

He turned around. He called out, tentatively: "Ray?"

"I was slightly off target," said Ray's voice from behind him. Adam spun round again. The big man was standing near the far edge of the clearing, grinning wryly at his own condition.

236

Ray's feet and legs were plastered with wet mud, up to above his knees.

Ray picked up a piece of dead bark and with a faint grimace began to scrape away some of the goo; there were still some human situations, it appeared, that no amount of intelligence, parapsych talent, or superb co-ordination were capable of dealing with gracefully.

Pointing with the defiled bark, Ray explained: "I was aiming for the top of that little hill over there; I was sort of curious about what was on the other side, which may be why I came down beyond it, in a mudhole." He raised his eyes to Adam's. "But the point is that the parapsych talent is not adversely affected by the Field."

Adam sat down on a handy log. After all that he had learned in the past few minutes, he felt he needed to sit down. "I thought the story was that all the Jovian parapsych talents were disappearing. That they've been fading steadily since you all passed adolescence."

"You're absolutely right, Ad. That's the story."

Ray's grin was, as of old, infectious. "You don't still believe all the stories you hear, do you?"

"You mean..." Adam let it trail off.

All he could think of for the moment was that Merit hadn't seen fit to enlighten him about the powerful talents that she, too, must still have at her disposal. But all he said was: "You're lucky you didn't land on one of those jagged stumps over there where I did my logging, for the cabin. Or come down right on top of a poison lizard in the swamp."

Ray shook his head. "That would be physical harm caused directly by the use of parapsych talent, within the meaning of the law—and that, leaving out minor bruises and such, is still a practical impossibility. Remember?"

"Still an impossibility for you. Not for the Field-builders. You were just telling me how they…"

"Yes… well, they may no longer enjoy a total monopoly on the ability to use parapsych as a weapon. We must develop, are developing, means of self defense. I can put it more precisely: violent harm from parapsych causes doesn't happen to us, to Jovians, by accident… teleportation is probably the safest form of transportation yet invented."

"If you say so… Ray, what's your plan? You said you were going to call the Field-builders to account."

"I am indeed," said Ray with calm confidence. He had now finished scraping most of the mud away, and he threw down the piece of bark and came to sit on the log beside Adam. "Our siblings have finished constructing a starship, at the old base on Ganymede where Doc—"

Adam held up a hand. "The Space Force knows about your ship. I was wondering if I should mention it to you, but then I assumed you already knew they did."

"Your assumption was quite correct. And General Lorsch I suppose is worried lest we be bringing our ship here, and planning to upset things for her somehow? Well, we are. Our ninety-eight siblings are bringing our ship along to Golden now. It'll be here when we need it."

Adam got to his feet. He walked a little distance and turned back. "Ray? I don't like this. I mean this between you and the Space Force. I know them, and I know Jovians, I suppose better than anyone else does."

"I'm sure you do, Adam. And what is it you don't like, precisely?"

"They don't understand you, Ray. And I'm not sure you understand them. As soon as that ship of yours arrives in normal space near Golden they're going to arrest whoever's operating it—or try to arrest them. They consider that kind of a ship illegal, and they take things like that seriously."

Ray threw back his head, and his laughter roared out, sudden and surprising. The log rocked under him. "No, Adam, we're not going to fight a battle against the Space Force—although we could. Sorry if I let you think that, even for a minute. We'll park our ship about six hundred kilometers above the Ringwall, and there they'll surround us with a large force—I hope—trying to arrest us as you say.

"We can keep them at arm's length, until events on the surface below have made it possible for them to join us in our endeavors, and convinced them that they should do so. Does that help to set your mind at ease?"

"No, Ray. No, not really. Events on the surface? What events? I don't understand. Look, I'm just a slow human. Take it easy and explain it all to me slowly."

"Adam, we're just going to have to show the Field-builders to the Space Force. It's a case where mere explaining and arguing won't do the job."

"Show them how?"

"Bring them out into the open, out of their dungeons into the light of day. Display them as they really are. I and a few others are going to teleport to the Ringwall from here—from in the Stem or somewhere near it. We ought to be able to reach the Ringwall in, I suppose, five or six jumps. We'll do that while our ship and the Space Force ships are above it. The enemy can be found there, at the Ringwall. And they have the key to the Field there with them, Adam. I've felt it. I've seen it in their minds.

Once we arrive there, we'll be able to take that key into our possession. We'll turn the place upside down and inside out if need be."

It was all coming at Adam too fast, much too fast. "You, and a few others, are just going to walk in on the Field-Builders and do all this to them? How many of them are there?"

Ray strode over to where he had dropped his bow. He picked the weapon up and stood there gripping it. "I'm not sure, but we can do it. Numbers won't count for that much, not in our part of the struggle. A little later we will need the ships and weapons of the Space Force—that's why I'm taking steps to make sure they'll be on hand. There'll be plenty for our brothers and sisters of the normal Earth-descended strain to do; but basically, primarily, this is Jovian business. We are not going to submit to being laboratory animals for the Field-builders; we don't intend to sit here like rats in a cage, tapping our noses against the Field."

Ray was obviously bitter, and deeply angry. Again, Adam thought that he had never seen Ray quite like this before.

Adam himself felt small and inadequate, as he rarely had since he had been a toddler. He asked Ray: "Why are you telling me all this?"

"Because you are a Jovian," Ray answered.

***

"Doc never knew about you," Ray was explaining, a little later, when Adam again felt capable of listening to explanations. "I was only two years old, myself, and a long way from being able to assume leadership, when the other children began trying to duplicate Doc's experiments. That Ganymede installation was and is a huge place. There were vast areas within it that Doc hardly ever entered, and we had a good deal of freedom. And we had abilities that Doc never imagined, at least until much later. He didn't miss a little genetic material from his stock.

"When you were decanted, Adam, one of the laboratory workers was bribed into seeing to it that you were transported to Earth safely. At that point, something about my colleagues' plan went wrong—they couldn't oversee the details from the distance of Ganymede, and you wound up in a public Home instead of a real one as they had intended. My elder siblings tell me they were sorry about that, and I believe them; but as events turned out, we all had to follow you into similar places, at least temporarily, as you know. By the time I was fourteen, I had learned about the experiment that produced you, and I was anxious to get a look at the result. I managed to get myself assigned to the Home that you were in, when it became necessary to go into one—the rest, as they say in stories, you know."

"... but I never guessed..."

Ray grinned at him. "Oh, and one more thing, Ad—Merit has never known. She'll be as surprised as you are."

It was all too much. Adam sat down on the log again, making a helpless gesture.

"I haven't told you any of this before," Ray went on, "because there have been times, many times in fact, when it seemed a distinct disadvantage to anyone to be known as a Jovian. Also, I admit, my older siblings expressed some curiosity about how you would develop, living in an environment substantially different from ours. Whether you've gained or lost by not knowing your heritage—who can say?"

Adam continued just to sit there. He felt numbed, stunned, like part of the log himself. He looked at Ray for a while, then stared into space, then looked back at Ray again. He couldn't doubt any of this, basically, that Ray was telling him.

He, Adam Mann, was a Jovian. He wondered if the curious kids who had created him had given him some other name at first. If so, he didn't think he wanted to know what it was.

No wonder that all his life he had known a sense of being different from the people he lived among, a chronic sense of outrage at the surrounding human idiocy.

"I am telling you this now," said Ray, "because very soon I am going to need the willing help of every Jovian mind and body. And you have it all, Adam. Whatever talents we have are yours, at least in potential." Ray was calmly ready to resume his archery practice, and now the big man's bowstring thrummed again.

Adam raised his eyes just in time to see the arrow hit home. A perfect shot, as always. And now, for himself too, for Adam Mann...

Gradually the realization was growing in him. A foretaste of the new world that he was about to enter. A Jovian world, in which he might climb to heights that were now beyond even his imagination.

***

"This is what I call the right way to convalesce," said Vito Ling, pulling two rabbit-like hoppers out of his game bag, and dropping them on a rock beside the cooking fire. The biochemistry of Golden's native life ran so closely parallel with that of Earth that an inhabitant of either world could generally provide safe nourishment for an inhabitant of the other.

"Convalesce!" Ray laughed. "I think you've just been loafing for the past week. Like me."

"And I'm glad," said Merit, on her knees beside the fire and feeding it with kindling. "I'm not eager for you two to vanish back into Fieldedge, and find a way to spoil this planet. I've decided I like Golden just the way it is."

"We'll convert our scientists to Field-lovers yet," Adam said. Several days had passed since he heard Ray's revelations. Ray had said he hadn't yet told Merit much about the coming struggle, though she was certainly aware of his perceptions of the Field-builders' minds. And Vito had as yet been told nothing.

Merit had been informed, by Ray, of the truth of Adam's Jovian origin. And, as far as Adam could tell, she had been as astonished by the news as he was himself.

Immediately afterward she had come to Adam with a strange look in her face: "Ray just told me…"

"About me?"

"Yes."

And those were the only words the two of them had yet exchanged on the subject. There had been little chance for them to be alone, with Vito now out of the hospital. But ever since that moment Merit had looked at Adam in a different way. Exactly what the difference was he could not analyze.

At the moment, Adam was sitting with his back against a tree, feeling comfortably tired and at peace in a way that he had never really known before. Since the day of Ray's revelations, Adam had been spending the mornings trying to develop his latent parapsych talents, under Ray's tutelage, and the afternoons in teaching Ray, Merit, and Vito his own hard-won skills of the primitive life. Ray had warned Adam that probably he would never be able to teleport unaided, but he had already learned to achieve some intermittent telepathic contacts.

243

And now, relaxed, Adam felt a sudden quick touch against his mind. It came like a glimpse of monstrous black wings overhead, foreshadowing some danger.

If Merit perceived the dark passage, she gave no sign; she and Vito were horseplaying like happy newly weds beside the fire. But Ray stood up, and with a beckoning motion of his head got Adam to walk away from the fire with him.

Once out of sight of the clearing where the four of them had camped, on a supposed vacation, Ray stopped, looking Adam in the eye. "By this time tomorrow, we must be ready to move."

"As soon as that."

"As soon as that." Ray was brisk and businesslike. "Are you with me?"

Adam shook his head. "I'm keeping up so far." His tone was almost plaintive.

Ray grinned and clapped him on the shoulder. *Like the old days, playing some game at Doc's.* The message came through plainly, without spoken words. "Good enough. Right now, jump with me into Stem City, okay? Let me guide."

Adam nodded and turned his back on Ray, who was standing just out of physical reach. They had taught him teleportation theory; they had held him back, so far, from the brink of actual movement. This would be the first time—if it worked—

Adam let the wall of trees before him slide out of focus in his eyes. His vision, his attention, came to be centered somewhere else—

—he felt the premonitory aura, stronger than it had ever been in practice—

—and then before his eyes there was a different wall, the interior surface of some building. They had arrived.

"A hotel room I use," said Ray. It was a cheap hotel, Adam decided; the small room was piled with loaded camping packs, canteens, axes, knives, arrows, enough to set up a small wilderness outfitting company. "Help me decide what to take to the Ringwall, Ad. We might be several days there, though I doubt it's going to take that long... something wrong?"

Adam drew a deep breath. "Just that your confidence strikes me as a touch overwhelming—you know, if it was anyone else suggesting this kind of an expedition to me, what I would tell them?"

"It's not anyone else."

"Right... so who's going on this expedition? The two of us, and... ?"

"And Merit. I want every Jovian to be there, in the action. All one hundred and one." Ray winked lightly. "There'll be ninety-eight of our siblings aboard the ship above us. I've had confirmation of the number."

"And what about Vito?"

"What about him? Oh, I think I see what you mean. Well, he can find his way from here back to Stem City, he's essentially recovered now. Or, we can carry him along if he insists, and Merit insists, as they both probably will."

"You think they will?"

"I'm reasonably sure. Don't you think so?"

Adam sighed. "All right. Three of us, or four. And when we get there?"

"Yes? What about when we get there?"

Adam picked up a pack, and tossed it down again. Knowing that he himself was equipped with the genes for Jovian intelligence seemed to make no difference in the difficulty of understanding Ray, when Ray started explaining his plans, or rather started actively not explaining them. Adam said: "I don't know what I'm supposed to do when I get there, Ray. That's what about it. I won't know a Field-builder from a fencepost if I bump into one."

But Ray was not perturbed. "You'll know. And you'll know what to do, when the time comes."

PART FOUR

Chapter Sixteen

"If she does go on any such expedition, I'm going too," said Vito Ling, speaking very firmly. There was in Vito's attitude a strong mixture of you're-all-crazy-but-I'm-going-to-humor-you, along with a good measure of grudging respect: some of the three of you at least *might* be smarter than I am, you Jovians have been right before, and you could be right about this too. This was not Vito's very first reaction. Merit had only kept her husband from immediately informing the authorities of the plan to teleport to the Ringwall, by not telling him about it until the party of four were out in the wilderness, with no possibility of quick communication with anyone back in the Stem. Still, when Vito was finally informed, it had required all the persuasive abilities of the other three to keep him from starting a solo hike back to Stem City immediately.

For perhaps the fourth time in the last few minutes, Vito looked at his wife and asked her: "Why are you going, Merit? Maybe these two guys have lost their minds... but why you?"

She gave him a strange smile. "Jovians together, against the world."

"If the ninety-nine others all walked off a cliff... all right, Adam, the hundred others." One more item had been revealed.

"Ray might be wrong about the Field-builders," Merit admitted suddenly, and looked suddenly at Ray, who gazed back at her calmly and did not appear particularly upset by the suggestion.

Merit went on: "If he is... there's only one way to prove it." She looked at her husband again. "And, if he's not..."

"That's about the way I see it," Adam said. Not that he really thought Ray might be wrong, but it was a good way of putting the situation to Vito. And the fact that Adam was convinced and was going along with Ray's plan had from the start made Vito stop and think; he had considerable respect for Adam.

But the argument wasn't won yet. "Then the only basis you have for this whole thing," said Vito, "is Ray's word."

"That's right," said Adam. Merit nodded.

Vito and Ray looked at each other.

"I'd be skeptical too, in your place," Ray said to him mildly.

Vito looked at his wife again. "Then you've never seen these Field-builders, except, as I understand it, in Ray's mind."

"No," she answered. "I never have. There are a number of parapsych things I'm not strong enough, or skilled enough, to do without Ray's help." Adam, listening, couldn't tell whether she was getting angry with her husband or not.

"But you're convinced you have to do this." There was a new finality in Vito's voice.

"I am."

"To teleport," said Vito, as if to himself, and Adam could see how fascinated he was, as a scientist doubtless, but not only in that way.

"That's what we're talking about, yes." Ray's voice was quiet, but held a certain challenge.

"If you go," said Vito to his wife again, "I'm going with you."

***

Darkness was falling now at their camp, in the archery-practice clearing only a hundred meters or so from Adam's cabin. Ray had announced that they should be ready to start within about twenty-four hours. He explained that it would take them about an hour, with several rest stops included, to teleport halfway around the world, and he wanted to arrive in the vicinity of the Ringwall soon after dawn there.

"I've explained the dangers," said Ray to Vito calmly now. "If you insist on going, we can take you." Then Ray looked at Merit, as if the final decision in this matter should be hers.

"My husband makes his own decisions," she told Ray firmly, before the angered Vito could speak for himself. "He has said that he accepts the risks, on your word that they are necessary. I accept them on the same basis."

"I thank you. All of you." Ray glanced up briefly toward the stars. "Obviously our ninety-eight siblings have already agreed with me. If not unanimously—near enough."

"Not unanimously?" Adam asked.

Ray looked at him, as if fearing to be disappointed by what he saw. "Near enough. They'll have the ship in place over the Ringwall tomorrow."

Merit closed her eyes, and nodded. "So be it, then."

When the next day's sun dipped out of sight behind the trees just to the west of their campsite, the four from Earth stood in a circle, packs, weapons, and other equipment strapped to their bodies. They faced each other across a close circle, not quite touching each other.

"We may be temporarily separated after the first jump," Ray warned the others. "But we should still commence the second jump at the same time, if not from exactly the same place. And I guarantee we'll get back together when it becomes necessary. After four or five jumps we should arrive together in the vicinity of the Ringwall—not in it, but in sight of it. Are you all ready? Then here we go—"

***

—and they were standing on another wooded hillside, a place Adam did not recognize; it was still dusk here, so they could not yet have traveled many kilometers toward their goal.

Vito was not with them. Merit, her sudden fear evident, looked around in all directions for her husband. But he was gone. She turned to Ray.

"It's all right," Ray told her, calmly, paternally. "The little feller isn't too scared—I've still got a touch on him."

Merit's eyes blazed briefly in anger, and Adam was glad they were not aimed at him.

The three of them waited, resting minds and bodies between jumps. They had warned Adam that teleportation could be physically draining, and he was learning that they were right. They walked about a little, restlessly, as individuals, but still kept close together. Dusk was deepening slowly. Limited conversation was exchanged. Ray had to keep reassuring Merit, or trying to do so. "I tell you he's all right."

"He'd better be. He'd better be."

"Time to go," Ray told the others presently. He was as calm as ever.

***

—and they were standing in the middle of an open space, a larger clearing surrounded by a different forest, and it was deep moonless night. The group was still three strong; Vito had rejoined it somehow, but now Ray was nowhere to be seen.

Merit almost crushed her husband hugging him, crying out softly in her relief. Then the three exchanged whispered information. Vito had spent his time of separation from the others in almost total darkness. Except that he had been under trees somewhere, evidently in a forest, he could offer no intelligent opinion as to where he had been, or how far from the others.

Overhead, the Galaxy sprawled across a velvet sky. From the position of the constellations Adam estimated the local time at about two hours after sunset. That meant that they were well on their way around the planet, standing now on Golden's surface at a point much farther from Stem City than any other Earth visitors had ever reached.

Vito was fumbling with something in the dark. Then he announced: "We're still in the Field here. Just as I was on my solo side trip. I thought we might strike a pocket of normality under the Field somewhere. Theoretical possibility, but we haven't come to it yet."

Adam whispered to Merit: "How long will we wait here, do you think?"

"Maybe as long as half an hour. I don't think the next jump can be delayed more than that—Adam?"

"What?"

"Did Ray show you—anything of the Field-builders, as he did me?"

"No. He evidently couldn't—I'm not able to see into his mind that clearly."

"He showed me. If he's right, well, what we're doing is more important than—almost more important than we can imagine."

"Great." Vito sounded more impatient than impressed. "Is that the sea I smell?"

They all sniffed the air. There was a certain alien tang; none of them could be sure if salt water was a component.

Adam said: "But we can't be far from the sea now, anyway. Do you think we'll make the other coast in one more jump, or will it be an island?"

"There's no way to be sure," said Merit.

Adam could feel an inner tide rising, an oncoming aura of teleportation. He opened his mouth to speak, but there was no time to speak. Then the ground dropped out from under Adam's feet, and he lost his surroundings in the darkness. He was aware, for just a moment, of a strong, cool wind blowing in his face from out of the continuing darkness, as he fell feet first through empty night.

And then he splashed into salt water, deep and rough.

He fought his way back to the surface, swimming desperately to keep afloat against the weight of pack and weapons. The pattern of the icy stars told his racing mind that the time here was near midnight, and that in turn meant that he must be somewhere near the middle of a great ocean.

Parapsych theory to the contrary, there seemed to be nothing to prevent his drowning here as a direct result of his teleportation. Adam slipped out of his pack straps, abandoned bow and quiver to the sea, and let the belt that held his knife and hatchet sink away from him. There was no choice.

The water was almost comfortably warm. At least it felt considerably warmer than the air, and now, relieved of his burden of equipment, Adam could swim quite easily. There was no need, at least as yet, to shed his boots. They were lightweight and non-absorbent, Space Force surplus like some of the rest of his clothing.

From moment to moment he expected to be rescued from the sea by another teleporting jump. But the usual premonitory sensation did not come to him, and no jump happened. Did that indicate that even in the middle of the ocean he was really not in serious danger? So Ray had reassured him. Adam wouldn't have cared to bet on it. But now he had no choice.

Adam bobbed about in moderate waves, turning to look and listen in every direction. He tried to keep a screen blank in his mind, ready for any telepathic message that might be sent his way. He called out vocally, but got no answer.

At first the night around him had appeared featureless. But as his eyes adjusted more fully to the dark, he thought he saw, in one direction, a dark mass at the horizon, blotting out stars in the lowest part of the sky. Having no other plan to follow, Adam paddled toward the blot. Still really expecting to be teleported away at any moment, he took his time, coasting relaxed face down in the water for long seconds, then coming up for a quick breath and a lunging stroke with arms and legs.

It was impossible to judge the distance of the land ahead. If indeed it was land—it still might be clouds, for all he knew. Whatever it was, Adam swam on toward it, through the alien sea and night, each moment half-expecting the next teleportation jump to whisk him away.

The stars informed him that something like an hour of steady swimming had passed, before he felt completely sure that the dark mass was solid and that he was definitely closer to it. Then almost at once he heard the sound of gentle waves on a beach, and touched sand with his feet.

He had been in excellent physical shape and well rested when the teleporting started, and the swim had not really tired him. With hardly a pause for rest, Adam walked up out of the water onto a sand spit which curved away toward a greater land mass, his original dark target bulk. There were no lights to be seen ahead, nothing but featureless darkness. Staring through the darkness, Adam tried to formulate a plan.

He was beginning to grow worried. He should have been swept away many minutes ago, together with his fellow Jovians, in another teleporting jump. But he had not been swept away. Something might have gone wrong. The telepathic world was dark and cloudy too, as far as his own limited, half-developed powers could show it to him.

It was borne in on him how much he was dependent on the others, on Ray especially. Too dependent. There was no help for it, but Adam didn't like it. He was going to have to develop his own powers.

Now was not the time to start on that. Still it was not in a planeteer's nature to just sit and wait and hope for the best— nor was it in a Jovian's nature, Adam told himself. He began to walk slowly and cautiously along the narrow curving spit of sand toward the dark amorphous mass ahead. He tried to probe ahead with his mind, willing to settle for a minimum, for the foreknowledge of a few meters of space, a few seconds of time. Even this modest effort failed.

Slowly the dark blur resolved itself. An island gradually grew and widened and took shape around Adam as he advanced. There were many trees, sheltering pools of deeper blackness. He could not guess at the island's size. For all that he could see, it might have been some portion of a mainland; but he was still sure that he was somewhere near midocean.

His steps slowed as the darkness thickened. The only artificial light he had with him was matches, and he feared they might only reveal him without letting him see much of his environment. He decided that it would after all be best to find some kind of hiding place in which to wait for daybreak. Then, when he could see, he would cope with the situation as best he could, assuming that teleportation had still not swept him on.

Adam was moving forward, one cautious step at a time, under a thick growth of trees, when the stench hit him. The overpoweringly evil smell came at him in a wave, as suddenly as if some huge beast with bad teeth that yawned in the midnight darkness immediately in front of him.

But it was not really the odor of rottenness, though it was just as bad. It was not only repugnant but totally strange. It stopped Adam in his tracks, and sent him centimetering his way cautiously backward.

And then there was a voice out of the darkness ahead, a kind of voice that formed words, though it was otherwise an utterly inhuman, belching sound.

"Earthman," it said, creating words in the common language of Earth, carving them out in a strange heavy accent. "Earthman, I like to think about your kind."

"Uh—uh—" Adam stuttered; he nearly fell. An impulse to giggle fought within him against an even stronger urge to turn and run. Planeteering training won out, and he neither ran nor fell into hysterics, but only backed away another step, his arms rising automatically to a defensive position.

Talk, his training urged him. If someone on a strange world spoke to a planeteer, the planeteer was supposed to answer.

Adam replied: "You like to think of us? Why?" He experienced a trivial satisfaction at the steadiness of his voice.

The voice came again. "Why? I marvel at your grasping of the small. And why do you kill each other with such enthusiasm?" The basso barking, belching at him out of the night had a tympanic sound, like the deepest roar of a lion. Still Adam was able to sense nothing else about the speaker, except the smell—the smell was gradually fading, and perhaps it did not really belong to him, or her, or it.

"I'm not sure why we do these things," Adam temporized. "What do you want of me?"

"You have come to an island where I am. Do you know why you have come here?" There was a pause, just long enough for Adam to have forced in an answer if he had had one ready. "Then follow me," the voice commanded.

There was a receding sound. Adam's imagination, trying to match that sound convincingly with something in the physical world, could picture nothing more likely than a hollow metal drum, being dragged away forcefully through dense thorny bushes.

Adam hesitated only briefly; then with a mental shrug he followed the sound, walking with slow lightless caution through the almost perfect darkness under the trees. Within a few strides, at approximately the location from which the voice had spoken to him, he stepped on something that quivered and scattered like small hard living creatures under his boots. A wave of the strange ugly odor rose overpoweringly about him, only to fade quickly as he moved on.

Under the trees Adam encountered neither thorn bushes nor metal drums, nor anything remotely like them. The ground was level and largely barren. The sound led him on steadily, at an easy pace. Adam paced cautiously after its maker through the darkness, sensing the tree trunks only just in time to avoid bumping into them.

Soon the source of the sound changed the direction of its movement sharply. Adam followed the change, and soon after that bumped up against a wall of something that felt like sandstone. His groping hands told him that the wall was no more than chest high, but thicker than he could reach across.

His guide seemed to be following the wall now, moving to the right.

After a few more turns, all made following the windings of the wall, Adam saw a yellowish light ahead. At about the same time, he and his guide emerged from under the trees. The starlight showed him the being he was following, but only as a vague shape, the size of a man perhaps. It was ten meters or so ahead of him and moving quite close to the ground. Whatever it might be, it was not a human of the primate theme.

The yellow glow ahead was coming from inside a one-story building. The structure was of a simple, flat-roofed design, with doorways and windows open to the tropic night. It appeared to be constructed of the same rough stone as the low wall. There was a gateway in the wall, and they passed through it, Adam still following his guide, toward the building's largest doorway.

"Go inside," said the tympanic voice of Adam's guide, who had stopped at a little distance to one side. "Go inside and look. I want to see what effect on your parapsych theories is had by the sight of a possible result. Did I phrase that correctly? I am not one who knows your speech behavior well. But go and look. Be my fellow scientist, hey?"

Adam walked toward the open doorway at the center of the low building. Inside he could see a large, plain, stone-walled room, illuminated by the bright yellow glow that was coming from no visible source. The room contained nothing but a large, open pit or tank sunk into the middle of the floor and defended by a circular low wall.

The sight of a possible result. The Field-builders' torture chamber, or one of them. Adam paused in the doorway, intuition whispering to him that in this room he was going to find the half-alive remains of Alexander Golden.

He didn't want to see that. He hoped more fiercely than ever that the next teleportation jump would quickly come, come now, and take him out of this. But he made himself cross the floor to the low wall around the tank, and look over the wall and down.

***

"They came in past the robot picket ships ten hours ago," said General Lorsch. For the first time in many days there was no tiredness in her voice. Her electronic pointer flashed as it marked the location of the sighting on the holographic model of the space around Golden. Around her the small, dimly lighted briefing room on the command deck of the flagship was quiet, the small group of people who filled it listening intently.

"The pickets have been following them," the General went on, "and no doubt they are aware of that. Now they're within fifteen hundred kilometers of planet surface, and holding position there. We're going to surround them as best we can with our three manned ships, and then we're going to ask them some questions. Yes, Colonel, what is it?"

Brazil stood up in the small group of senior officers present. "Ma'am, is an arrest certain?"

Lorsch paused for just a second before answering. "I'd say almost certain. This is the Jovian ship, and it's illegal; we can't have people jaunting anywhere they like in starships, involving all humanity in God knows what.

"I don't know if the Jovians intend to resist arrest. We don't know what weapons they may have. Considering their abilities, maybe something very new and very good." She looked around her solemnly. "We'll be three ships to one, but, frankly, this operation may develop into a battle. We must be ready for that."

Another officer stood up. "Boarding parties, ma'am, I presume?"

"Correct. Colonel Brazil is going to be in command of that part of the operation. Colonel, I want you to me right after this meeting."

Me and my hotshot record, Boris thought, sitting down again.

***

Adam stood looking down into the tank, feeling a kind of strained, puzzled relief, an anticlimax. Five meters below, an amphibious beast of a kind that he had never seen before splashed and wallowed in shallow water. There was nothing in the appearance of the beast to connect it with Alexander Golden, or indeed with humanity in any way; rather it looked vaguely like a seal. Assuming that the creature was native to Golden, it was hardly surprising that Adam had never encountered a member of its species before. Golden was after all an Earth-sized world, and he was standing in a hemisphere of that world that had never before been explored by Earth-descended humans.

There was a tiny splash in the water, just beside the seal-like creature. And then another splash and then another. Something, a slow hail of small objects, was falling into the tank.

Adam looked up at a blank stone ceiling, close above. He could see the tiny objects materializing in the air now, a thin rain of them, looking like pebbles, coming out of the air under the low ceiling to fall and patter around the thing living in the tank. Suddenly, like an animated rubber toy, the creature stretched its body completely out of its old shape and into a new one, altering its form completely into something like that of an octopus. Still it never at any stage of the change looked anything like Alexander Golden, or any other human being of Earth.

"Observe classic symptom of falling stones," boomed the guide's voice, from somewhere in the darkness outside the building. "But do you not detect the sickness? I thought you were a sensitive, teleporting as you were."

Adam turned to face the wide dark open doorway. All he could think of was to try to change the subject. In his growing state of shock, ingrained planteering methods won out again. "Will you tell me your name?" he asked.

"I am studying you, not the other way around. Co-operation, please."

"I only want to—"

Afterward Adam could not remember just what he had meant to say he wanted. He found himself sitting on the stone floor, with his back against the low wall that guarded the tank, and with no idea of how long he had been sitting there. He felt no pain and had no memory of any, but the feeling that he had driven his will into some analog of a stone wall, so that his will had been bent back upon itself. The effect was disorganizing, like an electric shock to the central nervous system.

The guide's concussive voice, patiently curious, now repeated its question from the outer darkness. "Do you sense the sickness of the one in the tank? Answer, please."

It seemed wise to avoid further argument. Adam got to his feet and looked into the tank again. No further change in the occupant was observable. "No. This being looks—strange to me. But I can sense nothing wrong, in the sense of sickness." *Merit, Ray, where are you?*

They were nowhere, as far as he could tell.

Could he somehow have missed, been left out from, a teleportation jump?

If Adam's guide was aware of his efforts at telepathy, it did not comment on them. "That being in the tank has deformed itself," the creature outside in the night explained. "Crippled its mind and body, by using what you call parapsych forces in an attack upon another being. Such is the usual result of attempting such use—" The guide interrupted itself with a sudden skreeking noise. "Did you think he was one of your kind? Not so, he is one of mine, and this planet is his native world. Such as he are brought to this island to reach for health, and I am here to help them. I think you came here because of that, and because I like to think about your kind."

Adam knew that straining anxiously for the teleporting jump would not help him to attain it. He strained anyway. He got nowhere.

Again he tried to contact Merit's mind, or Ray's, and again he had no success.

The guide asked him again, with patient interest: "Why do you of Earth destroy each other with such enthusiasm?"

Trying to think of a reasonable answer, Adam for the first time and without trying caught a flash of the guide's mind; a glimpse not of black threatening, foreshadowing wings, but of something incomprehensible but magnificent. Adam's mind supplied the image of a carven alien palace.

Was *this* a Field-Builder? But no, it couldn't be. Ray had been very vague in his physical descriptions of them, but he had said...

Now that Adam tried to think of it, he could not recall that Ray had given any physical description of his enemies at all. But their minds, their minds as Ray had pictured them, were vats of sickness.

Now the guide, with keen curiosity, was telepathically directing a question—Adam could not tell what question—to another of its kind. Adam sensed that other mind, too, for one instant, then both were gone from his perception. Through the open doorway he heard metallic scratching noises again, as his guide went moving away through darkness.

Adam was left alone with the thing, the creature, in the tank. *But do you not detect the sickness?* He could not. Remembering his hallucination on the Stem City slideway, he closed his eyes briefly; the low stone wall beneath his hands felt utterly and completely real.

Opening his eyes, he saw a light outside the building, and for an instant interpreted what he saw as the dawn. But this was a much closer fire, not far outside the doorway and moving nearer still.

After another glance at the wallowing, stretching thing in the tank, Adam went to the doorway and looked out.

The fire came walking quietly around the corner of the building and toward him, in the shape of a tall man. A man being consumed steadily by flame, pacing toward Adam, who backed away mechanically, with almost no capacity left for astonishment. With dim horror Adam saw that the flesh was already charred away from the bones of the man's arms and fingers. The figure turned a blackened horror that was no longer a face toward Adam. Sound came from it, a parody of speech.

Only then was Adam able to react with some semblance of purpose. He dashed back into the building, with the vague thought of somehow getting water to throw on the burning man, or some flame-smothering thing to wrap him in. But there was no way to scoop up water from the tank, nothing within his reach but stone, no way to help. The seal-like creature in the tank still sloshed gently, in water far down out of Adam's reach.

Adam turned away from the tank and ran outside again. He was just in time to see the flaming figure collapse. There was no writhing in pain or shock; the body was simply too structurally damaged to stand.

As Adam watched the body shrivel on the sand, the next teleporting jump swept him up unexpectedly.

Chapter Seventeen

Colonel Boris Brazil had just left a last briefing session with the General, and now he was conducting a similar meeting of his own, meanwhile wondering in odd moments how he had ever managed to get himself into this.

"We're about twenty-four thousand kilometers from them right now," he was telling the hundred potential space marines—most of them really planeteers—who sat in rows looking up at him. "We're keeping station. And they're just sitting there, eight hundred klicks directly above the Ringwall. They won't answer us, but they certainly know we're here. In a few hours we're going to start closing in on them from three directions, and do whatever we have to do to get their attention one way or another. If it does come to a fight, and the General does decide on a boarding action—well, you and I are elected."

The hundred faces arrayed before him were all sober, and the great majority of them were young. They asked him silently: Are you going to be able to lead an operation like that? What do you know about it? How many of us are going to get killed?

Boris went on: "I don't need to tell you that a genuine battle would be something new for all of us. I've been in a little fight or two, here and there. And I did get a high score the last time I played at maneuvers with robot ships, if that kind of thing reassures anyone."

His audience relieved him somewhat at this point by managing a faint perfunctory laugh, and he went on. "All right— let's see who among you had the highest ratings in boarding techniques, last time you practiced. Anybody with A-one, raise your hands. Good. How about A-two?"

In a matter of minutes he had squad leaders chosen. Dismissing the rest temporarily, he called the handful of squad leaders, a much more manageable number, into a smaller meeting to sketch in a tentative battle plan.

"We have half a dozen yesmen available for what look like the dirtiest jobs. So I'm going to volunteer six people, I want you to suggest names, for the comparative safety of puppet chambers aboard this ship."

Wish I had Adam Mann here for this job, Brazil thought to himself. He was remembering that first geryon hunt here on Golden, with Mann in the puppet chamber then. That seemed like so many years ago.

Adam came out of the last teleportation jump into broad daylight, standing almost upright at the bottom of a ravine overgrown with low vegetation. He staggered, off balance for an instant, crashing through bushes of unfamiliar types. The sky visible above the steep sides of the ravine was a clear blue, with a few clouds in it red-tinged by a sun quite low in the sky. The time was either shortly after dawn, or late in the afternoon.

There was a sound like steady thunder, coming from somewhere in the middle distance.

No one else was in sight.

Adam started up one side of the ravine. When he had climbed a few meters he could see drifting, mountainous clouds of spray in the lower sky ahead of him, and he knew that he was very near the Ringwall. The thunder in the air must issue from the vast falls and rapids of its surrounding rivers.

He climbed all the way up the side of the ravine, and stopped. He could see now that he was standing about halfway up the side of a larger slope. All along the wide valley below him, a wild nameless river tore itself over kilometers of rocks. Above the river's opposite shoreline, rainbow-haunted clouds of mist climbed steadily, as if impelled by a rising wind. The clouds were ascending a steep, barren slope, kilometers long, to fog the morning sky above the Ringwall itself.

Built atop that long opposite slope, the outer cliff-face of the Ringwall went curving and angling away from Adam in both directions. It had a look of unreality, like a surrealist painting on a stage backdrop; yet it was real. Flying birds were distant specks between him and its bulk.

And it was not really a cliff face, or at least it was not completely natural. Looking at it this closely, from this angle, Earthly eyes could at last be sure of that. The Ringwall was at least in part deliberate construction, made according to some intelligent design.

There were outcroppings, along its top and upon its flanks, with lines as straight as those of any structure ever built on Earth, their shapes suggesting turrets and battlements. There were calculated niches, and true columns, and real buttresses, appearing here and there along the length and height of that awesome wall. In the blue-shadowed recesses between the larger projections there might be room for small villages—but Adam knew somehow that villages would not be there.

The Ringwall. Adam Mann looked down at the foot of its island, then looked up, up a kilometer and more, at the face of the wall itself. He could see now how a million niches and a million windows of various depths and shapes had been cut into the white or brown or gray rock. There were streaks of pure crimson, straight or in perfect curves, that ran among the openings and marked the joinings of stone blocks whose sides were measurable in hectares. Trees grew on the wall in places, miniature forests less like window-gardens than like moss upon a castle wall.

Adam thought of the thousands of pictures taken from Space Force scoutships, ships driving or floating six hundred kilometers or more above this scene. No telescopic camera had been able to see detail anything like this, not through the eternally rising mist and through whatever it was that fogged the films in infrared. Not simple heat, apparently. Adam, at his distance on the ground, could feel no radiant heat.

There were certainly structures on Earth at least as high as this one. There might be one or two as big, measured by volumes and distances. Measured by sight and feel, there was nothing to compare with it.

Adam tore his eyes away from the Ringwall at last. On his own side of the river he scanned the long bushy slope, cut with small winding ravines, that extended for a great distance to his right and left. He was looking for his companions, and once he began actively looking for them he quickly spotted Ray. The huge man, his body tiny against the backdrop of the river valley, was standing some distance below Adam, on a little rocky plateau directly above the river's edge. Ray had his back turned to Adam, and was gazing steadily across the river, up to where the giants' stonework waited.

Adam cupped his hands to his mouth, but the yell he had been about to utter died in his throat. When he looked at Ray more closely, he saw that Ray was standing firmly in midair, his feet half a meter above the rock.

It was no news to Adam that Ray Kedro had the power to do such things; but the sight of a parapsych trick now, here in the face of the enemy, gave Adam a sense of something indefinably wrong. Was the trick meant to impress someone? The Field-builders? If not that, what?

Adam looked around again in all directions, but could see nothing of either Merit or Vito. He turned and scrambled back down to the bottom of his small ravine, then followed its sinuously eroded curve down the larger slope toward Ray. Adam had lost his weapons, his food, and his canteen, but such losses might not matter much. Not if they could quickly complete whatever job Ray had in mind.

Adam halted for a moment, closing his eyes. For the first time, doubt came over him with dizzying force. What job did Ray expect to do here, exactly? No one knew that but Ray.

And Adam hurried on. Yes, complete the job—or quickly abandon the attempt, Adam thought to himself—and jump out of here again within a few hours.

He wondered at himself, as he trotted down the ravine. Why had he ever agreed to come here? Three men, one woman, against…

Against what, exactly? Adam thought of the creature who had spoken to him on the island, and of the burning man he had encountered there.

If it had been anyone else but Ray who had suggested that four of them come here and attack the Field-builders, Adam would have called it madness. But because it was Ray…

And then I even used what we call projection to present our case, Ray had said to him once. *That method gives me very considerable powers of persuasion.*

Did Ray *actually* mean for only the four of them to—

Adam stopped again. Somewhere down the ravine ahead of him, a woman was wailing. It was a low sound, expressing terrible grief. Slowly Adam moved forward. A terrible buried suspicion was rising in his mind, and he could not yet let himself see exactly what the suspicion was.

He came in sight of the woman, and she was Merit, collapsed and weeping on the ground, huddled over a hiking pack. Adam knelt beside her, to lift and turn her gently. Her face was contorted, in agony of some kind, in an agony of grief, and her blank eyes seemed to look up through Adam to the sky.

He saw that the pack Merit was crouching over was the one that Vito had been wearing. Adam saw also that the shoulder straps of the pack now ended abruptly, in short stumps, and that the very ends of the straps were burned black, as if a slow laser might have cut them away.

Still not really looking at him, Merit spoke to him suddenly, in a hurried and mumbling voice. It was as if she were hardly conscious of who she was speaking to or what she said.

"… he said, the time has come for defiance—of something. He said that now was the time for a bold decisive step. He told me he was behind what they did to Vito in Stem City." Her eyes came to focus on Adam's face at last. "And he was the one who made Vito try to fight you, at Fieldedge. I thought so, then, I feared so, but I couldn't believe it."

"Who?" Adam asked her. As if he did not already know.

"Ray. Ray, Ray, Raymond Kedro. Then they burned my husband to death just now, he and the others."

"The others?" Adam whispered. He added dazedly: "I saw a burning man."

"The others. Most of our siblings, up in the ship. Most of them follow Ray. They have for years. I followed him too. I did everything he wanted, all these years. Almost everything. I had no children. But still he had to kill Vito. Vito, Vito!"

Merit bent again, swaying from side to side as if in physical agony, and a long keening moan, an almost animal sound, came from her.

Adam spoke to her. He petted her and stroked her hair. Then after a few moments he abandoned the effort and stood up. He could do nothing for Merit right now. He moved on down the ravine.

The raging water was near at hand, and the sound of it was loud, when Adam reached the foot of the rock that Ray was standing on, or rather standing above. Ray still gazed as if entranced across the river, at the Ringwall. Ray's right arm was now almost two meters long. The arm hung grotesquely out of its sleeve, the big hand trailing along the rock below Ray's feet like something Ray had forgotten. The arm was stretched out of all natural shape and proportion. It suggested the deformed members of the creature that Adam had seen on the island, confined in the sunken tank.

Ray, continuing to gaze at the Ringwall, paid no attention to his altered arm, or to Adam, calling up to him.

Adam climbed the rock, with difficulty. By the time he reached the flat top, Ray's feet were down on rock again, and his arm had regained a normal appearance. Adam noticed that Ray was also missing his pack and weapons and canteen.

The huge man looked at Adam, calmly and without surprise. "Ours," Ray said, raising an arm and pointing to the Ringwall. "Whenever we choose to take it. And after that, the Field. And, after that, the universe."

"Merit says you killed—"

Ray interrupted, his loud voice riding over Adam's as if he were not aware that anyone might be speaking. "I was wrong, before, when I thought that a greater race than ours might come after us. That would be impossible. I see now that we are the ultimate peak of evolution. I could have allowed pure-bred Jovian children to exist, for they could never have become our superiors. Never. But ... it's best after all that we've waited for them. All my decisions are for the best. When this little war is over, we will have a time of peace. There'll be time enough for children then."

Adam grabbed at Ray, seized the arm that a moment ago had been stretched. In his grasp it felt quite human and normal, plain flesh and bone. "You and the others killed Vito? Why?"

"Easy, Ad. Take it easy." Ray pulled his arm roughly away. "We had to spank Merit, but she'll be all right in a little while. You don't know yet what it is to be a Jovian. So don't try to tell me what to do."

"Spank her?" Adam could hear panic in his own voice. "What are you talking about? Who do you mean, we?"

Had the Field-builders somehow managed to drive Ray mad?

"Our ship's up there." Ray pointed overhead; listened to word by word, he sounded rational, as firmly in control of himself and of events as always. "Merit fought us, over that human husband of hers, and so we had to discipline her. I should never have allowed her to have him, to begin with—but she'll get over it. She'll be all right, soon."

Adam backed up, getting as far from Ray as he could on the little plateau. The river roared at the rocks below, not caring what people did.

Why do you kill each other with such enthusiasm?

Ray was looking at him now with an expression of—well, of annoyance. And meanwhile one of Ray's legs was beginning to elongate, doubling up under the big man's massive body. Ray shifted his balance, putting his weight on the other leg, but otherwise he did not appear to notice the new change.

Ray said to Adam: "Don't look so shocked. Remember, Ling was only human."

"Only human."

"Yes." Ray nodded soberly, as if he considered that he was making quite a serious point. "And he was keeping Merit away from us. Away from me especially. And what if she had become pregnant by him, and carried such a hybrid to term? That was a possibility, you know. Interbreeding is still possible, and the purity of the Jovian race must be preserved. She'll be glad, when she finally understands what it means to be a Jovian. Yes, the purity of the race must be preserved." A shadow crossed Ray's face, and he raised his voice. "I tell you, don't look that way at me! After all, we once did the same for you."

The river thundered in Adam's ears.

Alice.

Chapter Eighteen

For combat Brazil was buttoned into his boarding capsule, melded with the machine into a semi-robot that along with a swarm of others like it had been fired out of the flagship into the sunlit vacuum of six hundred kilometers altitude above the Ringwall, where it clung, a leech among other leeches, to the huge hull of the Jovian ship. Instruments now reported to Boris Brazil, the man inside this particular semi-robot, that one of its metal arms was gone, burned or blown away already and that the temperature of the capsule's outer surface had risen well past the melting point of lead.

The heat inside the Colonel's capsule was still survivable. It was the hole in the armored hull of it, near his left foot, that might be going to finish him. Something had pierced the capsule at its foot, and had come through the leg of the armored suit the Colonel wore inside it, and clobbered his own left foot and ankle. The suit's hypos and tourniquet had bitten him. Flesh and blood had no business, he thought, mixing into this kind of a fight.

The capsule had sealed itself again around him, and Brazil had no time to worry about his numbed leg. Now he was scrambling his boarding capsule, under semi-automatic control, over the surface of the Jovian's hull, probing for some weak spot where he could hang on successfully and start trying to dig in. At the same time he was trying to coordinate the similar activities of the rest of the boarding party, which was under his command.

Until about half an hour ago, the Jovians on their ship had behaved like relatively sane people, talking calmly if a bit unreasonably to the three Space Force ships confronting them, while the four of them rode together in formation around the planet, leaving the dawn terminator behind them and keeping the Ringwall below.

Then a disturbance had erupted inside the Jovian ship. It had begun, as far as the Space Force listeners could tell, suddenly. First there was the background noise of verbal wrangling, coming plain over the communications channel open between the ships. Then there were sounds of some more violent trouble.

It began with one voice, that was heard over the radio channel for the first time as it broke into a wrangle over space law and the rights of travelers, crying jubilantly: "We've done it, we've killed with our minds alone!"

Then protest, from other voices, equally fierce and sudden: "It's wrong!"

"And what of the reaction, have you thought of that?"

But the protestors had been obviously a minority aboard the Jovian, for they were shouted down. Then pandemonium. They had forgotten to turn off their radio transmitter over there, or they had scorned to do so, or else they had deliberately wanted the human world to hear. To Boris and other outsiders listening, it was as if everyone aboard the Jovian ship had suddenly got drunk, or gone mad.

"For the purity of the race!" one voice, a woman's, had cried out from there, exultantly. And on that note the Jovians, or their prevailing majority, had started the firefight without warning, aiming what must have been everything they had at Lorsch's flagship. The flagship was hurled a hundred and fifty kilometers away, her outer hull punctured in spite of ready defenses, and three of her crew killed instantly.

Lorsch had driven her ship back as fast as possible to where the others were roasting each other, and her three ships had clamped on to the Jovian with forcefields, the flagship using all the power of her space-bending engines, so that the four ships hung locked together, like atoms in some giant molecule.

While their computers fenced, striking at one another with their flickering hammers of weaponry, women and men huddled in their cocoons of metal and padding, waiting for computers to present them with the next decision that could be made slowly enough for humans to have competency.

General Lorsch made one such decision, and the boarding party was launched, led by yesmen in the first six capsules. The Jovians' smaller weapons picked out and destroyed the yesmen, and killed or wounded the first six human beings to launch, Brazil among them, before any of the boarders reached the enemy hull. And here and there, in a capsule-cocoon that had been penetrated by no apparent physical force, a Space Force man or woman burned silently and perhaps painlessly to death.

To Boris, the battle was experienced largely as electronic signals inside his capsule, and the movements he made with the capsule's inhuman limbs; the gabble of question and answer and noise inside his helmet, and heat and shock and pain. And the gradual conviction that his left foot and ankle were completely gone.

In his helmet a voice said, at intervals: "We're holding, we're holding." The Colonel understood what the voice meant: the engines of the Space Force ships, acting as generators now, were standing the overload of combat, resisting the enemy, and striking at him with weapons of heat and force and disruption, powers like something out of the heart of a sun.

And the enemy was still resisting too, and still hitting back hard, but it seemed that he could spare none of his incredible strength to pick the metal gnats of the boarding party from his armored surface.

Each metal gnat was protected from Space Force weapons by its own friend-or-foe radar beacon; the racing combat computers on the big ships picked the tiny voices of friendship out of the inferno of battle noise, and channeled their violence elsewhere—at least, so matters went in hopeful theory. Practice, to Boris, was being bounced off the hull time and again, when something heavy hit nearby, then getting back to the hull again with his capsule's jets, and scrambling again for a hold.

He was bounced off again, more violently than before, and coming back saw on his capsule's viewscreen a red-rimmed dark hole, a couple of meters in diameter, piercing the smooth bright Jovian hull just ahead of him.

"Breach! Breach!" someone else was shouting, having spotted the hole at the same time.

"Thor, this is Bee, we are entering a breach," Boris called back to the flagship, giving the machine called Fire Control the information that fragile friendly human flesh was about to do just that.

"We're gaining!" shouted the voice that usually said *We're holding*—the voice of someone who watched an indication of the total force being exerted by the Jovian. The enemy had been hurt—either that or he was faking, pretending weakness, gathering his strength for an even greater effort to come.

Brazil led his boarding party into the torn-open hull, hoping to stay alive, trying to take the enemy alive. Weapons ready, he scrambled his capsule forward through a slick patch of still semi-molten metal, into the breach.

***

"You killed Alice. You were behind everything they did to her." Adam spoke as he stood facing Ray on the flat rock, with the wide river roaring below them and the Ringwall looking down.

Ray looked at him calmly, and made a slight dismissive gesture. "Oh yes. Your wife. But never mind that now. We knew best. You have to admit that we always know best." The answer was delivered almost absently, as if Ray were overwhelmingly distracted. Even before he finished speaking he had turned his face partly away from Adam, and was looking up at the Ringwall again.

Ray said: "The Field-builders are in there, with their victims—and they're aware of us out here. Aware at this moment of me here, looking in at them... but our ship is overhead—did I tell you that?" He looked back at Adam, calmly and inquiringly.

Adam stared back. Even rage had to pause. "You've forgotten telling me that, two minutes ago?"

Ray blinked at him, as if Adam's question had no possible relevance. Then Ray, as if continuing with some subject already under discussion, said: "It was years ago when we first began to weed the human garden. For a time, a long time, we were too conservative. We removed only certain very objectionable people—the power-mad, the organizers of hate groups and of crime syndicates—obscene little creatures, unworthy even of our true human ancestors. Then gradually we began to feel more confident, and to do more.

"From now on, we will do more still. You of course were wrong to mate with a human female. But you didn't know then that you were Jovian. We can forgive you."

"You—can forgive me Alice."

Ray ignored the answer. "We were right, of course, to dispose of her. But I see now that we were in—can I call it error?" He shook his head, muttering for a moment to himself. "Of course I can call it error, I can say whatever I like..."

He looked closely again at Adam, and for a moment Ray's old infectious grin was visible. Then the grin as gone, replaced by—something else. A look that would have gone better with a long, scaly neck. "... in error, in our choice of methods. Hired physical violence." Ray's voice expressed contempt, and he shook his head. "You foiled the attempt on Ling in Stem City, and I'm glad that you did. The use of such means is really beneath us. *Now*, after we have killed with our minds alone, I understand that... I think my intellect is growing tremendously now, hour by hour, even minute by minute... now I understand that, and now I see the true glory of... of... what was I saying?"

A pebble fell, from out of the clear blue sky. Adam saw it clearly as it fell, as it struck Ray on the shoulder and bounced off to come to rest with minor clatter on the huge flat rock where they were standing.

Ray looked up, puzzling at the sky with slow, vague eyes.

276

The mighty intelligence was crumbling, the godlike powers falling in upon their center. Adam watched the collapse with cold rejoicing, violent hatred.

Adam said: "Damn you to hell, you deserve what you're getting!"

"Ohhh?" Ray again tore his gaze down from the Ringwall. And, for the first time since Adam had climbed up on the rock with him, he gave Adam his full attention. Ray's body came jerkily back to normal shape, the elongated leg restoring itself as in some dream, or some conjuror's trick.

Ray said: "One thing you must remember, one thing about being a Jovian. It is that I am your leader, and I am always right. If you dispute that, you must and will be disciplined. We have begun with Merit. I think that it will be preferable to destroy her personality entirely, and then rebuild—"

A trigger pulled in Adam's brain, sending him two steps forward, left, right, and then the front snap kick with the left foot, snapped faster than the eye could follow.

Ray moved almost as fast, and very lightly for all his bulk, sidestepping perfectly. He smiled pityingly, and shook his head. "Adam, Adam, will I have to rebuild you too? How can you hope to fight a telepath physically? One who is bigger and stronger than you are?

"I think I will remove both you and Merit to the ship, and begin the process there, as soon as the difficulty with the human ships is over." Ray squinted up into the misty sky. "That should be soon." He turned his back on Adam again to gaze up at the Ringwall. "Later I can return to deal with the—creatures—who live there." Without looking Ray dodged Adam's chop at the back of his neck. Then the huge man spun around, avoiding a driving knee, and swung.

Adam saw the enormous fist coming at him, and thought he had it ducked, but it seemed to swing lower, following the movement of his head. There was a flash in his head and his consciousness was gone—

—for what must have been only a second or two; he found himself rolling onto his back, hands and feet ready for defensive work. There was a numb fogging pressure on his mind, and his eyes were blurring.

Ray was standing back, calm and safe, talking and talking, delivering a lecture:

"—acting like a human—cannot condone—"

Ray, Ray, who was Ray? Alice's killer, Merit's tormentor, freely confessed, standing there in front of him. Adam rolled up into a catlike crouch, and heard himself muttering the gutter words and threats of his childhood. In a few seconds the cold computer in his head was clear enough, the body ready. He started forward in a half-crouch.

"You cannot fight a telepath in such a way." Ray was leaning forward, speaking very distinctly, as if to a child. Then a shade of alarm crossed his face and he started his dodging motion in time to avoid the first kick and the second. Then he parried the smashing backfist strike with his forearm, and launched a kick of his own that Adam was expecting and easily avoided.

There was not much room on the little table of rock for stalking, the cold computer commented unhappily to Adam. He moved in again on Ray, and saw knowledge of his own intentions in Ray's eyes, knowledge disregarded by Ray's supreme confidence.

Adam threw another combination of kicks and blows. Again Ray could not totally avoid the final impact, though he almost succeeded in dodging it, so much of the force was lost. But the last kick caught him just above the knee. This time Ray's counterpunch went only halfway before he jerked it back, just in time to keep from being grabbed by arm and shoulder, levered off his feet, and slammed down onto rock.

Adam and Ray moved hesitantly closer, then alertly jerked away from each other. Now, whenever Ray's weight came on his right leg, he limped.

A purple welt from one of the exchanges was rising on Ray's hairy forearm. But he was able to make himself stop limping. "You are a true Jovian," he said, sounding like a proud father. "A true—"

He got his guard up just barely in time. Again the last phase of the attack damaged him; he could not move swiftly enough to escape entirely what he perceived was coming. Nor could he strike back with Adam's unthinking speed.

Adam made no conscious tactical plan. He moved in on Ray, and let the years of training and practice take over.

Adam was knocked down again. Then when Ray stepped close to kick at him, Adam blocked the kick with his own feet, tripped Ray and threw him back and down. Both men got to their feet, almost grappling, breaking apart at the last instant. Then they lunged and fell together, lungs sobbing for air, arms locking and twisting for advantage. Ray's greater strength began to tell. Adam got an arm free, and jabbed his enemy in the throat, and broke away.

Timeless and bloody, the fight wore on.

Adam stood watching Ray's head sway back and forth. It was an almost hypnotic movement against the background of the Ringwall, and Adam could not tell how much of the unsteadiness was Ray's and how much was his own. But Adam had to pause for a moment, to gasp for breath, he had to rest. He felt as if a gang had been beating him, though he could remember no details of the times that Ray had been able to get to him.

Ray's head swayed farther to one side; then all at once the huge man sank into a half-sitting, half-kneeling position. His hands lay down at his sides, his arms moving, quivering as if he were trying to lift them and could not. His throat made a choking whistle with each breath, and before he could speak he had to spit out something bloody.

"I must conquer you." Ray could get out the words only a few at a time, with little sobbing breaths between. "Or I must kill you. Can't you see. I am the leader. I am. The greatest. Jovian of all."

Adam could still stand up. And he could still talk. "You killed Alice."

The blue eyes of the superman were filled with pain. Once before, long ago, Adam had seen those eyes look just like that. But now Adam bent and picked up a sharp piece of rock. Just the right size. His hard hands hurt, and a rock would be a handy thing with which to crush a skull.

Ray was trying to say something more. "I—I—if you *are* the leader, Adam—" He gasped, and shook his head. "Lead them well, Adam." He looked up, pleading. "Don't get them into trouble. I—I—sometimes I feel sick—"

Ray managed to lift his hands all the way up to his head. Then he rolled over sideways, writhing on the rock. From the clear sky there came a fall of pebbles to patter around him.

The rock in Adam's hand felt far too heavy; his bruised hand was trembling under the weight of it. He turned and pitched it out into the river. Now there was nothing left.

No, one thing, one person. Merit. He had to get to her.

Climbing down from the little plateau of rock was painful. And after he had climbed down he could not rest, but had to go staggering back up the little ravine. Because Merit was there.

From across the river the Ringwall looked down on him, as indifferent as the sun. Someday, he told it, we'll learn what you really are. But now he had no emotion left for it.

Merit was sitting almost where he had left her. No more contortions of grief, but apathetic calm.

Adam sank down beside her, looked into her eyes that followed him gently, and reached out with his hand. Without meaning to, his fingers left blood on her cheek. Maybe it was the feel of the blood that pulled her up to full awareness.

"Adam, you're hurt." Gently she took him by the neck, and pulled his head down into her lap and held it there, her hands pressing and rubbing the back of his head tenderly. "I was afraid for a long time that they'd do something to Vito," she said softly. "Still when it happened I couldn't believe it."

Adam closed his eyes. His whole body trembled violently for a moment, then was able to let go in utter relaxation. "I fought with Ray," he told her. As if he were a child hoping for an explanation from Merit, for reassurance, for something that would make sense. "He's still alive, sitting up there."

"I know, I know." Her fingers soothed him. "Later we'll worry about him. Rest now. Heal."

Time passed. Adam felt the strengthening morning sun on his back. Suddenly he became aware of two things: he was intensely thirsty, and his cheek was resting on the thigh of a very desirable woman.

He raised his head and opened his eyes, and saw a geryon looking at him, from only thirty meters up the ravine.

Chapter Nineteen

They had one knife between the two of them, one small blade with which to try to defend themselves. Looking over the upper edge of their little ravine, Adam spotted four more geryons, higher on the broad slope, and working their way slowly down. The hides of these animals were darker than those of the geryons of the Stem area, and these were perhaps on the average a little larger; but from what Adam could see of them so far, their hunting formation appeared to be the same. He had no doubt that they were hunting, and little doubt of what they had selected as their prey.

He held a quick discussion with Merit, and they began to make their way down toward the river; no other direction appeared to offer any chance at all of avoiding the animals.

When they came in sight of the high rock on the shoreline, Ray was no longer there. He was nowhere to be seen.

"Adam."

He paused. They were almost at the shoreline. "What?"

Merit was holding both hands to her head. Then she looked up, as Ray had, squinting toward the few high clouds that trailed through the calm silent sky above the endlessly rising mist. She said: "Something terrible is happening—there's killing and killing, out there."

"The Field-builders?"

"No. I don't know if they even exist. All I know about them is what Ray... I mean our people, and... our people. We can't expect any help, down here, from anyone."

"You teleport," said Adam. "Jump out of here. Try to get back to the Stem, or up to a ship, whatever. We'll forget about the Field-builders, they don't seem to be bothering us. I'll be all right, until you can get some kind of help back to me."

"No." She looked at him. "I wouldn't leave you."

"Go, I tell you. I'm used to this kind of thing. I enjoy it. I'll be all right."

"No. Anyway, you don't understand. I can't teleport alone. Not now."

Adam had no breath or strength left in him for argument. He looked back. The things with human faces were getting closer, coming slowly and methodically down the slope in their fan-shaped formation. A couple more of them had appeared from somewhere. They were able to smell the blood on him, of course, Ray's blood and some of his own; they could tell a kilometer away when something was hurt and weakened.

Should he separate from Merit? Not yet, anyway; there were advantages for her as well as for him in the two of them being together. He would try to get away with her down the river, or across it; the water ought to wash him clean of blood and that might help.

They forced their way through a shoreline row of tall bushes, and emerged from it with the river right at their feet. They were in full view now of the Ringwall, towering distantly atop the rocky slope that went up from the far shore. The river here was swift foaming water a hundred meters wide, everywhere shallow and dotted with small rocky islets. Not far from where Adam and Merit were standing, a fallen tree made a bridge from shore out to the nearest of these islands.

The geryons were closing in on the two humans quickly, their hunting formation only fifty meters away. Adam urged Merit out onto the fallen tree.

It was sturdy enough to bear them, and they both reached the nearest island easily. But the island promised no safety. Within a minute there were seven geryons gathered only a log's length away, on the shore that the two people had just left. The animals began cautiously testing the water with massive feet.

"They're going to come after us," said Adam.

"Then we'll have to cross the river."

"All right. Let's go." It did not look absolutely impossible—and there really was no other choice.

Gripping hands, they slid into the water, that was here about waist deep.

Behind them, the animals were entering the water together, beginning a slow swimming and wading progress toward the first island.

The crossing would have been a perilous one, even starting fresh and with no danger in pursuit. Wherever the water was deep, the man and woman swam and were swept downstream. When a sandbar or one of the small islands came within reach, or the stream shallowed sufficiently, they would brace their feet on the bottom and wade again, or grip and climb on rock.

Their lead over the cautious animals steadily lengthened.

There were periods of time, some of them lasting for many seconds, when Adam found that his mind and Merit's were in contact, when without using precious breath they could trade exact pictures of grips and footing and the distance of the pursuing animals. Perhaps it was this mental contact that tipped the scales, and brought them across the river alive.

284

Adam crawled out upon the shore of the Ringwall's vast island feeling that another three meters of river to cross might have been too much. He could imagine no experience in life finer than just to lie on firm ground, without moving, and concentrate upon the enormous job of breathing that there was to be done.

The geryons were still following them, so far as inexorably as death. But they had made the crossing with their usual prudence, and without the help of human hands to cling to island rock. Therefore they had been swept well downstream, and were visible only as a scattered cluster of small dots in the distance, still in the water. The animals' crossing of the river was not yet finished; it might well be half an hour before they reached this spot. But their presence downstream killed any idea of escape by simply drifting or floating in that direction.

Merit had recovered enough to sit up. But all was not well with her. "Damn it. I've done something to my ankle."

Adam raised himself on his elbows. "Teleport. Get out of here. Bring back help. Do it for me. I'd do it if I could."

"I tried, Adam. A moment ago. I tried to teleport to a spot just in front of the geryons. I thought it might scare them off. But I couldn't jump. Anywhere. Not even ten meters." Merit gave a little watersoaked smile that quickly faded. "When Vito died, and the others who were burned like him, up in their ships, there was some kind of terrible— backlash. A parapsych reaction. None of the talents are working properly any more."

Adam grunted. Finding himself able to move again, he got over to where Merit was sitting and started to examine her ankle.

From behind him, a familiar voice said: "I plan to rebuild your minds. Both of you."

Ray was there, seated crosslegged in the air, two meters above the ground. His eyes looked vacantly out at them from his battered face. Ray's arms both hung limply at his sides; one of them was elongating and shortening again, over and over, bone and flesh and even the sleeve included. Ray did not appear to notice the varying deformity at all.

"*I* crossed the river easily," said Ray. He spoke in a cheery voice that made the rest of him infinitely more horrible. "I can still teleport. I am the unique leader. The Field-builders won't be able to hide from me now. What do you suppose they think of that? Watch."

And he flickered out of sight.

Merit buried her face in her hands.

Adam stood up, and took her by the hand, and tried to get her up on her feet. "Never mind about Ray. Don't think about Vito. Those animals haven't given up. We've got to keep ahead of them, till we get somewhere they can't follow."

Merit managed to stand up. She even found a laugh from somewhere, though the sound of her laugh was far from reassuring. "At least we've had a good drink," she said, and hobbled to refill their single canteen from the river. Their course was going to take them uphill, away from water.

Adam asked: "How's the ankle?"

"I can block that kind of pain. And I think there's no great damage. I can walk."

Adam's beaten body had already stiffened from the short rest, he straightened up fully, with a grunt, and looked up the long rock-strewn slope toward the Ringwall's overwhelming pile.

"Then let's start up the hill," he said. "Who knows, if there's anyone home, we might even get some help."

From a rich supply of shoreline driftwood they chose two broken, dead branches to serve as staffs. They started up the slope, saving strength at the start by going slowly. Not that they were capable of much speed anyway. The pursuing geryons were still only distantly in sight.

Ahead of them, Ray sat on a rock, waiting.

Merit cried out to him: "Ray, do you know me? Can you understand me? We need help."

"I know you, both of you." Ray nodded wisely. "I understand you better than you understand yourselves."

"Ray, we need help."

"Against the Field-builders—yes, of course. And it's only right, only proper, that you should pray to a superior being for the help you need. Yes. Only right." Ray's face still showed some effects of the battering Adam had given him, but Ray no longer appeared dazed. Rather there was a look of profound wisdom in the blue eyes.

Adam glanced back over his shoulder. The geryon pack was completely across the river now, and were coming along the shore at a loping pace. Already they had gained a hundred meters or more. He said: "Ray, what do you want from us? Either do something to help us, or go away."

Ray looked at him keenly. "Adam, I want…"

"What?"

"I want you… I want you to come and visit our school when you can… Doc and Regina will be glad."

Ray still looked wise and confident. He presented the image of a leader that any human might be glad to follow.

In Adam's memory rose the events he had witnessed during the night on the ocean island. He let the picture rise, and pushed it forward in his thoughts; he could see in Merit's eyes, turned now to him in desperation, that she was reading it, and he could see that the implications of it hit her hard.

Adam took her by the arm. "Never mind. No time to think about all that. Come along."

There was still only one way to go; animals and fate were driving them up to the Ringwall itself.

They walked around Ray, and in the moment of their passage he disappeared again.

The sun rose higher as they climbed. It burned down on them through the high rolling clouds of mist that here went up eternally from the great confluence of rivers. The rocks nearby, the great angled pile of the Ringwall ahead, the methodical animals steadily gaining in their pursuit, all shimmered faintly in the heat. Merit and Adam alternately drank from the canteen, a swallow at a time, and climbed on, not daring to pause for even a moment's rest. Not when each backward glance showed the unhurried geryons a few meters closer.

We'll make it, Adam thought, trying to project encouragement to Merit. With his imagination at least he reached forward, trying to anchor himself on that approaching moment when they would stagger into the shadow of one of the Ringwall's mighty buttresses. There was no use trying to look beyond that moment, to see what form safety was going to take.

But they were not going to win the race. There was no moment when the hope of escape vanished; it faded away slowly. The geryons were closing in more rapidly, still without appearing to exert themselves. One of their commoner tactics was to let prey exhaust itself in flight, thus weakening the final resistance.

Merit stumbled suddenly—Adam had forgotten about her injured ankle—and he caught her by the arm. "Teleport out of here," he told her. "If you love me, go."

She shook her head, her body swaying in exhaustion. "I can't." She clung to him briefly, then pushed herself away, standing on her own feet. "I won't."

He took a last drink from the canteen and handed it to Merit. "Finish it," he ordered. Then he bent and picked up a small rock and threw it thirty meters downhill at the nearest animal. The stone missed the arrogant, handsome face, and bounced harmlessly off the dark hide of one shoulder. The animal stopped for a moment, then took another hesitant step forward.

Adam screamed at it, a brief volley of obscenities. "We didn't come all this way to finish in your rotten guts!" Now all of the geryons paused briefly in their patient climbing, to watch and listen to him.

His throwing arm possessed no yesman power, so it was unlikely that he could damage the animals seriously with rocks. He climbed again, with Merit. He had not thought, looking at this slope from the other side of the river, that the way up would be so long, the Ringwall so remote. The very size of it had fooled him. Human strength was failing, draining from their trembling legs and sliding feet.

As always, the pack followed. Suddenly one animal pulled out of it, and ran past Adam and Merit up the slope, grunting and wheezing in its brief effort for speed. It got ahead of them easily, cutting them off from the foot of the Ringwall. Blocking them from the towering mass of shimmering convoluted stone, laced with shadows, whose foot Adam estimated was only a hundred meters ahead.

"There must be something there," Merit croaked to him. "There must be some kind of help there, if they trouble to cut us off from it." She was hardly able to stand, and her hands were bleeding from the sharp rocks that she had gripped and fallen on. It would be of no help to Merit if he were to separate himself from her now.

"Come on." And Adam led her on, climbing straight toward the waiting geryon. The beast weighed ten times what they weighed together, and its yellowed teeth were the size of human hands. Yet it shook its head nervously when they moved straight at it. Adam pulled out the knife from Merit's belt, and used it to slash a rough point on the end of his driftwood staff. His legs kept working under him, somehow still driving him upward, slow step after slow step.

"Give me that." Merit took the pointed staff from him. "I can't throw as well as you can. You keep the others off."

Adam picked up rocks. There was always some chance, with geryons, if you could fight back enough to hurt them at all. Geryons waited and watched, and followed, and waited some more. They always waited, if they could, until you were too weak to hurt them. Adam hurled rocks downslope at the following pack, and kept on climbing.

Now he diverged slightly from Merit's course, hoping that the animal ahead of them would be more likely to retreat if they came at it from two different directions. He still had the hunting knife, and he held it ready, out where the geryon could see it. Adam was sure that the damned things were able to recognize a weapon.

Merit climbed straight toward the waiting beast, leveling the pointed stick at its head.

"Wait!" Adam staggered closer. "Let me get—"

She jabbed the spear at the geryon's face, just a second too soon, before the animal might have backed away. Adam heard its teeth bite through the foolish stick as he lurched forward, stabbing the hunting knife into the beast's leathery neck, trying to turn it away from Merit. The geryon's lunge at her became panicky flight the instant it felt the knife. It trampled Merit blindly and galloped downhill, seeking the safety of the pack; and again the rest of the pack hung back briefly, startled.

Merit lay on the rocky ground. For a moment Adam could touch the blurred confusion of her mind. He put the knife between his teeth, tasting geryon blood, picked up Merit and slung her across his shoulders.

He staggered up the hill again. The pursuing geryons still delayed, watching the wounded one as it leaped and twisted, trying to bend its long neck enough to snap at its own wound. Adam ceased looking back; before the animals got near enough to attack, he would be able to hear them coming on the loose rock.

He climbed. Merit on his back was still breathing, and was not bleeding very much. He would stop when he could, and do what he could to help her.

He climbed. Until a time came when there was deep, cool shade around him...

***

... then he was aware that more time had passed, and he was lying on his back, after someone or something had just rolled him over. His eyes opened to the sight of a geryon face half a meter from his own, and he slashed up at it instantly with the knife that was still in his hand, carving the human nose.

The animal screamed and reared up like a horse. As it spun around to flee, its foreleg struck Adam's right arm. The knife flew away, and he thought for a long instant that his arm had been torn off. But the limb still hung from his shoulder, bleeding, and with a heavy numb pressure inside it that was soon going to turn into pain.

The pack of animals had backed away again, and were content now to sit in the sunshine twenty meters away, and wait. Merit was lying close beside him, but just out of reach.

He called to her, but she did not move or answer. She was still breathing. Her eyes were closed, her face was drawn, but there were no geryon teeth marks on her yet. Adam looked for the knife but could not see it anywhere. That was almost a relief; if he could see the knife he would have to try to crawl to it and get it back.

Sitting up, he got his back against cool stone. Slowly he realized just where he was. They had reached the shadowed base of the Ringwall. He knew the great smooth stones around him towered on up into the sky, but he could see neither the stones nor the sky very well, nor think about them clearly.

Adam saw that one of the waiting geryons had caught a little animal of some kind. And now the pack found some amusement in killing the creature as slowly as they could. They never allowed themselves to become completely distracted by the lesser game. Always one of the pack was watching Adam. *Soon, you will be weak enough*, the patient yellow eyes informed him. *We can make you last much longer than this little animal.*

Adam got to his feet, without thinking about whether such movement might still be possible. The packs were long gone, food and medicine gone with them. Canteen still here—Merit had it clipped to her belt—but Adam knew that the canteen was empty. Water gone, then. And the knife gone too.

He got himself over to Merit somehow, and got his one operational arm around her, and picked her up. Then he half carried, half dragged her deeper into the cool shadow. There was a doorway waiting for them there, within a recess and then another recess of the towering stone, or at least they came upon an opening of the proper size to be a door. Adam looked at it as calmly as he would have looked now at blank hopeless walls. Holding Merit, keeping her from falling, he limped forward into a passage that was large enough to let the geryons follow.

Adam followed the passage. He knew without looking that the geryons still pursued. There were no branches, no agonizing choices of which way to go. There was light enough to see the way, daylight, he supposed, filtering in somehow from overhead. He wasted no effort in trying to fix the source of light. Merit moaned as she walked, leaning on him. She said nothing, and half the time her eyes were closed. There were odd blocks of stone, projecting from the floor and the walls. Adam bumped into them and fell on them frequently.

He thanked whoever might be responsible that his injured arm had not yet begun to hurt. Or maybe it was hurting, and he was just too far gone to know the difference.

There were many turns in the passage, all of them with sharp, right-angled corners. Sometimes at a corner Adam looked back, and when he looked there was always a geryon head sticking around the last corner, watching him carefully. Here the animals could follow only in single file, and they were being very cautious. The thing for prey to do was to get into a smaller passage, where geryons could not follow. But there was only this one wide passage, filled with light enough to see, when Adam's eyes could see, and stone blocks on which to fall.

Adam stumbled into a pool of water a few inches deep, formed by a small stream that came gurgling merrily and for no apparent reason from a plain fount in the wall. He drank and wallowed in the pool, and took the canteen from Merit's belt and filled it up again. He waved his useful arm, and shouted echoes at the geryons when they dared creep closer. He splashed Merit, and thought he got her to swallow a little water from his cupped hand. He himself felt shivering and sick and unreal after his drink; he didn't want to revive, didn't want to know what was happening to him.

He was moving on again, somehow, holding Merit up with his good left arm. They came upon Ray, sitting crosslegged in the passage.

"I've thought about the geryon," said Ray, in conversational greeting. Ray's face that was changing in and out of its proper shape, altering, bulging, sagging like wet plaster. But Ray did not mind. He said: "They're not just animals, you know. They're something more."

"They're after us, Ray. They're right behind us." Adam slumped down, unwillingly, his legs just giving out beneath him.

"I know what they are," said Ray.

"They're animals and they want to kill us and eat us. Ray. Can you—"

"No, not mere animals, Adam. I am considering, evaluating, the possibility that the geryons are really the Field-builders themselves. They are the ones who really built..."

Ray paused. His face, handsome once again, frowned lightly. "What was it that they really built?"

"Ray. Listen. Can you get Merit out of here somehow? Teleport with her?"

"You see, Adam. First, at the bottom of the scale, there are vegetables... no, start with viruses. Or perhaps one should really start with rocks..."

"Ray."

"... and vegetables, and then there are animals, and then comes good old Earth-descended Homo. Sap. And then at the top are Jovians."

"Ray, I'll listen to it all some other—"

"The ladder of created being," said Ray in a loud firm voice. "That's what C.S. Lewis—do you know him?—wrote somewhere... but he was wrong. Very wrong. Because that is all there are..."

"Ray."

"Rock, vegetable, animal, human, Jovian. We're at the top. Now I am considering the possi—the possi—I am thinking about..."

"Ray."

"Lemme think. I—can't—think—" Ray's body distorted into new frightfulness; a moment later he once more flickered away out of sight.

Adam stared stupidly; had Ray really been there at all, this time? Adam's arm was throbbing violently. He must be feverish. He looked around and saw a geryon watching him, from the last bend in the passage, watching with those yellow eyes, like those of a dead thing. The geryons were real enough.

The animal stretched its neck forward, the human face as always lacking any expression except for the illusion of pride. Was it at long last impatient, ready to charge? Adam got to his feet.

Merit's mind touched his again; it was as if he could hear her calling to him, out of a foggy distance. *Adam, leave me, go on, look for help.*

It took no courage to say no to that. There was no place in the world for him to go, if he left her.

Some time later, they were again limping along in glaring sunlight. Adam realized that they were inside the Ringwall, because the day-light was much brighter, and around him there were tall trees and tall stones, and towering, unidentifiable shapes that he had not seen outside. But it didn't matter. Soon everything would be over. He kept expecting to feel teeth.

At one point he realized clearly that he was crawling up a little slope, moving on his knees and his one good hand, and that Merit was standing beside him, trying to pull him along. Then they were sitting together, side by side, backs propped against a wall, looking down a little slope to where the familiar geryons— almost old friends by now— peered from among tall rocks to see if their victims were yet weak enough. Merit looked as if she had passed out again. Good. That was good. She might never feel the teeth.

Chapter Twenty

A frightening thought came to disturb Adam's calm. It was that he might be able to get up and go on farther if he really tried. It would be much easier just to sit here and be chewed to death. But he couldn't just sit here, that was impossible. There welled up in Adam a terrible puny rage, a fury like that of a sick old man, against the animals. He would not let them defeat him, destroy him and his woman. He could not. He groped with his left hand for something, anything, to use as a weapon. Like an animal, he growled at the other animals that menaced him.

They cringed away uneasily. But not from Adam. They looked around, raising their leathery ears beside their human faces. They turned and looked behind them, aiming their tails in his direction. Then they retreated prudently between tall rocks, to watch and wait. Someone was approaching from that direction. Or something was.

A figure wearing heavy Space Force ground armor emerged from among the tall rocks, a little distance beyond the geryons. The figure came walking, with steady powerful strides, straight toward Adam and Merit.

"Our plan has succeeded," said a voice at Adam's side. Ray's voice. Ray sat there on the ground. His face still showed what Adam's hands had done to him, but his shape was normal again, as he sat watching the walking figure approach.

The newcomer halted a few meters in front of them. Through the transparent front of the ground-suit's helmet a man's face was plainly visible… and Adam thought that he had seen that face somewhere before. Somewhere, somewhere.

"You're not real," Adam accused him suddenly. "We're in the Field here. Your groundsuit wouldn't work if you were real."

"But my suit does work," the stranger's air-speaker replied calmly, in what sounded like a native Earthman's voice. "Therefore we are not in the Field. Not right here."

Ray stood up, towering taller than the other. "Now I have you," Ray said to him majestically. "Your race is in my power. I am the supreme being of the universe, do you realize that? I have come to harrow your dungeons, release your prisoners, destroy your power."

Merit was still passed out.

Ray's mad rambling voice seemed to be reaching Adam's ears from a distance. *Not in the Field,* the man in the groundsuit had said. *Not right here.* What did that mean? Adam couldn't think. His mind was running itself to death in a little circle of animals and rocks.

The man in the suit had said something to Ray, and now Ray was speaking again, arguing with him: "—no, I am not human. I am much more than that."

"But you *are* human," the stranger answered. "And so are we. Did you think that we who built the Field were more than that? You have a small idea of what being human means."

"I am not human."

"I have never understood you Earth-descended, though I know you better than most of my kind know you. Because I have lived among you."

"Alex Golden," Adam croaked, suddenly remembering. Both of the other men turned to look at him. Merit did not turn her head. She was still out cold.

Ray only seemed annoyed by the interruption, but Golden—yes, it was he all right—gave Adam interested attention.

"Yeah, that's me," the man in the suit said, in a different, more ordinary voice. "The only Alex Golden that ever was. This is my planeteering outfit." He raised a gauntleted hand and gestured at himself; whether he meant the suit alone, or suit and body both, Adam could not tell.

Ray's annoyance had grown. "Lived among us, did you? That's nothing! I can change my shape, too!" He demonstrated. "I can get free your prisoners."

"We have no prisoners. Your mind has torn itself on its own weapons," Golden told him, watching bizarre alterations with little apparent interest.

Adam could feel a wave of faintness coming over him. "Help us," he asked, of anyone who would listen.

Golden turned back to him. "Most of my kind would not take notice of you here. It's not that we're your enemies; Kedro here sees our minds only through his own hate, he fills our images with his own sickness. There are no torture chambers here, except the ones he has imagined. But most of us would simply not take notice. Our minds and yours are vastly different. I think it's only because I lived so long on Earth that I realized you were here now."

"I am no human. And I can do more than you can do! I am going to turn you into a telepathic frequency converter." Ray stood beside Golden, grabbing at the smaller man's armored sleeve. But even Ray was not going to be able to push around someone wearing heavy ground armor, and Golden was not perturbed. The Jovian towered beside him like a giant child, fretting and plucking, demanding more attention.

"Help, then," Adam whispered.

"I've already told you," said Golden. "All you need to know. You can do the rest."

There was a silence. Ray stood clenching his hands and staring helplessly at Golden. But Ray was being ignored.

Adam suddenly pushed himself almost erect, leaning against the rock behind him. Every time he blinked his eyes, the figure in armor wavered, like everything else in his field of vision. But it did not disappear.

"Your suit works," Adam croaked. "So there's no Field here, inside the Ringwall."

Golden regarded him calmly, but gave no other answer.

"So seven years ago your scoutship had room enough, altitude enough under the Field, to pull out of its fall. It landed here, as you knew it would."

Maybe Golden smiled, just a little, inside the helmet.

Ray sank down on his knees, suddenly, with a loud cry. "No! I must be more than human!"

Golden immediately crouched down too, as if he wanted to keep on a level with Ray to speak to him. He waved at the skulking geryons. "Those are only animals, no more than animals, no matter what their faces say. Once—they were more. Consider that. We are above them, you and I. Above the human, there is nothing, or one life-form only. Is there not pride enough for anyone in that?"

"One life-form only…"

"Not you, my sick man, no, not you. Those sane beings who say they see it call it God."

Ray shook his head slowly, slowly. "I am more than a man. More than a man."

"There is much pain, too, in being human," Golden said. "But there is only one way we can turn to rid ourselves of that. And that is backward."

"I defy you, Field-builder, torturer." It came out as a mad scream. "I will destroy you yet!"

Adam could no longer see Ray anywhere. The big man had disappeared again. But Adam could spare no time or strength for Ray, wherever he might be. Adam was thinking, and thinking now was as hard as climbing a cliff. He dared not slacken his grip for a moment.

"The scoutship is still here, then," he said aloud, staring at Alexander Golden. Adam could feel the throbbing in his arm, going faster and faster. The sun shone down on him. He was awake, he must be. "Even if you're not real, it's still here, crashed or landed. A lot of it would survive a crash. At least there'll be a first aid kit."

Golden stood erect again. His head turned to one side, so that his eyes looked toward the open space, the vast unroofed center of the Ringwall. Then he too was gone.

Adam stood up straight with a gasp, lurching away from the rock that had supported him. Only Merit was still with him. He bent over her and slapped her, trying to wake her up; she only moaned. With his one good arm he dragged her to her feet. His bad arm had started to hurt like hell. Good. It would keep him awake.

He laughed aloud, and there was a mad horrible echo from the laugh, and the geryons who had started to come out shrank back again among the rocks. Maybe he had been keeping the pack at bay for an hour with the loud sounds of delirium, maybe this time neither Ray nor Golden had been any more than fever dreams. But it didn't matter. Because, somewhere near here, landed or crashed, the scoutship had to be real.

He shook Merit by the hair. "C'mon, get moving, kid! We've got to travel!"

He got her walking down the slope, angling away from the geryons, taking the direction in which Golden had turned his head.

***

In the middle of a grassy meadow the scoutship waited undamaged, in perfect landing position. As Adam finished the last dragging step, he could hear the geryons moaning behind him, still not quite daring to charge and kill the beings who had fought them for so long.

If an illusion cast a long shadow in the afternoon sun, if it felt like solid smooth metal when you leaned against it, then an illusion was enough, no one could ask for more. Adam was gathering his strength to knock on the ground level hatch, when it swung open. The standard model planeteering robot stepped out and caught him as he started to fall.

***

He was aware of not hurting anywhere—not until he tried to move. Even then, a blanket of protective numbness enfolded his body, thickly enough to constitute a vast improvement. He tried the fingers of his right hand and thought that he could feel them rub against each other. Not bad, then. It wasn't bad at all.

Adam opened his eyes to find himself in the familiar setting of a scoutship's small control room, strapped into the right seat. Maybe the last seven years had been all a dream, and when he turned his head he would see Boris—but no, the robot was bending over him.

"How do you feel, sir?" the robot asked.

"The woman who was with me—"

The robot pointed, and Adam turned his head, heavy skull swiveling on neck muscles that cried out with pain when forced to work again. There was Merit, securely tucked into a bunk.

"She is asleep now, sir, and seems to be in no immediate danger from her injuries, though she needs further medical attention as you doubtless know. I have administered first aid treatment to both of you. Will you please identify yourself to me, sir?"

"My name is Adam Mann." It sounded strange, it even tasted strange as he pronounced it. "I used to be a planeteer. Oh, one thing, very important. I'm a human being, nothing more."

"Certainly, sir," said the robot, unperturbed. It knew a human when it saw one, or it thought it did. Probably its programming included instructions to humor crazed wanderers, or accident victims, when they said strange things.

But the robot wasn't going to let his identification go at that. "Please answer this question," it requested, and then queried him on a technical detail of scoutship operation. Not one civilian in ten thousand would know the answer, but not one planeteer, or former planeteer, in ten thousand would have forgotten it.

Adam consulted his memory, and gave the correct reply.

"I accept that you have had planeteering training," said the machine. "I place myself, within limits, under your orders."

Adam took thought. Thinking, at least, was not painful. "What were your last orders?"

"My last orders were given me more than seven years ago, by Chief Planeteer Alexander Golden." As the robot quoted, it reproduced the tones of Golden's voice: " 'Stay with the ship and keep it in good shape until another Earth-descended human comes.' The type of order is unique in my experience, as are the conditions under which this scoutship landed here."

"You fell, through a condition we have named the Field, which surrounds this planet almost completely."

"I was inoperative through the fall," said the robot, "but since landing I have observed this Field, as you term it, on the radar screens."

"What happened to Golden, after the landing?"

"Immediately after giving me the order I have just quoted, he walked away. I have had no contact with him, or any other human, since then."

"So." Adam drew a deep breath; his ribs hurt too. "Can we take off from here, and get back into space?"

"Yes. I have computed that there is room enough under the Field for the necessary acceleration. The scoutship can be made to coast upward through the Field, on a ballistic path, if it is assumed that control and power can be re-established above six hundred kilometers altitude."

"They can be." Adam let his eyes close; a robot could make the takeoff, if it could be made. "Let's go, then. You'll probably see some Space Force ships when we get above the Field. There may be fighting in progress."

"Fighting, sir? In space?"

"Yes. If you see any, avoid the fighting ships and drive around the planet to the antipodal point—there's a shuttle port there now."

"First there is another matter."

Adam opened his eyes again.

"It requires human judgment to decide," said the machine. "Since shortly after your arrival, a creature I cannot identify has been outside the ship, moving among the large animals that pursued you. I cannot decide whether or not it is human."

The robot switched on a viewscreen in front of Adam, showing the meadow outside the scout. Adam watched, for long, long seconds.

"Did you say 'no'?" the robot asked.

"Yes," said Adam. "Yes, he's human. Go out and bring him in. Lock him in the alien room. You must stun him if he resists; I order that, and take responsibility. He is mentally and physically ill."

"I will obey. Then we must leave the surface and obtain medical help."

"Yes." Adam let himself slump back in his seat.

He could let go, now. Drifting toward a pleasant stupor, he watched the screen, where a somewhat smaller animal cavorted among the geryons. It had a scaly body and furred legs, like one of their young, but it lacked the true geryon shape. It lacked true shape of any kind. Suddenly the creature went down, as if hit by a stun beam; a second later the robot appeared in the viewscreen's picture, to drive off the larger beasts and lift the small one carefully. Its head swung loosely, dangling on the long geryon neck, and it had the wide powerful geryon jaws. But the nose and eyes and forehead were those of Raymond Kedro.

***

Adam realized that he was lying in a bed. He blinked his eyes open and shut a couple of times, without really comprehending anything they saw. He rolled over, and grunted when his arm twinged fiercely.

"The beauty sleepeth," said a familiar male voice, quite near at hand. "And where in all the realm can be found a maiden desperate enough to awakeneth him with a kiss?"

Adam opened his eyes again. "Boris."

Brazil sat bathrobed in a wheelchair, his left leg sealed into a cabled mold. "Howdy, bub. Anything interesting happen to you lately?"

They were in the sick bay of some big Space Force ship, Adam realized. The place was crowded, with casualties overflowing into extra beds. The background feeling and faint sounds suggested that they were in space.

"Yeah, she's all right," Brazil said. "No need to strain your neck looking. She's up and walking around already."

Adam lay back. "You lanky ape," he said. "Looks like you had a fight and won."

"You looked like you had one and lost, when that robot flew you in. In Golden's scoutship, yet... yeah, we had quite a scrap here. We took about fifty people alive out of that hundred. We might even have come out on the short end, but they started fighting among themselves. About someone being burned, whether it was right or not— maybe you can enlighten us on that."

"Yeah—but it's a long story."

"That fellow we took out of the alien room of that scoutship—he's Kedro?"

"Yes."

"Some of the other people were pretty sick, in the same way. I wonder what got into them? All we wanted to do here was hand 'em a parking ticket, so to speak. And they opened up on us with everything at once. And they kept talking about burning this fellow Ling. And a couple of my people got burned to death too, in a most peculiar way."

Maybe this is my first official interrogation, Adam realized suddenly. Just Boris sitting there in his bathrobe, talking things over. He thought about the question.

"It started a long time ago," Adam answered after a while. "They had a plan—Ray Kedro had a plan—that didn't work. As I say, it's a long story."

"Yeah. Well, not all of 'em thought that way."

Adam looked at him.

"I mean your girl Merit, among others."

"If you think that she—"

"At ease! Calm down. Nobody wants to hang her. Unless some evidence comes up that I don't know about yet. It's no crime to have had your chromosomes manipulated. I merely remarked that she seems like a nice kid."

Adam let out a long sigh. "One part of the long story I'll tell you now. Ray Kedro told me that I was one of them too. Maybe he was lying; maybe not. I don't think he was, about that."

Brazil thought that over with raised eyebrows. Then he shrugged. "Well, I can stand it if you can. I expect it'll be a long time before Raymond Kedro can tell us a straight story, assuming that he wants to. The medics have him in a deep freeze. Do you know what shape he was in when they took him out of that scout?"

"I know what shape he was in when we left the planet," said Adam. *I can stand it if you can*, Brazil had said. To hell with it. I'm a man whether or not I came out of Doc Nowell's lab. I am what I am.

And another voice, remembered but already fading: *You have a small idea of what being human means.*

"I assume I'm not under arrest for anything?" he asked. "Unauthorized exploration, maybe?"

Boris shrugged. "We asked your help in the situation, if you remember. I assume you were doing what you could to help. We've got enough prisoners, what do we need with one more?"

"And Merit?"

"I told you, no. Be reasonable, what would we charge her with? Teasing the geryons? Unless something new shows up when we get your stories in detail. Hey, now, about that scoutship—"

"Later." Adam relaxed, closing his eyes in peaceful weariness. He opened them again to see Brazil wheeling away. Adam called after him: "Hey. When we're both in one piece again, I just may be calling on you. To look for a job."

Boris nodded, his long craggy face solemn, and turned away again. He wheeled a little distance, suddenly roared with laughter, and turned back. "I don't know—look what we started the last time we worked together."

Adam groped with his good hand for something suitable to throw, but could find nothing. Never mind. He began to doze off, smiling. He could hear Boris's muttering, receding into the distance: "The sleeping beauty sleepeth again, and where in all the realm can be found a maiden of such courage as to—oh. Beg your pardon, ma'am."

Then there followed a silence. It took no exercise of parapsych talent for Adam to feel her approaching his bed. The aura of her mind was subtle and sweet as fine perfume. He opened his eyes and stretched out his good left arm.

THE WATER OF THOUGHT

THE WATER OF THOUGHT

Chapter One

In the dream a faceless figure came pacing after Boris. Clad in a groundsuit, it groped toward him with hands whose fingers writhed like snakes, menacing and venomous.

No, Boris told the figure, it's not me you want. Those are your hands, not mine. And then he realized that he was waking up.

***

He lay in the bottom of a little two-passenger sportboat with a float-cushion tucked under his head. The boat was pulled into the shore of a tiny river island, and the light of an alien though very Sol-like sun came dappling down on him through alien trees, making leaf-shadows of shapes that to Earth-descended eyes were subtly wrong. The sun reflected from the quiet water to shimmer upward on Brenda's laughing face and her dark brown hair as she bent over him.

Boris was blond and bony and tall, with innocent blue eyes in a rough face; it crossed his mind that Brenda was his opposite in just about every physical detail. He had met her ten days ago, when he had arrived on the planet, and though he hadn't been alone with her for any length of time until today, he had been looking forward to the chance.

Her manner now was one of playful reproach and overlain with just a little concern. "I don't mind your dozing off," she told him. "But must you have nightmares?"

"I guess I must. Was I making noises?" He stretched luxuriously, trying to remember the dream. But already the burden of it was slipping away.

"What were you dreaming about?"

He sighed. The sound was part contentment with this, his waking world, part something else. "I think it probably had something to do with my last job."

Brenda became more sympathetic. His work impressed her. "Where was that?"

"Oh. Parsecs away from here."

"Well, of course. But what happened? If you don't mind my asking."

"I don't mind. What happened was a man on my crew opened his helmet when he shouldn't have. As simple as that. Something got in and began eating at him."

"Oh, horrible. Now I wish I hadn't asked. Was he..."

She had never heard of the man before, and still it hurt her personally to hear about it. "The medics saved him. He's getting a new face built."

Brenda looked at Boris silently for a long moment. Then with some hesitation she asked: "Did they blame you for it?"

"No." Boris sat up, making the boat rock soft ripples into the gentle river. He looked round at the peaceful green wilderness that filled island and shores alike. Hayashi was, or had been, a planeteer, not an infant. He shouldn't have needed extra warnings, and leading by the hand.

Once, more years and planets ago than he cared to think about, Boris had been young and green. Then a planeteering scheme of his had led to the drowning of a number of men. But why should he recall that old disaster, on this pleasant afternoon? He didn't know. And why should Brenda immediately ask him if he had been blamed for what happened to Hayashi? Did he look guilty? By any professional standard he was far from being a failure.

He needed this leave; and an idyllic layover on the way home to Sol was a special bonus. Lately, even before the Hayashi incident, he had been feeling tired and stale.

He grinned abruptly at Brenda. "Enough about nightmares!" And he caught her by the arm and gently pulled.

"Oh, oh," said Brenda, gently chiding, and gently resisting. But her opposition was not very intense, and perhaps would not be too prolonged—

The communicator was chiming at them from under the dashboard of the little sportboat.

With a quick little gasp that sounded more like vexation than relief, Brenda suddenly exerted strength impressive for a young woman of her size and pulled away from him. "It must be important, or they wouldn't call."

She twisted around to touch a switch. "Brenda here. And Colonel Brazil. What's up?"

A male voice from the instrument at once began shouting at them, telling a confused story about a killing. Boris let the babble go on while he disengaged himself fully from Brenda and got the boat moving, away from the island and into open water. He steered carefully around a bend in the river, then accelerated downstream at the top thrust of the sporter's waterjets. A few kilometers ahead, he could see above the treetops the insubstantial-looking forcefield screens that were activated on occasion to shield the tiny colony of Earth-descended people.

Brenda, in shock over what the communicator was telling her, was silent. Boris put practiced calm into his voice as he answered it. "Is that you, Morton?" If Boris remembered correctly, Don Morton was the name of the colonist who happened to be presently standing the routine defensive watch. If any serious trouble had arisen, Morton might be forgiven a tendency to over-excitement. For ten years there had been a colony of Earth-descended humans on this lonely, lovely planet called Kappa. Ten quite peaceful years, according to what Boris had heard about it, and no doubt by now the colonists were beginning to imagine that they understood the place.

"Yes, it's me. This is Don Morton. The defense tower."

"All right, fine. What's happened? This is Colonel Brazil. Start again, will you?"

"It's Jones." Morton's voice had regained some self-control. "He's gone crazy and killed a native. And now he's run away."

Hang on. I'll be there in about two minutes."

Almost all that Boris knew about Edmund Jones was that like himself the man was a planeteer, and that he was spending a lengthy leave here on Kappa pursuing an interest in anthropology that he said was both professional and personal. Boris too was on leave, but only stopping over, waiting for a ship that would carry him home to Sol System.

Boris Brazil and Edmund Jones had started out a few hours ago on a picnic with Brenda and Jane, another currently unattached young woman of the colony. But Jones had a standing request that he be notified at once whenever a native medicine man visited the colony, and so Morton had called Jones on his boat radio about noon to tell him that a shaman had arrived and was setting up camp near the colony's main gate.

Certainly Jones had not been drunk or otherwise deranged when, accompanied by a disappointed Jane, he deserted the picnic and hurried back to see the witch doctor. That gave him less than a standard hour to somehow get in shape for craziness, killing, and running away.

The sportboat skimmed the placid stream, between shores covered with growth just a bit too open and pleasant to be called jungle. Something in the air and sun of Kappa gave to chlorophyll in leaves a greener-than-reality travel advertisement look. Had it been easier of access, the planet might have more tourists and make an excellent site for a big colony, thought Boris. As things were, dust clouds and more or less permanent atomic storms peppered the whole section of Galactic arm around Kappa, making c-plus travel permanently uncertain.

Boris slowed the boat as it passed the riverside landing field where shuttles came down from visiting starships. The landing field was empty now. Just ahead, the colony's defensive forcefield opened a gate in itself at the place where it bulged out over and into the river. Driving in through the gate, he docked beside a rank of miscellaneous water craft. Brenda stepped up to the dock beside him, and together they strode toward the defense tower. This was a neglected-looking building four or five stories high near the center of the small residential compound. The compound contained only a couple of dozen structures altogether, built mostly of glass and native wood and stone, and inhabited by fewer than three hundred Earth-descended people. The colonists lived here, while automated machinery did the routine work of running mines and farms and ranches out in the zones of Kappa's grimmer climates, where intelligent natives were few or none.

The Space Force, with its planeteers and research teams, was gone from Kappa, moved on to worlds yet unexplored. The colonists were people who liked the life of an isolated small town, or they would not have remained on Kappa long, maintaining a foothold for Earth, and making themselves comfortably prosperous. Kappa had never offered them worse than incidental and occasional danger.

But now Boris found half a dozen anxious people, including Brenda's friend Jane, gathered in the room that occupied the whole top level of the defense tower. All were crowded around Morton's sentry chair, watching his viewscreens.

Pete Kaleta, the colony's pudgy mayor, was speaking. "It all looks normal at the silver mine; he went in the other direction anyway. Oh, Brazil, very glad you're here."

"What's it all about?"

The colonists looked uncertainly at each other. When no one else seemed eager to speak, Jane began. "Jones—Eddie—hardly said a word all the way back here in the boat. But he didn't seem wild or anything. Just thoughtful."

Boris asked: "So what happened when he got here?"

Kaleta took a deep breath, and spoke. "A pair of men from a tribe just west of here arrived shortly after you four had left on your picnic. They started to set up camp just outside our main gate. One of them, a witch doctor by his face paint, said he wanted to see Jones—Jones has been talking to all the local witchmen. So Morton got Jones on the radio and Jones came back, put on a groundsuit, and walked out through the main gate."

"Put on a groundsuit?" asked Boris. "Why?"

Kaleta gestured nervously. "He didn't say. I suppose he wanted to impress the natives. Or maybe he just wanted to have the radio handy."

There were handier ways than putting on a suit, thought Boris, to carry a radio around.

The big viewscreen in front of the sentry chair showed the area just outside the main gate. The grass there was littered with bright bits of fabric, scattered wooden boxes, and primitive utensils. In the foreground stood a native pack animal, grazing placidly. Heavy leather straps hung broken from its back; someone or something had torn the panniers from its sides and scattered the contents.

Don Morton, a powerfully-built young man, swung round in his sentry chair, and took up the story. "Jones went out there in the groundsuit and talked to the natives. I wasn't paying any particular attention to just what he said—I'm not even sure he had his suit radio on then." Morton looked at Boris belligerently, as if expecting to be accused of something.

"All right, go on."

When Morton hesitated, Jane said: "I came up here to watch, after Eddie told me he'd rather go out and talk to them alone. The first thing I saw was one of the Kappans outside offering Eddie a drink. He poured it from a funny kind of bottle—I've never seen one just like it before. And then Eddie did radio in. He said something like, 'Hey, better have a stomach pump ready, just in case.' He didn't drink whatever it was right away. He still had his helmet on, and was standing there talking to the witch doctor."

"Morton, I wish you'd called me," said Mayor Kaleta, staring into the viewscreen.

Morton shifted nervously in his chair. "Well, anyway, Jones sounded like he was serious about the stomach pump. So I called up the infirmary, and talked to Doc, here."

Doc pulled thoughtfully at a heavy mustache. "What that stuff was, I can't imagine. I wouldn't expect a small amount of any Kappan drink to have much effect on an Earthman—unless it was meant to be a poison. You know, Kappans and Earth-descended are remarkably similar in their biology, even for two prime-theme human races; I've seen experimental skin grafts made to take from one to the other. Anyway, as Morton says, I did get a stomach cleaner ready."

Morton took up the story again. "By the time I finished talking to Doc, Jones had his helmet off, and was starting to drink, from a little cup. He took a sip, and then he stood there talking for another minute; I don't know what about. Then he gulped the rest of the stuff down. Then, first thing I knew, he and the Kappans were arguing. I was just starting to pay closer attention when I guess he must have shut off his radio. I have no idea what the fight was about." Morton looked at Jane.

She said: "Well, I saw Eddie step forward, shouting at the Kappans. I guess he was threatening them. They backed away; they looked frightened and surprised."

"Jones grabbed at them," said Morton. "He knocked them down behind those bushes there. I think he must have killed them; you know the power in those suits. Then he tore the baskets off the pack animal and scattered all the stuff inside, as if he were looking for something. By that time I was already calling you and the mayor."

Mayor Kaleta seemed much worried. But he had nothing to say, for the moment.

"What kind of suit did Jones put on?" Boris asked.

"Heavy ground armor," Morton answered. "We keep two suits of it ready, just in case. We've never needed it."

"Ugh." It seemed to Boris that things just might get much worse before they started getting better. He decided that he had better put on the other armored suit himself before going out to investigate.

Jane said: "And then Eddie found the bottle, where the Kappans had put it away, all wrapped up. He took another little drink, in a hurry, and then he set the bottle down in the grass as if it were something precious. Then he came back in through the gate."

"What?"

"Oh, yes." Morton had an angry look. "He radioed: 'Open up the outer gate, you fool, I need a rifle.' Well, I didn't know what the hell was going on. When he came back like that, I thought he must have some good reason. I mean, he's a planeteer, isn't he? He's supposed to know what he's doing in... in strange situations. Right?"

Boris said: "Well, let's find out how strange the situation is. So you opened the outer gate, and he came in again?"

"Right. And I opened the little door to the arms room, and he went in and got an energy rifle. We keep a couple of them handy, like the suits. And then he trotted off without another word, heading west."

Jane added: "And he picked up the odd little bottle and took it along with him."

The silent mayor had one hand over his eyes.

"I'd better get out there," said Boris. He adjourned the meeting to the arms room at the main gate, where he could get himself fitted into the remaining suit of heavy ground armor while the talk went on.

So, it seemed that Jones was running amok, with equipment that would make the average man as dangerous as a troop of saber-wielding cavalry. And Jones was not an average man, but a planeteer, with all the skills, including combat skills, of the professional interstellar explorer. Boris was a chief planeteer himself, when not on leave enjoying rest and recreation as he was now. So, it was quite logical for the colonists to call on him in an emergency like this one, and let him take over. Set one to catch one.

Possibly, he thought as he began cladding himself in armor, Jones is still rational. It's just that he's discovered something that makes it right for him to manhandle a couple of natives, arm himself even further, and then run off without a word of explanation. Boris couldn't imagine what such a discovery might be.

"Anything else peculiar around here? Unexplained?" he asked, while a couple of the colonists helped him with the fittings and fastenings of the armored suit.

"Things have been pretty dull," Kaleta said.

"Since Magnuson disappeared," said Doc. When Boris looked at him, he amplified: "An anthropologist, named Emanuel Magnuson. Used to work for the Space Force, spent most of his time out in the hills near Great Lake. He was supposed to leave when the last of the Space Force people pulled out, but instead he vanished. Looked like some carnivore probably got him."

"But you weren't sure?" Boris probed. "Could the Kappans have done him in?"

"We've always kept on good terms with them," said Mayor Kaleta, looking at Doc. "The Space Force seemed to be satisfied that Magnuson was killed by animals."

Doc, squatting to work on one of Boris's boots, contrived to shrug. "Maybe they were. He was a strange one. He'd argue his theories... there, how's that feel?"

"Okay." Boris brought an arm in from one suit sleeve and fastened his helmet from the inside. Then, checking his breathing apparatus as he went, he headed for the outer gate. For all the suit's weight and bulk, walking in it was easier than without it. Its limbs, powered by a tiny hydrogen fusion power lamp, were driven by servomechanisms that followed the movements of the wearer.

As he passed the door to the arms room Boris stepped in, took down the remaining energy rifle, and checked the charge. Such a weapon was effective at close range even against heavy groundsuit armor. If it should ever come to that.

When the main gate shimmered open for him, Boris went out and saw the scattered Kappan goods, and the grazing, phlegmatic animal. It would be nice, he thought, to find tracks indicating that the two Kappans had departed the area at a speed impossible for seriously injured men, and to find Jones sleeping off his strange intoxication behind a bush. Sometimes, Boris had noticed, the world was not nice.

Kappans were a leathery-skinned people, with very wide-set eyes and bulging foreheads, grotesque by Earthly standards of appearance. The first man Boris found in the bushes was quite dead, with the insects at him already. The appearance of his head suggested that he might well have died of a blow from the power-driven arm of a groundsuit.

Boris's helmet radio brought him the collective gasp of the people in the defense tower; they were watching through the television eye that rode on his shoulder.

"That's not the witch doctor," someone commented.

Boris turned up the sensitivity of his suit's air mikes and kept on searching, holding the rifle ready with the safety off. When he had moved on a few more meters he caught the sound of ragged breathing. The second Kappan had crawled under a bush to hide. The wide-set eyes were open, and from behind oozing blood and witchman's paint they followed Boris.

"Send out a couple of stretcher bearers," he radioed. "And someone tell me a few soothing words to use."

Boris, helmet under one arm but still wearing the rest of the groundsuit, stood beside the hospital bed in which the injured Kappan lay. While Doc worked on the man, Brenda acted as translator.

"He says, just as soon as Jones had smacked his lips over the drink, he demanded to know where it came from. Jones was being initiated into the—well, the Kappan witch doctors' union, I guess you'd call it—so they told him the truth. It comes in trade from the western hill people, near the Great Lake. Then Jones demanded that they give him more of the drink, and when they wouldn't do that he went after it. They tried to stop him from tearing up their goods, but he just knocked them aside."

"What was in the drink?"

The Kappan hesitated for some time before giving his short answer. Brenda glanced around at the blank faces of the other colonists present, frowned, and translated for Boris. "He says, 'The Water of Thought.' "

"What's that mean?"

Everyone still looked blank. "I've never heard of it," said Kaleta, who had just come into the infirmary. "And I've been here eight years, always in contact with the natives."

"Maybe this guy's making it up," said Morton, shaking his head.

Boris said: "Well, an Earth-sized planet can hold a lot of secrets. I'd be out of a job if it couldn't." He drummed metal fingers on the helmet under his arm. "You're all sure that there was nothing in the Space Force reports about such a drink, or poison, or whatever?"

Everyone nodded or murmured assent. "I can check the memory banks," the mayor said. "But I'm sure already. We practically memorized all those reports."

"Then maybe this man *is* lying about it. Or it's something new."

Brenda again questioned the Kappan, then passed along his reply, which was fairly lengthy. "He says it's old, very old. The Water of Thought lets a man communicate with his animal ancestors; very powerful medicine. He can tell us about it now, because we've saved his life. No one else has ever reacted to it the way Jones did, he says; he says he guesses Earth-descended men are just different."

"If only Jones had remembered that simple fact," said Doc morosely. "Well, you people had better all clear out of here for a while. My patient needs some rest."

"Two anthropologists," said Boris, thinking aloud as he walked to the door of the infirmary. "One vanishes somewhere near this Great Lake, and the other is last seen running toward it. It is west of here, isn't it? Or is there more than one Great Lake?"

The colonists, most of them coming along with Boris, probed one another with the quick searching looks of people who have known one another for a long time.

"There's just one that I know about," said the mayor finally. "I don't see any connection, though, between what happened to Magnuson and what Jones is doing."

323

Brenda was keeping thoughtfully silent.

"Excellent man in his field, he was," said Morton, leading the way out into the sunlight. "Magnuson, I mean."

Time was passing, and Boris was in a hurry to get moving. But he had the feeling there was something relevant that he was not being told. "I've got to go after Jones. If any of you know anything that might help me, I'd better hear it."

Mayor Kaleta shrugged irritably. "We're telling you all we know, Brazil. No doubt you're right; someone must stop Jones, or there's no telling what he'll do, what problems he'll involve us in with the natives. Frankly I'm glad you're willing to take the risk of going after him. I don't want to send out a lot of untrained people, not knowing what he's up to with that suit and rifle, or what the natives might..." He looked back uncertainly toward the infirmary.

"You're right," Boris said. "Better keep your people here, inside the defenses, as much as possible. I'll need a copter and a pilot, though."

"Right. I'll see that a machine's ready." Kaleta hurried off.

"I'm as good a pilot as there is around," said Brenda.

Chapter Two

At an altitude of seven or eight hundred meters they had no trouble in following the trail that Jones had left. It ran as straight as some fanatical assassin's lunge, through bush and swamp and an occasional cultivated field, toward the western hills that were still eighty kilometers and more away.

Jones might be napping as he traveled, or unconscious, or even dead. The semi-robotic suit could be set to balance itself and walk, or even run at thirty kilometers an hour, holding to a course and steering itself around major obstacles. With its self-contained recycling systems and stock of emergency rations, it could keep a continuously sealed in wearer almost comfortable for a week, and functioning for a standard month.

Boris to his relief could see no signs along the trail that Jones had had any more trouble with the natives. Any Kappan who saw the suited figure pass would be likely to stay clear; Jones had knocked down rows of small trees that stood in his path.

"What do we do when we catch up with him?" Brenda asked coolly.

Boris reflected that he seemed to have made a good choice for pilot. "You set me down on his trail before then," he answered. "This copter makes too good a target for that rifle of his."

"You think he'd shoot us down?"

"We'd better think so." Boris watched Brenda's profile, which remained calm. Something about the behavior of the other colonists still bothered him, and he shot a sudden question: "What was this Emanuel Magnuson like?"

Brenda's eyes, watching the terrain and air ahead, were briefly clouded. "I think he was a fine man. He was good to Jane and me—in a fatherly sort of way. He was nice. But still there's something so—intense—about him."

"You speak as if you think he might be still alive."

"Do I? I guess I do. I get the impression sometimes—oh, I don't know."

"Tell me."

"It's like a feeling in the air, around the colony, that Dr. Magnuson didn't just die in a simple accident. Though I don't recall anything definite ever being said. Do you know what life in a small town's like? Or maybe our small town's unique."

"I was born in a small town. Under a dome on Mars. It's starting to puzzle me a little why you stay here, Brenda."

"Oh. When my parents died, I just stayed on. All the people are my family and friends. Jane and I are like the two orphans; maybe we're spoiled." She glanced over at Boris. "Sometimes I—we—get restless. We took a trip out once—"

Boris interrupted: "Better start down now. I don't think he can be more than six or eight klicks ahead of us. See that second meadow up there? Aim for it, but when you get about halfway there peel off sharply to the right. We'll take a little evasive action, just to be on the safe—"

The accustomed drone of the copter's engine had suddenly disappeared; in the heavy silence Boris looked overhead to see the jet-spun rotor idling toward a halt. In his stomach he felt the familiar start of free fall. His hands moved instinctively to the copter's controls, but Brenda's fingers were already there, doing the proper things.

But to no avail. The engine remained dead; Jones must have hit it squarely with a jolt from his energy rifle. The copter tilted forward, and forest replaced sky in front of Boris, ranks of trees coming closer in a long hard rush. The machine was not dropping quite like a rock, but neither could you describe what it was doing as a satisfactory glide.

"Bail out!" Boris yelled at Brenda. He reached to take what control was left out of her hands. "I've got the suit!"

Her fingers were already tightening the parachute straps over her coverall, but she hesitated momentarily, her wide brown eyes looking into his, checking in her own mind to make sure that what he said made sense. Then, just as Boris was about to shove her clear, she popped open the cabin door on her side and leaped out.

With metal arms he fought the controls until the steering column bent. And then the trees were upon him.

Bounce and bang. Bounce again, and smash. He held his arms before his faceplate, until he had shocked and jolted to a halt. Blessed be heavy ground armor.

Boris's seat belt was holding him, upside down, among splintered branches. The copter was a mass of torn metal around him; no way that it was ever going to fly again. The afternoon sun beamed through a fine haze of leaves and sawdust, still drifting and settling.

Taking inventory of his sensations, Boris could find nothing worse than a couple of probable bruises. He began to break his way out of the wreckage. It had been a frustrating day, up to now, and there was a certain satisfaction in bashing aside obstructions. As soon as the way was clear, he undid his belt, hung for a moment by one arm, then dropped with a clanging thud to the ground. He retrieved his rifle, which had landed nearby, and saw with relief that it was undamaged—for all he knew, Jones might be coming round for another shot.

Now for Brenda. After getting his directions from the sun, Boris moved off through the forest at a fast lope, toward the area where he judged her parachute ought to have come down. After a few minutes of coursing back and forth he spotted the bright cloth spread on the ground.

"Boris!" Her voice came from above. She sat four meters high in a tree, clasping the shag-barked trunk. Her face was pale, but her voice was pretty good, all things considered. "My ankle's hurt. No, I'm all right, really; I climbed up here. I thought I might be able to see where you had come down."

"Well." Boris allowed himself a grin. "You can relax now, your knight in shining alloy's here. If you're not injured it looks like we're in pretty good shape. Even if your ankle's hurting I can carry you back to the colony in five or six hours with this suit. Of course wearing the suit I won't enjoy the task nearly so much."

"What about Jones?" Brenda asked. "Are we just going to give up on finding him?"

"I was hoping you'd take that attitude. Just let me go check his trail, at least. He might be still nearby somewhere. Tell you what, suppose you come down from that tree and hide in a bush, and I'll call your name when I get back. My suit is number Two—see? I suppose that Jones must have on number One."

"Okay, go ahead. I'll be all right." Brenda started to get herself down from the tree. Boris observed that she was definitely favoring one leg.

There seemed little point in trying to tell her what to do if he didn't come back. So without further delay he moved out into the woods, slipping his bulk of metal along as quietly as possible. When he was out of Brenda's view he halted, waiting for a minute, watching to see if Jones would appear near her. Jones might have seen the chute come down, and he determined, for some mad reason, on more murder.

Jones did not materialize, and Boris soon moved on. Just about where he expected to find Jones's trail, he came upon it— a line of brush and saplings trampled down and bent toward the west. Evidently Jones still did not care a damn whether anyone was following him or not. Boris stayed with the trail for another hundred meters, and then noted hopefully that it had begun to waver. Soon it looped around as if the man making it were no longer sure of his directions.

And then Boris saw a silvery gleam ahead—Jones's suit, fallen on its faceplate in low grass. Boris let out a little sigh of relief, and moved forward, watching alertly—

"Freeze in your tracks, Brazil," said a voice not far behind him. "I've got a rifle on you."

There seemed to be little future in any other course. "Now drop the rifle, and take off your helmet."

He did.

After a moment Jones came walking around to face him, well out of reach but easily close enough for the energy rifle he held to puncture Boris's armor. And the weapon stayed center-aimed at Boris.

Jones was almost as tall as Boris, and built more heavily. He sported a short black beard. More dark hair grew thickly on his bare massive forearms, and from the throat of his coverall. He looked happy.

"Well, what's the matter, Jones?" Boris asked. "I'd like to hear your side of this." He made his voice a trifle loud; it was conceivable that Brenda had worked a cramp out of her leg and had decided to follow him.

Jones showed white teeth, and looked Boris's suit up and down with an expert eye. "No sidearms, eh? That's fine. Sit down against that tree over there, and I'll tell you my side, as you put it. Understand that I'll kill you, if need be, but I don't want to kill you. I've thought of a much better way."

"That's good to hear," said Boris, sitting down as directed. Then he nodded toward Jones's fallen armor. "Neat ambush."

Jones ignored the compliment. "Brazil, I've tasted the Water of Thought—that's what the witchman said they call it. And I've come to know—" Jones paused, giving his head a little shake. "There's no use my trying to explain. I wouldn't have believed anyone who tried to tell me. You'll have to taste it yourself before you'll understand." Keeping an eye on Boris, he walked to the fallen groundsuit, and from somewhere inside it brought out what could only be the medicine man's bottle.

"No, now, wait, maybe I *can* understand," said Boris smoothly. "I'd like to try. You tore up those people's property back there and ran off, just to find more of this Water of Thought?"

"Tore up their property. I did more than that. I killed someone. Oh, I know that at least one of them is dead. But I had to do it, they were keeping me from the Water. You'll see when you taste it. Nothing could mean more to me now than it does; not food, or relief from pain, or women, or anything else. I sound like a madman, don't I? But you'll see how it is." Jones put a hand to his forehead. His face and eyes looked as if he might be developing a fever.

Boris thought rapidly. "Jones, do you have a family?"

"Never mind my family!" For the first time, though, Jones showed a hint of inner conflict. "I know I won't see them for a long time. Maybe never. How can I, when the Water of Thought is here on Kappa?"

"All right, so it's necessary to get more of this Water of Thought. Most likely it'll take a large expedition just to find out where the stuff comes from."

"Oh, no, Brazil." Jones chuckled. "No, you're not sweet-talking me back to the colony. They'd just stick me in the infirmary, and they wouldn't give me any more Thought-Water if they had any, which they don't. Right now, the only way I can get along with another Earthman is to convert him to my way of thinking." So saying, Jones held up his stone bottle. "You will be my first disciple."

Keep him talking, thought Boris. Maybe the stuff will wear off, or he'll pass out. "Jones, are you religious?"

Jones accepted the question as relevant. "You know, I wasn't."

"And now you are? I don't understand."

"Of course you don't. But you will. You will." Still keeping the rifle steady, Jones used his teeth to loosen the carved top of the bottle. Removed, it made a little drinking cup. He set the cup down on a level spot of ground and very carefully poured it half full of clear liquid from the bottle.

"This is God, Brazil. That's what I mean. God's in my little bottle here." It was only with great evident effort that Jones was able to keep from drinking the contents of the cup himself. But he backed away from it, still holding the bottle and the rifle. "Now drink that!" he ordered. "Move forward slowly and drink it."

"If I take any, there'll be less for you."

Jones bit his lip. "It's an investment, to get more. That's the only reason I can stand to give it away. One man alone can always be tricked or trapped somehow, but with two of us, in ground armor, working together, the Kappans will never be able to keep us from getting at the source of the Water. Now drink! I'm in a hurry. If I must, I'll kill you and go on alone."

Boris stood up slowly, and walked slowly forward; he had heard the sincere intent of murder before, and recognized it now. But experience gave no protection against the cutting edge of fear.

"Just let me walk away, Jones," he said loudly. "Even without my groundsuit. I could just walk back to the colony." Possibly Brenda was listening, wondering what to do, and

331

would accept the hint. "It would take me a couple of days, and you'd get away."

Jones only moved the rifle muzzle slightly, motioning toward the cup. It would be plain suicide to try to rush Jones. Swallowing the Water of Thought might be suicide of a different kind, but it seemed to Boris that if he drank he would at least keep on breathing. And while breath lasted, there was always hope. Three or four days should see the arrival in Kappan orbit of the cruiser that Boris had been expecting to ride home to Sol; the cruiser would have the people and the equipment to mount a massive search.

Boris decided to try one last argument. "Jones, I—"

"One more stalling word and you're dead."

Boris bent down, reaching for the cup. He noticed that his fingers were still steady. As if that meant anything.

"Brazil, if you spill even one drop, I'll take the time to kill you slowly, before I go on."

Carefully, Boris picked up the cup. The liquid in it was as clear and thin as spring water, or raw corn whisky. A subtle, slightly fishy odor rose from it.

"Drink!"

As a man threatened with drowning would clutch for physical support, so Boris tried to clamp a mental hold on sanity. He hoped that Brenda would somehow know enough to run from him if he went mad. The fluid in the cup rose before his face, a tidal wave to sweep his mind away. I am the master of my fate—

"Drink!"

Boris sipped. The stuff had an alien tang, not unpleasant, but with a ghost of fishiness. He swallowed the half-cupful of the Water of Thought, and found it pleasantly cooling to his throat.

Boris brought his hand down with the empty cup in it, being careful not to spill a single drop. He tried to brace his mind against the overwhelming lust for another drink, that any second must strike.

Jones relaxed, sure of himself now, slinging the rifle over his shoulder. "Brazil, I'll pour you another little shot, if you like. Share and share alike with this bottle. You don't have to rush me for it. It might spill, and we wouldn't want that, would we?" His chuckle had an obscene sound.

Boris felt a moment of mental confusion; but it seemed to pass. He still had no craving for the Water of Thought. Could he hope to be immune? He would play along with Jones, hold out the cup as if demanding another drink, and as soon as Jones had poured it Boris would throw down the cup and grab—

And then Boris discovered that he was unable to move a muscle.

He still breathed, and obviously his heart was still beating. He didn't feel numb. But he couldn't move. He felt sweat break out on his forehead.

Jones stepped closer to him. "What's the matter with you? Brazil. Look at me. Answer me!"

As if with a life of their own, Boris's eyes swiveled obediently to look at Jones. Boris's voice, speaking without his volition, said: "The matter with me is I can't move."

"Hah!" said Jones, an incredulous snort.

***

"So, you can't move without being ordered," said Jones, three minutes later, pacing back and forth. "You can't be faking. If you were faking, you'd pretend to feel the way I do. I'd have fallen for that. Then you'd take me by surprise, and drag me back to the colony." Jones shuddered. "They'd keep me there, alive, but without the Water. They'd try to *cure* me."

With a quick move Jones grabbed the empty cup from Boris's statue-hand, tilted the bottle again, and rationed himself a tiny drink. He swallowed it, gasped, and stood for a moment with his eyes closed. Then he carefully capped up the bottle again. "Oh, put your arm down," he said in preoccupied annoyance.

Boris's arm relaxed. But the rest of his body remained frozen, save for his eyes. They still helplessly followed Jones, who had begun to pace again.

"You don't have to watch me all the time!" Jones barked. Then, in an apologetic tone, he added: "Look—you can stand easy, or whatever you want to call it. Just don't try to attack me, or run away, or disobey me—or communicate with the colony. Outside of that you can move any way you like. All right?"

Boris's neural circuits seemed to close again.

"I guess it'll have to do," he said. The paralysis had left him so shaky that he sat down and closed his eyes. He hoped that Brenda was hiking toward the colony by this time. Probably, though, she would spend the approaching night in a tree somewhere near here. And it seemed likely that the colonists would come searching out this way in the morning, and spot her parachute and the copter wreckage. Boris wished he knew more about Mayor Kaleta and the other people back at the colony.

"Well, maybe this is all right!" said Jones, suddenly pleased. "Yes, I think so. You'll have to help me, and when we find more of the Thought-Water I won't have to share it with you."

Opening his eyes, Boris saw Jones climbing cheerfully back into his groundsuit. If Boris moved quickly, he could beat Jones to one of the rifles. Boris decided to leap for the weapon, grab it up, and kill Jones if need be. Boris decided to do it, but that was as far as he could get. His body would not even consider a translation of the plan into action.

At least, he thought, I still have my sanity, upon which I took so tight a grip. But what good is sanity to me now? And how long will it last?

***

Jones resumed his westward march. By his order, Boris walked beside him. I am a semi-robotic man, Boris thought, walking inside a semi-robotic suit, that adds up to one whole robot, plus a little extra machinery. Plus a little something else, all that is left of me. Or might the little bit of something else be an illusion?

Darkness found them on the first slopes of the western hills, and there Jones called a halt. Ahead lay hundreds of thousands of square kilometers of rough, forest-covered country, almost completely unexplored.

"There'll be more copters out looking for us, sooner or later," said Jones, turning his faceplate up to the first stars of the night. "So we'll light no fire. And we'll take turns standing watch, just in case. Wake me in two hours, or sooner if you see or hear anything I'd want to know about."

So Jones lay down to sleep; and Boris found himself unable to do anything but stand guard against those who might be coming to rescue him.

At first, the passage of time gave him some hope. The effects of any drug would surely wear off, sooner or later. Probably, he thought, in a matter of no more than hours. But

335

two hours passed, and then he had no choice but to awaken Jones. Then Boris, on command, lay down and drifted off into a daze of sickly dreams, bad dreams, in which he was compelled to fight with a child's thin arms against an overwhelming faceless Something—

Jones was shaking his suit to awaken him. Jones had been on watch for more than two hours, for it was almost dawn. Twenty meters or so away a figure was standing motionless, partially hidden by the thick morning mist.

It's a man, was Boris's first thought, it's a short Kappan savage without clothes. The apparition was at least a head shorter than Boris, male, with grayish leathery skin and a heavy growth of dark hair at crotch and armpits, on the forearms and lower legs. The overall configuration was undoubtedly prime theme.

Standing up slowly, with his open hands spread out, Jones made the planeteers' basic gesture for greeting primitive prime theme people. With a bobbing, somehow apelike motion of its upper body, the figure half-turned away from Boris and Jones. It hesitated in that attitude, as if on the verge of flight but looking back over a shoulder at the two men. Its arms were muscular, but short, not apelike. Boris imagined he saw intelligence in the pale eyes, and then imagined he saw the lack of it. Jones gestured again, and the creature turned and sped away into the mist, running easily, like a man.

"So," said Jones, in a tone suggesting that he was not greatly surprised. "The Kappan hominid does exist. It was carrying something in one hand."

"Yes. I believe it had a rock." So might Earth's first tool-maker have looked, Boris thought, a few million years ago. "You'd say that it was pre-human, then?"

"Wouldn't want to stake my life on it." Briefly Jones had become a planeteer again. "The survey missed the hominids completely. Only in the last couple of years a few stories have leaked out of these hills. The other Kappans who live in this area call the hominids the Forest People."

"Our survey missed a whole species? A large, mammalian species at that?"

Jones removed his helmet and rubbed his neck. He looked tired, but no longer particularly feverish. "Sounds like sloppy work, sure. But just look at this country around here; you can see how it'd be easy to miss a lot. High-crowned forest, very difficult to see under it."

"That's true."

"What we just saw looked a lot like a Kappan human. But the hominids in my opinion are probably a separate species." Then Jones grew distracted, surveying the morning sky. "The trees will help to hide us, too—we'll need that." He picked up his energy rifle and adjusted the vernier for a fine beam. "Think I'll take a little walk, scout around, and try to get us some meat for breakfast. Why don't you get a small fire started?"

Boris got to his feet and automatically began to look around for usable wood. "That was a neat shot that you made yesterday."

Jones looked blank. "What?"

"Hitting my copter."

Jones blinked. "I never saw your copter after it started down. Didn't you just land it?

Chapter Three

Brenda was awakened from uneasy sleep by the sound of a copter's rotors. She had dozed off in spite of everything, after tying herself into the crotch of a tree five meters up, a tactic she thought likely to foil any of the local predators with which she was more or less familiar. The sun was barely up, burning away a low ground mist. Above the mist the greenish sky was clear.

The copter was circling slowly, a hundred meters or so above her head. Before climbing this tree she had managed to spread the bright cloth of her parachute to its widest stretch, making a marker visible a long way off.

Brenda waved energetically. The copter circled once more, then started down to land a little distance off, where trees were thinner. She unknotted the belt with which she had secured herself to the tree, and started to climb down. Sharp pain awoke in her right ankle whenever she put weight on it, and she could feel that it was swollen above her low-cut shoe. Should have worn boots.

When she reached the ground, she remained where she was, clinging to the tree trunk. Presently Kaleta appeared, coming toward her from the direction of the landed copter. The mayor was carrying a machine pistol, and he looked around him warily.

"Mayor Pete! Am I glad to see you!"

Something was wrong about the way the mayor looked at her. "Where's Brazil?" he asked.

"He went on chasing after Jones, yesterday before dark. Boris said he'd come back in a few minutes, but he never did. I was worried, but I couldn't go looking for him—my ankle's hurt.

Something's happened to him, and we've got to get more people out here and start searching, right away."

"Hm. We've got to find him, all right. Here, if you can't walk, lean on me." They started toward the mayor's copter.

"I'm sorry, Brenda," the mayor said, watching her limp as they drew near the machine. "I didn't intend—well, now you're in this, I suppose. There's nothing to be done about it."

"What's up?" Don Morton demanded, leaning from the pilot's seat of the copter. Jane, looking small and frightened, sat beside him.

"Brazil's gone west, I guess," said Kaleta, motioning in that direction with his gun. "After Jones, or with him."

"I don't like it." Morton shut off the copter's idling engine and hopped out. "Why couldn't we have had a couple more energy rifles?" he complained to the world at large. He slapped his own holstered pistol. "I don't know about one of these things— against those suits."

"Are you going to call for help?" Brenda demanded, trying to cope with growing astonishment.

"No," said Don Morton. "Shut up and get in the back seat."

Brenda had seen Morton in ugly moods before, but this looked like the worst. She kept quiet for the moment, and climbed up into the rear of the copter. Jane gave her a hand up, and then sat beside her. The men moved away a little, talking to each other in low, urgent voices.

"What's going on?" Brenda whispered.

Jane was near tears. "Oh, Brenda, honey, I'm sorry. I knew Don and Mayor Pete were up to something. I guess I knew it was smuggling. But I didn't know that crazy business yesterday had any connection with it. And there I was, telling everyone just what Eddie did outside the gate, before Don could hush me up. I thought he was going to kill me, later."

"Smuggling? Smuggling what?"

"That—damned drink. It's some kind of drug..." Jane bowed her face into her hands.

Right now, to Brenda, the most pressing thing was still that Boris needed help. Intending to call the colony herself, she reached forward to the copter's radio—and found that all power was off, not to be restored by pressing switches.

She leaned out of the cabin. "Please, Mayor Pete! Don!"

The mayor would not meet her eye. And Don Morton held up the copter's power key, showing her that he had it. His smile was ugly indeed. "Just behave," he said. "The good mayor and I are going to do our own searching. In our own good time."

***

"You're not drinking much from your bottle," Boris commented, when he and Jones were on their way again, striding up a long slope through open forest. After a breakfast of roast meat, Jones had taken a single swallow of the Water of Thought; he had otherwise been content with the ordinary water in his suit's canteen unit.

"I know something about drug addiction." Jones smiled faintly behind his faceplate. "This is something different from any addiction I've ever heard of. In fact I'm not an addict, in the sense that I don't suffer physically from abstaining.

"No, the effect seems almost purely—mental. I can't describe it. I don't think that any doctor could—or any poet. All I know is that nothing else will matter to me, for the rest of my life."

"How did you come to take the first drink?" Boris asked, and felt the ghost of humor at sounding like someone interviewing an old alcoholic.

"Why, I wanted to get in good with the witchmen." Jones laughed without humor. "I told you I know something about drug addiction. I'm here on Kappa for Space Force Intelligence. The crime syndicate's taken an interest in this planet lately, and we've wondered about the attraction. Some kind of exotic dope seemed like a good bet, but I swallowed the stuff before I knew I'd found it. And once I'd swallowed it I wasn't about to try any of the possible antidotes available. All I really wanted from the witchmen was information about the tribes up in these hills, and to try to get a line on Magnuson. He seems to be involved somehow, that story about his being eaten by predators was never very convincing."

"He worked for the Space Force too, didn't he?"

"Yes. Toward the end he seems to have spent most of his time arguing with his boss. There was research he wasn't being allowed to carry out; it seems he wanted to make anthropology an experimental science. He had theories about reinforcing natural selection, weeding out the unfit. Of course the Tribunes vetoed any such scheme."

"So you think he went into hiding here, to work in secret?"

"That's what SFI thought when they sent me. Now, I think he might have tasted the Water too." Jones looked at Boris. "It's hit you one way and me another. There's no telling what it might have done to him."

***

In the afternoon Boris and Jones passed four Kappans, who stood in a group at some distance, watching them. These were not hominids, but tall spear-carrying warriors who closely

341

resembled the men of the tribes nearer the colony and were certainly of the same species. Jones waved at them in passing, but when he got no reply did not attempt a closer approach.

"They don't seem too surprised by our suits," observed Jones thoughtfully. "Evidently they've had some contact with colonists. Maybe with Magnuson."

"So, what do we do?"

"For now we just walk on some more. Let ourselves be seen."

At sunset Boris and Jones dined again on fresh-killed meat. And again Boris was assigned the first watch after dark.

He had not asked a second time for his freedom. It was not something to be given him, but something to take when he was able.

He would try, with all the will that he could muster. Jones slept, stretched out beside the little fire, whose flickering light made ancient armor of his suit.

Boris picked up a rifle. Experimentally, he tried to aim the weapon at Jones, and found that he could not. There was nothing that could be described as a struggle with himself; it was simply that his hands and arms refused to make the required motions.

At last he threw the rifle down, and looked up through the treetops at the stars. Killing Jones, or threatening him, was not really the answer anyway. The trouble was inside himself.

Boris faced in the proper direction, back toward the colony, and drew a deep breath. He willed himself to walk quietly away. But his feet would not move. After a long time he sat down.

***

Again Jones's shaking awakened Boris to a cool and misty dawn. What had looked in the evening twilight like another valley about a kilometer distant Boris now saw to be a lake, at least six or eight kilometers wide. Much of its extent was obscured by patches of morning haze.

Eight Kappan men, armed with spears and wearing loincloths, stood about twenty meters off, watching the two Earthmen stolidly. The visitors were obviously not much impressed by groundsuits.

When he saw that Boris was awake Jones slowly stood up, making the peace gesture. Boris imitated him, without being ordered. He welcomed the appearance of the natives, on the theory that his predicament was so bad that any random change was likely to be for the better.

Some of the Kappans imitated the peace gesture. Others conferred among themselves. At last the tallest one stepped forward and spoke, clearly, in the language of Earth's colonies and Space Force: "You men of Earth, why do you walk here?" He had an odd accent, but Boris had understood worse.

Jones answered: "We are looking for another Earthman, called Magnuson. We are the enemies of his enemies, so we want to be his friends."

The tall warrior looked them over for another minute. Then he raised one arm, as if waving to someone a considerable distance away. "Wait," he said. "Magnuson is not far. But if you try to use your far-speakers, he will hear them. And then you will not find him."

"We will wait," said Jones. He turned to Boris. "If Magnuson has radio equipment out here, it means that he's been getting help."

Boris came to a decision. "Jones, I don't think you're my worst enemy on this planet. I'd better tell you something. You know that accidental failure of one of these copters is very unlikely. If you didn't shoot at mine, then someone probably sabotaged it."

"So. Probably our smuggler didn't want you to catch me. Wants us both out of the way. Who do you think it was?"

"Probably the mayor. Another thing—Brenda was with me in the copter, and she had to parachute. She's back there somewhere with a twisted ankle. I didn't want to tell you when I thought you were wildly murderous."

Jones turned away, then back. "If she's in trouble, I'm sorry about it. But if my own family means nothing to me now, then how much do you suppose Brenda means?"

The two Earthmen waited, not looking at each other for a while. The warriors still leaned on their spears, watching impassively. Perhaps half a standard hour passed, and the mist lifted slowly into the greenish sky, revealing most of the lake's shoreline. Two or three kilometers away, set back a little from the shore, the huts of a village slowly became visible. The settlement straddled the mouth of a small river and was almost concealed under the forest's edge.

In the direction of the village, but much closer, another Kappan warrior suddenly appeared on a hillock, waving his arms.

"Walk," said the tallest warrior, the one who had spoken in Earth-colonial. He had circles of red paint or clay that Boris was later to learn denoted both his name and his rank daubed round his thick arms, and his flint-bladed spear was longer by two hand-spans than any of those of the men with him. He motioned with it toward the distant village. Jones and Boris started in that direction; the Kappans followed.

Coming closer to the village, Boris was mildly surprised to see how well built it was, with an air of permanence. The houses—you could hardly call them huts—were of dressed logs and shingles, a few even of stone, and stone paths neatly connected them. There was a central building, larger than the rest, which appeared to be a temple of some kind. It was constructed half of smooth-cut stone, half of elaborately carved wood. Boris was certain that other villages of the same or tributary tribes must be nearby; there were not enough dwellings visible here to support the social superstructure that was implied by the temple.

It was quite possible that the Space Force survey, done ten years before, had not even touched these people. The whole planet would of course have been mapped by aerial and orbital photography, but ninety-five percent of the surface could have received no more attention than that.

A little mob of village children promptly formed as men and women came out of the houses. They seemed to be no more than calmly curious as Jones and Boris drew near. The people of this village wore robe-like garments, and their gestures were gentle. They were of the same stock as the eight hard-muscled warriors, but obviously of some different class or caste.

The tall spearman with the red-circled arms came to the front of the procession to lead Jones and Boris through the village. Boris's planeteering eye judged that the warriors were not conquerors here, for they moved courteously enough among the soft-robed people.

Spanning twenty meters of quiet river, a wooden bridge thumped and squeaked under the booted weight of groundsuits.

Just ahead was the temple building, and now in its doorway there appeared a lean and shaggy Earthman, dressed in worn coverall and boots. He had the bearing of a leader, and the robed villagers who were near made way for him deferentially.

Jones halted a few paces from the temple doorway, and made its occupant a slight bow. "Dr. Magnuson. I'm glad to meet you at last."

The man returned the nod almost casually. He was casting quick, appraising glances over Jones and Boris. "Gentlemen, you puzzle me," he announced in a cool, detached voice. Boris felt that the tone contained an assumption of superiority. "You've been walking for at least a day in this area, but you've made no radio contact with the colony."

"Magnuson, they say that your enemies are theirs also," the tall warrior informed him.

Jones smiled. "That's right, Doctor. I've come to prefer your way of life."

Boris thought that the appraising eyes were puzzled by this. But they turned calmly enough to him. "And you, sir?"

"He's drugged," Jones cut in. "Never mind about him for the moment. Magnuson, I want to speak to you alone, right away. It's urgent."

"Why not? Come inside and we can talk." Magnuson gestured toward the entrance to the temple.

Boris, compelled by a quick nod, followed Jones inside; Magnuson came in after them. The interior was dim, divided into several rooms, and held nothing immediately startling to an experienced planeteer's eye. A couple of the soft-robed people were there. Magnuson said a few words to them, and after hesitating for a moment they made graceful gestures and went out.

Magnuson turned to Jones. "Very well. What is it?"

"I want the source of the Water of Thought," said Jones in a deliberate voice. "And I want it right away."

"So." Magnuson hesitated thoughtfully. "Once I wanted very much to find that myself. I should still like to, but... may I ask what your reason is for wanting it?"

"I don't want to steal it, or smuggle it offworld. I just want some for myself. I could agree to any of a number of different arrangements, provided I'm guaranteed a steady supply. A few mouthfuls a day would be enough. But that much I mean to have, make no mistakes. I've already killed men for the Water. You know the power in these suits?"

"I'm not a fool," said Magnuson shortly. Boris thought he was more offended than worried by Jones's demand.

Magnuson went on: "Some of the Water of Thought is available, right here in this village. I'll undertake to guarantee the amount you say you need. Provided that you work with me."

"Where does it come from?"

"The warriors make periodic raids into territory upstream along the Yunoee—that's the river running through the village. They capture the Water somewhere up there, and bring it back with them in pails." Magnuson gestured at some containers stacked against a wall. "I don't really know any more than that. I've made myself a person of some importance here, as you'll see, but I'm still not privy to the tribal secrets. In fact I am in some ways a dictator, yet I am still not a full member of the people. Perhaps I shall be, soon." He smiled suddenly, with surprising magnetism.

Jones was looking about. "You say there's some of the Water here in the village? Show me."

Magnuson's brow creased in a small frown. "Remember, it's a sacred thing to these people."

"Show me."

Magnuson hesitated briefly. "All right. Come this way." He led them behind a stone altar, and through a door into another room. This was a windowless place, lighted only by a few oil lamps on low stone pedestals. Half a dozen of the robed men were here; two of them lay supine on a mat of woven branches, and Boris was not sure that those two breathed.

"They've drunk the Water of Thought," said Magnuson, indicating the two men on the mat. "Kappans claim to experience racial memories under its influence."

It seemed to be all things to all men, thought Boris. He found himself able to speak up. "What did it do to you, Doctor?"

Magnuson's vital eyes flicked at him. "Nothing of importance."

"Where is it?" Jones demanded.

Magnuson bent down. From the floor near one side of the room he lifted another woven mat, and then a tight-fitting hardwood cover. A sunken bathtub-sized vat was revealed. The liquid in the vat looked black in the dim light.

Jones took a step forward, peering at it. "You mean, that whole tubful is—the Water?"

"Yes. The priests here try to keep a stock—what are you doing?"

Jones had dropped to his knees beside the sunken vat. He pulled his helmet off and tossed it aside. Turning to Boris then, he ordered: "Brazil, watch them. If any of them starts to do anything dangerous to me, kill him. Say you'll obey me."

Boris's hands moved to unsling his rifle, and his finger flicked the safety off. His chest forced air up through his throat, and his throat and his mouth made a word out of it: "Yes."

Jones bent over the vat, and there was a stir among the watching Kappans. Magnuson gestured sharply, and said something; the robed ones muttered but stood still Jones dipped a finger into the vat, then raised it to his mouth, tasting. A moment later he had stretched himself out prone on the stone floor, and was thrusting down his head to drink.

Boris had to watch Magnuson and the Kappans, to see if they might be going to do anything dangerous to Jones: To judge by their faces they were not pleased at what was happening. There was a bubbling sound; Boris wondered what his own fate was going to be if his master drowned himself.

At last there came a louder gurgle, followed by a gasp, and Boris was able to look down. Jones was rolling over on the floor, his armor clanking on stone. His whole head was wet, and his eyes moved like a baby's, chasing things unseen by others. For an instant Boris thought that the man had been poisoned, but then he saw that Jones' ecstasy was of pleasure and not of pain.

Jones cracked the stone floor with a metal fist. "Brazil, let them kill me if they want to!" But a moment later he thought better of that order, and sat up. "No, don't let them! I can drink again tomorrow, and the day after, and every day, for years and years." As if his body were a new and unfamiliar thing, Jones got unsteadily to his feet, and leaned for support against a carven temple post.

An oil lamp sputtered. Everyone else in the room was silent, while Jones's gasping breath slowly returned to normal.

His eyes came back at last to look at the others. To Magnuson he said: "There's plenty of the stuff here for both of us. We have no quarrel."

Magnuson was as coldly controlled as before. "I don't use the drug. And you are forgetting those who do, the owners. My friends here will not allow you unlimited wallowing in that vat. No. I told you it was sacred to them."

"We'll see about that."

"Oh, I don't doubt that in those suits you could destroy this village. But doing that won't help you find the source of the Water. Not if you kill the whole tribe."

Jones let go of his support. "I don't want any more killing. But I'll do anything to find that source."

Magnuson moved two paces away, and stood for a moment with his back to everyone. Then he spun around. "You say you'll do anything. Will you join this tribe? I'm supposed to be initiated into it soon. The ceremony can be moved up, held a day or two from now."

"What'll I gain by doing that?"

"More than you know." Again, that sudden, magnetic smile. "Once initiated, we will be entitled to know all the tribal secrets. And these people will help and defend us like brothers."

Jones thought it over. "Might be a good idea at that."

Magnuson nodded. "I'll explain the details presently. But right now, things will be easier if you'll leave the temple."

Jones delayed, looking down at the Water of Thought in its dark vat. "Funny. Now, when I try to imagine the source, I can almost see… a green, peaceful place. But it's like—like trying to recall a dream that's almost slipped away." Abstractedly, shaking his head, he moved to the door and out of the room.

Magnuson shook his head also, looking after Jones. "It's not good that he should drink so much of it." Then he put a hand on Boris's suited arm. "You must follow his orders?"

"That's right."

"When did you first drink the Water of Thought—both of you?"

Boris thought back. It seemed like a year. "This is the third day."

"I drank the Water once myself, and in five days its effects had left me. I offer you this hope; and I trust you'll remember me when I in turn need help."

Boris could not let himself start hoping very hard. "What did it do to you, Magnuson? What was the effect that passed away in five days?"

"I told you it was nothing of importance. But that isn't really true; the Water brought me here." Magnuson looked round the temple. "To more important things than drugs." The smile flashed. "Come. You are both my guests tonight, and we are going to have a feast."

Chapter Four

The calm water of Great Lake mirrored the greenish sunset. In front of Magnuson's hut, or house, torches were set up on poles and lighted. A low table was brought from somewhere, and platters of food prepared. Acting as cooks and waiters and furniture-movers were Kappans who wore neither the warrior's loincloth nor the priests' robes, but a kind of kilt. The kilted workers, men and women alike, wore their hair in long braids.

351

Emerging from his dwelling, Magnuson addressed Jones cheerfully. "I would suggest that you and Brazil get out of those suits, if you want the people here to accept you. You'll certainly have to remove the helmets if you're going to share their food."

"All right, we can't live sealed in forever." Jones's eyes were still distant, and his face had a feverish look again. He had spent most of the day after his drink sitting alone, as if preoccupied with thought. "Let's relax for a while, Brazil."

A minute later, the empty suits lay with the rifles on the ground. Five seconds after that, the necks of Boris and Jones were each ringed by half a dozen spearpoints. Boris, at least, was not greatly surprised.

Magnuson was pleased, but also worried. He chided the spearmen in their own language, and pulled gently at their arms. The rings of flinty points widened by a few centimeters.

"I'm sorry to frighten you," said Magnuson, sounding sincere. "Still, my Kappan friends here have the right idea. You must be subject to my plans, not I to yours. A great deal more than your lives or mine is at stake here. Humanity itself. Yes."

Red Circles, who Boris had decided was probably chief of all the warriors, appeared, and smiled to see the groundsuits and rifles already separated from their owners. Red Circles held a brief dialogue with Magnuson, then issued a few sharp orders. The ring of threatening spears dissolved. Teams of kilted workers carried away the suits and rifles.

Magnuson excused himself briefly. "I have a short radio message to send, and I'd better do it before nightfall. There are nocturnal atmospheric changes, as you doubtless know, that can make radio privacy harder to maintain." He paused, nodding to his prisoners. "Soon enough, the colony and the galaxy will know where I am and what I'm doing. But not just yet." He turned and went into his house.

Jones looked round. A couple of spearmen at a little distance were watching. "Brazil," he said. "I'm sorry."

"That we've lost our suits? I don't think I am."

"I mean sorry about compelling you to help me. But then I didn't really have any choice."

"I know how that goes," Boris said.

In a minute, Magnuson had rejoined them. "Gentlemen, shall we dine?" He motioned them to places at the low table. "Sit down. Relax. Believe me, I mean you no harm. No. There is suffering enough."

With a slave's fatalism, Boris squatted on a mat and began to eat. He was just getting a good start on his portion of roast meat when he heard the sound of an approaching copter.

Beside him, Jones jumped to his feet, shouting: "Our suits! Quick! Bring them back!"

But Magnuson, showing no great excitement, simply stood up from the table and walked away, motioning his two guests to remain where they were. The copter's sound grew louder in the darkness, slowed, and then died abruptly, as if the machine might have made a radar landing nearby. In a few minutes Magnuson was back, and Boris was not much astonished to see Pete Kaleta, a pistol strapped on his hip, walking beside him. Don Morton and Jane were a little more of a surprise; and then, provoking an unexpectedly sharp reaction in Boris, Brenda walked into the firelight Her hands were behind her as if they might be tied, and she was limping rather badly, but she appeared otherwise unhurt. The relief in her eyes when they discovered Boris tore at the raw wound of his helplessness.

353

Kaleta stopped in front of him. "I meant you no harm, Brazil. Or Brenda. I didn't expect your copter would fail quite so suddenly. I'm no expert at sabotage."

"No one on this planet has yet meant me any harm," said Boris. "How far behind you is the Space Force?"

"I meant I wasn't trying to kill you." The mayor stared thoughtfully at Boris; the past tense hung in the air; the stare was all the worse in that it did not seem intended to frighten.

Magnuson suddenly noticed Brenda's bound hands. He yanked a knife from a sheath at his belt and cut her free. "There's no need for this damnable business!" He hurled pieces of cord away.

"Who said you could—" Morton's move toward Magnuson was stopped by Red Circles' spear leveled at his chest. Morton took a step back, his hand going to the holster at his side.

"No!" Kaleta grabbed at Morton. "Take it easy. We can't afford—take it easy, will you? We'll talk this over later."

There was a little silence. Morton, glowering, at last relaxed a little.

"Go ahead, tough guy," said Jane to him at last. "Get us all killed." With a little shudder she moved away from him, toward the table. "I see supper's ready. Are we all invited?"

"You are indeed," said Magnuson. He looked big, standing protectively beside little Brenda. Beside him she looked very young. She rubbed her freed hands, her brown hair hanging loose around her face.

"Thank you," she said to Magnuson. Then she looked across the table at Boris. "Are you all right? Our *mayor* came and *rescued* me this morning, as you see."

"I'm alive; I'm drugged," Boris told her. Her eyes went wide.

Magnuson sheathed his knife. "Let's all have something to eat," he advised calmly. "Then we can talk."

While eating, Boris kept a planeteer's eye turned on the Kappans. None of them were sharing Magnuson's table tonight, yet Boris got the impression that they might be at the next meal. Their relationship with Magnuson was undoubtedly complex; the robed priests deferred to him, the warriors defended him and took his orders about some things at least, and the kilted workers served him. Yet he had said that they would not tell him the secret of the source of the Water of Thought; not that he now seemed to be very much interested in finding out.

Brenda from her seat across the table was silently appealing to Boris for reassurance if not active help. He found himself resenting the way that she was looking at him. He wanted to scream at Brenda that he was more helpless than she was, that there was nothing he could do for her, not a thing, whatever happened. With an effort he kept his face calm, kept himself from screaming; that was about all that he could do.

Jane was a frightened young woman, and showed it, eating almost nothing, looking from one face to another for some sign of hope.

Kaleta and Morton and Jones were all dining in poker-faced silence.

Even now, relaxed, Magnuson still had the bearing of a chief. He ate sparingly, though with evident enjoyment. At last he wiped greasy fingers on a cloth handed him by a kilted worker-girl, and belched with healthy satisfaction. The worker-chef, standing nearby, smiled at this sign of approval.

"On Kappa," Magnuson began the conversation, "Eden is here and now."

At Boris's side, Jones raised his head. He turned his face, with an odd expression, down the table toward Magnuson.

Magnuson gestured at the villagers nearby. "Oh, for these people, and for the rest of their species scattered round the planet, Eden of course has passed. But nevertheless, for some other creatures in the wilderness near here, its time is now."

The Kappan night was deep around the little torch-lit table, and vast. Sounds from without the village indicated that various nocturnal animals had wakened. Jane giggled nervously, and Morton ostentatiously yawned.

Magnuson looked at Jones. "I told you that more than our individuals lives is here at stake. We find ourselves privileged to aid the forces that on another world created us. To become evolution's conscious and willing tools. The Kappan hominid is on the verge of becoming human, and chance has given us the opportunity to help."

Red Circles had been leaning on his spear, a few paces from the table. Now he stirred restlessly.

Magnuson looked over at him, as if accepting a challenge implied by the movement. "What are the Forest People, Red Circles? Are they men?"

"They are enemies or slaves, Magnuson."

"But, when some of them have become men, full men like you and me, what then?"

"Magnuson you know they are our enemies. I have seen you torture them, and it was good. Now these others from Earth will help us kill the grown Forest People and make the young ones our slaves. And we will hide all of you, when your enemies come flying to find you. All this will be good too."

Magnuson sighed with weary impatience. "Red Circles, I do not mean to kill the Forest People or to make them slaves, and well you know it. You have learned new speech from me, with great skill; can you not learn more than speech? When the Forest People have become full men, like you and me, then it will be wrong to kill them, or to keep them at work by whipping."

"Yes," said Red Circles. "When they are men." He was not arguing with Magnuson, but neither was he giving way.

Magnuson looked round the table at his fellow Earth-descended. "How many men and women, do you think, upon how many worlds, have lived out the lives of baboons, among families of less-than-man? How many bearing within them the spark of humanity have spent their days and years grubbing for insects, beside their animal parents and siblings? I tell you, it is happening here and now, on Kappa.

"Tomorrow, we are all going up the river to the Workers' Village. The council of chiefs has decided that a new temple is to be built, and the stone quarry up there is busy. You will see how the hominids are used in the quarry. They are beasts of burden, but among those beasts I fear that there are slaves."

"Helping the poor slaves is all very fine," said Pete Kaleta, wiping grease from his hands. "But you know what we want."

"I sent you some of the Water of Thought," Magnuson replied stiffly. "In payment for the radio and the other things you got for me. And for your silence. As if you didn't want silence for yourselves."

"Yes, you gave us a little of the stuff. But just a sample. Well, the people in the Outfit want some more. They like something with a real kick to it, I understand. Don't look so disgusted. You knew who we were doing business with. Now I swear to you, Magnuson, I mean to deliver the stuff we've contracted for." Kaleta looked round; Red Circles had walked away, and no other Kappan was listening, but he lowered his voice anyway. "That's going to take a lot of Thought-Water, and it's going to mean a lot of money. A lot. We'll give you a share of the profits. You can spend it doing things for these hominids, if that's what you live for. But understand, you're going to help us make the delivery."

Magnuson looked at Kaleta and Morton as if they were filth just dropped onto his supper table. Then he turned to Jones and Boris. "Gentlemen, as you know, I have quarreled with the Space Force. Daily I violate its narrow-minded rules restricting anthropological research, but I still respect it and I respect you. When I see such as these…"

"Don't get tough." Morton's voice was icy. Then he smiled over at Jones. "I understand you're going to make a good customer for the Water from now on. Stick with us and we'll see that you're taken care of."

Jones stared back. Then he put his face down in his hands on the table.

In the small hut where he and Boris were quartered for the night, Jones poured himself a sip of the Water of Thought. Then he sat on a stool silently clutching his stone bottle, which appeared to be nearly empty.

"You look sick," said Boris, rocking on his own stool. They had been allowed a small oil lamp, but no table to put it on, so it burned on the dirt floor.

"I am sick. Feverish. Magnuson hasn't given me any more of the stuff yet. It may be killing me, but I don't mind if it does. If only I wouldn't imagine strange things. That's the part that gets me." Jones got up, went to the open doorway of the hut and looked out. Then he came back and stretched out on a sleeping mat. He had recapped his bottle and he still held it tightly.

"What sort of things?"

Jones did not answer. After a while he seemed to sleep.

Boris went to the doorway and sat down there cross-legged, looking out at the fire-spotted village night. He wondered where the groundsuits and the rifles were being kept. Not that the knowledge would do him much good if he had it. Against a tree in the middle distance there leaned a warrior with a spear, visible in silhouette, probably watching Boris.

Kaleta and Morton had not seemed to be worried about the Space Force. Doubtless the cruiser was late, and doubtless before it got here the smugglers planned to have a barrel of Thought-Water stowed away, and no inconvenient witnesses on hand.

The rest of the colonists were probably staying close to their firesides on the mayor's advice, and thinking with admiration of heroic Mayor Kaleta, brave Don Morton, and fearless Jane whatever-her-name-was, who were all out risking their necks in the wilderness to rescue Brenda and Boris from the berserk killer Jones.

On the other side of the village common, a slender figure had just appeared beside a small fire. It was Jane, and she was looking about her as if in search of someone or something.

Boris found himself free to stand up and walk out of the hut. Jane watched his approach, and smiled tentatively when he drew near.

"How goes the plotting?" Boris asked, moving up beside her. Though the night was not cold, he spread his hands out toward the fire. It seemed an ancient, almost instinctive gesture.

"Not too well, I think." Jane's voice was like her body, small, firm, and quick. Her hair was lighter than Brenda's, her face thinner, to Boris less suggestive of sensuality. "Don and the good mayor have walked back to the copter; they're going to radio back to the colony that all's well with them and me but we haven't found you or Brenda yet. I suppose you're worried about Brenda?"

"Sure, not to mention myself. But how about you?"

"What do you mean, how about me?"

"I mean should I be worrying over what might be done to you—or what you might do?"

Jane gave her nervous laugh. "Both, I guess. I admit I'd like to be rich, and I'd like to get off this planet permanently with Don. Or someone, not Don if I can help it. But I really don't want to hurt anyone in the process. And I don't want to get arrested. Isn't that a laugh?"

"No."

"No." Jane's eyes became sympathetic. "Boris, what's happened to you? I can see something's—wrong."

"I drank the Water of Thought. I lost my—free will." Boris's voice cracked, and he realized that he was suddenly very close to breaking down. He had lost count of the hours and days of his helplessness. "I have to follow Jones's orders. If he told me to stick my head into this fire, I would do it."

"Don't say that!" Jane cried, quietly, impulsively. Her sympathy was undoubtedly sincere. She took a step toward Boris, and gripped his arm as if to save him from the flames.

Having her do that was more help than he would have believed. "I'll be all right," he said in a moment, and put his big hand over hers. "Are you involved in this dope-peddling? Not yet, eh?"

"No. Not yet." Jane let go of him, and shivered. Now it was her turn to spread her hands to the fire as if for warmth. "But I'm afraid of Don. Why haven't you asked about Brenda?"

360

"How is she?" He had judged it wiser not to show concern.

"All right, except for her sore ankle. Magnuson treated that for her. She's sleeping now. Boris, you don't think I'm ugly, do you?"

"Not by Earth-descended standards, certainly. Under normal conditions I might well be chasing you around the fire."

"No, you'd be chasing Brenda. Oh, I'm her friend, really, Boris, but I do have this streak of… envy. Whenever she has someone or something that I don't have, I envy her. Maybe that's how I got started with Don. He was after her, though she was too smart to ever be much interested in him."

"What kind of a guy is Morton?"

"Not very nice. He can be mean, very mean, Boris. I've been around him enough to know."

"And you never guessed what he and Kaleta were up to?"

"That's fairly recent. I knew something was going on. I was hoping it was something that would make enough money for Don to take me offworld with him. I guess I was afraid to find out what it really was, but I didn't think it'd be anything this bad!"

"But you knew it was connected, somehow with Magnuson?"

"I found out little bits of things, here and there. Dr. Magnuson made himself vanish, out here in the hills. Then he sent a Kappan he trusted to Don at the colony, telling Don there was something up that might make a lot of money. Oh, he knew what Donnie boy is like, all right. And the mayor, too. Magnuson scares me."

"What kind of help did Magnuson want?"

"Oh, radio equipment, so he could listen in and tell if anyone was searching for him. Other things, some scientific equipment, I don't know. You ask a lot of questions."

"It's about all I can do."

"Oh, Boris, I wish it wasn't so. And to handle everything Don had to cut the mayor in. Mayor Pete's greedy, too. Even greedier than Don, I guess."

"So they're using Magnuson and he's using them. Interesting. Any one else in on it?"

"No. Oh, you mean Brenda?" Jane gave him a cold, bright smile, and shook her head almost regretfully. "No. I'm good at keeping secrets."

Boris returned the smile. "So, here we are. You still think you might get rich, and get away from this planet, and not have dope-smuggling and maybe murder on your conscience when you do. But really you know that the Space Force is almost sure to uncover all this sooner or later, because so many people are involved." Boris himself was not so sure as he made himself sound. "And when that time comes, you'd like to have me as your friend. If I'm still alive."

Jane put her hand on his arm again. "I'll do what I can for you, Boris. Yes, for Brenda too. But I can't do much." She raised the hand and traced with one finger the line of his jaw. "You know, I could wish you were under *my* control, not Eddie's. But Don will be coming back. I'd better go."

***

Boris was almost back at the doorway of his hut when he realized that a man was standing motionless in the shadows beside it. It was Magnuson.

When Boris stopped, the doctor took a step forward, cleared his throat, and said self-consciously: "I order you to stand on your head."

"What?" Boris felt an almost hysterical urge to giggle. Then he understood. "Oh, a test. No, Doctor, I don't have to obey your orders. Only Jones's."

"Good. Then you will not obey Morton or Kaleta either. Will you step into the hut?"

Inside, three warriors held Jones. His arms were bound, and there was a flint knife at his throat.

"Jones controls you. And now, as you see, I control Jones." Magnuson was not boasting; he was miserable. "Oh, this is all horrible. But I must remain in control, and there is no other way to do it."

Jones spoke without moving his head. "Brazil, he wants you to get into a groundsuit and disarm Morton and Kaleta. Wait until they finish with the radio and come back to the village. It shouldn't be too hard a job."

Boris looked from Jones to Magnuson. "You don't need to compel me to do that— just give me permission."

"I hate to use you as a slave." Magnuson was suffering. "But I have done worse things. Yes.

"I know you'd escape in a moment if you could. Perhaps you'd kill me, and that would end my work. So I must control you in the groundsuit and get you out of it again. I hope that I can soon convince you that what I do here is the work of Man. But in the meantime—"

There came a muffled clanking at the doorway of the hut. Red Circles and two others bore a groundsuit in.

Jones gave precise orders. "Brazil, put the ground-suit on. Disarm Kaleta and Morton, but don't hurt them if you can help

363

it. Then come at once back to this hut and take off the suit." He glanced at Magnuson, who nodded. The flint knife was eased a few centimeters away from Jones's throat.

"I think I will be the one to take the weapons from the two Earthmen," Red Circles said.

"No." Magnuson looked steadily at the war chief. "They will be on their guard, and you might have to kill them, especially if you went alone against them."

Muscles bunched along Red Circles' jaw. "Magnuson does not say that I might fail."

"I know you better than that. But bad as they are, I do not want the two Earthmen killed. I mean to provide them with a chance to prove themselves true men."

Red Circles appeared to understand, if not to agree.

Magnuson stared off briefly into space, fascinated by something that only he could see. "Like a baptism," he mused. "It may wash away past sins."

Boris, getting into the suit, thought that he understood. Magnuson had said earlier that all of the Earthmen present would become members of this tribe. Then the "baptism" would be an initiation ceremony.

"There may be shooting," Boris said to Magnuson. "Better see that the village people keep their heads down."

"Yes, that's right." Magnuson hurried out of the hut.

"One thing," said Boris to Jones.

"What?" Jones opened his eyes. He had seemed to be resting on his stool, almost oblivious to the Kappans who stood by ready to kill him at a moment's notice.

"Let me make sure that Brenda's safe."

Jones sighed. "I'll ask them to bring her over here so you can see she's healthy—as soon as you come back here and get out of that suit."

And that had to suffice. Boris went out of the hut, wrapped in the familiar fluid power of a groundsuit, but as helpless as ever. Outside, he met Magnuson and strode across the village common with him.

"They'll come back to the village along that path," Magnuson whispered to him, pointing in the starlight. "The copter is in a clearing over there. Remember, no bloodshed."

"I want none."

"Of course. Good luck." Magnuson moved silently away.

I don't need luck now, thought Boris, watching the greater darkness of the path where it emerged from the forest. Later he would need all the luck available, when he tried to resist his orders, when he attempted to keep the suit on and pick up Brenda and carry her away to safety.

A flashlight appeared, far down the path. Moving expertly in the bulky suit, Boris took shelter behind some bushes. He turned up the sensitivity of his helmet's microphones, and picked up a low murmur of voices.

"—anything fatal to Brenda, at least not right away. That'd be a terrible waste," Don Morton chuckled.

"Let's get the *business* settled." Kaleta sounded angry. "We'll be lucky to manage that, without playing around."

"All right, all right. Anyone who's dead or missing can be blamed on Jones afterwards. I suppose eventually there's bound to be some kind of investigation."

"So we want to get the Kappans on our side. And we play along with Magnuson until we find out where the stuff comes from."

They were very close to Boris now, and evidently Kaleta caught the gleam of his suit through the bushes. He stopped, grabbing at Morton; the flashlight in Morton's hand swung suddenly to shine into the thicket.

"Who?" demanded Kaleta sharply.

"Me," said Boris, and plunged after Morton, who had spun around and was dashing back along the path toward the copter. The race was no contest. Morton heard the metal footfalls closing in, turned, and fired. Bullets whanged off the armored suit before Boris got a grip on the barrel of the machine pistol, yanked it from Morton's grasp, and bent it into uselessness.

"Come along." With compelled gentleness, Boris took Morton's arm and towed him back toward the village. Morton made choking sounds of rage and fear, but offered no more resistance.

The good mayor had been smart enough to raise his hands and stand still. Boris plucked Kaleta's firearm from its holster and squeezed it into junk. Then, gripping one man's arm lightly in each metal gauntlet, Boris marched his prisoners back into the village and across the common.

Magnuson met them, an escort of warriors at his back. His face showed relief. Jane and Brenda stood beside him.

"I'm all right, Boris," Brenda called to him. There was hope in her eyes again.

Nothing would be easier now than to rage through them all, knocking them aside until he had Brenda safe in his metal arms; then, to run with her, spears bouncing from his back, trees crashing under his feet, carrying her safe through the night toward the sheltering forcefield walls of the colony.

Boris removed his helmet, then his suit. He could not even try to disobey.

Chapter Five

In the morning, again transmitting his orders through Jones, Magnuson had Boris once more put on a groundsuit, then drag the other suit to the river and throw it into a deep pool, together with the energy rifles.

"We are going upstream," Magnuson announced, when the rest of his prisoners had been assembled to hear him. "A few kilometers north of here at the Workers' Village there are some things that I want all of you to see. Probably we will stay at the Workers' Village tonight, and tomorrow go on upstream again. Farther that way lies the Warriors' Village. There, in a day or two, we shall all of us learn whether we are acceptable to the Spirit of Man."

"You're out of your head," Morton told him.

"I know you think so. But come."

When the march upstream was organized, Magnuson led the way, with Red Circles and an elaborately robbed chief priest at his sides. Boris, still wearing the groundsuit, followed, accompanied by Brenda and Jane. Then Kaleta and Morton, both sullenly silent. After a few more priests, a small band of warriors brought up the rear, with Jones secured among them, gagged so he could shout no sudden orders to Boris.

The path between villages was a well-worn trail, but steep in places and fairly difficult. It zigzagged uphill among boulders and under overshadowing trees. Brenda was still limping, though Magnuson had treated her ankle. Boris helped her over the rougher spots. He found that he was hardly able to speak to her. Her eyes were sympathetic and not accusing—but still it was harder and harder for him to meet them with his own.

After the first kilometer and a half the trail climbed beside a low waterfall and then smoothed out. Now it wound along beside the Yunoee through cultivated fields in a broad, flat valley. Trees were widely scattered here; anyone scouting in a copter could easily have seen the procession, spotted the Earth-descended people and the glinting groundsuit. Magnuson kept looking up and around at the sky, but it was empty of machines.

A few kilted fields hands looked up, from their labor or rest, to gape at the procession as it passed. Soon another cluster of small buildings came into view ahead.

The Workers' Village, like the Temple Village, straddled the narrow Yunoee. But instead of a temple this settlement was centered on sheds, where logs and stone were worked and stored. A kilted worker-chief came forth to greet Magnuson and the other two chiefs as equals. The six captive Earth-descended people caused much curiosity, almost all of it polite, among the workers.

Again Boris was ordered out of the groundsuit, and it was carried away to some hiding place; then Jones could be relieved of his gag. After that Magnuson's prisoners were only casually watched.

After talking privately until mid-day with the other chiefs, Magnuson came to share a meal with the six other Earth-descended. He ate quickly and sparingly, as usual, then rose to speak.

"I have persuaded the other chiefs to begin the annual rite of passage tomorrow night. When this year's class of young Kappans face their test, we all of us will go with them." He smiled happily at the two young women. "You of course will go to the women's ceremony, somewhat earlier. Things will be much easier for you than they will for us."

Kaleta jumped to his feet. "What are you getting us into?"

Magnuson smiled at him briefly. "Why, Mr. Mayor, I am giving you a chance."

"To enter a tribe of savages?"

"One who promotes organized crime has no right to use that word of others. It is true, that if you survive, you will find the tribal secrets open to you, and these warriors sworn to defend you like a brother. But what I am talking about is a greater chance that that. If you can prove your own humanity and your own manhood, to yourself, I think you will care less for peddling dope."

"And if I can't—prove myself, as you put it—to you?"

"Not to me, Mr. Mayor. To yourself, and to the tribe. I'll be beside you, undergoing the same things. And if we fail? Why, then we will die—deservedly."

Kaleta sat down, as if his legs were suddenly too weak to hold him; his plump face had turned grayish. Morton sat beside him, smoldering. Boris, watching, derived a certain satisfaction from the look of the two smart operators as they revised their opinion of the crackpot who wanted to be a savage and could somehow be disposed of easily when the time was ripe.

Magnuson turned from the table. "Come along, all of you. This afternoon I want to show you something of my work."

He led them west from the Workers' Village, at right angles to the river's course. The path here was wide and dusty, scarred as if by the frequent dragging of heavy objects. When they had gone a few hundred meters, staccato shouting and the cracking of whips could be heard from a short distance ahead, behind a screen of trees.

The path, emerging from the forest, spread to form a broad grassless area rimming a quarry pit. Over the wide pit dust hung in the air. Along its edge kilted workers were shaping blocks of stone with saws of copper or bronze, the first metal tools that Boris had seen in native Kappan hands.

But stonecutting and metal tools were not what Magnuson had in mind to show them. "There," he said, and pointed.

Up over the lip of the quarry-pit, moving with painful slowness through a haze of dust, beasts of burden came into view. They appeared a pair at a time, gripping a crude rope with their human hands, hauling upward with all their strength. There were eight of the short, two-legged beasts in the team, and they dragged uphill a sledge weighted with a single stone block. Under the flicking whip of a kilted overseer, the hominids moved their load without outcry. Their naked leathery skins were white with the dry dust of the quarry. One of the two females in the team was obviously pregnant.

Magnuson gestured for his little group of sightseers to accompany him as he moved forward to the rim of the pit. Now Boris could see down into the quarry, where other groups of hominids were toiling. He had seen slaves before; he had seen humanity in most of its known themes abused and brutalized upon a score of planets. The sight before him was somehow different from anything that he had seen before, and he could not decide at once if it was worse or not as bad. These hominid faces, prime theme though they were, outwardly resembling *homo sapiens*, showed nothing Boris could identify as human hope or hate, fear or resentment. Their five-fingered hands expressed nothing, hung limp when not gripping rope or pushing stone. None of the beasts had been given work requiring tools. The kilted men with whips barked out their orders in repeated monosyllables, as if to horses.

If these beasts were the product of some brain-washer's art, then the most accomplished tyrants of the Galaxy might be able to learn new skills on Kappa. But no, thought Boris. These two-legged brutes have never been human.

Jane had turned away from the sight. But Brenda watched, and Boris saw tears in her eyes.

"It is not as simple as it seems," said Magnuson to her gently. "If they had the bodies of horses, and you saw them given food and water and rest, you would not weep for them. They are given those things."

"But they're not horses," objected Brenda.

"Ah, that's the point, yes. Weep for those who are not. Perhaps as many as one in five, even one in three, must bear in their brains the spark of humanity. And that spark has never been fanned."

"Why do you say they must?" Kaleta asked.

"Look at them. Think about them. They can hardly be anywhere else on the evolutionary tree. In the wild state they are quite capable of using weapons, to fight the villagers and no doubt in hunting also. Biology is not really my field, but their cranial capacity seems quite adequate for abstract thought. It's true that apes will now and then use tools. But the ape brain is always smaller, and the forelimbs adapted primarily for travel, whether brachiating or walking. In the prime theme tree only man and his immediate ancestors habitually stand erect. Come this way. I'll show you my laboratory."

Magnuson led them away from the quarry, along a narrow, little-used path that curved through the woods for a hundred meters and ended at a big, new-looking cabin of solid log construction. At one end of this building was a pen of upright logs, like a prison stockade.

Inside the stockade were eight hominids. The one female and one of the males looked old and completely crippled, obviously unable to any longer haul stone in the quarry. The remaining six were all younger males, all comparatively healthy-looking, though one of them was minus a hand. Looking more carefully at the six, Boris saw that each bore the scar of some serious but now healed injury. Probably primitive ropes broke often in the quarry, and heavy stones slipped and slid and fell.

A water trough ran into the pen. "Dry again," sighed Magnuson, taking up a pail. He began to fill the trough up from a nearby well. "I can't get the villagers to feed or water a hominid that does no work. They give me the ones that are badly injured in quarry accidents, and my first aid and Earth drugs save some of them, as you see. Red Circles will not understand that my treatments are not meant as torture. There, you were all thirsty, weren't you?"

Inside the pen, the hominids had clustered along the trough, cupping up water in their hands, or bending over to slurp noisily. The one-handed male drank, then turned and reached out between the logs of the palisade toward Magnuson. Magnuson touched the gray leathery hand, as if knowing that was all the creature wanted.

"Have they any speech?" Jones asked. He was staring with an odd expression at the hominids.

"No. Oh, according to the villagers, the wild adults have a language of their own. But I doubt it's more than a system of warning cries such as monkeys use. I've never been close enough to a wild adult to hear it myself."

"But they must have a speech. I can remember—" Jones abruptly stopped speaking. He stared at the hominids as if something about them frightened him. They were paying him no attention.

Magnuson shook his head, watching Jones carefully. "No, they have no speech. The young ones are captured when they wander away from the wild troop, then brought here and trained like horses or dogs. I've tried to teach them to speak a few words, but I think none of them is psychically ready for symbolic thought. So I mean for the six young males here to go with us tomorrow night, into the rite of passage."

Boris, having followed Magnuson's thought this far, was not surprised. He tried to picture members of three species being initiated into the same tribe—he didn't yet know the details of the initiation, but he could imagine what it would be like. Still, he refrained for the time being from arguing.

Jones was surprised. He asked: "Will the villagers stand for it?"

Magnuson nodded. "Just barely. Oh, perhaps all six of these will die in the ordeal, for no mere animal can pass through alive. But in pain and shock is man born, as an individual or as a race. If the ordeal awakens none of these six to manhood, why I must try again; I must somehow get time to try again. In the end I must succeed. Then I shall have made man, and what our so-called civilization does to me will not matter."

Morton, who had been silently expressing disdain, now laughed. "You'll play hell starting a tribe with those. Six males."

Magnuson was unruffled. "The female is not so important." He bowed, smiling, to the two young women in the tour. "Until civilization is attained. And even then a psychic difference remains, which we ignore to our cost. What we now call civilization abandons the formal rite of passage, and thereby enfeebles the race. Eventually we must return on our home planets to the ordeal of the weeding-out. Only males who can prove their manhood should survive long enough to reproduce."

Magnuson's Earth-descended audience heard him in silence, angry, fearful, or indifferent. Maybe, thought Boris, some of them half believed him. But Magnuson was not interested right now in their reactions. The one-armed hominid still stood at the palisade, thrusting out both hand and stump between the logs. Magnuson touched the gray hand again.

After feeding his hominids, throwing leaves and roots from a bin into the pen, he beckoned again to his visitors. "Come inside, all of you."

Most of the interior of the large cabin was a single room, floored with stone slabs. There were village-made worktables and shelves, holding a scattering of books and papers, a small computer, various chemical and electrical apparatus.

"I took a chance, stealing this for you," said Kaleta, pointing to a microscope under a dusty plastic cover. "Why'd you want it, if you're not working with the Water of Thought?"

"I was mainly interested in the Water, at first. Drinking it, as I have mentioned, brought me here. But once here I turned to more important things. Yes. I've now almost entirely given over the physical and chemical sides of research. But here, here's an interesting bit of physical evidence."

From a table Magnuson picked up a skull of somewhat less than adult Earthman size but still, thought Boris, of a brain capacity probably sufficient for intelligence. It was certainly prime theme shape. The teeth were omnivorous, human-looking, and noticeably worn—probably a quarry-beast chewed a lot of grit along with its rough food. The jaw was short, heavy, almost chinless. Below a receding forehead the supraorbital ridges stood out boldly, joining together between the eyes.

"What do you think about it, gentlemen?" Magnuson spoke to Jones and Boris.

Jones, briefly a planeteer again, accepted the skull. He turned it in his hands, looking at the face, the sides, and the top of the cranium. "Prime theme pre-sapient hominid. Rare, but hardly astonishing."

"Correct. Now, tell me, upon how many planets has the transition from beast to human been observed? The achievement of sapience, in any theme, prime or otherwise?"

Jones shrugged. "It's never been observed, as far as I know, but that's not surprising. If you want to talk technical evolutionary theory, it's an instance of the automatic suppression of a peduncle. The beginnings of anything tend to be out of sight and out of reach."

"Right again." Magnuson nodded, smiling and intent. "But here and now, upon this world, the rare moment is before us. Or it will be, if we choose to create it. And I so choose."

Jones put down the skull, and leaned wearily against the table. "All this has ceased to concern me, or I'd argue with your methods."

"Argue, then. I've told you that your slavery to the Water of Thought will probably soon be over."

"If I'm soon dead, it will." Jones displayed a sickly smile. "If I argue with you, will that induce you to refill my bottle?"

"No. But I can promise you that you'll drink the Water of Thought at least once more. We all will, on beginning the initiation ceremony."

Kaleta and Morton almost jumped at Magnuson, cursing him and demanding explanations; Boris came near joining them.

"I tried to have you all exempted from drinking," Magnuson said. "But the chiefs refused. They gave in to me on the more important point of letting the hominids participate, so I would not press them on this."

Only Jones relaxed. "Then I won't argue. I'll accept as true any theory that brings me more of the Water."

"If you won't argue," Boris said, "I will. Our going through a paddling to join some half-wit fraternity is not going to prove anything, except that we'd rather suffer than die. Neither will it prove much about your hominid pupils here, as far as I can see. If you can't educate them now, a torture session won't make them any smarter. What's wrong with just letting them alone, to go to hell in their own way? That's all the Space Force wants, as I see it. And for once I tend to agree with my bosses."

But it was no use; he was not getting through to Magnuson. They were thinking in different coordinate systems. Well, Boris had expected argument to fail, but he had had to try.

Magnuson faced Boris more in sadness than in anger. Or perhaps he was controlling his anger well. "Oh, yes. I am—what is the phrase?—a do-gooder. I interfere. My interference in evolutionary processes has been forbidden, on this and other planets. I remember the words of one Tribune—she said my work would be cruel, cruel to animals and humans both. As if hominids and humans alike were not already on the anvil of evolution! The only mercy granted the Kappan hominids is their ignorance of the transformation that lies just beyond their reach. Cruel! Perhaps that Tribune would forbid a woman to give birth, because the experience would be likely to traumatize her child."

"Well, I can't stop you." Boris picked up the hominid skull from the table, and on a hunch turned it upside down. The *foramen magnum* had been enlarged by crude hacking into a gaping hole, big enough to have permitted extraction of the brain.

Magnuson was smiling at Boris's discovery. "Yes, more evidence of proto-humanity. When one of the hominids dies in the quarry, the others usually cut or break open the skull, and devour at least part of the brain. Unpleasant, yes. But still, as a twentieth-century anthropologist wrote: 'Nearly the most ancient human trick we know.' "

***

Boris sat on a log at one side of the sunny common of the Workers' Village, while Brenda stood behind him, massaging his tired neck. Children, kilted and kiltless, goggled shyly and laughed at them.

"How's your ankle now?" he asked.

"Not bad. Better than it was. Afraid I wouldn't get far, though, if I tried to run for help."

"I can't do that, or anything," he said. "I've tried."

"I know you have. You'll get over it, though. You will."

"Magnuson thinks that Jones and I will recover in another day or two. I suppose just in time to drink more of the stuff for the ceremony. But Magnuson isn't trusting me in the groundsuit anymore."

"That's a good sign. Isn't it?"

"I suppose it is. But I can't afford to start hoping." That was a shameful thing to say, especially to anyone as brave as Brenda

377

was turning out to be. But Boris said it. He could feel himself hitting bottom.

***

Quartered that night with Jones in a hut in the Workers' Village, Boris dreamed again. He was a hominid, dragging a heavy sledge up the side of a quarry-pit. He felt a whip. Planeteer Hayashi was behind him, pulling desperately with one hand at the monstrous growth upon his face, and lashing Boris with the other.

Chapter Six

In the morning the Earth-descended were served a breakfast of fruit, stewed meat, and freshly baked bread. A pair of robed priests arrived from the lower village, and helped Magnuson lead his six young hominids from their pen, after first roping them together like hand-bound mountaineers. Then the procession of the day before, enlarged now by hominids and more priests, moved on upstream. This time the groundsuit was left behind, and Jones was no longer so closely guarded.

After a couple of kilometers the flat valley pinched in again, becoming a gorge through which the Yunoee tumbled. Again the trail became difficult; but the group moved at an unhurried pace, and the journey was short.

The Warriors' Village at the influx of a tributary creek, straddled the Yunoee as had the two settlements below. In this settlement the huts were roughly made, and crudely shingled with thorny bark.

Here the villagers' greeting was a screaming mob scene. Boris put his arms protectively round both Jane and Brenda as howling warriors leaped past them, brandishing knives and clubs. But the Earth-descended were not really menaced. It was the roped-together hominids that drew the brunt of the threatening uproar. It took all the shouting and gesturing that Magnuson and the robed witch-men could manage to keep the hominids from being physically assailed and probably slaughtered. The hominids cowered and snarled, huddling together inside a ring of screaming warriors and squaws. Magnuson needed half an hour to get his pupils into the village, to the comparative safety of a pen that had been built for them.

Boris had little worry to spare for hominids. He was relieved when the village women took gentle custody of Brenda and Jane and led them away, evidently to some ceremony which males were forbidden to attend.

While Magnuson conferred with the chiefs, the four other Earthmen were shown where they were to stay. Kaleta and Morton sat down and whispered together. Jones paced restlessly around the portion of the village where he was allowed to go. Boris sat down in the abandoned hut in which he and Jones had been billeted, and tried to keep out of trouble.

He had been there only a few minutes when a shadow darkened the green brightness of the doorway, and Morton stepped in.

"Brazil, you're still under Jones's orders, huh?"

"Yes. But I can defend myself if need be."

I didn't come in to start a fight." Morton seated himself on the dirt floor. "Look, do you know anything about this initiation business Magnuson's got us into?"

"Not this one in particular. I've seen 'em on other planets."

"What's the best way to get through one?"

"You're asking me for help? When do you plan to murder me?"

379

"All right, so I've got a lot of nerve. I said I didn't come in here for trouble, but you don't scare me a damn bit, colonel, or whatever the hell you are. You don't have your tin suit on now."

Jones came in. "What's this all about?"

Morton stood up. "Maybe *you'll* tell me something about this initiation thing. After it's all over you're going to want me around to fill your bottle for you."

Jones's cheek started twitching. "There's no big secret about getting through an initiation. As Brazil says, it's not much different from joining some halfwit fraternity. Just grit your teeth and follow orders, and don't try to fight back."

Morton nodded slowly. "That's about what I thought. And it might get pretty rough, right? Suppose we tried to get out of here, today or tonight, what do you think our chances would be?"

"Just about zero," said Jones, "and I don't want to get away."

"That's right, you'll do anything to stay near the Thought-Water." Morton thought for a moment. "Well, I agree with you, for once. I've gone through a lot already to get my hands on that stuff. I'm not about to give up now."

When Morton had gone out, Jones sat down, his cheek still twitching. He pulled his little stone bottle out of a coverall pocket. "Brazil, you're lucky. If and when you're cured, you're a free man. If I'm cured of this I'm still a murderer."

"Temporary insanity might be a good defense."

"Legally, I suppose. But I'll still know what I've done, and why, and how it felt to give up everything for this. For water. You know if I lose the Water, I won't have anything."

"You think we'll be cured, Jones?"

"Magnuson thinks so. And he's so calmly sure of everything it's hard to argue with him. Right now he's debating with the chiefs again. They still don't like the idea of initiating his six hominids, but he's still insisting, and he'll probably win. He's quite a man."

"He is. But what chance will his hominids have in an initiation?"

"Almost none. They don't know what it's all about, ritual, ties of blood, sacrifice. They're just simple, ignorant people."

"People?"

Jones raised the dry bottle to his mouth, holding it vertical to drain any last possible drop. Then he hurled it across the hut, and began to laugh, in quiet near-hysteria.

"They're people," Jones said. "I'm mad, but I know. Don't ask me how." With that he collapsed, laughing or sobbing.

Boris sat quietly, looking out into the green Kappan sunshine.

Somehow, the day passed, and most of the night.

***

In the dark pre-dawn Boris found himself suddenly awake, listening to a distant rumble of drums, and to a howl like that of whirled bull-roarers. Across the hut, Jones too was awake, and sitting up. Before either could speak, the hut was filled with warriors, masked and painted as Boris had never seen them before. He was jerked to his feet and dragged from the hut with Jones beside him. Their escort was joined by another little swarm of warriors surrounding Morton and Kaleta, and the whole mob moved out of the village, taking by torchlight the path that climbed yet farther upstream beside the riverbank. Magnuson was ahead of them on the path, going in the same direction under his own power, holding the lead end of a rope which the six cowering hominids gripped like blind men traversing a place of danger.

There was much howling and jostling. Boris staggered and scrambled and was pushed along. Torchlight fell on frenzied or frightened faces, on night-black river water and the white curl of rapids. Ahead the sky was lit by a huge fire, and from there came the sounds of drum and bull-roarer.

The steep riverbanks fell away again as the place of the fire drew near. The procession moved on into the glare and the heat of the flames before it halted. The young villagers who were candidates for initiation were standing beside the fire already, in kilt or robe or loincloth, frightened but trying to be stoic. The five Earthmen and the six hominids were pushed in among their group. The drums were very loud.

"Tell Brazil that he is free," Magnuson shouted to Jones. "Until he has passed through the ordeal, or failed it, he must act for himself. Tell him!"

"All right." Jones turned to Boris. "So be it. You're on your own, sink or swim."

Boris hated both of them. He was not property, not a robot to be turned off or on. And at the moment, any talk of his having freedom was a bad joke. The hands of half a dozen warriors were on him, pulling off his clothes. Each candidate for tribal membership was first stripped, then draped with a net-like garment of tough fibers, weighted with fist-sized stones. Someone thrust another such rock, painted with a crude design, into Boris's hand, making sure that his fingers gripped it tightly.

"Hold on to your rock at all costs," Magnuson was shouting at the other Earthmen. "To drop it means to reject the use of tools, and if you drop it you will be killed."

The candidates were pushed into a ring, scorchingly close to the fire. A warrior thrust a cup under Boris's nose; he drank, draining the vessel, and the Water of Thought was cool and familiar in his throat. Beside him, Jones gasped, and drank; they had to tear the empty cup away from him. The hominids gulped, like so many thirsty animals. The young villagers, tasting the drug for the first time, swallowed it with reverence. Boris could not see how Magnuson and Kaleta and Morton faced the moment; they were now somewhere on the other side of the fire from him.

Someone screamed a signal and a dance began, the candidates circling the fire, the warriors keeping pace with them in an outer ring, flourishing weapons and leaping in the firelight, to the roar of drums.

Boris, positioned in the inner ring between a village youth and one of the hominids, jigged and hopped, doing what seemed to be expected of him. Somehow the hominids were moving with the others, so far at least, not dancing but keeping their relative places in the ring. What would the Water of Thought do to them? At least it had not paralyzed Boris again; he felt nothing from it yet.

One warrior leaped in from the outer circle, and slashed lightly with a small flint knife across the chest of one of the young villagers, who gave no sign of pain or shock. Then the man whirled back to his place in the outer ring, and others danced in, each to single out a different victim.

Boris felt a sudden sharp gouge on the back of one leg, and managed to keep himself from showing any reaction. The man who had wounded him now spun dancing past in front of Boris. He was masked, but Boris recognized Red Circles by his size and his painted arms. It was undoubtedly a compliment to be

383

favored with the personal attention of the war chief, though not one that Boris could fully appreciate.

The creeping hypnosis of the drums and the dance was available, and Boris knew that it could help. He let himself move into it, gradually. He concentrated on holding a part of his mind ultimately clear, ready to take control.

Abruptly, screaming hell broke loose; the warriors had started to torment one of the hominids. Boris turned just in time to see the victim react with the simple directness of an animal, striking back with the sacred rock that it had been given to hold in its fist. In the next instant the hominid's body seemed to sprout spears like porcupine quills. Then it was only a gory and lifeless thing, being dragged away.

In the next moment, another hominid fought back, and died. And in the next, another. Between the explosions of violence only seconds elapsed, but Boris found himself able to think as if leisurely minutes were passing. The hypnotic influence of the dance had brought him to a state of observant detachment; he felt he was able to calculate long plans between throbs of the hammering drum. He saw the warriors with torture-knife and killing-spear, getting rid of their hominid enemies one after another, killing them within the rules of the ordeal, but with hair-trigger good will for the task. He saw Magnuson, standing still, arms half raised, ignoring his own fate, watching while his work and hope died on Kappan spear points.

And with this detached clarity, and tremendous speed of thought, Boris saw the fifth and sixth hominids still standing in their places behind Magnuson, while the fourth was dying before Magnuson's eyes.

Those remaining two hominids still stood, moving obediently with the circle, holding firmly to their ritual rocks, while one warrior jabbed at them with a point and another scorched them with a glowing stick. The two hominids watched Magnuson like dogs, and they obeyed him like trusting men, amid this violence and death. And Boris saw two warriors look at each other, look and come to silent agreement. They thrust with their spears, and the fifth hominid died, not by the rules of the passage, but by racist murder.

Then the two murderers saw Magnuson turn toward them. And though he turned too late to see what they had done, they moved away as if ashamed, and so the sixth hominid still lived, under Magnuson's watchful eye.

To Boris all these things seemed to hold deep mystical significance. He knew that he was sliding deeper and still deeper into the hypnosis of rhythm and pain and the Water of Thought, and whatever else might be here at work; he knew it with the corner of his mind that was still normal, and had been assigned to hold control, but kept shrinking into less and less importance. Boris was not frightened. Mayor Pete Kaleta hopped past him, glaring wildly, muttering his terror, but that meant nothing to Boris. Even Red Circles had become an unimportant figure, who now and then approached bringing unimportant torment.

That fifth hominid had died unjustly, killed by murderers who were false to the tribe and false to the spirit of man. Sometime Boris would tell the story, and see the murderers punished. Sometime in the future. But there was no future, really; this dance was eternal.

The figure of Magnuson drifted past, dancing mechanically, bending to look at the stained earth where his hominids had died, then looking up again, eyes prayerfully following the lone hominid survivor.

It was the young hominid with one hand.

Magnuson should be praying, now. There should be some atheists' prayer, to the Spirit of Man, that he could say.

Let us call you down, Man, from your abode of evolutionary law. Let our fire and the sound of our drum bring you descending through this planet's night to enter the brain's of those who dance for you. Make us all men. Make us all men. Boris could almost see the Spirit, brooding in the rolling heat above the tongues of fire, coming and going with the heartbeat of the heaviest drum.

Then there was a disturbing noise that served to give his mind a foothold, and he fought his way up from deepening trance, pushing spirits and dreams away. One of the village adolescents had cracked and gone wild, had screamed and tried to run from the torture and the dance. And spearmen, ruthlessly obedient to the law of the ritual, forced their weapons home. The young Kappan died with a bubbling scream. Magnuson did not care about this one; Magnuson did not take his eyes from his hominid. But Boris saw the corpse dragged away. The sacred rock had fallen from the boy's hand, and a man kicked it into the fire.

Don Morton danced past; Boris was vaguely surprised to see him still alive. Morton's eyes were glazed, and he shouted incoherently. He did not blink when a warrior jabbed him.

The next thing Boris realized clearly was that the dance was over. The sun was touching the eastern horizon, and he and the other survivors were being led through the gloomy woods in torchlit silence. Was the ordeal finished? Not very likely.

Boris heard one awakening bird, and then found himself entering the mouth of a cave. His head still echoed with the now-silent drums, and his minor wounds blended into one pervasive ache, but it was not over yet. He was herded forward with the others, into damp and stony silence.

The twisty passages of the cave linked together chambers so big that in some of them the torchlight died out without revealing all the walls. Feet shuffled behind Boris and ahead of him, along a well-worn trail, and from somewhere came the sound of trickling water. His throat burned with thirst, but he knew there was no use hoping for a drink.

The procession of candidates for manhood wound to a halt at last inside another enormous chamber. Here each candidate was made to sit in a separate niche among the rocks, isolated from sight of the others. Boris sat down with relief; there was a moment of rest and almost of peace.

Magnuson walked past him, croaking: "Do not move from where you have been placed, under pain of death. Do not move from where you have been placed—" He went on, repeating the warning, evidently for the other Earth-descended.

Sitting in his rocky niche, probably carved out many generations ago, Boris could see no one. In most directions, his field of view in the wavering, indirect torchlight extended hardly farther than his arm could reach. Directly behind him was a shadowy opening between rocks; it looked as if Something might crawl out of it at any moment. Directly in front of it was a sizable open space. Niches and folds of rock and stalagmites surrounded the open space like rows of seats around an arena; and now in the arena there gathered half a dozen robed medicine men, carrying torches and chanting.

As they sang, the witchmen began extinguishing their torches, one by one, so that the darkness grew up a leap at a time. Boris waited, fatalistically ready for whatever might come next. He was sitting tailor-fashion, holding his sacred rock on

387

one knee, while the other stones tied to his net-garment dragged wearily down upon his shoulders.

Only one torch still burned; the rocks of the cave all leaned and swayed with its light. The medicine men were close around it, doing something—Boris squinted through bleary eyes, and at last decided that they were lighting small shielded lanterns of some kind. And now the priest-chief, wearing the biggest mask and longest robe of all, had appeared in the arena. Another animal-skin robe, dripping wet, was in his hands. He raised the wet robe above his head, and slowly brought the night down with it, putting out the light. The last syllable of the chant died with the sputtering of the torch.

With sight gone, the sound of trickling water seemed louder. And Boris was able to notice that the air in the cave was fresh, and that it was moving subtly past him. Probably there were several exits. A clever man might crawl silently through this darkness, find his way out, and be kilometers away in the woods, drinking safely from a fresh stream, before his tormentors even missed him. Never mind; any man who thought himself that clever would be certain to crawl into a trap and get himself speared to death. Still Boris could not free himself of the thought that escape was a possibility. This cave seemed to have been designed for concealed movement.

At least, he told himself, he was now free to try. Or had his free will really been restored? Was Magnuson planning on the ordeal as part of the cure—

A hideous scream tore through the blackness, echoing and re-echoing, like some frenzied animal leaping from one wall to another of its cage. Boris kept himself under control. He continued to sit still. There was a shuffle of movement nearby and the sound of heavy breathing. The sounds died out again.

Somewhere a Kappan boy began a hesitant, groping chant, as if inventing prayer.

Boris's eyes had slowly grown more sensitive in the darkness. Now he could detect a faint blur of light across the upper part of the cave.

"Brazil? Magnuson? Anyone near me?" The quiet voice was that of Jones, and it came from somewhere nearby on Boris's right.

No one jumped at Jones to kill him for speaking, so Boris judged it was probably safe to answer. "Brazil here. What's up?"

"Good. Listen, Brazil, some of these guys with the spears may have taken a drug to sharpen their night vision. Before this started I heard one of the women saying something about it."

"One of the women?" Talking was rough on the dried-out throat, but it might help the cause of sanity.

"Yes. Judging from what I heard, the women have their initiation in this cave too. None of them ever get killed; Brenda and Jane are probably having a feast with their new sisters right now. How long do you suppose we've been in here?"

"I don't know."

No one else seemed disposed to join the conversation. Either the other Earth-descended were out of earshot, or they thought that talking was too risky. Or they were simply saving their throats. There was silence for a little while.

"Brazil, you don't think I really wanted to leave my family, do you? Leave, abandon, everything I had and everything I was? Maybe you wanted to be a slave to this Water of Thought, but I didn't."

Boris's head jerked around. He stared into the darkness, toward the invisible Jones. "What do you mean, maybe I wanted to be a slave?"

"Well. Some people do want to get rid of all responsibility. It occurred to me."

For a moment Boris was unable to reply. He felt a great, hollow rage. *There's no truth at all in that, he thought. Not in my case. I wasn't tired of being responsible for myself.*

God. It couldn't be true, could it? He shivered, sitting still in the damp, moving air. It couldn't. But suppose...

Suppose that the effect of the Water of Thought upon an Earth-descended human, or human male at least, was this: to push the mind in whichever direction it happened to be leaning, making a fatal obsession out of what had been only a potential weakness.

Was this realization in itself the cure that Magnuson had predicted? Or was it the cure, but Magnuson didn't realize it?

From off among the rocks there came a sudden weak flash of light—one of the dark lanterns flicked open for just an instant. There was a startled gasp from someone and then a return of darkness and silence. After some timeless interval, another lantern flashed in another part of the cave, accompanied by sounds of sudden movement and a cry of fear. Boris made his muscles relax and tried to keep his mind on things other than thirst and physical danger.

Perhaps it was well that he did, for the next light that flashed illuminated the area just in front of Boris, and he saw that between him and the lantern crawled the figure of Red Circles, knife in hand. In the next instant blackness had returned. Don't move, Boris reminded himself, under penalty of death. He would like to crack Red Circles on the knuckles with a kilogram or so of sacred rock, that would be more fun than moving even, but it too might be considered bad form.

Surprise. Instead of the now-familiar pain of Red Circles' dull knife, the lantern beam came again, in the same place. Red Circles was not in sight. A couple of meters in front of Boris on the cave floor, just far enough so he would have to leave his place to reach it, was a large cup holding something that looked like water. The light went out again.

He was not to move from where they had placed him; they would know, somehow, if he moved. But Boris's memory held and enlarged the sight of that cup, full to overflowing, a little water sloshed out carelessly onto the stone floor as if the cup had just been hastily set down. Boris's thirsty throat argued that no one could notice a difference if a mouthful of water were taken out. But his brain knew it was a trap. The cup might even be poisoned. If he had to, he could go a long time yet without drinking. And he had to.

He shifted and stretched his fingers, which were growing stiff from gripping the sacred tool-rock; it would not do to drop the thing by accident. Then he gave a little jump, and cursed, as Red Circles jabbed him nastily from behind, out of utter silence and darkness. Boris felt sure it had been Red Circles again; he thought that he could recognize the technique by now. He kept himself from trying to kill Red Circles.

What price free will now?

From somewhere in the cave there came an animal sound, a growling and snuffling that spoke plainly of a prowling predator. Boris's intellect insisted that it must be only a warrior doing imitations, and with some effort Boris kept his intellect firmly in control.

Soon, from close in front of him, came the faintest possible sound. As if someone might be there, examining the cup, or removing it.

391

Immeasurable time hung in the cave. Its darkness swarmed with ghosts of sound, like the murmur in a man's ears of his own bloodstream. Like the unimaginable sounds inside an anthill whose inhabitants are seeking a way to climb out toward sentience. Growing louder in the mind, a whispering that might have been blind cells; evolving, pre-conscious still, but desperate to grow, to find the long, hard way to Thought.

This was becoming much worse than the dance. Boris ached to leap up, to fight, to run away; but he made himself sit still. When the animal snuffling sounded again, it was almost a relief.

Now Boris could hear Red Circles coming to stick him again, behind the rocks to his left rear. It was a very faint sound of movement, but Boris heard it. How good it would be to turn around and smash the Sacred Rock into—

"Boris?" It was only the tiny ghost of a whisper, but he knew immediately that it came from Brenda. Great Gods of all the Themes! He wanted to whisper to her to get out of here, but his dry throat choked.

"Boris, it's Brenda. I can see, a little. Do you need water?"

"Yes," he got out, in a faint whisper. "But—"

She was moving away already, crawling in almost perfect silence, apparently going to get him a drink. She must be mad, completely mad. But what was he to do, call her back and start an argument?"

Then Jones's voice came again, from somewhere on Boris's right.

"Brazil, I did want to. I've thought it out, I've faced it."

"Jones? What's that?"

"I did want to give up everything. I sit here in the dark, and I can see into myself. I left Kitty, and I left my work, and everything else I had. I wanted to be a fanatic, to give up my whole life for something, and I did. For the Water."

"It—may work out." Boris could hardly understand what Jones was talking about. He was listening for Brenda, expecting every second to hear the sounds of her capture or murder. He wondered if any of the warriors who must be listening could understand his talk with Jones. Quietly Boris stretched and flexed his legs, getting ready for the hopeless running fight that seemed inevitable. At least such a distraction might give Brenda some chance to escape. But how had she got into the cave? and where was she?

"It'll work out, all right, Brazil. I'll tell you how it will. I gave up everything for the Water, and now it's given me up. I'm cured." Jones's voice was dead.

"What?"

"That last drink we had, starting this initiation business. It tasted the same, but it meant nothing to me—it had no effect. I'm dead, Brazil. My life has gone, for nothing."

Boris was listening and listening for Brenda, sifting every whisper of sound from the far reaches of the cave. He almost shouted for Jones to shut up. "Maybe so, Jones," he said.

"Maybe so? Maybe so? Listen, Brazil, they put a cup here, right in front of me. I wonder what's in it."

"They set a cup here too but I didn't taste it."

"No, you wouldn't. You're not the kind to give up your life for something. Nobody's ever understood me. Not my wife or anyone else. If I thought that this cup had the real Water in it, and that I might feel it again—"

"Can't you keep quiet?"

"Quiet? Quiet? Gods of Space, I'm dead, and you say keep quiet. All right, Brazil, I'm putting you back under orders, right now. Don't move unless I tell you, and don't lie to me."

Boris heard a faint sound behind him, and he knew somehow that it was Brenda coming back, bringing him water. He was afraid to try to move. His freedom had been only an illusion, and at a word from his master it had flickered away into nothing. Boris could do nothing for Brenda, or for himself, or for anyone else. Whatever happened was not going to be his fault, no, not this time.

Jones said, "Brazil, is your cup still there? Taste it and tell me what it is."

"I don't know if it's here."

"Boris." It was Brenda's whisper, from behind him. Boris realized suddenly that they must have given her the Water of Thought during the women's ceremony, and that it must have unbalanced her in some way. That was what brought her here now, trying in this mad fashion to help him.

Jones said: "Brazil, I order you."

"Boris." She whispered his name again, and this time one of the warriors heard her. Boris could vaguely see the man's upper body; he was passing nearby, turned at the sound of Brenda's voice. He stood for a moment without moving, probably incredulous, and then, soft-footed as a cat, came closer to investigate. In ghostly silence the warrior passed so near that Boris could see he carried a short spear, and was going to probe with the spear for Brenda.

Boris moved, without thinking of whether it might be possible—the terrible thing called freedom was his again.

He should have used the sacred rock, but for some reason he set it down before he rose up silently behind the warrior.

Boris's left hand shoved low into the Kappan's back, ready to break his balance, and Boris's right arm whipped around in the silent-killing throat attack. Boris was stiff and weak; the man was not properly caught but retained balance enough to twist around and gasp in air, getting ready to yell. Boris drove knuckles into the man's throat, preventing any intelligible outcry, and then grappled for the spear.

A second later the silhouette of the warrior's head bent backward; hands had reached from behind him to claw at his face. Boris managed to wrench the spear away, spun it end for end, and drove it home. A dying weight sagged away, sliding quietly to the floor of the cave.

Then Brenda had Boris by the hand. She was kissing his hand and tugging on it at the same time, pulling him away. He let her lead him. The only hope was to get out of the cave, and quickly, by whatever route she had used to sneak in. Other warriors must already be approaching to check out what had caused the scuffle.

Behind Boris, a far louder struggle exploded in the darkness. Jones's voice bellowed: "Brazil! There is no cure! Obey me! Fight for me!"

Lantern beams were springing alive, centered upon Jones. He had captured a spear, and was fighting like some mad Norseman. Another spear had already been thrust through his body. One warrior lay at his feet, while more of them closed in.

There was nothing to do but go with Brenda and get out of there. Boris followed her insistent tugging, away from the lights and the struggle, under an overhang of rock that forced them both down to hands and knees, an after that into still deeper darkness.

"Brazil, fight for me! I'll have the Water—before—"

395

Jones's voice died away, and the sounds of fighting with it. The faint reflected glow of the lanterns had vanished entirely from Boris's vision. *Jones is cured*, he thought suddenly.

It was as dark as total blindness here. Brenda had released Boris's hand and crawled ahead of him. Now and then his hand, groping for the way, fell on her shoe or ankle. The way had become a tight, low passage through which he was almost too big to scrape. He lost the rocks from his net-suit, and he lost a little more skin, but he got through, still gripping his captured spear. After perhaps thirty meters of this kind of crawling he could hear insects. A few meters more and the overhead suddenly receded. Raising his head he glimpsed a sliver of comparative brightness, like the night sky. And there, a star.

There was room now for him to move beside Brenda. "This way out is the women's secret," she whispered. "One of them showed it to me today. And I took some of their night-vision drug."

At last there was room for them to stand and walk; the secret passage emerged into the open air through an otherwise almost inaccessible hole in the rocky hillside. Only now did Boris fully understand, with dull surprise, that night had indeed fallen again; he had been all day inside the cave.

They were standing on a sort of rocky balcony, in front of which a boulder made a crude, chest-high parapet. Anyone starting up the hillside from below would have a hard climb getting to them, and they were going to have a hard time getting down.

"We'll be safe here, for a while," Brenda whispered. "All alone." She put her arms around Boris and pulled his head down and kissed him fiercely. Then she let go of him abruptly. He could see in the starlight that her hands were busy with the front of her own coverall.

He was so stupid with thirst and fatigue and weary pain that for a moment he did not comprehend what she was doing. "What…?"

"Boris, please. I can't help myself." She had started to take off her coverall; it was pulled down to her waist; and now Brenda threw an undergarment aside. "Here." She grabbed his hand and pulled it to her breasts.

"No," he croaked. Stupid as he was, he realized that it was the damned Thought-Water making her do this. She had been leaning toward loving him, and the Water had pushed her, as it had pushed them all. Anyway, the only animal urge he was able to feel at the moment was thirst. "Water," he croaked, looking downhill over the starlit forest.

"Boris! Boris?"

But he was already climbing over the irregular natural parapet. He scraped himself some more, but hardly felt the damage. Down under those trees somewhere was water, real water, cool and drinkable. He hadn't staggered far down the slope before Brenda was with him, her clothing more or less arranged again, holding his arm to keep him from falling on his face. "The river's this way," she said. Her voice sounded as if she might be weeping.

He was headed that way already; it was obvious from the shape of the land where the Yunoee must lie. He reeled toward it with only elementary caution, and when he came to it at once threw himself down on the bank. He thrust in his head, he drank and wallowed. He emerged with a sharpened awareness of all his pains and problems, but he felt able again to think with something like clarity.

397

Brenda was lying beside him on the bank, waiting for him. "Now, Boris. Please. Love me." Again the coverall was open. Almost off, not quite. He understood with pity that she was trying to be as provocative as possible.

"Brenda, not here, not now. I've got to run for my life, they'll be out here after me any minute. It's the drug making you do this—"

She gave a little scream, pure suffering, as if he had burned her with a hot iron. Her hand lashed out to slap across his face. "You filth! I risked my life to save you!"

"Brenda—" He hesitated. Was it worse to bring her with him or to leave her here? Was her ankle ready to stand a long flight? He didn't know how fast he himself was going to be able to move, shoeless and battered as he was. If she stayed here, and they didn't know she had sneaked into the cave, Magnuson might protect her; whereas if she fled with Boris, and they were caught ... but Morton and Kaleta were here, too.

Brenda lay on her back. She spoke in a sober voice: "Boris, I tell you I've got to have you. I can't help it. Otherwise I'll kill myself."

Chapter Seven

Boris scrambled to his feet and reached to pull Brenda up beside him. "Then come," he said, and kissed her quickly, once, and turned and trotted away, dodging among the trees as if flint points were already hurtling at his back—as well they might be, at any moment.

Brenda kept pace at his side. Her ankle must be healed, or very near it, or else she was ignoring pain—as he was. They ran in silence, saving breath. Once Brenda, with her augmented night vision, pulled at his arm to steer him clear of an almost invisible stump.

After a few minutes of this Boris halted, in a small clearing, breathing hard, long enough to get his bearings from the stars. Then they were off again. Boris had decided to set a course northward, at right angles to the easterly direction of the colony. Some of Red Circles' men were sure to be sent to the east, to get ahead of the fugitives and cut them off. Boris meant to go far enough to the north to get around them.

But the most immediately important thing to do was to put distance between themselves and the warriors' village. So far the grassy footing was fairly easy, and Boris meant to make the most of it. With daylight they would have to find a place to hide and rest; then he could think about improvising shoes as well as scrounging food.

Brenda, who had not spoken since he had pulled her up from the riverbank, still matched the speed of his long strides through the night. She at least had shoes on. But her ankle ... so far she was giving no sign that it might be a difficulty.

More minutes had passed, and there was no sign of pursuit as yet. A small ridge of land cut across their way, and Boris, saving breath, indicated silently that they should climb it. Going up, he avoided any way that looked in the starlight like a path, for beside a trail on this rim would be an ideal spot for a sentry. Red Circles, he thought, you're going to have quite a chase before you catch us, giving us this much of a start. In fact you'll find to your surprise that you can't catch us at all—positive thinking is the thing.

At the top of the ridge they paused again for breath. Boris looked back along the way they had come, and reached to grip Brenda's hand tightly in his. Now there were torches visible among the trees; but the searchers' lights were scattered widely and uncertainly, and Boris and Brenda had several hundred meters on the nearest of them.

Her face was turned up to him in the starlight; an anxious, trusting face, very beautiful to him now. "Are you all right?" she whispered. "Can you go on?"

"I'm all right. Your ankle?"

"It doesn't hurt." He was about to remind her that it was not too late for her to turn back and seek Magnuson's protection. But something in the way that Brenda was looking at him reminded him of her pledge to kill herself if Boris abandoned her. "That's good," he said. "Come on."

He set a course along one side of the ridge, north into the hills. Brenda with night-seeing eyes chose the easiest path among trees and brush. Again they were silent as they traveled, and Boris used the time for thought.

As he read the situation, once the ordeal was over Magnuson would willingly join in the pursuit. When officially a member of the tribe he would be a great Kappan chief, and could have no tolerance for those who fled from baptism. That Morton and Kaleta, if they survived the test, would also join the chase was obvious.

His thinking seemed to be discovering nothing but new problems, not ways out of them. When the ridge they were following mingled with a jumble of other hills, Boris continued to direct their flight northward, angling a little to the east. Their pursuers seemed not to be prospering, for when he looked back from high spots he saw no more torches. But the real pursuit had not got started yet. The Kappans would probably wind up the initiation ceremony, and wait until dawn, before organizing an all-out search.

For a while north was downhill, and the going correspondingly faster. Presently they came to a stream. Boris was almost sure it was the Yunoee again, here upstream from the villages. Brenda agreed with his judgment that there were probably no more villages up this way; neither of them had heard any mentioned. He drank deeply again, and this time she drank at his side.

"We've got to keep going," he told her. "But first I have to rest a minute." He sat down for a moment on the grassy bank beside the star-reflecting water.

A vivid flash of memory came, a picture of Jones, fighting in the cave, his body transfixed by a spear. Boris's head jerked up in alarm. He had dozed into sleep, sitting slumped over on the bank of the murmuring stream; he woke with his head pillowed on Brenda's lap.

Gods of Space, he had more than dozed, the eastern sky was gray! Boris jumped to his feet in a near panic. He turned his head this way and that, looking and listening, ignoring Brenda's soft protests that she had been on guard all the time.

"You should have wakened me!"

"You looked so bad, so worn out. I was afraid you'd collapse if you tried to go on without rest."

Muttering, he waded into the stream, and bent to drink again.

The water here tasted faintly fishy. Well, what was so strange about that? There were doubtless a number of different things that could make a stream taste fishy. Fish, for one.

"What is it, Boris?"

"I don't know. Nothing. Come on, we've got to move. We'll travel in the water." Brenda followed him. The Yunoee flowed dark and quiet around their knees, swallowing their trail as they waded upstream. Boris stopped now and then to bathe his stiffening little wounds. He washed the dried Kappan blood from the spear that he still carried.

Dawn was becoming a fact. Boris tasted the river again. It wasn't just fishy; there was no use trying to deny that here it savored faintly of the Water of Thought. That was one taste that he was never going to forget.

Tangled thickets nearby grew right down to the water's edge. Boris probed his way with the spear into the densest growth, where midnight gloom still held. "There's a little space in here. We'd better rest here through the day."

***

When with the second dawn the ordeal came to an end, Magnuson with the other survivors returned to a joyful welcome in the Warriors' Village. Their wounds were treated, and the new members of the tribe drank and ate and rested beside the old. The festivities were marred and somewhat rushed by the news of Brazil's so-far-successful flight. But before allowing himself to think much about that problem, to sleep, or even to relax, Magnuson had first to see that the new man, the one-handed hominid, was safely housed in the pen where he had been one of six confined animals the day before yesterday. Then, planning the new man's protection and education, Magnuson fell asleep.

He was awakened by a not-too-gentle prodding. Standing over him was a figure wearing a groundsuit. Startled, Magnuson jumped to his feet.

It was Morton's face inside the helmet. "Magnuson, you're coming with me. They haven't caught Brazil yet, and we can't let him reach the colony, him, or Brenda either. I can run them down easy in this suit, if I can get on their trail. But I need some

402

guides and trackers to do that, and I need you along to interpret. Also I want to keep you under my eye."

Magnuson thought about Brazil. It was too bad, but... "Yes, he must be caught. And I suppose the girl too."

"Damn right. I'm glad you see things straight for once."

Jane, excited, came running up to them. "I'll come with you, Don. I'll help."

"Woman on a war party? I don't think the spear-carriers would go for that."

"I suppose you're right." Jane was pale, breathing heavily. "But you'll catch them, won't you? Both of them, and bring them back?"

"You just a little jealous, Janey?" Morton grinned.

The young woman's face twisted into a mask of insane excitement; of hate, the like of which Magnuson had never seen on a rational human. Jane raised clawed fingers. "When I get my hands on her again..."

Magnuson, watching, felt a weary concern. He had too much to do, too many responsibilities. Jane and Brenda had both been given the Water of Thought for the first time, and he, under the press of other worries, had all but forgotten to consider the fact. Of course the Water was likely to have a drastic effect on their psyches. Not so great as if they were males, of course but... and Morton! Again Magnuson was going to have to deal with a madman clothed in the power of a groundsuit.

Magnuson looked closely at Morton. "How do you feel?" he asked, carefully.

"Feel? I'll feel fine, as soon as I get Brazil in these." Morton raised the suit's armored hands, and smiled again. "You look a little surprised to see me dressed up, Doctor. Why, you told me the whole tribe would be my brothers now. Nobody stopped me putting it on."

"Will you two get going, then?" urged Jane, her fingers twisting nervously at her hair. "Catch them. Why should *she* ever have him?"

"She's right, Professor," said Morton. "Come on, let's get the show on the road."

"All right. All right, I'll come with you. Where's Kaleta? I'll have to leave some instructions with him."

"In there, still sleeping it off. Hurry up!"

Magnuson entered the indicated hut and shook the mayor awake. "Kaleta, can I trust you to do something important?"

"Uh. I can hardly move."

"You needn't move much. I've got to go off with Morton, for days perhaps. My hominid is in the pen, here in the village. I don't really expect any of the villagers to attack him, but I want you to guard him, just in case. And give him food and water. It is supremely important that he survive. You must watch over him till I get back."

"Awright. When I wake up."

"You're awake now. You can move out there and sleep in front of the pen. No one will bother you."

From outside, Morton shouted: "Get the lead out, Magnuson! I'm taking a regular war party north! That's the way they went!"

But Magnuson persisted. Half-dragging, half-cajoling, he got Kaleta out of the hut and posted where he wanted him. Then there were a few other preparations to be made as rapidly as possible. Morton fumed, but had to concede grudgingly that the prospect of an extended march made them necessary.

Setting out at last with Morton and six warriors, Magnuson glanced back into the empty-looking village. Kaleta's plump form was stretched out in sleep beside the pen. Above him the one-handed hominid reached out through the palings, as if still asking some patient question.

***

Boris woke to find the sun near the zenith, one greenish glint of its surface coming through the close tangle of the thicket to strike him in the eyes. His head was on something yielding... not Brenda's thigh this time, but her folded coverall. The bare softness of her body lay curled and snuggled at his side. Last night... yes, last night.

The thicket was quiet. The river murmured just out of sight. Boris eased himself up to a sitting position, his cuts and bruises protesting fiercely. He was ravenously hungry, and reached out at once for a sample of the juicy stalk of a likely-looking plant. While awaiting his stomach's judgement on this morsel, and for Brenda to awake, he maneuvered himself into a crouching position under the close overhang of branches, and pulled off one of the small rocks still hanging to his net-garment. With this he set about quietly trying to detach the sleeves of Brenda's coverall, with a view to making himself some kind of footgear.

His moving around soon woke her, and she looked up at him unreadably. Even before she moved, she asked him: "Boris, do you love me?"

"Yes." He knew he was answering the Water. But what else could he have said?

Brenda sat up and looked at what he was doing. "Let me help you with that," she offered, having grasped at once what he was trying to do.

405

After a little discussion of the project he let her take over, and crawled about cautiously prospecting for more food. A few trees grew up through the thicket, and under the loose, shaggy bark on their trunks Boris discovered some grub-like things. These creatures were no doubt rich in protein and fat and the first one he sampled was quite palatable, at least to an experienced planeteer who thought about something else while swallowing. Brenda made a face at the idea of such fare, but then she wasn't really hungry yet. Boris wasn't either—that is, not approaching starvation—but he didn't need to let things go that far before he could suppress his civilized tastes. Today even raw and hairy food meant strength, and strength meant life.

Brenda did try some of the juicy plant, whose sampling had not as yet made Boris sick.

"I wish they hadn't made this damn thing so well," she muttered, working awkwardly with rock and spearpoint to separate the coverall's seams. Naked, crouching over her primitive job, she looked like a primitive herself. Not really, though.

"Hey."

She looked up, from under a tangle of soft brown hair.

"I do love you."

They ate a little more, and lay together once more and rested, and then worked again on the job of making footwear. At last Boris had, if not shoes, at least a pair of very tough socks bound onto his ankles with net-strings. The loss of the net garment didn't bother Boris much; it had provided neither modesty nor protection. Then they slept.

It was nearly dark again when they were wakened by men's voices, moving along the opposite bank of the stream, no more than ten meters away. It sounded like the villagers' language. The two in the thicket, he with spear in hand, she gripping a rock, waited silent and motionless until the sounds of speech had faded out into the distance.

"What do we do now?" Brenda whispered coolly.

"Let's discuss." It was nearly six days, to the best of Boris's calculations, since Jones had pointed an energy rifle at him and compelled him to swallow the Water of Thought. It was a couple of days since the ordeal had started, and doubtless that had been over for some time. For nearly twenty standard hours Boris and Brenda had been free, a state of affairs that would not sit well with the Kappans, or with Magnuson, or with the smugglers either.

"The Kappans probably won't care a whole lot one way or the other about you," he whispered to Brenda, watching her work her way as quietly as possible back into what was left of the coverall.

"I suppose; what's one female more or less? But Don Morton and our dear mayor will have other ideas." She reached for her shoes.

"But I think Magnuson is probably still in charge."

"Are you telling me I should give myself up?" Her fingers, ready to pull on a shoe, were still.

"No. Only that if worst ever comes to worst... your ankle's still swollen, isn't it?

You're having trouble getting that shoe on."

"I can walk."

"We ought to be able to tie some-kind of bandage on it."

They did. By that time it was quite dark, and Boris, spear in hand, led the way out of the thicket and into the river again. When he drank, he was again aware of the taste of the Water of Thought. It was faint but undeniable. This time he spoke of it to

Brenda, and she agreed with him. Now was not the time to debate possible explanations. They moved on upstream.

Within a kilometer, as Boris had more or less expected, they ran into steep rapids. Here they had to climb from the stream; and when he stood on the high bank looking back he got a nasty shock. There were lanterns bobbing about near the thicket where they had spent the day. His plan had used up their strength and time, and had moved them a score of kilometers farther from the colony, but their pursuers were now as close on their trail as ever. Or at least some of them were. He had succeeded in scattering and worrying his tribe of enemies somewhat, but that was about all.

There was a reasonable path here following the course of the river, and he led Brenda upstream along it. If they struck off through the bush they might slow themselves down critically and would certainly leave a plainer trail. The sleeve-socks were an enormous help; getting, even this far without them would probably have been impossible; but Boris doubted whether they were going to be enough. Tonight, he thought, my feet will give out on rocks or plant-stubble somewhere. From then on I crawl.

As before they spoke little on the trail, giving them both plenty of time for private thoughts. Boris looked up frequently at the stars. The cruiser had been scheduled to arrive three days ago, and it might very well be up there in orbit now. But then, the difficulties of astrogation being what they were, the ship might very well be three days more, or even longer, in reaching the system. And when it did arrive, and the people on board learned something of the colonists' difficulties, they would hardly start their search during the hours of darkness.

These were not very positive thoughts that Boris was entertaining himself with, but they were the best he could do at the moment.

It was a nightmare of a night. All through it, four or five lanterns stayed on their trail in the dark, becoming visible whenever Boris and Brenda topped a rise. At last the undergrowth beside the riverbank trail thinned somewhat, and they could move away from the river long enough to start a false trail or two. These seemed temporarily effective; each took their pursuers a little time to figure out.

His feet. His weary muscles. He was debating with himself whether to try sending Brenda on ahead; and then he saw in the starlight how her mouth was set. When he looked at her movements closely he could see that she was trying to conceal a limp.

"Your ankle. I thought it was all right now."

"I must have given it another little twist back there. One of those underwater rocks. Boris, go on ahead. They won't hurt me if they catch me, you said so yourself. But they'll kill you."

He might have laughed, if his throat wasn't so sore. If several other things. "I'm moving at about top speed right now, girl. I was about to send you running on ahead."

After that there seemed no more to say.

At dawn there were no dense thickets to hide in readily available, and the last look at the lanterns had shown them so close behind that Boris dared not delay even a minute to look for a good hiding place. They were following the spine of a high, wooded ridge, and they just kept moving along it. Boris considered going downhill into the ravine, hoping to find a wadable stretch of the Yunoee, or some other stream to drown their trail; but if he went foothill and then missed finding an escape, the hunters would be down on them like an avalanche. He didn't think that he could climb another hill.

Having just admitted that to himself, he saw a place just ahead where the ridge that they were following angled higher. A sketch of a path led upward, and in the soft dust were several sets of prints, from what certainly looked like bare prime-theme-human feet. He pointed a finger at them and croaked something.

"Boris, I can't make it." Brenda stumbled, tried to get up, then stayed down on her knees. "Go on. I'm going to try to hide."

If he tried to help her walk they were both going to fall down. "I shouldn't..." He wanted to say that he shouldn't have brought her, let her come along, however it had happened. Too late now. He bent over Brenda where she sat in the dust and they clasped their hands, all four of them, together.

He could do nothing for her unless he got away.

"They won't hurt me. Go on."

Actually he thought she was going to be better off being caught separately from him. He croaked some kind of a farewell and turned and tried the hill. Somewhat to his surprise he found that he could manage it, at least on this soft dusty trail. His feet had once been useful things, and he supposed they might someday be so again, but right now he would prefer not to know them. As for things like water and food and rest... rest...

He was getting lightheaded, and all he had to do was faint and roll back downhill; that would fix everything nicely. Scion of the Martian Brazils, famous bon vivant and adventurer, adjudged not quite human by Red Circles, scion of the Kappan Circles.

Boris topped a small rise in the trail and stopped to breathe. Brenda had managed to get out of sight somewhere, he couldn't see her. He could see the warriors coming, though, only two hundred meters behind him, and they undoubtedly saw him. There were ten of them, and one had something over his eyes as if to shield them from the light. So, one had taken the night-vision drug, that was how they had tracked the fugitives through the night with only torches and lanterns to light the trail. It seemed unfair.

Boris climbed on. He had to pause now at every second or third step to rest, and he looked back each time he paused. The warriors saw him, all right, for they pointed at him, and waved their weapons as if to urge one another on. But still they advanced only hesitantly, making no real speed. Could they possibly fear him? Did they think he had magic powers which had let him escape the ordeal?

Gritting his teeth and gripping his spear, Boris kept going. They weren't gong to take him prisoner, no, not again. His hunters continued to gain on him, but as it were reluctantly. Maybe from down there he looked like a man walking deliberately, contemptuous of his pursuers. Maybe if he turned around and walked toward them they would run.

He glanced back once more and nearly fell, for his hunters were indeed retreating, backing downhill with nocked arrows and leveled spears. Boris looked uphill, and saw the hominid troop coming down in a slow semi-circle, dozens of wild adults, armed with stones and crude clubs. He faced immediately toward the retreating hunters and hurled his spear after them, staggering with the effort. The spear fell ludicrously short, but the gesture just might suggest to the hominids that his heart was in the right place.

About half of the hominid numbers charged downhill past Boris, howling at his erstwhile pursuers, who turned and fled.

The other half surrounded him, yipping and jabbering about him, not knowing what to make of him. These were no dead-eyed quarry beasts. It seemed to Boris, groggy as he was, that these might very well be men. He made a planeteers' gesture designed for communicating with Apparent Primitives, and aroused some interest. The hominids formed a loose squatting circle around Boris, and took turns jabbering. They shooed insects, and panted and yawned, incidentally displaying their human teeth.

Boris's head was spinning, but he kept on making gestures, and tried a few words of this and that, being careful not to sound like a villager. His audience gaped unappreciatively. To blazes with them all, and also with the idea of preserving a show of something or other. If he was going to die here, it would not be while standing on these feet. He sat down in the dust, and by probing gingerly through the fabric of his improvised socks tried to decide how much was left of his soles.

From somewhere downhill came cries and shouts that sounded like a fight in progress. Most of the crowd lost interest in Boris and charged off in that direction. But half a dozen stayed behind, still watching him.

Should he try to tell them about Brenda?

First he was going to have to try to ask them for some water. Because the sun was so hot...

***

He was being carried, his head on a leathery shoulder, other arms and shoulders supporting his body. Hominid smell was thick about him. Overhead, treetops flowed by at a fast walk. Boris's mouth was wet; it seemed that water had been poured on him, and he had a memory of recent choking and swallowing. It was dim here under the tall trees, though what

412

little Boris could see of the sky was still bright with daylight. The trail he was on was narrow and twisting, overhung by many branches. His unspeaking bearers were carrying him into some secret fastness of the dim green forest.

Chapter Eight

Capture, thought Brenda, had been something of an anticlimax.

The scowling warriors who had at last come upon her trying to hide in the woods had jabbered contemptuously. Obviously they were at first of two minds as to whether to take her into custody, or simply hurry on with the important part of the chase, ignoring the alien female with the flat forehead, close-set eyes, and what they must think of as disgustingly soft skin.

But in the end they had collected her, and one of the junior members of the party after some protest had been delegated to lead her back toward the Warriors' Village. Once deprived of his part in the glorious chase, her disgruntled guard had seemed in no great hurry to get home, which was a relief. Brenda hobbled along in front of him as best she could, wishing that she had a crutch. And she thought about Boris as she went.

Looking back now, she was abruptly horrified at the memory of how she had acted on first getting him out of the cave, how close she had come to getting them both killed.

But he knew what the Water of Thought could do; he would understand. After going through one day of it himself, Brenda wondered how Boris could possibly have retained his basic sanity through five.

Hobbling through the woods, almost back at the village, she smiled, lightly and briefly, remembering that day in the thicket. There was something good to be said for madness. If you could only turn it on and off.

She had felt the madness and now she knew it for what it was. And she considered herself free of it. And she would be ready this moment to rejoin Boris if by doing so she could be of any help.

He hadn't been caught. He hadn't been caught yet. There had been yelling on the trail ahead, immediately after they had separated, when Brenda had crawled off the trail and tried to hide. But those yells had not been cries of triumph, she was sure of that. And now, on her way back to the Warriors' Village as a prisoner again, another search party, outward bound, passed her and her escort. And the warriors in it were made angry by what her escort had to say to them. And, when no one could see her, Brenda smiled.

As with her capture, there was no particular excitement about her arrival, when she limped at last back into the village common, and was allowed to sit down there in the dust. The few children playing nearby took little notice. Nor did the women who were passing to and fro, stolidly engaged with their eternal chores. Brenda was one of the tribe now, and the women made friendly gestures to her across the barrier of language. They didn't mind that she had run away. Probably they had done that, or felt like doing it, themselves.

"Brenda!" It was Jane, her face showing relief, running toward her. "Brenda, honey. Oh, I'm so glad you're all right. You are, aren't you?"

"Basically. How about you? Where are the others?" Brenda let Jane help her to her feet, and lead her to a nearby log that served the village as a bench.

"Nothing's happened to me, honey. Except... Don went wild when Boris got away. Worse than any of the Kappans. He's out chasing Boris, and Dr. Magnuson is too." Jane, her face troubled, sat down at Brenda's side. "Eddie was killed, in the ordeal."

"I know. I'm sorry."

"Yes. I don't think he'd have taken me offworld anyway. I think he had one of those permanent marriages." Jane pulled her arm from Brenda's touch. "Bren, I have to confess something. It must have been that drug that made me do it. When I heard that Boris had run away with you, I—I was hoping that they'd catch you. In fact I ran around here screaming, like some terrible... I wanted to see him *dead*, and you too, rather than see you with a good man I couldn't have." Jane began to cry. "I don't suppose you can understand. How could you?"

"Oh, Janey, it *was* that awful drug. I know. It—it made me do things too."

The two small town girls who had grown up together sat side by side, trying to comfort each other, both of them weeping.

"Where's Mayor Pete?" Brenda asked, finally, dabbing at her eyes and looking around the village.

"Lying around somewhere. He hasn't got over the initiation yet. I wish I'd never heard of him, or Don Morton either. I knew they were both rotten, and still I played along with them."

***

Pete Kaleta peered cautiously around the corner of the hominid's pen, looking across the village common at the two girls, who were crying on each other's shoulders again.

Probably they were set to talk and weep the rest of the day. They were not likely to interfere with anything he did.

The hominid inside the pen reached out through the palings to touch Kaleta's coverall; Kaleta brushed the single leathery hand away with distaste.

"So, you and I belong to the same club now," he said aloud, looking at the hominid. Both bore practically the same ritual wounds from the ordeal. "I hope you feel as lousy as I do."

The pale eyes looked back at Kaleta with what might be frustration, as if the creature wanted to talk to him, and almost but not quite knew how.

Kaleta turned away. Since the ordeal he had not been able to think for long of anything, not even his injuries, but one thing: what he had seen in the Temple Village, only a few kilometers away—a vat, filled with many liters of the Water of Thought.

The interstellar crime syndicate would pay a fortune, a vast fortune, for the contents of that vat. And now the warriors were gone from all the villages, Magnuson and Morton were gone too, Jones and Brazil were out of the way. There was no one, really, between Kaleta and all that wealth down in the village.

And the copter was still parked in concealment down there near the Temple Village. Magnuson believed himself to have the only power key for that copter, but Magnuson was wrong, not as smart as he thought he was. Kaleta had hidden an extra power key inside the copter's cabin, and he had also concealed a weapon there.

It was not likely that Kaleta would ever get a better chance than this. He could walk downstream right now, go to the copter, and arm himself. Then he could raid the virtually undefended Temple, and fly away with buckets full of the Water

416

of Thought. He would hide the stuff somewhere nearer the colony, and when the Space Force came he would put them on a false trail and try to keep them away from these villages. Of course there were great risks involved. But the possible reward was so great as to be worth any imaginable risk.

Kaleta saw himself safely away from Kappa and the wife who had gradually become no more than an irritation, amid the fleshpots of Earth or Planet Golden, maybe allowing a few of the more beautiful women there to help him spend some of his money.

He drew a deep breath, and found that his decision was already made. He would do it; he would gamble everything. A helpful idea immediately suggested itself, and Kaleta smiled and opened the door of the hominid's pen. Let the creature wander away. Then Magnuson, returning here, might think Kaleta had gone chasing after the escaped hominid. Or, Magnuson might even blame the villagers for both disappearances. Either way there would be a diversion.

Without waiting to see whether the hominid took immediate advantage of the open door, Kaleta turned and walked calmly away himself, as if he was just going into the woods to relieve himself. No special preparations were necessary for his plan. The few Kappan women and children in sight ignored him; he didn't think Jane or Brenda were aware of him at all.

Once the trees were solidly around him, Kaleta quickened his pace. Going downhill, he hoped to be able to reach the Temple Village in two hours or less.

As he emerged from the woods onto the riverside path, he stumbled awkwardly, and cursed. He was still worn out, aching all over, from the ordeal. He had had only about six hours sleep before Magnuson awakened him, and very little since then. Plenty of reason to worry. His original plan with Morton now appeared hopeless. Morton in a groundsuit was another good reason for Kaleta to get out; he didn't trust Morton a bit. But overriding all details was the thought of that vat of the Water of Thought, and the price that the Outfit would pay for it.

He would get away with twenty or thirty liters if he got a drop; maybe he could get a lot more. He could force some of the Temple Villagers to help him carry pails. All Earth-descended men probably looked a lot alike to them, and he might easily manage to blame his actions on someone else. There were all kinds of possibilities as well as dangers in his plan; he would just have to work it out as he went along. But he could not turn down this chance of enormous wealth—because nothing else mattered, by comparison.

His legs were already weary, but still Kaleta walked quickly, sliding and scrambling down the steeper places in the path. As a member of the tribe, he expected no trouble from any Kappans he might meet. Even Magnuson halfway trusted him now, and that was the biggest joke yet. Magnuson was, must be, highly intelligent. And yet, blinded by his obsession with ordeals and weeding out the unfit, wanting to be God and decide who could live and who couldn't, creating men from baboons.

It was strange, thought Kaleta, how everyone among the Earth-descended except himself had been mentally twisted by their draughts of the Water of Thought. Jones, driven to give up everything else just to get another drink of it. Brazil curiously paralyzed in his will. Magnuson probably confirmed in his pseudo-religious fanaticism. Jane driven mad with envy of Brenda, and Brenda... Kaleta hadn't seen enough of her since the ordeal to know what the effect on her had been. And

Morton... Kaleta hadn't seen much of Morton either, but enough to get the idea. He looked over his shoulder and shivered slightly. Morton in his right mind was bad enough.

A collection of nuts, all of them. Psychos. It seemed that he, Pete Kaleta, was the only one who had not been unbalanced by drinking the Water of Thought. Probably that was because he was the only tough-minded realist among them to begin with.

Could he be that firmly certain of his own sanity? As he hurried downstream he frowned, trying to step back mentally and view his present actions with complete fairness, objectivity. His basic goal, realistically enough, was wealth. Very well. Then it was perfectly logical for him to steal the most valuable property within reach (which happened to be the Water), hide it somewhere, and sell it later on. Of course, he repeated to himself, it was a dangerous plan, but you never gained anything important without taking risks.

After he had somehow weathered the inevitable Space Force investigation, the smart thing would be to smuggle the stolen Water offworld in small batches. That way the whole thing could never be lost at once. He had his contact with the Outfit. They would know ways. But he would have to be very careful that they didn't cheat him.

He would have to be careful in other ways, too. For example, about suddenly leaving Kappa to enjoy his new wealth. That would look very suspicious. If need be, he could forego the fleshpots and continue to put up with his wife's whining and nagging. Once wealth was his, nothing else would bother him greatly.

Maybe, with a little luck, Morton and Magnuson and Brazil would all eliminate one another. That would help a lot, if Kaleta didn't have to try to kill them himself, or cut them in. And the two young women would have to be put out of the way somehow; he had known them since they were just children, and it was sad, but there it was. They were all dangerous to Kaleta's wealth.

Anyway, back to the heart of the plan: when he had surmounted all such dangers in one way or another, he would smuggle his stolen Thought-Water off world in small batches. He would have his payment smuggled in, in installments, just as the Water went out. None of your electronic credits, not in this case. He wanted something more tangible. He would arrange to be paid in bills of high denomination, which would take up little space, and so could easily be hidden.

Puffing with effort, his feet hurting, Kaleta still smiled and maintained his rapid pace downhill. His vision of wealth, before vague and abstract, had taken concrete form. He could almost see the money, the dozens of crisp bills coming into his hands. Possibly he'd get away with forty liters of the Water today, and possibly the Outfit would pay him five million for that much. Maybe just the first installment, for the first small batch smuggled offworld, would be half a million. He would bury it in the woods, probably, somewhere fairly near the colony. Interstellar currency was made to last, physically, and it would stay buried years and years without any special precautions and still be fresh and crackling whenever he went to dig it out and look at it and fondle it. Kaleta could almost see that first payment of half a million, maybe three-quarters of a million right now, he could see the numbers and the zeros on the bills—

A rock tripped him, and he sprawled painfully on the path, skinning the hands he used to break his fall, awaking pain in all his wounds from the ordeal. He cursed and scrambled to his feet and hurried on.

After he had stolen and sold this first barrel-full of the Water of Thought, collecting his first five or six million and putting it away, what was to prevent him from raiding these villages again and again, getting away with more and more of the stuff? Maybe the Space Force could be put off somehow. Maybe he could bribe someone, even a Tribune. Kaleta grimaced. He would try that only as a last resort, for bribing anyone important would mean giving up a substantial portion of his wealth. A crooked Tribune would certainly be very greedy. Kaleta groaned aloud, hurrying through the woods. It seemed he was doomed to share his money, with Morton or with someone else.

A sudden thought stopped Kaleta in the rocky path, and made him face back upstream. The real wealth, the source of the Water was somewhere back up there. Immediately after the ordeal, he and the other new members of the tribe had been told something of its secrets, Magnuson translating for the others. Most of what had been revealed was magical nonsense about this and that, but one real secret was that the Water of Thought was obtained by raiding the territory of the Forest People, north of the villages. Kaleta had been too groggy then to think or care about it, but now he saw how this offered unlimited possibilities for the future. When he had weapons, and a copter, and time.

But the vat in the temple was a sure thing, and he had better concentrate on today's job. When he had that vat emptied he could go on with further plans. Kaleta faced downstream again, and hurried on.

The Workers' Village was just ahead. A branching trail joined in here, and along it a few kilted Kappan men were approaching, dragging with them a half-grown male hominid, gagged by a stick tied into its mouth, its arms bound. The men were laughing and pleased with themselves; evidently they had just caught a beast that would be useful in the quarry. When they saw Kaleta they stopped and stared at him, letting him pass the intersection ahead of them.

He waved and smiled at the workers, as he would have done on meeting Kappans near the colony. He half-understood these villagers' speech, but he did not want to try to say anything. All he wanted was to pass these men without alarming them.

He apparently succeeded in this, and in another minute was entering the Workers' Village. The few people he saw were, appropriately enough, at work, and paid him little attention. Trying to look like a man on a casual stroll, he stopped at the village well, where the river water came up mudless after filtering through twenty meters of sand. Taking his time, Kaleta hauled up a bucket and then drank from a gourd hung at the well. He smiled at some watching children, and then walked on along the downstream trail.

When he was a couple of hundred meters below the Workers' Village, he looked about to make sure that he was unobserved, then waded out into the Yunoee. If he had all his directions straight, the copter should be less than a kilometer from him. It was hidden at the edge of a landing clearing in the woods on the other side of the river, just a minute's walk from the Temple Village. Probably there would be a Kappan guard or two watching the copter, but Kaleta now had the wounds of the ordeal to prove that he was one of them. The half-wit fraternity, Brazil had said. Right now Brazil was probably wishing he had joined.

The river, nowhere more than a stone's throw wide, was not swift at this point. Kaleta did not even bother to remove his light boots, though he had to swim a few strokes near the center of the channel. Then he was wading again, reaching the opposite shore, and climbing out. The only people in sight were a few kilted laborers, and they were a long way off and paying him no attention. He walked away from the river, across a cultivated field, and then into woods again.

He located the copter's hiding place with little trouble. It was just a little natural clearing whose two or three obstructing trees had been hacked or burned away. The copter was just where Kaleta had last seen it—pulled a little way back out of the clearing, under high trees whose canopy of branches would make it virtually invisible from the air. There were two guards in sight—not fierce warriors, Kaleta saw thankfully, but a pair of robed priests who looked as if they did not know what to do with the clubs in their hands. Evidently Red Circles' men were all busy hunting Brazil.

Kaleta approached casually, and walked calmly out into the clearing. He smiled and waved to the priests when they saw him; though not very martial, they were muscular youngsters, and he was going to have to be careful.

"I must enter bird," he said—or tried to say—in their language, as he walked toward them. He pointed at the copter to show what he meant, and continued to smile.

The two regarded him with some dislike, he thought, but no real suspicion. They gave the impression of being uncertain about the duties of guards, and jabbered between themselves, saying something about the chiefs. Finally they made way for Kaleta to approach the copter.

Still smiling, he stepped past them. He opened the door to the cabin, and felt inside a small storage compartment under the front seat, letting out a breath of relief when his fingers located the machine pistol and the spare power key exactly where he had hidden them, taped to the top of the compartment out of the way of a casual inspection. There were also a couple of extra clips of ammunition for the pistol, which he pulled out and stowed in a pocket of his coverall.

Then he climbed up into the copter and looked over the controls. Everything appeared to be in order, ready to go. Now all he had to do was collect his cargo.

As he hopped down from the copter and approached the guards with the gun aimed, his hands were shaking. He had never killed anyone before, and he felt almost sick at what he was going to do. But then he visualized the money again, and saw these two Kappans standing between himself and it. They would never stand by and let him load buckets of the Water of Thought and fly away with it.

The pistol made a low, ripping sound, like heavy cloth tearing. It was not very loud, but the two young Kappans were twitching on the ground, amid a great deal of blood. Kaleta saw that he had used up half a clip, and reloaded. His hands were steady. He dragged the riddled bodies into the bushes, out of sight, and kicked leaves over the blood.

So far, so good. Should he fly the copter into the village? Easier to get the Water aboard that way. But that would attract the attention of everyone in the area; and, Kaleta recalled, there were enough trees in the village to make it difficult at best to land. He wasn't all that great a pilot. He made sure there were no bloodstains on his hands or clothing, stuck the pistol inside his coverall, and started briskly along the path to the village.

424

This was where Brazil in a suit had once confronted and disarmed him. Not this time, Brazil.

At one point along the path he had a good view of Great Lake, which was as calm as ever, rimmed by distant green hills under the greenish Kappan sky. Lake and hills and sky made a peaceful scene, and Kaleta stopped for a moment to look at it. He felt a twinge of yearning. Why did life have to be the grim and ugly thing it was? But there was no getting around it, the game of life had to be played by the rules of harsh reality.

He went on. A few seconds' walk took him past the spot where Brazil had jumped out in the ground-suit. Kaleta smiled.

His smile grew broader as he entered the Temple Village; it was, if anything, more nearly deserted than the other two settlements had been. Kaleta proceeded straight to the Temple and went in. He found no one in the first chamber. The door behind the stone altar led him into the room where the Water of Thought was buried. An old priest and a young one were sitting on mats. They looked up as Kaleta came in, and were astonished when he went straight to the sunken vat and pulled aside its coverings. The priests both shouted angrily at him, and he drew the pistol, wondering if they even knew what it was.

The older man came forward, waving his arms and yelling. Kaleta shot him, knocking him back across the room. The young man just stood still, gaping, frozen with shock.

Against one wall was a neat stack of wooden buckets with fiber handles, clean and painted utensils. Possibly, thought Kaleta, they were the means by which the warriors who raided hominid territory brought back the Water of Thought. He grabbed up a pair of the buckets, one nested inside the other, with his left hand, and held them out. The young man remained frozen. Kaleta cursed him with no effect, and had to kick him a couple of times before he would start to move.

"Fill them! Like this!" Kaleta got himself a third pail, and dipped it into the opened vat. He would be able to carry only one himself; he had to keep the pistol ready.

At last the young man got the idea, and obeyed. Then Kaleta prodded him toward the exit. "Go on! No, stupid, take the pails with you! Carry them!"

A woman saw them come out of the Temple. She saw what they were carrying, and ran away screaming before Kaleta could decide whether or not to shoot at her. It was too bad, but he would probably have to do some more killing before he got away.

"Go—that way—go on!" Kaleta urged his coolie through the village. The Kappan moved ahead slowly, carrying his two buckets dripping with the Water of Thought, stopping every few feet to look back in unbelieving terror, as if he expected Kaleta to vanish at any moment. Kaleta snarled at him and jabbed him on with the pistol.

"Don't slop that stuff around, you—" But if he hit the man, more of the Water would certainly be spilled. They made slow progress, but fortunately the village remained empty, as if the only effect of the woman's screams had been to scare the remaining people away. It seemed to Kaleta that it took him an hour to urge his trembling, laden captive as far as the copter.

Luckily the young man had set down the buckets before he saw the four dead hands of the two guards that protruded from a thicket; at that sight, he went completely to pieces. Kaleta shoved him aside, and carefully hoisted his thirty or thirty-five liters of wealth into the rear of the copter, a pail at a time. He found a roll of sealing-plastic in the copter, and wrapped the pails to minimize any further spillage during flight. Everything was working out.

He hopped down from the copter, and was about to shoot the only potential witness who might be able to identify him, when there flashed before his mind's eye the picture of those other empty pails inside the Temple.

It was agonizing. There had been so much Thought-Water left in the vat. Should he attempt another trip? The delay meant risking what he had already gained.

Maybe he could make ten million today. Or even twelve. All for himself.

Instead of shooting the blubbering youth, Kaleta grabbed him by one arm and slung him staggering back toward the village.

"We go again. Hurry!" Kaleta made the youth run, and ran beside him. At the edge of the village Kaleta had to stop for a moment. He was still weak from the ordeal If he fainted now—

But the vision of his wealth was plain before him, and he knew he would not faint. "Come along, hurry!" The village still looked empty of people; Kaleta gasped with relief. Only the old priest's dead body inhabited the Temple. Kaleta handed two more of the pails to his unwilling partner, and again took another for himself.

This time the Kappan youth knew what was wanted, and moved a trifle faster, filling the pails and starting off to the Temple again. He kept darting fearful glances at Kaleta's pistol, but he was starting to think again, and Kaleta watched him carefully.

Kaleta felt a rising certainty that he was going to be able to get away with it; he could almost feel and smell the money. From here on it was easy. Even if half a dozen warriors came at

427

him now, he thought, he could fight them off with the pistol, and get away.

They left the village and traveled the long-seeming path again, with its view of the calm lake. They were halfway across the landing clearing when Kaleta heard a boy's voice shouting. A half-grown robed youth ran out of the forest near the copter, Red Circles gasping four steps behind him. Kaleta's porter set down his buckets and fell on his face. Red Circles had a bow and arrow in his hands, small things that it seemed a child might use for practice. The angle was wrong for Kaleta; if he shot Red Circles from here, some of the bullets might hit the copter, and could drain priceless wealth from the Water-laden buckets already stowed inside.

Kaleta sidestepped for a better angle. The bow twanged, and the little arrow came so swiftly that it was sprouted between Kaleta's ribs before he could try to dodge.

He looked down at the arrow in surprise, found that he could not breathe, and dropped his pistol. He managed to set down his pail of the Water of Thought without spilling any before he fell.

Chapter Nine

Don Morton dug in his metal-shod feet and with his servo-powered gauntlets took a good grip on the trunk of a sapling. He bent his legs, then straightened them, lifting, grunting a little at the tree's resistance. With a mighty ripping sound, roots snapping like shots, the sapling gave up its hold on the soil.

It was a satisfying feeling. Morton stood up straight, waving the tree in one hand almost as easily as a feathered wand. "There. I'm getting pretty good, huh?"

Magnuson was busy studying the rugged landscape through a pair of binoculars, and did not answer at once. He and Morton were alone, for the moment, atop a ridge somewhere near the hidden headwaters of the Yunoee, deep in hominid territory. The six warriors who had accompanied them here as trackers on the search for Brazil were out hunting down an evening meal.

In Morton's view, Magnuson's behavior ever since the ordeal, had been even more arrogant than usual, as if the professor deliberately wanted to anger everyone he dealt with, Morton in particular. The scientist gave no evidence of having heard what Morton had just said to him. And Morton had spoken plainly.

"How about an answer, huh?"

At last Magnuson put down the binoculars. "If the other party's report is true," he said abstractedly, "the hominids could easily have killed him."

Talking about Brazil. Changing the subject without answering. Was this man trying to get himself killed?

"I SAID, I'M GETTING PRETTY GOOD WITH THE SUIT!" Morton roared, turning up his helmet's speakers to amplify his voice. "ANSWER ME! ANSWER!"

Magnuson heard him this time all right. He looked vaguely sick and uneasy. "I'm sorry," he said. "Very sorry. Yes, you are getting good with the suit. Better than Brazil was. When you find him, he won't talk to you the way he did last time."

"Damn right he won't." Morton took the tree in both gauntlets and cracked it over his armored knee, and threw the shattered wood away. "And I don't believe that the hominids got him, either. I'm gonna get him."

429

Brazil was the kind of guy who liked to get into one of these superman suits himself, and then push people around. Morton remembered Brazil disarming him, back in the Temple Village. And then Brazil had somehow escaped from the cave of the ordeal. Doubtless he had been laughing again as he sneaked out of that and ran away, while Morton had had to stay there, and suffer, and…

"I'LL KILL HIM!" Morton bellowed. Then he remembered to turn the speakers in his helmet down again. "A rotten bastard like that. I'll break his arms and his legs, and then his neck, when I get these hands on him." Morton raised the steel fingers that trembled in sympathy with his rage; oh, this suit was a wonderful thing!

"Yes." Magnuson heaved a tired sigh, put his binoculars back into their case, and sat down on a log. "In another day or two we may find him."

"Any idiot knows that; we *may* find him." Morton mimicked Magnuson's voice; then he puffed out a sigh of his own, and let the subject drop. He wished he could reach a hand up inside his helmet and rub the back of his neck; he was getting a headache. He felt weary. There hadn't been much time to rest after the ordeal, and he had worked hard today, practicing with the suit, and climbing cliffs and trees to look for Brazil. And the world seemed to be against him, as it had always been.

Ever since the start of the ordeal, when he had tasted the Water of Thought, all the causes of just rage that Morton had been forced to endure in his lifetime had seemed to take on doubled force. The Water of Thought was good stuff after all, for a real man; it just made him see clearly the way things really were.

The Water had made Morton fully aware of all the injustices that had ever been heaped on him, culminating in the ordeal itself. And during the ordeal his rage had been so great and pure that for a while it had made him meek. Morton had endured the sufferings of the initiation with what amounted to calm patience, because that was the only way he could survive to eventually enjoy revenge. When he had finished Brazil and got back to the village, Morton was going to look up the warrior who had tormented him during the ordeal, and devise for him some elaborate, slow, and particularly horrible death. Morton wanted to spend a lot of time and thought on that project, not to hurry it.

Thinking of his enemies, Morton, tired or not, was unable to stand still a moment longer. He spun around, pacing nervously this way and that, his armored hands flexing.

"Oh, sit down," said Magnuson peevishly. "Better save some of that energy."

That tore it. With the gorilla-strong arms of the suit, Morton grabbed Magnuson and hauled him to his feet. He aimed a backhanded slap at Magnuson's face, but at the last instant pulled it, stopped it almost completely. He was going to need Magnuson yet for a while.

Magnuson fell back over the log. He lay there with his mouth bloody, conscious but making no move to get up.

"Why don't you stop making me mad?" Morton demanded. "You just keep asking for trouble."

"I'll try to stop."

Magnuson's cold eyes were uncomfortable things to face, and Morton turned away from him. "Where are those goods?" he wondered aloud. "They're supposed to be hunters, and it takes 'em all day to catch one animal. I'm gonna see what they're up to." He trotted away down the hill, moving heavily.

When Morton was out of sight, and he was alone, Magnuson struggled wearily back up to a sitting position on the log. He spat out some blood, and tested his loosened teeth with tongue and fingers. It was a narrow, extremely dangerous path he had to walk with Morton, every moment, until the effect of the drug had worn off. And then? He could not shake the conviction that Morton would still be deadly dangerous in the suit. Magnuson would never be able to fully trust him.

And yet, Morton had come through the rite of passage, had proved himself a man.

Magnuson shook his head. Morton's case proved only that real men could do bad things—as the case of Brazil proved that apparently strong, complete men could have fatal, hidden flaws that showed up only under the X-ray probing of the ordeal.

Magnuson was certain that only by such ritual testing of all its men could galactic, or at least prime-theme human, civilization save itself from decadence. What ritual might be applicable or necessary to humanity in other themes—squid-like folk with tentacles were not the farthest removed from *homo sapiens*, and some forms were completely sexless—was an ultimately fascinating question, but far beyond the scope of his own life's work. He had dedicated, consecrated himself, to the cause of prime-theme Man, here and now, on Kappa. To help the cause, Magnuson had stolen and lied, and worked with the dope-smuggling scum of the very civilization he detested, making himself doubly a criminal in its eyes. He had interfered with fatal effect in Kappan affairs, and he would be prepared to commit worse crimes still—but if prime theme civilization survived in the galaxy, Magnuson felt sure of being remembered as one of its saviors. And again it struck him as ironic that two planeteers, members of that civilization's elite Space Force, had failed Man's test.

Magnuson remembered his first drink of the Water of Thought, which he had taken about a year ago. It had been part of his first initiation. Then, in the peculiar Kappan way, he had become a shaman without first becoming a member of a tribe. On that day, immediately after he had taken the drug, while the drums pounded and the chant soared, he had seen with new and overpowering certainty how right and necessary was the work he had already chosen to do—to pull the Kappan hominids through the sieve of testing, extracting from them the new branch of humanity which some of them must be ready to form. This mystical certainty had continued during the four or five days it had taken Magnuson to arrange his own disappearance and flee to these remote villages. Then, though he had never begun to doubt his work, a certain transcendent quality in his belief had faded. He understood now that the drug had brought that quality about, and had given him the courage that he might otherwise have lacked, to act on his convictions.

But the truth of his convictions had in no way depended on the drug. During his first weeks among these villagers, he had taken a good deal of interest in the Water of Thought. But he was more anthropologist than biologist or chemist, and in those early days the Kappans had not trusted him with free access to the Water-vat in the Temple. Soon his work with the hominids from the quarry had absorbed him, and he had thought less and less about the Water. In fact he had never tasted it again until just before the recent initiation, when all the candidates drank. It had been a pleasant surprise to find that his earlier draught had evidently given him immunity; if that was the usual case with Earthmen, the crime syndicate was due to suffer a disappointment, which made Magnuson feel somewhat better about his indirect involvement with them.

Now, the Water of Thought interested him hardly at all. On Kappa or on Earth, the key to Man's future lay in his deliberate evolutionary selection of himself, not in drugs. He yearned intensely to get back to the Warriors' Village, where the new man-hominid waited, newly human intelligence in his eyes. Living proof, who must convince the Space Force that Magnuson's way was right! Oh, in the name of Man, if only Kaleta was taking good care of the hominid!

Some distance below Magnuson, at the foot of the ridge, the suited figure of Morton reappeared. The six warriors were with him, and one of them was carrying game. There was water down there, a small tributary of the Yunoee. It would make a good place to camp for the night.

Morton looked up and waved imperiously for Magnuson to come down. It might be fatal to irritate Morton again. Magnuson stood up with a sigh, and began to descend the hill.

***

The sun was warm above. It came and went on Boris's eyelids as if perhaps moving leaf-shadows intervened. Before he even opened his eyes, he tried to remember where he was. He could tell that he was sitting on grassy earth, his back propped against a rough-barked tree. Oh yes, of course, the picnic. Brenda was so beautiful—

An unearthly voice jabbered nearby, and memory returned with a rush. Boris cracked his eyelids open cautiously. He beheld a daylight scene in the shady forest. Nearby and in the middle distance, a number of gray, two-legged forms moved about. None of them seemed to be paying him any particular attention at the moment.

Had they carried him here to be guest or dinner? He was still alive, which argued for the former. And they had given him water, which was also a most hopeful sign. Boris tried to think his situation over, before he moved so much as a finger, or even opened his eyes completely, while his accumulated physical discomforts were still soothed by inertia.

At least he had escaped the villagers, Magnuson, Morton and Kaleta. Of course Jones had died in the ordeal, and for all Boris knew the other Earth-descended men might have also. It would be ironic indeed if Magnuson were killed in the very ritual he loved so well and prescribed for all—but Boris couldn't really believe that he had been. Magnuson would survive if anyone did.

And Brenda—at the thought of her, Boris opened his eyes wide, and raised himself a little from his position against the tree. She was either crawling about lost in the woods or the Kappans had taken her. If Boris was going to have any hope of ever doing anything for her, he had to start from where he was, by first finding out just what these hominids intended to do with him.

A few of the gray figures noticed his movement, and heard the accompanying groan. They turned toward him with mild interest. There was nothing like a general alarm, no monkey-cry of alert. What jabbering took place was between individuals. Watching and listening, Boris got a strong impression that it was genuine though doubtless primitive speech.

This was a gathering-place, obviously, but he could not call it a camp. The hominids who had driven off the village warriors had been carrying rocks and dead branches as weapons, but here not an artifact was in sight. There was not a lean-to, a fire, a bed, a shred of clothing or an ornament. With only his sleeve-socks and the remains of his net-garment, Boris could feel overdressed among these leathery nudists.

On other planets he had seen primitive prime-theme people who lived almost this simply. Yet something was very different here. Something was wrong in this Eden, something missing. A small crowd had accumulated and was watching Boris with curiosity before he realized what the odd thing was. There were babes in female arms, and there were hominids who appeared to be not quite fully grown. But above the age of beginning toddlers, there were no pre-pubescent children anywhere in sight.

Maybe it was a school day.

Boris decided that if anything like a joke could still occur to him, he was probably not yet dead. That made it necessary to sooner or later try to get to his feet. Slow movement, with many grunts and pauses, interested his primitive audience but did not startle them. Not that he could have moved fast enough to startle anyone anyway. At last he reached something like his full height, and began a planeteer's routine of supposedly friendly gestures.

He towered, a bit unsteadily, over the crowd, whose taller heads reached just about up to his armpits. These creatures were of the same form as the quarry-beasts that Boris had seen—and yet they were completely different. Apart from any moral or intellectual problems posed, the others had struck Boris as repulsive. He would personally have preferred to be away from them, to look at something else. But seen like this, in their own world, the hominids did not strike him as ugly creatures. Somehow the thickness of their grayish, leathery skins appeared to be perceptible, and was not unattractive.

As he went slowly through the sign-language routines meant to demonstrate his admirable qualities of goodwill and fearlessness, Boris became especially aware of one individual in his audience—this was a male, taller than the average and probably a little older, if silver in hominid hair meant age.

The others seemed to make way for him, with slight and perhaps unconscious movements. Boris paused in his presentation and looked at this individual, who took the opportunity to toss something toward Boris. Boris found himself catching and holding the raw hind-quarter of a small warm-blooded creature.

The haunch did not smell especially appetizing, but at least it was fresh, and Boris's stomach rumbled approval. He made his best thank-you gesture, peeled away some fur, bit, chewed, and swallowed.

The food-giving one said something to Boris. Boris wished him good health in return. In his professional judgment, the odds that these were human beings had just risen enormously. Near-humans might use tools to fight and hunt; but when a dominant male went about handing out food instead of grabbing it, it seemed a good bet that the sometimes blurry-looking line at the border of humanity had been crossed.

But the prime-theme human slot on Kappa was firmly occupied by the villagers' species. That they were true prime theme was proven beyond doubt by their extremely close biochemical kinship with Earth-descended humans. On a planet as Earthlike as Kappa, theory predicted, demanded, evolution of life in the prime theme, with earthlike humanity at the top... but could evolution on Kappa have two heads?

Anyway, today's dinner was not where a planeteer was eaten, but where he ate. The raw meat tasted better than the grubs that Boris could remember devouring in a certain thicket—though not a whole lot better, actually. Boris stopped gesturing for the time being and attended to his food.

The food-giver, watching him, alternately smiled and frowned, as if he might be considering the obvious language problem. Or perhaps he was only stretching his face.

Before attempts at communication were resumed, a real monkey-troop alarm was called. The hominids all scrambled away in one direction, jumping and shrieking. The food-giver ran with the others, trying like any leader to get ahead of his followers as soon as he could be sure where they were headed.

The mass movement turned out to be not a flight or an attack, but a greeting. It seemed that a war party, or at least some all-male group, was returning to the gathering place. Boris could not recognize the individuals in it, but he thought it was probably the aggressive gang who had gone skirmishing after the village warriors. This was borne out by the fact that several of the arriving hominids were wounded, two of them badly enough to require their being carried by others. One of the two had a disabled leg, and clung to a stretcher improvised from a springy branch. The other one looked dead.

There was a great deal of jabbering on all sides, and Boris was almost forgotten in the excitement. He noticed that the dead hominid was receiving more attention than the wounded ones. This struck Boris as odd, and he moved to a position where he could watch what was going on around the corpse. He could pick out no chief mourner, but it seemed to be an indignation meeting.

People as primitive as these were probably basically quite non-aggressive. Still it made Boris uneasy to be the lone outsider around when they were angry about something. It was a time to be unobtrusive, though not too timid; and that was a balance hard to strike, for a man who stood two heads taller than the crowd and came from a different planet.

But Boris, to his relief, found himself almost ignored for the moment. Here came a man with an edged stone in his hand, and Food-Giver beside him, making their way through the small crowd around the corpse. They both squatted down by the head of the body, and the man with the rough hand-ax went to work on the neck.

This was intriguing. Boris watched closely, with a hardened planeteer's interest. He thought he could guess what was coming next, for he remembered the hacked-open hominid skull that he had seen in Magnuson's laboratory near the quarry.

By now there were nearly a hundred hominids gathered around the dead man, watching. But Boris's height still let him see. The head came free, and was more or less peeled. Then the man with the hand-axe turned the skull upside down and attacked the base, enlarging the *foramen magnum* to get at the brain.

Boris was expecting an immediate ritual cannibalism of the brain. But to his surprise nothing of the kind was performed. He missed some details of what was being done, but what he did see astonished him. Perhaps half a cup of clear liquid, only faintly tinted with blood, was drained from the skull into a gourd held ready by Food-Giver.

And that appeared to be that, for the present. The crowd gradually began to disperse. Boris saw that some of them were weeping, but this did not surprise him as it almost certainly would have a few days earlier. Here, after observing the hominids in their natural state for only minutes, he had seen and heard enough to convince himself of their human status.

The question was, what had been drained into that gourd, and what was going to be done with it? The clearness of the fluid suggested lymph; Boris wasn't at all sure of the details of hominid physiology, except that it must be somewhat different from his own, and even from the Kappan villagers'. Boris had a wild and horrible suspicion about that clear liquid.

Some of the females were gathering closely about the dismembered corpse. Boris did not wait to see what they were going to do with it. Wincing along on painful feet, he followed Food-Giver and a couple of others who were walking away with the gourd.

They took it without ceremony a couple of hundred meters into the woods, to a small clearing centered by a smoldering pile of logs. The grass near the logs had long since been burned away. A faint, worn path surrounding the blackened area showed that there was more or less regular foot traffic here. Possibly lightning had once fired a dead tree, and the embers had been fed and maintained for some unguessable time since then.

At one side of the blackened area stood a crude, knee-high cairn of rocks, and a couple of hominids were already pushing a portion of the smoldering fire in that direction, scooping with sticks and leading the fire to the base of the cairn with a lure of fresh, dry wood. Others in the group had gathered large, thick leaves, which were now wrapped around the gourd. Then the gourd was settled on the cairn. Its exact positioning took some time. Boris thought it was left too far from the fire to cook, but where it would be heated. One man squatted down nearby, concentrating carefully on the fire's progress; the other hominids drifted away.

Boris found himself ignored for the time being. He was thirsty, and limped downhill, following the lay of the land toward the probable location of a watercourse. Though he had no plans for immediate flight, it was reassuring that no one hindered his movement. Before he started once more for the colony he meant to eat, and rest, and do something about improvising shoes, if not pants—the sleeve-socks had probably saved his life, but they were not what you could call adequate footgear for hiking.

At the foot of the slope, only a few score meters down, he came upon the small stream that he had expected to find; he wondered if it was the upper Yunoee. Boris lay down at the edge of it and drank, and felt a chill as if he had seen a great snake about to strike at him from the water. This stream was, though much diluted, undoubtedly the Water of Thought.

The stuff could hardly run in every river on the planet, or it would have been found long ago by Space Force people or colonists. So this must be the Yunoee, or a key tributary. The farther upstream, evidently, the stronger the taste. Down at the villages, it was indistinguishable from ordinary river water. What would be found at the source?

Boris took off his sleeve-socks and sat for a few minutes, cooling his sore feet in the stream, and telling himself that mere survival in his situation presented enough problems without trying to do exploration and research as well. But he could not shake the idea that here, especially, knowledge and survival were connected. At last curiosity won out, and he tied his footwear on again and began to hobble upstream along the bank. After a couple of bends in the watercourse he could see a waterfall not far ahead, a high slender curtain of crashing spray.

Studying the bank on behalf of his sore feet, Boris's eyes spotted an arrowhead; then another, a few steps farther on, half buried in dried mud. It was more than likely that Red Circles' men had once been here.

Now, looking for more clues, he could see in a nearby bush a broken pail, with a rotted handle of twisted fiber. Where had Boris seen the like before?

In the temple of the lower village, he remembered. Pails like this one had been stacked in the room where the vat of the Water of Thought was buried.

He stepped into the river, and bent and tasted it again. The unforgettable flavor was there; it seemed to be growing stronger with every few meters he advanced, to the very foot of the waterfall. But still it was a flavoring only, not the strong Water itself.

Climbing the rocks beside the fall was a tricky job, but Boris was determined. He took his time about it, and at last gained the highest rock and sat on it, getting his breath, nursing his feet, looking ahead on a level at a green meadow of Eden. Above the narrow fall, rocks held the river back into a long, sinuous spring-fed pool, enclosed on three sides by a park of stately trees. When he had rested briefly, Boris stood up and walked through the lush, well-watered grass that rimmed the pool. All was so peaceful that he thought of serpents.

It was no serpent's head that rose from the grass at the very edge of the water. The head was that of a half-grown hominid, who had evidently thrown himself down to drink.

Boris made a peace gesture. The boy stared back at him for long seconds, then rolled over toward the water and drank again, as if still deeply thirsty. Boris wondered if he might be sick. He was the youngest-looking hominid, except for infants and beginning toddlers, that Boris had yet seen in the forest.

The youth took his time about drinking. At last, with a sigh and a gurgling belch, he rolled back to look once more at Boris. Something in the look brought back the snaky chill Boris had felt on discovering what the stream just below the waterfall contained.

Boris stepped carefully toward the upper pool meaning to taste it. But for all his caution, the young hominid was alarmed. The hominid was a gaping boy no longer, but a startled ape, leaping up heavy with drink, grabbing a fallen branch as weapon, hooting and snarling wordless threats. Boris stood still.

In response to the noise, another hominid torso rose from the tall grass on the other side of the pool, this one showing the budding breasts of a young female. She hooted a questioning response to the male. She too had obviously been drinking, for silvery drops fell from her chin.

Boris stood quietly waiting. He was not physically afraid of the two small ones, but he wanted no misunderstanding with the tribe. Soon, the head of the girl on the other side of the pool bent down again to drink. But the young male on the near side was not so easily placated; he still crouched, baring his teeth and growling at Boris, a dog, an ape, an animal.

Then a thing happened that was perhaps one of the ordinary miracles of the universe; but Boris was to remember it with perfect clarity for the rest of his life. A critical synapse closed, perhaps, somewhere in the hominid brain; or some other threshold was reached, some other trigger clicked. The hominid body stood a little straighter, and a human being looked out of the hominid eyes. The boy distinctly spoke some words, which sounded to Boris like a slowed-down version of the adult hominids' jabber.

An answer came, from not far behind Boris. He whirled; Food-Giver stood there, a club held with apparent absent-mindedness in one hand. Food-Giver was a head shorter than Boris, but his limbs were heavily muscled; Boris had a rough moment or two before he could be sure that Food-Giver was not annoyed with him.

The young hominid dropped his own branch, and sighed. He gave the impression of having understood Food-Giver's words, and being reassured by them. Then he sprawled prone again at the edge of the pool to drink.

Food-Giver stood quietly watching Boris. Cautiously Boris stepped to the edge of the pool, bent, and put out a hand toward the calm surface. It seemed that he was committing no offense. He cupped up a few drops in his hand, and tasted; it was the Water of Thought, nearly as strong as what he had been forced to drink from Jones's stone bottle, and again before the ordeal.

Boris sighed, and started away from the pool, heading slowly downhill out of Eden. If he was allowed to, he meant to do nothing but rest and think and eat and drink for a day and a night. He was very weary and there was much to think about.

Food-Giver tossed aside his club and walked beside him.

Chapter Ten

Getting food, as long as he was willing to accept what the hominids thought of as food, posed no particular problem. The moment Boris showed interest in anything that an adult hominid had and considered eatable, some of it was sure to be handed him. It was not, he observed, that he was being

444

regarded with any special favor; the hominids did the same thing constantly among themselves. It was not surprising in such an extremely primitive culture. Food-Giver had probably achieved what dominance he had simply by being a better provider than anyone else around. The other side of the coin was probably that there were drawbacks to accepting too much charity, and Boris made sure to dig up some food for himself, lest he lose all status before his career in society could get off the ground. He even managed to give away a couple of juicy roots, and a few fat grubs that he felt no reluctance to part with.

At night the tribe bedded down under the trees, mostly paired male and female. Boris found himself a comfortable spot near the edge of the fire-clearing, and when he woke during the night made himself useful and kept warm by adding a log or two from a pile that other people had brought in. The leaf-wrapped gourd still waited on its cairn, and he was careful not to disturb it.

***

It was morning, and Food-Giver was prodding Boris awake. Grunting and stiff, Boris arose from his grassy nest, and saw at once that something important must be going on. Four or five of the graying elders of the tribe were inspecting the gourd.

Evidently they decided that whatever purpose had made them put it by the fire was accomplished. It was handed to Food-Giver; and he, surrounded by the irregular honor guard of the others, took it off through the forest. Boris's feet were feeling a little better this morning, and he kept up with them. They looked at him curiously, and talked about him, but made no objection. Actually he thought that Food-Giver at least was pleased.

By a roundabout way that avoided any steep rock-climbing they reached the pool of the Water of Thought, above the waterfall. Food-Giver waded out a couple of steps and poured into the pool, carefully but without any ceremony, half the contents of the gourd. Then, using as dipper another gourd that was handed to him, he added Water from the pool to the original vessel until it was once more full.

The path to the fire-clearing was retraced; a gathering of the younger adult males awaited the elders and Boris there, and things were solemn. Attention was centered on the gourd in Food-Giver's hands. Boris, noting some serious looks directed at himself, was willing to fade into the background, until even sharper looks and some jabber made it obvious that he was expected to stay.

There were no drums or chants here. Still, what followed was certainly ritual, the first that Boris had observed among the hominids. The young men sat down in a circle facing the leaders; Food-Giver motioned Boris to take the place at the end of the young men's line. Food-Giver then solemnly handed the gourd to the man at the other end, who took a sip and passed it down. Each man sipped in turn, and the gourd moved down the line from hand to hand.

Well, it hadn't killed Boris before he knew what it was; and there was no way to avoid it now. When the gourd reached him, Boris was ready. He touched his lips to the stuff inside.

It was the Water of Thought, and, as far as he could tell, nothing but. Far stronger than he had ever tasted it before. What was the connection between the clear Yunoee and the lymph inside hominid craniums? Almost absently, Boris handed the gourd to Food-Giver, who had walked over to stand directly in front of Boris with what might be termed an expectant expression.

Food-Giver gently pushed the cup back, then raised his own empty hands in a pantomime of a man draining a drink to the last drop.

Well, Boris's second deep draught, just before the ordeal, hadn't seemed to affect him at all. What with his drinking from the tainted river, he might be building up an immunity. There was a good cupful left in the gourd, and like a good diplomat Boris drank it all.

The taste was not bad, really, but it was very strong.

With that, the meeting was abruptly over. The members of the council with one accord returned to their individual problems of digging roots and scratching parasites. Boris, finding that his hosts had begun to share with him other things than food and drink, made his way again to the river below the falls with an idea of drowning some of these gifts or persuading them to leave.

After some moderate success with that job, he hunted up a good flint point among the wasted arrowheads along the bank, and started to get some tough green bark from a tree. He had rather enjoyed planeteers' survival school; he thought he might try his hand at making himself some moccasins.

Before he even got as far as peeling the bark for them, he knew he had a fever which was rapidly getting worse. He tried to keep working for a time, but then gave up and threw himself down in the shade; he was not only burning up, but getting lightheaded. Damn the Water of Thought, you thought you had it beaten, and then... Jones, too, had been feverish from drinking a lot of it. What now, plenty of bed rest?

He tossed restlessly on the grass, wondering if he ought to go back to the river and try to cool himself. What a mad shivering chill that would produce. Someone came to sit beside him, and he looked up to see Food-Giver.

"I hope you can talk soon, Swimmer-With-Berries," Food-Giver said.

"Soon, but I feel sick," answered Boris, abstractedly, speaking the hominid language. The jabber felt strange on his tongue, and yet not strange. Then Boris sat up straight, gazing in awe at Food-Giver, who looked back in mild alarm.

"Great Gods of the Galaxy," said Boris softly, in Space Force-Colonial. There were no hominid words for that.

***

Fortunately the fever leveled off before he became delirious, though all he was able to do for it was lie in the shade and hope. Food-Giver and a revolving delegation of other adults stood or squatted around him, now and then questioning him softly and mournfully—or rather, questioning Swimmer-With-Berries, who had died yesterday from a villager's spear thrust. Boris of course was still Yellow Monster, his original self, but as the newest male around he had been chosen to bear the reincarnation of Swimmer too.

Boris fairly well understood all these things without asking about them, for he found himself possessed of a profusion of hominid memories in addition to his new knowledge of the language. And yet, fever and all, he knew himself still as Boris Brazil; there was for him no real confusion of identity, no sense of any alien personality crowding him inside his skull.

Food-Giver (which was a correct title) and the others asked polite questions of Swimmer-With-Berries. Was he comfortable? Had it been painful, they asked, to die?

No, it hadn't been, Boris remembered. Not very. He could plainly recall looking down at his own gray leathery chest, watching his own spilling blood, glimpsing near his feet, where his failing hands had dropped them, the rocks he had carried into the fight. Vaguely he remembered seeing the grotesquely tall, pale-yellowish monster who had thrown a spear at the villagers following him.

Much farther back, he remembered himself at other sessions like this one, asking the traditional mourners' questions of the newly dead, who through the Water of Thought were merged again with the living.

But it was Boris who remembered all these things. Squatting around him now were not old friends talking with Swimmer-With-Berries, though they thought of themselves that way. They were in fact still Kappan hominids talking to a Mars-born, Earth-descended planeteer. As Boris saw it, Swimmer was dead and gone, but parts of his memory had been implanted like segments of recording tape in Boris's brain.

Like cronies at a wake, Food-Giver and the others chatted of old times, growing more cheerful as the conversation moved along. Boris could not recall many of the events they spoke of, and this did not surprise them. That was the way the Water worked; some parts of the life of the departed one were always lost to death.

But Boris had Swimmer's memories of many everyday routine things, of eating and mating and—on comparatively rare occasions—fighting. And Boris searched those memories for information.

449

There was a scene in which the dead body of a young female was being ritually buried. Rows of hominid faces looked at Swimmer as his hands scooped earth into the grave where food and flowers had been placed already. There had been tears on Swimmer's face, but there was no emotional content for Boris, in this or any of the other memories.

The earliest of Swimmer's memories that Boris could find was one in which he lay beside the Sacred Pool, drinking and drinking. His belly was already bloated with the Water of Thought, but it was still pleasant, even necessary, to drink more.

Of course. Young hominids after being weaned ran free in the forest, on the fringes of the tribal territory, surviving there as best they might. No adult tried to teach them anything, for they were not yet real Thinking People. They were Dark People still, like other animals. And sometimes the hated villagers trapped the young ones, and took them away to a terrible place where they were tortured, and made to spend their lives in moving stones. There they remained Dark People as long as they lived, because they were kept from the Sacred Pool.

At about the same time that a free young wild one grew into the power of sex, the taste of the Sacred Pool, which had been repugnant, suddenly became irresistibly attractive. For long days the young ones spent most of their time lying by the banks of the pool, drinking until their bellies bloated, hardly leaving the place even to seek food. Then there came a time when the taste of the Water no longer pleased them greatly. Then they came and joined the tribe, bringing with them the powers of speech and thought, and the tribal memories.

The tribal memories?

Why, of course.

Now that he thought about it, Boris could easily remember himself in a female hominid body, gathering sweet roots along the base of a great ice wall that blocked the upper end of a valley.

As a planeteer, Boris could recognize the great ice wall as a glacier. But his Kappan memory brought back the looming size of it, and made him feel again its cold breath on his leathery skin, as if he had passed it yesterday.

Might that memory be ten thousand years old? Boris knew that at least that much time had passed since glaciers last scoured these subtropical valleys.

Restless with his persisting fever, and with the awe of what was happening to him, Boris got up and walked unsteadily away from the mourners. He made his way to the Yunoee again, and splashed its fresh water on his fevered face. The Yunoee was cool, but Boris could find no memory of its ever being frozen, not even when the glaciers were near. All adult hominids knew that its Sacred Pool had to be defended. It was the Water of Thought, a River of Thought that flowed in the brains of men, generation after generation.

After drinking of the Thought-tainted water—there was nothing else available to drink—Boris scooped up a shaky palmful and held it close to his eyes. It looked perfectly clear.

Hypothesis. A microscopic organism of some kind—call it the X-bug—lives and thrives and reproduces in the Sacred Pool, and perhaps nowhere else. Some X-bugs are naturally carried out over the waterfall, but for some reason they die or lose their potency as they drift downstream; after a few kilometers, only the fading taste of them is left.

A hominid drinks from the pool. Suppose that the X-bugs resist digestion and are taken live into the drinker's bloodstream. Suppose that they have an affinity for the brain, and suppose further, if it is not too feverish a thought, that they become a loosely integrated but necessary part of the hominid brain, serving some critical synaptic function and also bringing information that is henceforth available to the hominid as memory. And also, while in the brain, they record at least some part of what the hominid experiences.

Boris discarded his handful of water and started groggily back uphill. He rather liked his theory. There were the planarian worms of Earth, one of which could acquire part of the simple learning of another by eating the educated one's minced body. There were analogs among lower forms in the other common themes of known Galactic life.

How did the X-bugs manage to keep storing up new data, century after century, and still retain at least something of the very old information from ten thousand years ago? Perhaps the X-bug reproductive process started out each new individual with half its data-capacity blank.

Boris was not a biologist, only a feverish and beaten-up jack of all trades; but he thought that his theory could not be too far from the truth.

The doctor, back at the colony, had said that Earth-descended humans and the Kappan villagers were remarkably alike, biologically. But after all, Earthfolk were not meant to imbibe their memories and the neural connections of their speech centers. So when an Earth-descended person drank the Water of Thought, the X-bugs rushing to the brain found no ready welcome; they just raised frustrated hell there until eventually the body's defense systems did them in. A Kappan of the villagers' species who drank the Water probably experienced much the same thing in milder form—they spoke of going into trance under the Water's influence, and tapping racial memories. But it was small wonder that the Water of Thought should cause mental imbalance in the Earth-descended.

The mental effect of Boris's first drink had been so overwhelming that he had noticed no particular physical effects. But Jones had been feverish. Come to think of it, Jones had said things suggesting that he had picked up at least a few hominid memories with his draughts of Water. Then, after four or five days, both of them had recovered. Boris had regained his freedom, and Jones had discovered that the object of his fanatic passion no longer satisfied.

Perhaps their first drinks had given them a certain immunity, for their second drinks, at the beginning of the ordeal, had seemed to have little or no effect. Kaleta and Morton on the other hand had taken their first drinks only when the ordeal started, and therefore were probably still crazed in one way or another.

And Brenda—Gods, he had to get out of here and help her, or at least find out what was happening. But at the moment Boris was very glad just to be able to reach his shaded nest again, and sink down weakly into the grass.

"I am sick," he told Food-Giver, who was still waiting nearby. Food-Giver grunted sympathetically, and offered him half a mouse. Boris waved the gift away and closed his eyes.

Why should the third drink have sickened him, if he had been immune to the second? Well, for one thing, the third drink had tasted much stronger than the other two, and for another, he had been forced to swallow more of it. If his theory was correct, that third drink had brought X-bugs to his brain in such concentration that the data they carried somehow became available to him. Such close biochemical coordination was not unheard of between two races or species of the same theme from different worlds. Skin grafts could be made to take from Kappan to Earthman, Doc back at the colony had said.

But this time, though the drink had been stronger, Boris had not been mentally unbalanced by it. Maybe his psyche had actually been strengthened by that first bout of temporary madness—another intriguing theory. The Water of Thought was going to keep a lot of research people busy for a long time.

Magnuson was, or had been, a scientist of reputable standing. But he had swallowed the Water, and then apparently had never tried to work on it, to solve its puzzles.

Wearily puzzling about Magnuson, Boris fell into a fevered sleep. The mass animal-screeching of animal children awakened him. Swimmer's memory knew that particular sound, though faint with distance, to be an important warning, and it brought Boris jumping up from sleep. His first clear impression was that he felt much better. His fever had broken, and he was in a cold sweat.

Boris ran with other members of the tribe toward the distant sounds of alarm, picking up a club as he went. A couple of adult scouts who had gone out to investigate an earlier outcry were already hurrying back with their report to where the tribe was assembling.

"There are six villagers coming this way," one reported.

"And another monster, like this one," said the second scout, pointing to Boris. "And yet another monster, who is even stranger. It has no face or hair, but shines all over like the sun on water. They are all coming this way in a group, along the river, four or five shouts from here."

Food-Giver turned slowly to Boris, silently asking for expert advice on the subject of monsters.

Boris's fever was gone. If his theory was correct, the last living cells of Swimmer-With-Berries had been repelled from Boris's Earth-descended brain, and were food for phagocytes in his alien circulatory system.

But Boris found that he still understood the hominid language. With a moment's thought he could still recall the image of the glacier, though perhaps some of the detail had been lost. Evidently his own brain had somehow re-recorded much of what Swimmer's cells had tried to bring to it.

"I know this monster-who-shines," said Boris. "I think he and the other monster have come to find me and kill me."

"If they come with the villagers, they must be our enemies, too," said someone. There was general agreement.

Boris was thinking that whoever was in the groundsuit could hardly be a real expert in its use. And would doubtless be demented in some way by the Water of Thought. Mentally tilted in some aggressive way, probably, since he came hunting.

Boris asked the scouts: "Did one of these monsters have shaggy hair on his face and head?"

"Yes, the one who did not shine had much hair, darker than yours."

Magnuson. Which meant that either Morton or Kaleta must be in the suit; and Morton was the tough-posing one. If it was true, as it seemed to be, that the Water of Thought pushed an Earth-descended man toward his weakness, Morton might well be afflicted with blind rages. This suggested a plan; it was rather a scary plan, and Boris looked for another one. Unfortunately without success.

He interrupted a strategy conference to say: "This shining monster is a very great fighter. Clubs and little stones will not hurt him."

There was an awed murmur at this; all eyes were turned on Boris.

Swimmer's segmented memories were unclear about something, and Boris asked for information. "Food-Giver, have The People ever attacked the villages?"

Food-Giver was perhaps astonished at having to explain any historical matter to Swimmer. But he was tolerant of monsters, and finally answered: "Yes. The last time was six father's-times ago."

"If we go to fight in the villages, the villagers will kill us," observed another large man standing nearby. There were grunts of agreement. The Sacred Pool meant humanity to future generations of The People, so it would always be defended to the death. But what good reason was there for going to fight in an enemy village?

"I think that today all their warriors are busy in other places," said Boris. "And if we go to the villages we will frighten their whole tribe very much, so tomorrow their warriors may stay home instead of coming here. But first there is the shining monster to think about, who may kill all of us if we let him."

Again there was murmuring; but Swimmer's word seemed to be trusted.

"I wanted two of you young men, the most agile, to come with me," Boris said. "We will fight the monster among the high rocks, two shouts below the Sacred Pool." It was a bend of the Yunoee that Boris's eyes had never seen, but he could remember how it looked. "Then the rest of The People can easily drive off the six warriors and the other monster."

456

The Home Guard was much astonished; they were not at all used to such strong suggestions. For fanatically poor discipline, this army would have made Old American backwoodsmen look like Prussian regulars. Still, this proliferation of monsters was an unheard-of situation, and Boris's try for leadership was therefore at least tolerable to The People.

"We know six villagers are coming this way," said Food-Giver, sticking conservatively to facts. "Maybe there are more. I'm getting ready to fight." He made no appeal for others to join him, had no comment on the plans of yellow monsters. He might have argued jealously against such plans if his culture had been slightly less primitive, but leaders in the simplest human societies everywhere rarely argued. Everyone did much as they pleased, anyway.

Boris called firmly for two volunteers. "You," he said. "And you. Will you come with me? And will you do as I say? We will have a hard fight, and a strange fight, against the Shining Monster. We will save many of The People from being killed."

The two young males he had chosen had youth in their eyes, as well as in their supple bodies. They came with him. They knew no more of groundsuits than of quadratic equations, and quite likely he was going to get them mangled; but he told himself it was for Brenda. And for The People, too.

Chapter Eleven

"Now something's gone wrong with the damned suit," growled Don Morton, standing knee-deep in the swift rapids of the upper Yunoee. The suit's left arm had developed some kind

457

of a hitch in movement; he couldn't control it precisely any more.

Magnuson, breathing heavily with his effort to keep up with Morton, was ascending the steep riverside path. The six village warriors were all out somewhere ahead, scouting. Or more probably loafing, Morton thought.

"I said, there's something gone wrong with this!" Morton waved the defective arm.

"Yes." Magnuson nodded agreement. It was easy to tell what he was thinking, though.

Morton demanded: "I suppose you think I shouldn't have broken all those rocks back there. Well, they kept slipping under my feet. Why shouldn't I hit 'em?"

"You know more about the suit than I do," said Magnuson.

"Damn right I do."

Morton climbed a little higher, enjoying the way the water roared at him, and couldn't push him back, as long as he had solid footing. He paused, scanning the hillsides around him. Here, the hills were very steep, the bones of rock thrusting up through the soil, into occasional crags and pinnacles. Brazil could be hiding out right here, somewhere, thinking himself safe. Oh, to catch one glimpse of Brazil, who was the cause of all this effort and trouble! When he got a grip on Brazil he was going to tear him into handfuls. Slowly.

Magnuson had stopped to drink from the river. When he arose from the bank, he had a funny expression on his face; he smacked his lips, and looked thoughtfully upstream.

"Well, you got any more bright ideas?" Morton demanded.

"At the moment, no," said Magnuson, at once giving Morton his full, polite attention. Magnuson wasn't really such a bad guy; ever since Morton had slapped him he had been polite and respectful. It just showed that people needed a bit of rough treatment every now and then; it was good for them.

Morton got a drink, too, turning his head inside the helmet and sucking insipid water from the suit's small tank. Blah. Maybe he should chance taking off his helmet, so he could get a real drink too.

"Look! There!" Magnuson was crouched, his arm pointing, body tensed.

Morton whirled, sending up a spray of water. A few hundred meters distant, a figure moved along a steep hillside. An Earthman, tall and blond and nearly naked.

Morton hesitated momentarily.

"Go after him!" urged Magnuson. He straightened, groping for his binoculars. "There's something burning between those little hills near there—see all the smoke?"

"So what?" Morton took some slow steps in the direction of the distant figure. "I'm gonna get him!" Rage came to a focus. Running, the suit's legs ripped sheets of water from the river. Morton sprinted up the steep bank, smashing aside brush and saplings, his eyes fixed on his enemy who was at last in sight. The figure of Brazil soon vanished behind some rocks, as if he had seen Morton coming. Morton exulted. Go on, run, try to get away! This time, I've got the suit!

Running in the groundsuit was an athlete's dream come true, a joy that Morton experienced more keenly with every trial. Almost effortlessly he made the first rough hillside flow down past him. Rocks spurned by his heels flew back like missiles.

He pounded along the top of a rocky ridge for fifty meters or so, heading toward the broken hills and pinnacles among which Brazil had vanished. Something was indeed burning there, something sizable to judge by the size of the smoke-pall that hung between the rocky hills.

Was Brazil trying to send up a signal? Morton stopped momentarily, anxiously scanning the sky. There were no copters in sight, no Space Force shuttle craft.

Was the smoke, then, part of some kind of trick? But he was invulnerable! Morton laughed aloud, and flew on. At the end of the ridge, he recklessly broadjumped a ravine; misjudging his landing on the other side, he fell, sprawling and sliding halfway down the next slope, among rocks. He was unhurt, but even a second's delay was maddening. Cursing and scrambling, he got himself reoriented and rushed on.

Here, he was sure, was the very spot where he had last seen Brazil. And now—there he was! The tall, unmistakable figure was hurrying away along a dangerous rocky slope, toward the heaviest smoke. Morton could see that the dark gray clouds were rising from a row of fires, banked with smoldering greenery, arranged along the foot of the hill. Did Brazil really hope to confuse him with smoke? Morton laughed again at the futility of such a plan, and launched himself after his enemy.

Something struck with a sharp clang against his helmet. On the precipitous slope above Morton, a hominid snarled and jabbered, hurling down fist-sized rocks at him. Morton growled in rage and charged the hillside. Sand and loose gravel flew out from under his metal feet; he fell, then slid down into the greasy-looking smoke.

The air inside his helmet stayed fresh—as fresh as it ever got—but now it was difficult to see. Again, a thrown rock clanged from his suit. He saw no one, but he could hear the chittering of his enemies plainly. As if they were laughing at him.

460

Were a whole group of hominids helping Brazil? That was fine with Morton. It would simply mean more targets for his revenge. He stood up, trying to see through the smoke, smiling coldly. Let them laugh all they wanted, let them think they might make fun of him and then escape. He could afford to let them laugh a minute longer.

Rocks pelted around him, here and there into the burning brush. As long as he stayed down here he could see almost nothing. He climbed, carefully. But when he emerged from the smoke he found that he had got turned around somehow, and was on a different slope from the one he had slid down. Over there was the hominid, still in sight—but over here was another one, atop another peak. Morton tried to make up his mind which one to go after first, while more rocks clattered insultingly around him. As soon as he started after the nearest hominid, he heard a shout behind him. Brazil was there, up on another pinnacle, hurling rocks like an ape himself. So! Hominids forgotten, Morton reversed himself again. The shortest way to Brazil lay straight through the fires. But when he had kicked his way through the smoldering piles of brush, he found that the suit's faceplate was fogged over with greasy soot and adhering dust. Looking out through it, Morton could hardly have distinguished a crouching man from a boulder. He stopped, fumbling around inside the suit. There should be a washing system for the faceplate.

A hominid raced by, running like a mountain goat not ten meters away, and with a shriek hurled some kind of filthy muck at Morton. It spattered all over him, and part of it hit his faceplate, obscuring his vision even more. Morton roared, and gave chase. But where had the ape gone? He couldn't take his helmet off to clean it, they were pitching those stones much too accurately. But he had to stop for a moment and get his faceplate cleaned. Forgetfully, he brought his left arm up in a wiping motion, to try to scrape off some of the mess. The erratic arm smashed against the faceplate glass and the helmet just above it. That did it. In a frenzy, Morton pounded his own helmet again and again, with raging fists. The suit-builders had turned out junk, useless junk!

But the helmet and faceplate withstood the beating; and when Morton's fury had abated enough for him to finally locate the interior control for the washer, even it still partially worked, cleaning half of his faceplate.

He looked up, and was just in time to see Brazil, rolling a boulder down at him. With a yell, Morton charged. He meant to catch the rock and hurl it back, flattening his enemy like an insect on a wall.

The rock hit him before he realized that it was too big to catch, on this loose footing anyway. The boulder bore him downhill, and he screamed in terror as it bounded with him, spinning and rolling him helplessly among other rocks, shooting him finally against immobile masses of stone, with a clanging like the end of the world.

In an awkward position, almost standing on his head, Morton lay gasping for long seconds, before he could feel sure that he was not killed or maimed. In fact, he gradually realized, he had hardly been hurt at all. Just bruises here and there, and the wind knocked out of him.

"I'm gonna break your arms and legs, Brazil, and then your neck!" he called aloud, when he had got back on his feet at last. The threat sounded weak and somehow inadequate to his ears; but he was almost incoherent. He knew his enemies were right up on one of these hilltops. They would be laughing at him, as they got ready to roll down more rocks.

Both sides could play that game! With a sudden inspiration, Morton picked up some small rocks, and looked around him for a target. Now where was Brazil? It was almost impossible to see anything clearly through this smeared and damaged faceplate. Morton would like to get his hands on the madman, the degenerate, who built this suit, and—

There was a hominid, looking down at him, gesturing what must be insults. Morton threw an egg-sized stone. It seemed to go like a bullet, but it missed the target, whizzing off harmlessly into space.

He could swear he heard them laughing. They would be getting more boulders ready to roll down on him. He started climbing; he had to come to grips with them. He picked up half a dozen throwing pebbles, but then his maniacal left arm dropped and scattered them, halfway up the slope. Another rock hit his helmet. Smoke drifted around him.

Morton was beyond rage. He made a crooning sound, like a lover singing. When he saw Brazil, he charged at full speed paying no heed to anything else. A wide chasm was almost under his feet before he saw it. Morton leaped desperately, and the edge of the far side struck him in the chest. He clung there with his arms, emptiness under his feet, and the suit's left arm failed him again just as Brazil hit him with another big rock. Then Morton was endlessly falling, bouncing and falling again, with the world of rocks and sky spinning around him and suddenly going dark.

***

"Is the shining monster dead?" one of the young men with Boris asked him.

Boris had sat down shakily, collapsed would be more like it, on a ledge. His hands were bleeding from the edges of that last rock, and his chest was heaving. It had been a very near thing.

"I doubt it," he answered, when he could afford the breath for speech. "But I hope he will be hurt at least. Enough to make him stop fighting us."

"It will take—" The hominid held up a hand against the course of the sun. "This long, for us to climb down there and see whether or not the monster is dead. If the river does not carry him away. I think he finished falling in the river."

"You are a good fighter, Yellow Monster," said the other hominid, climbing up to join them.

"Thank you. Both of you are good fighters also. Let's just leave the Shining One where he is. I want to lead some of The People downstream against the villages."

***

An hour had passed since Morton had gone charging away after Brazil. Magnuson was crouching behind a log, still within earshot of the murmuring Yunoee. The six village warriors were scattered around near him, also in concealed positions. Shortly after Morton had left, another band of hominids had appeared, and launched a stone-throwing attack, but the villagers' arrows had driven them off.

Some yelling had come from the rocks into which Morton had charged, but now all was quiet. Could Morton be still venting some fiendish vengeance upon his enemy? Or had Brazil out-thought him and escaped, or even found a way to defeat him?

Magnuson rather suspected the latter. It was hard for Magnuson not to admire a man of Brazil's capabilities. Maybe

THE WATER OF THOUGHT

Brazil hadn't simply broken and fled from the ordeal. Perhaps there could be some deeper reason.

Magnuson, when Morton was dashing off an hour ago, had been on the verge of calling some final warning after him, a caution to be careful. But Magnuson hadn't called. It probably would have been a waste of breath anyway, at best. But also he must have been hoping that Morton, the proven man, would somehow be eliminated.

"Magnuson, someone comes."

The whispered warning roused him from deep and troubled thought. Around him the warriors were stirring cautiously, turning their attention downstream, to the south. Were the hominids trying to encircle and trap them? But Magnuson felt sure that such tactics would be beyond them, in the wild state.

And it was Red Circles who came into view on the riverside path. He was leading a comparatively strong war party, twelve or fifteen men, and as they came into sight Magnuson saw that all were carrying the painted buckets from the Temple. This, then, was meant to be a raid after the Water of Thought.

Red Circles came forward, walking tall, a bow and arrow in his hands, his eyes scouting the woods and cliffs. He stopped, and Magnuson stood up to greet him.

Reserved triumph, and perhaps amusement, were in Red Circles' eyes. "Magnuson, the Earthman Ka-le-ta is dead."

"What? How?"

Red Circles put a hand to his belt and pulled out a machine pistol, holding it awkwardly by the barrel. "Ka-le-ta violated the Temple, and he killed three men with this. So I killed him."

"What of the hominid-man?" Magnuson asked. "Be careful with that weapon; it is dangerous." He couldn't see if the safety was on. Kaleta must have had the pistol hidden somewhere; and he had still been drugged by the Water.

Red Circles curled at his lip at the mention of danger; but he held the pistol out to Magnuson. "Maybe you can kill some of the Forest People with this, Magnuson, though you have no skill with the bow. Maybe you will kill your hominid-man, for he has run away." Now the triumph in Red Circles' eyes was plainer.

"Run away?" Magnuson took a step forward, almost grabbing at Red Circles. "Where? How do you know?"

"The pen stands open."

Red Circles would not lie, but his tone was insolent. Magnuson accepted the pistol put the safety on, and stuck it in his belt. Then he drew himself up.

"Red Circles, you will speak to me with respect. The Spirit of Man speaks to this world through me, and that is a greater thing than you can understand." Magnuson understood that there was no Spirit, no God, and there would be none until Man had evolved himself upward to infinite power. But Magnuson's work brought that moment closer, so he was not lying to Red Circles. Red Circles had perhaps some dim appreciation of all these things, but he could not know them as a civilized man knew them, so their weight was all with Magnuson.

The war chief scowled, but he was still unable to look Magnuson in the eye for very long.

"We must find the man-hominid," Magnuson said firmly. "He is one of our tribe now. Have you any idea where he is?"

Red Circles gave the Kappan equivalent of a shrug. "Who can say where one of the Forest People might hide?"

"We must search for him."

Red Circles shifted his feet uneasily, but his voice was stubborn. "I and these men are busy, and the men who were with you here are going to have to come with me as well. We are going to get more Thought-Water. Kaleta defiled the vat, and the chief priest tells me it must be restocked at once. So we are going all the way upstream, to the Sacred Pool. Once you asked many questions about the Water of Thought, Magnuson. Now you are one of us, and you can learn all about it."

This time it appeared that Red Circles was not going to knuckle under. Still it was plain that he wanted no quarrel, that he was trying to persuade Magnuson. Once Magnuson would have needed no persuading; he would have made a great effort to discover the source of the Water of Thought. Even now, the idea was tempting. This would be his last chance for any such discovery, for tomorrow or the next day the Space Force would be here, and he expected to be under arrest.

But there was no time to spare for any purpose but the most important one.

"We go downstream," said Magnuson, putting his full authority into his voice. "We must track down the man-hominid, and keep him with us. He is alone and confused, and I can understand why he runs away. But he is the proof of a very great magic, much more important even than the Water of Thought; he is a man made from an animal!"

All Magnuson's authority availed him nothing. "You go downstream, if you want," Red Circles said. "But I am chief of all these warriors." He turned, and shouted commandingly to his men: "We go up!"

***

Boris was beginning to suspect that he just might, after all, be the dynamic-leader type. He had persuaded about twenty-five of the younger hominid men to follow him downriver against the villages. The two who had fought the Shining Monster with him had come back to the tribal gathering-place unscathed, and had been a great help in recruiting, with their tale of an easy dance through combat following Yellow Monster's instructions. It was against all the Space Force rules, of course, to exacerbate local warfare, but Boris could see no other way to go that offered so good a chance of getting his pursuers off his neck and perhaps even of rescuing Brenda. He was gambling that only a few villagers would be at home, that those who were there would flee, and that casualties on both sides would be at a minimum. He would gamble more than that to help Brenda.

"Run forward and make much noise when we come to the first village," Boris told his company as they were setting out. "And remember to look for a female monster; she is my friend."

His boys grunted cheerful assent; following a determined leader was still a new and exciting game to them.

When they got to the Warriors' Village they charged whooping downhill, with Boris in the van, and took the place by surprise. As Boris had hoped, there was not a warrior home. The women and children all evacuated the huts with miraculous speed, and went screaming panic and murder down the path toward the Workers' Village.

Thankfully there was no real murder, or even injury; the hominids were not culturally advanced enough to enjoy pillage and rapine. They shrieked good-naturedly to urge the fleeing enemy on, and waved good-by with clubs.

"Remember, look for female monsters!" Boris led a hut-to-hut search, aided by those of his irregulars who chose to help. It did not take long to make sure that Brenda and Jane were elsewhere. Nor was there any sign of Kaleta.

All this was fun! The hominids were ready to follow Boris downhill again.

"We will frighten another village!" he shouted encouragingly, waving them on. He had a hard time keeping up with them, though he had stopped to borrow a pair of some warrior's new moccasins, which were an excellent fit, or at least felt like it after the sleeve-socks, which Boris joyfully discarded. Shoes were a higher invention than the wheel, and he meant to insist on the point at the next scholarly meeting he attended.

Boris and his small, leathery army swept into the Workers' Village to find that panic had preceded them, and the huts and workshops were already empty of people. From the direction of the quarry there came a querulous hominid yipping; not words, but the frightened monkey-call of the young, though here in deeper, adult voices.

"It is the Dark People," said the hominid standing nearest Boris. In the next instant he ran toward the quarry, yipping a response. The others all cascaded after him.

"Wait! Not yet!" Boris had not foreseen this. "We'll get them out of there, but not yet!"

He might as well have shouted to recall the wind. His army was gone. But he could not blame them.

Seemingly alone in a deserted village, he ran from hut to hut.

"Brenda? Jane!" No one. No answer.

In one hut he noticed a quivering mass of bedding, but pulling it aside uncovered only an ancient and terrified villager.

Boris took the downstream path again, this time alone. For the thousandth time he scanned the empty greenish sky for any sign of rescuing or searching copters. Nothing. There was no use expecting any help beyond what he could give himself.

As he neared the Temple Village he studied the banks of the stream closely, and its shape. He was looking for the pool where Magnuson had ordered him to throw in the second groundsuit, and the energy rifles. The suit might well be full of mud by now, but Magnuson had not realized that an energy rifle would not be fouled by submersion.

He recognized the pool at once when he came to it, and waded out into the dark water, searching the muddy bottom with arms and legs. The current was not particularly strong here, and what he was looking for could not be far away. Unless someone had beaten him to it.

Boris went under water to examine the deepest part of the bottom. When he came up for a breath, Morton was standing on the bank twenty meters away, still wearing the battered suit, Number One. He was watching Boris.

"The river's not going to hide you," the suit's speaker said.

"Are you still drugged, Morton?" Boris asked. And just then one of his groping feet found the second groundsuit on the bottom of the river. Neck-deep in water, he stepped back, moving his feet this way and that, searching further.

"Oh no," said Morton calmly. "It's worn off. I won't knock myself out anymore. But you know too much about our little business now, I can't let you stay alive. You and the others can be blamed on the Kappans."

"Where's Brenda?" Boris asked, as his foot contacted one of the energy rifles. His actions concealed by the muddy water, he scooped up the rifle with his foot, into his hands. But Morton was still too far away.

Morton smiled. In a clear pleasant voice he announced, in obscene fantasy, just how he had disposed of Brenda. In the next instant Morton rushed Boris, charging with resistless speed into the water. He came on so quickly that Boris fired without raising the rifle above the surface.

A needle-jet of steam leapt up, at a sharp angle to the surface, and the groundsuit sounded, loudly, like a struck gong. Morton fell forward in a great splash as Boris dove out of the way. The suited figure floated, face down, hissing, and Boris could feel a wave of warmed water pass with it. On the back of the cuirass, where the power lamp rode, a blackened place the size of a saucer now showed; the suit's radio would be useless, even if a way could be found to get at it.

Holding the rifle, Boris climbed again from the river to the path, and put on again the moccasins he had left on the bank. For a little while, before the suit started to sink and wedged in shallows, he and Morton kept pace toward the Temple Village and the vast, quiet expanse of Great Lake that lay beyond.

When he reached the third village, he found that the wave of panic sweeping before the supposed hominid onslaught had emptied it just like the others. Again Boris walked among deserted dwellings, shouting uselessly for Brenda and Jane.

Pete Kaleta's head greeted him from atop a crude wooden pole newly fixed in the ground just in front of the Temple. With shaky relief Boris made sure that there was only one such pole. Brenda and Jane and Magnuson still remained unaccounted for.

Boris entered the Temple, and poked his head and his rifle into the inner room. Four trembling priests stood there before the Water-vat, clumsily holding spears more or less leveled.

Boris had as yet been able to absorb next to nothing of the villagers' language, but he tried.

471

"Woman!" he said, or meant to say. "Woman. Me. Mine." He swept an arm ground in a great gesture, asking where.

At last one of the priests appeared to get the idea, and raised a pointing arm.

Chapter Twelve

Red Circles and his augmented raiding party were out of Magnuson's sight, on their way upstream. Magnuson, alone, was walking in the opposite direction, going downhill, back toward the familiar territory around the villages.

He had been living and working in and around those villages for approximately a year. As he walked, he could see this rainy season's first towering thunderheads in the eastern sky, and he recalled that last year's rainy season had just been starting when he staged his disappearance.

There were times when he wished he might have devoted his life to some science as impersonal and plain as meteorology. But the Spirit of Man had called him, and he had been given no real choice. He had been forced to spend much of his life out of touch with the busy worlds of galactic civilization, to bury himself at last in these remote hills on this backwater planet. He had dedicated himself to his work, committed crimes in its name, was now hunting for a man to kill him to fulfill the demands of the ordeal. It would seem to most people a strange way to serve the cause of Life. But it was not really strange when you saw it clearly. Death was a necessary part of life. Failure had to die in order that success might live.

Prime-theme galactic civilization had much to learn, or re-learn, about the need for a continuous weeding-out of its members. In his heart Magnuson welcomed his approaching arrest and trial. Whatever the exact charges might be, he meant to make his defense an indictment and a lesson for civilization.

His defense was going to be basically an explanation of his successful work. He had raised an ape-like, gibbering thing to the rank of Man, and in the end the courts would not be able to deny the living evidence of that one hominid; sooner or later, the work of refining and perfecting humanity would proceed, on every prime-theme planet, and that was all that ultimately mattered.

Sooner or later; ultimately; but his own successful defense was going to depend on his one living man-hominid, and he had no guarantee that that one creature was still alive.

As soon as he came in sight of the Warriors' Village, Magnuson paused, sensing something wrong ahead. The village was too quiet, it looked too empty. There was no smoke of any kind.

There was a crackling in a nearby bush. Magnuson turned alertly; it was only a couple of old village women who had seen and recognized him, and were now emerging from hiding. In excited voices, sounding almost gleeful, they began a jumbled tale of great massacre and destruction by a thousand raging, wild hominids. The raiding horde had been led, they swore, by the very same yellow-haired, Earth-descended man who had so magically escaped from the ordeal.

Magnuson soothed the women as best he could, and tried to find out some hard facts. That proved to be impossible, or nearly so. Then, despite their dire warnings and refusals to go with him, he hurried into the depopulated village. No corpses and no damage were visible; but hominid droppings were visible in several places, testifying to a core of truth in the women's wild story. Making Brazil a leader of the enemy forces was certainly an imaginative touch. Of course it was possible that Brazil had discovered that the village was empty and then had dared to pass through it. Perhaps he had been fleeing from the animals.

Approaching the pen, Magnuson discovered it undamaged, though as Red Circles had said its door stood open and the one-handed hominid was gone. Magnuson had believed Red Circles, but seeing this for himself was still a blow. At least, he noted with relief, there were no signs of violence in or around the pen.

As quickly as he could, he searched the whole village, hut by hut, calling gently. There was no hominid.

The creature might possibly have gone back to the familiar laboratory-pen, near the quarry. As soon as he had checked the last empty hut, Magnuson hurried in that direction, toward the Workers' Village.

From ahead of him, somewhere downstream, there came an odd sound that he could not identify—as of a metal gong being struck sharply, once. Magnuson paused, listening for a few seconds, but the noise was not repeated. He hurried on.

***

When the young men of The People ran off in a howling gang with Yellow Monster, Food-Giver watched them out of sight, and then debated with himself what he should do. He had said that he thought the attack on the villages was unwise, but it looked like it was going to be made anyway.

At last, Food-Giver followed the attackers downstream. He was not jealous—at least not consciously so—but he was very curious. Yellow Monster said what he wanted done in a way that made the listener feel it would be wrong to do anything else. Even though Yellow Monster rarely gave food to anyone, still the young men were eager to follow him toward the dangerous villages. There was a great power in Yellow Monster somewhere.

It was necessary to go slow when approaching the villages. Food-Giver found himself a big club to take along, and he was ready at every step to turn around and run for his life. When Yellow Monster and the young hominids ran shouting into the first village, Food-Giver stayed back and waited to see what would happen. Not much of anything seemed to happen, which surprised him; at least there were no sounds of fighting.

Food-Giver was still not convinced. He skirted the empty village suspiciously. The young hominids and Yellow Monster had got too far ahead for him to see them, but his ears and his nose told him that they were going on downstream.

Remembering another raid of six generations ago, Food-Giver visualized the location of the next village. He made himself go a little faster; he wanted to know whatever was going to happen next, good or bad.

He was drawing near the next village when he heard a call like that of wild hominid children in distress, but in deeper adult voices. It came from ahead and to his right.

"The Dark People," Food-Giver whispered aloud. He took a tight grip on his club. He was alone in enemy territory, and afraid, but he could not ignore that cry. He was a leader because nothing meant more to him than helping his people, and now the Dark People were calling for help.

Food-Giver had a memory, many generations old, of their place of torture, a deep senseless hole dug into stone. He knew where it was, and he moved toward it with slow caution.

On a path ahead, he saw a couple of elderly villagers in kilts hurrying through the woods in frightened silence, coming toward him. They had not seen him, and it would be an easy matter to kill them. But any noise might bring warriors, so Food-Giver hid and waited for the two old people to pass. Then when they were out of sight he went carefully on toward the quarry he remembered but had never seen with his own eyes.

Very slowly, senses alert, he came out of the woods near the lip of the quarry. Here he found much fresh hominid sign, and could recognize the scent of one or two individuals. After considering the sign for a while, he interpreted it to mean that the twenty-five young men, or most of them anyway, had here turned north again in the general direction of home. They were going scattered out through the woods, and taking with them other hominids who could only be the Dark People from the pit.

Food-Giver made a sound and gesture of relief. All this was good, very good. The villagers had been robbed of their slaves. The People, instead of suffering great loss on this expedition as Food-Giver had feared, would have their numbers increased. The Dark People could be given to drink from the Sacred Pool, and then thought would come into their eyes, and speech to their tongues, and they would be real people at last. The tribe had been strengthened. Yellow Monster and his strange powers had done very well.

Moving forward to peek down into the quarry-pit, which was considerably deeper than he remembered it, Food-Giver saw three gray figures huddled together far below him. He saw that they were not bound, or confined inside a pen. They were alive, and free to climb out, but still they stayed in the pit.

"Hey there!" he shouted to them, forgetting caution for a moment. "Do you want to be Dark People always?"

But they only huddled together and stared at him, as if they wanted him to go away.

476

So. If they refused help, he would not try to force it on them. He would go home, where he belonged. But he had left the quarry only a few paces behind him when he caught a glimpse among the trees of a thing he did not remember. A strange, big hut, not such as the villagers usually made but built of the branchless bodies of many trees placed close together. Curious as always, Food-Giver approached the structure. The area near it smelled very little of villagers, but strongly of both monster and hominid. That seemed to Food-Giver like a friendly combination, and he was emboldened to go closer.

There was a dark hole, like a cave, let into the cleverly arranged log-pile. Inside, someone moved, making timid sounds.

The freshest smell was hominid, so Food-Give dared to go to the door and look inside. A one-handed male hominid was there, bedraggled and frightened-looking. Food-Giver noted the recent small wounds that marked the other's body, and stared at the old scar that ended the arm-stump. It was astonishing how neatly the hand had been removed, and how its owner had survived such a loss.

Then Food-Giver remembered to be courteous. "Are you Dark?" he asked. "Or do you think?"

The eyes of the one-handed hominid were strange and wild, as if thought were flickering up and down like firelight behind them. His mouth worked uncertainly. "I... I... I..."

"Maybe you drank once and no more from the Sacred Pool," said Food-Giver. "That's not enough. You will come with me now and drink some more." Food-Giver tried to talk the way Yellow Monster did, stating positively what should be done. It seemed that great things could be accomplished by using such a method. "Also you probably need food and ordinary water."

Something small squeaked and scuttled in a corner of the cabin. With an unthinking flash of movement, Food-Giver knocked obstructions aside and struck at the rat with a hunting thrust of his club. The sudden movement and noise made the one-handed one scream as if he were being attacked, and cower away into a corner.

Food-Giver had just made certain of the crippled rat, when he heard running footsteps outside the cabin. He turned sharply, but the breeze brought only a fresh whiff of monster. Food-Giver waited expectantly.

***

Walking quickly past the rim of the quarry, Magnuson peered down. Sledges and ropes and other tools were scattered carelessly. There had evidently been a hominid raid, the kilted overseers and artisans had fled, the quarry hominids had been taken away. But three of them were still down there in the pit. Perhaps because they knew no other place, perhaps because fear of their masters still held them when their masters were gone. Their upturned faces, as expressionless as those of cows, followed Magnuson as he walked along the rim. I will not fail you, Magnuson pledged silently, looking down at them. I will yet raise you up into the sun.

There came a sharp clatter and a thump from ahead of him, followed at once by a hominid scream. Inside his laboratory! If the wild ones were in there, and the one-handed man—

Magnuson ran forward. He found the machine pistol ready in his hand.

As Magnuson burst into the cabin he saw the one-handed hominid huddled down in a corner, looking up at him beseechingly. Before Magnuson could say or do anything, a big wild one lunged at him out of the gloom.

The automatic pistol hammered, the repeated concussion deafening in the enclosed space. One-Hand screamed once more, and was silent, cowering away from the noise. The wild one was hurled back across the room, and torn nearly in half. A table had already been upset, lab equipment broken, and a murderous club lay on the floor.

There were no others. Shakily, Magnuson lowered the pistol. He had come just barely in time, it seemed, but the new human life was safe.

Something curious struck his eye, and he prodded with a toe at the nerve-twitching gray hand that had almost reached him. Beside the hand lay half the body of a rat. Curious.

**

Boris, still walking in the direction in which the priest had pointed, halted when he reached the edge of the clearing and saw the copter under the trees on the other side.

"Brenda?"

"Boris?" And her blessed head appeared in one of the copter ports, to be joined a second later by Jane's. "Boris, this thing won't fly, the controls are all smashed. But whoever did it forgot the radio. I got a message off half an hour ago, when the villagers all ran away. The colony took a bearing on us, they're sending an armed copter. Oh, you look so ridiculous in that little net. But you're alive." And even before she got out of the copter, Brenda began to sob.

Boris kissed her, and gobbled half of an emergency ration that Jane found in the copter and brought to him. He kissed both girls, ate the other half of the ration, then crawled into the copter himself and found a spare coverall and put it on.

479

"Don't want to look ridiculous. Let's start hiking, ladies."

Brenda was still limping a trifle, but ready to go. They had made about three hundred meters east along the shore of Great Lake when the copter from the colony arrived and picked them up.

***

Seven days later, Boris was walking once more across the common of the Temple Village, through pouring rain. The landing clearing nearby had been enlarged, but was still full of copters. All three of the muddy villages were swarming with Space Force uniforms. The cruiser had arrived at last, and was in orbit above the greenish clouds.

In the middle of the common, Boris passed a villager who stood still, as if perhaps too bewildered to shelter himself from rain. The steady downpour had washed the colored clay from his arms, but Boris knew him. When Boris made a peace gesture, the war chief only looked the more bewildered. After giving Boris a brief sullen stare he turned and walked heavily away, a man whose normal world had been yanked out from under him, never to return.

Some of the Earth's old primitives had believed that a rain such as this fell to mark the death of a great chief. Magnuson was not dead, not the one for whom the heavens groaned and wept today; Magnuson sat alone in his well-built hut, his face tired but showing an inner contentment.

He looked up at his visitor without much surprise, as if perhaps Boris had been in his thoughts. "Brazil. It wasn't personal enmity that made me help them hunt you. You understand that?"

"You mean Morton forced you?"

Magnuson hesitated. "He would have tried to force me. But I can't say that he did."

"You mean it was for the cause. The great purification of mankind."

Magnuson folded his hands on the rude table before him. "I told you once that none of us matter, much, as individuals."

Boris shook his head slightly. "Anyway, I've already given my statement to the Tribune. Have you heard it or read it?"

"No. I've been ordered to stay in this hut. They'll charge me formally when I've obtained counsel," Magnuson was sitting while Boris stood, but still Boris got the impression that Magnuson was looking down at him. "You know, my hominid is alive and well."

"Your hominid?"

"I think I may claim credit for him. There are Space Force people examining him now. The day before the Space Force came, I succeeded in teaching him a word or two of speech. So you see that the rite of passage was effective."

Boris, sure that Magnuson did not yet know the truth about the hominids and the Water, stood there feeling weary, and could discover in himself no wish to destroy the smiling assurance before him. It would be short-lived before the Tribune's coming wrath—or else it would perpetuate itself by sliding completely into self-delusion.

Magnuson said: "I was only just in time to save him from a wild one, you know. I wonder what name he'll choose, when he starts to understand about names."

" 'Food-Giver' is a good name," said Boris. "Might call him that."

"I don't believe I understand."

481

"No, I don't believe you do." Boris had just come from viewing Food-Giver's corpse. There had been none of his people nearby when he died, no one to open the skull properly and in time, to drain and preserve the observations of his generous life for future generations.

The rain of the chiefs was falling.

The People: grunting, flea-picking, much abused and cheerful. Nasty, virtuous, and short. They were Boris's people too, now, in a real sense, and he meant to do what he could for them in the future.

But Boris could also remember Brenda being led into this village, to this very hut, helpless in the hands of those who might have killed her in their greed and lust. And he remembered Magnuson cutting the cord that bound her hands, throwing the cord aside, cursing whatever bound human beings, whatever stunted them or made them less than perfect.

"Magnuson, I'll do what I can to help you. You've drunk the Water of Thought several times. What you've done here you may have done under its influence."

"No, we both know that the effect soon passes. My actions here have been sane and responsible. The credit or blame is mine."

"The big charge will be manslaughter, or maybe even murder."

"Why, I don't see any way they can base that. I didn't kill Jones, he was quite willing to enter the ordeal. I didn't kill Kaleta. I've killed no one."

Boris could not stay in the hut any longer, and walked out into the rain. Behind him he could still hear the proud, dedicated voice: "In fact, no one can deny that I have *created* a new human life from..."

***

Back from a trip to hominid territory, where he had introduced the Tribune's representatives as friends, Boris found Brenda waiting for him outside the colony's main gate. She was wearing a rain hood, which she lifted obligingly so he could kiss her. Then she snuggled up against him.

So young. Never been anywhere, really. Offworld once, she had told him, on one quick trip. Such a small-town girl. In the last week he had seen her hunger for children and home-making.

Boris experienced a terrible sinking feeling, akin to what he had heard about drowning. Visions of future changes and responsibilities rose before him. But he was helpless, as if again in the grip of the Water of Thought.

"Listen." He started to walk with Brenda in the rain. "I'm a planeteer. I'm stationed here and there, and I'm moving around all the time. At least that's the kind of work I've always done. I've never been married. I've never wanted to settle down—before. I... am I going to have to struggle through this whole speech before you tell me yes or no?"

"You've never said no to me," she said.

ABOUT THE AUTHOR

Fred Saberhagen is widely published in many areas of speculative fiction. He is best known for his Berserker, Swords, and Dracula series. Less known are the myth-based fantasies Books of the Gods. Fred also authored a number of non-series fantasy and science fiction novels and a great number of short stories. For more information on Fred visit his website: www.fredsaberhagen.com

www.ingramcontent.com/pod-product-compliance
Lightning Source LLC
Chambersburg PA
CBHW071338020726
47502CB00001B/153